The man who knew Kennedy

i

To invert an epigraph,
    News from the Southwest.
        In the summer of the valve trombone;
          Tag up, Tag up.

ii

A salesman calls.
    The battle with Betty Beep.
        Our highways are haunted.
          Night in Wonamasset.

iii

The cigarette age.
    St. Thomas to first fish.
      To Guanahani.
        Nassau and Essex, Connecticut (outside).

If you lived in Arlington, you'd be home now.

The Man Who Knew Kennedy

A NOVEL BY

Vance Bourjaily

THE DIAL PRESS
NEW YORK

Manufactured in the United States of America

First Dial paperback edition—1978

ISBN: 0-8037-5291-1

This novel is dedicated, inevitably, to the memory of President John F. Kennedy, but it is an oblique sort of monument. If I were a musician, a poet or a sculptor, then I might strike a chord, a stanza or a stone with which I could try to express my feeling for the subject quite directly. But a novelist's eyes are not particularly suited to looking at the sun. We are more moles than eagles, at home in the roots and depths of things.

Probably this book is not a monument at all, but something more like a medallion. Historians and the public recollection have already fixed the image of our late president on the bright side of it—the novelist's job, as I see it, is to suggest some scenes and images for the other side.

V.B.

Contents

i

To invert an epigraph,   3
News from the Southwest.   7
In the summer of the valve trombone;   35
Tag up, Tag up.   67

ii

A salesman calls.   91
The battle with Betty Beep.   114
Our highways are haunted.   124
Night in Wonamasset.   143

iii

The cigarette age.   199
St. Thomas to first fish.   225
To Guanahani.   250
Nassau and Essex, Connecticut (outside).   279

If you lived in Arlington, you'd be home now.   296

To invert an epigraph,

I used to read a lot when I was a kid. I'd be telling myself a lie if I pretended not to understand why I don't much any more. It's because most evenings I've taken in enough gin and vermouth before dinner so that I'm too stupid to pay attention to a book afterwards.

I'm not stupid enough for the TV, but what else I do with my ordinary evenings at home isn't all that much more demanding—I talk with my wife and kids, or with people who come by, saying things I suppose I've said before and will probably say again. I look at a newspaper or an aviation magazine; study camera catalogues or bird guides; play old swing songs on the piano, quite a nice Baldwin grand; or even do a little work if I've had to bring some home. Work takes less mental presence than reading books.

But when I was a schoolboy in St. Louis, I read every evening, read whole authors. I read, among others—getting the books two at a time from the neighborhood branch library—the entire published work of Sinclair Lewis.

I read a book of his called *The Man Who Knew Coolidge*. But when I thought about it the other day I found that nothing had stayed with me but the title. By the time you're forty, the books you read at fourteen are books you never read.

So I got a copy of *The Man Who Knew Coolidge* from the library in the town where I live now—Scott's Fort, Connecticut, west of Hartford, north of Litchfield. The book hadn't been off the shelf for fifteen years, according to the list of dates stamped in front. I don't know what made me think that reading it might help straighten out my feelings about Dave Doremus, but when the title bobbed up in my head I thought I'd see if there was some connection. Dave was, among my friends, the man who knew Kennedy. Knew him, off and on, all his life.

I've never grown completely out of sympathy with Sinclair Lewis. I can read *Babbitt* and *Arrowsmith* with pleasure still—did it in the hospital a couple of years ago. Broken leg, trying to ski a slope I had no business on. I could probably even go *Main Street* one more time.

But *The Man Who Knew Coolidge* is really a bad little book. It's Lewis himself who's out of sympathy, as he wasn't in the bigger books. The Man is an office-supply dealer called Lowell Schmaltz. He lives in Zenith; he even has the Babbitts over to dinner as a matter of fact, admires George a lot. But Lewis makes Lowell Schmaltz a real offensive idiot. Reading *Babbitt* (no, I'd rather make that *Dodsworth,* as far as I'm able to recall the Dodsworths), I'd be willing to agree that I'm reading about my mother and father or, let's say, their friends; but nobody could have been a friend of Lowell Schmaltz. I don't believe the Babbitts ever returned that dinner. Sinclair Lewis seems to have let himself get bitter enough, late in the Coolidge era, to want to teach his readers to be desperate.

Still, Lewis's sonar was a pretty precise piece of equipment. I'm perfectly convinced when he picks up Lowell Schmaltz summing up Coolidge: "Maybe he isn't what my daughter would call so 'ritzy' . . . he may not shoot off a lot of fireworks, but you know what he is? HE'S SAFE."

I feel sure that's an American voice of the time speaking, voting confidence in our last-but-one New England president.

Then, as we were growing up, presidents came and went from Iowa, New York, my home state of Missouri, and from Kansas, and things turned upside down. That's why even the best of Lewis's novels are history books now, and no present help in understanding what has happened to us—to Dave Doremus and us all. Things are totally inverted. Look at that quotation.

John Kennedy was just exactly what *my* daughter, Mary Bliss James, would have called "so 'ritzy' " if she'd used the word; I think the fifth-grade word just then was "neat-o." And as for shooting off a lot of fireworks? And did we care to elect a man who was, in Schmaltz's capitals, SAFE?

I think events merge, like notes on a keyboard played in sequence, to produce tonality. There've been enough great events since the Lewis book came out, thirty-eight long American years ago, to change the sound of any century. We live and die, children of Sinclair Lewis's people, lives and deaths that echo very differently.

Mr. Coolidge died, for example, old and at home, neither honored nor dishonored; no one paid much attention. That's not the way John Kennedy went.

As for Mr. Lewis: life these days, sir, seems to teach a different desperation. We are sad where you were bitter, scarred where you were stung, and the things we see around us aren't really jolly enough to satirize—we're lucky when we can find them jolly enough to be revolting. Speaking for myself, most of the time I just don't think at all. And when something makes me think, I feel about the way I did in Nicaragua once: a kid named Ricardo took me on his motorcycle, up through steep, rocky fields till we had to leave the bike and walk, then scramble, climb, and finally go down on our hands and knees and crawl, to look over the edge, into the crater of a live volcano. I felt scared and precarious; I couldn't have made myself stand up. The ledge under my chest was hard and thin, brittle perhaps, and down under us, three or four hundred feet, was molten, smelly, indecipherable stuff that sent up heat and fear. I couldn't contemplate much of that, and for relief I raised my eyes and watched wild parrots, out over the center, flying in and out of the steam.

News from the Southwest.

Helen and I were on an airliner, half an hour away from landing in San Juan, Puerto Rico.

Helen is my wife. I'm Barney James, in my middle forties now, and seldom go back to St. Louis any more. I run a plant in Connecticut that does an old-fashioned thing—we make hardwood products. We make pitman rods, wooden bearings, tool handles and stock racks; we supply blanks to people who finish them into skis and gunstocks; we make oars and paddles and hockey sticks.

We don't do much cabinetwork any longer, though Gibson Hardwood Products of Scott's Fort was started as a cabinet shop more than a century ago, by one of Helen's great-grandfathers. That went down gradually in the depression, and in the years just before I joined the family and the firm, the plant was in war production, making instrument cases for the Navy.

I'm sorry we're out of cabinetmaking, and sometimes I think of starting it up again. But that would mean getting into veneers and plastic finishes, and buying fancy hardware. I like solid wood, lacquer, varnish and paint, and the feeling that we don't buy anything else except screws and bolts and glue. I'm one of the people who likes meeting a payroll every week. There are one hundred and ninety-two checks to countersign on Friday afternoons; I do it by hand and know the face that goes with the name on every one of them. We have a company plane, a Cessna 180. I fly it, having learned to in the Air Force, sometimes to meetings. Sometimes into places like Canada or the Midwest where I grew up: places the wood comes from. But I don't fly it as often as I used to; take an airbus, Dad, and leave the flying to us.

Late fall is a quiet time in my kind of manufacturing. There's a grandparents' house across town for the kids to stay at, so Helen and I can sometimes get away that time of year.

Our plans were to change to a local airline in Puerto Rico

and fly east another seventy miles to St. Thomas, in the Virgin Islands off the Puerto Rican coast. In St. Thomas we were going on board a charter boat, a fifty-two-foot schooner called *The Bosun Bird,* to cruise for a week with Dave Doremus and meet his new wife.

Dave had called me at the plant a couple of weeks before, from Cape Cod where he lived, and said: "Barney, I'm getting married again. Can you and Helen come to the honeymoon?"

He and I had been friends for a long time, starting when his father's career as a New Deal administrator brought the family to St. Louis for a school year: '35-'36, tenth grade for Dave and me. We both turned sixteen towards the end of it. Mr. Doremus was a man of some importance in the Roosevelt government, a specialist in setting up new agencies or branches of old ones; he operated on about the fourth level down from the Cabinet, a man who made things run, and might be loaned from Ickes to Morgenthau to Perkins, wherever there was his kind of problem. He worked for Joe Kennedy on the S.E.C., for a time, went to England with him briefly in 1938. During the war Mr. Doremus got to be a presidential advisor and had office space in the White House. My own father was the kind of Republican who didn't want to meet Dave's father, which was a disappointment to me but not the sort boys dwell on much.

2

What happened in the airplane, about ten minutes before the bad news came, was that Helen started one of her little quarrels. She does it for recreation, when time works loose, if I don't see it coming and refuse to play.

Helen James is a good quarreller, fast and deceptive, a little lacking in straight power maybe, but full of desire to win. The kind who'll come up smiling, half an hour after you thought it was over, and hit you again.

She started this one with a feint, which I should have recognized.

"I'm going to rest," she said.

"All right."

"I just want to close my eyes for a minute."

"Good."

"Is this the button that makes the seat go back?" She opened and closed the armrest ashtray a couple of times.

"Other arm," I said. I'd shown it to her when we first got on the plane, but Helen's far from being so stupid mechanically as to think she can make an airplane seat recline by opening the ashtray; there's nothing Helen is actually stupid about. I was supposed to say something impatient, or she was seeing if I would. But all I added was:

"Try the forward edge."

"You mean this little toad-colored thing?"

"Yes." The plastic from which the button was made was tan, with a greenish black mottling under the surface.

"Ick. Do you think touching it will give me warts?"

"Little warts, with propellers on them," I said.

"Barney, I can't make it work." Pout.

"If Madame will be so accommodating as to lean back. . . ."

I turned, raised up in my seat to reach across her, and pressed the button. Helen sank back. When I straightened around, all I could see were her lap and her pretty knees. Feeling that my defenses had been lightly probed and found firm, I let this suit me a little too well; Helen's feint had worked. I didn't think to register that she was now in a position to speak, unseen, at a moment of her own choosing, directly into my left ear from a distance of half an inch.

Lee Oswald must have had his rifle in position on the window ledge by then, and been watching the crowd form.

You were playing your office comedy, I imagine, or cutting your factory capers—up to your old housewife hijinks, grinning down a customer, barbecuing a client or doing something hilarious to a patient. If you weren't already out to lunch and half-bagged. I was starting on vacation with my wife, whom I still found childishly irritating and girlishly pretty (if womanly sad sometimes) after sixteen years and three children. So my farce was domestic.

Smooth air.

There was no sensation of movement in the plane. I opened a news magazine. The magazine was in a red plastic folder, the folder was in my lap, and the plane hung between sea and sky. I started to read the lead story. It was about Kennedy, as a matter of fact: "The president will be taking his first-string fence-mending team into Texas. . . ." News of any week. News warmed over. Soporific. I sometimes buy a news magazine if I'm taking a trip on public transportation and can't find a mystery or a spy story that looks good.

Better than escape. A warm bath for the brain. I let it wash my lobes. News seemed to be moving no more than the plane was.

"Barney, sweet." Something moist and penetrating happened to my undefended ear. "Barney, try not to resent the fact that I'm experienced."

"Huh?"

"It's natural, of course, if you're feeling all trembly and pro-vincial about not having sailed in a beautiful big boat before."

The Ozark Kid leapt for his horse. Horse sidestepped. "It's, huh?"

"I mean if there are things you don't understand, don't get cross about it the way you do."

"No," said the Kid, getting slowly to his feet. "No, I certainly won't."

"You can ask me, or Dave. Or Captain Clark, even. I'm sure we'll all want to help."

"What are you talking about?" I asked. "Or did you just start out and hope a subject would creep in?"

Oswald may have been sighting through his scope on the hel-mets of the motorcycle men leading the procession.

Helen's line seemed to have something to do with the fact that while I've sailed small boats some since we were married, it's been day sailing. The only nights I ever stayed on a boat were during the summer after the war, which I spent on a very sturdy, very shabby, Friendship sloop that Dave bought from a girl in Maine.

But I'd never even been on board a gold-plater, which is what Helen was talking about, and she had. All through her girlhood she went ocean cruising, sometimes on famous boats. She'd even gone on a Bermuda race, once, as cook for a crew of Yale boys, the year before we were married. Her first cousin Troy was sailing master, and she admitted there wasn't much cooking to it—they were all too busy to take a lot of time to eat. Now and then we've been invited to go sailing on that kind of boat since our marriage; sometimes she's been able to go.

Once we were going on a summer race, the Off Soundings, with Dave and his first wife, but I got too busy. Unexpected orders. Another time, with other people, I could have gotten away but didn't want to. The owners were friends of the Gibsons, Helen's family, and were people I get annoyed with. There's a kind of rich couple whose idea of how to be attractive is to take a more-bourgeois-than-thou attitude about money—fifty grand a year of unearned income and the big excitement in their lives recently was discovering colored margarine. So Helen went alone, and afterwards said I was right: "Last year we sailed down the Sound and went ashore for dinner and stayed at a marvelous hotel. And got dressed up and danced," she told me. "This year they thought it would be cosy to stay on the boat and play word games. We were at the same mooring, and I could see the hotel all beautifully lit up, across the water. And there I was wondering if the wind would change so I could hear the music, and trying to think of a six-letter bird, starting with 'A.'"

It didn't give me any sense of small triumph—I don't react to Helen that way. It made me feel I'd want to put off cruising until I could buy my own boat; it might be $15,000 or $20,000 but I was beginning to discover that there were banks around that would put together sums like that for sober, home-owning, slightly overextended borrowers like me.

Avocet.

Then, after a summer in which Helen didn't get to sail, came that perfect cue from Dave: wouldn't we want to charter with him, and the new wife we hadn't met, a late-fall cruise in tropic waters on a lovely boat he knew? The moment he said it, I thought it sounded like just what Helen and I would want to do. The moment I told Helen, she thought so too.

"What I'm talking about," she said now, "is you saying not to buy foul-weather gear, in New York."

"I only said it wasn't on the list of things Dave thought we'd need."

"Dave Doremus is an utterly charming man," said Helen, who'd seen Dave off and on through the years, but didn't really know him well. "Does he always think of everything? That's a very unusual quality."

I sighed, and she went brightly on.

"I'll bet you first noticed it when you were in nursery school, and he was the one who made sure everybody had crayolas."

"The point could be that foul-weather gear is that sort of thing charter boats have plenty of."

"Suppose they don't have it in my size?"

"Look, Miss Sweets." I decided to try encirclement. "Trembly and provincial though I am, and in spite of your staggering physique, I do know that there are exactly three sizes. Now, we have *women's small*. . . ." I stopped, right there, feeling pretty silly for getting drawn into this at all.

Oswald might have seen the car he was waiting for then, coming slowly, out beyond the underpass.

"I bought some anyway," Helen said, as pert and ready for protest as if the point had really been a big issue between us in New York.

"Sure you did," I said, and showed teeth.

She returned the same sort of false smile, but she does it better than I do. There's a mock sweetness about Helen's features that's suited to the whole range of ironic faces, and she makes them expertly.

It had been eighteen years, and she was eighteen, when I saw her for the first time, and she had changed of course. But even back then I'd found her kind of prettiness more irritating than seemed quite fitting for a girl brought up so comfortably. By now I think a man meeting her feels distinctly more provoked than allured; it's the mockery of the features, and the mettlesome eyes. The pigment is thin in her pupils, so that they look almost transparent, and they snap and sparkle at you, and change color, from blue to green, depending on what she's wearing. The eyes lead you on, while the smile says how silly you are to be led.

Helen's hair is dark, very soft and shiny. Apparently it's easier to keep that way than other women's—at least, she's hardly ever at a hairdresser's. Her nose seems sharp to me in profile when she's tired, and her mouth is probably a shade too thin, but very neat and smooth-lipped. Her bosom is plump and, as a matter of fact, freckled, but she keeps the rest of her body slim without much trouble, and she's always had good legs.

Men like to look at Helen. She likes being looked at. That's where the sadness starts, sometimes.

"A lovely suit of foul-weather gear," she was saying. "I never had my own, and there's never enough extra when a storm comes up." Poor beggar child. "It's blue. In the package from Abercrombie's with the bathing suit."

Cocked his gun.

"Blue," I said, trying to get back into my narcotic magazine.

"It was rather expensive, imported from England." She crooned it into my ear. "Navy blue, I should say. . . ."

"Splendid!" I yelled, jerking my head away and twisting towards her. "Good show. Top hole." I slammed the magazine against my knee. "Royal Navy. First line of defense. Tight little island, wouldn't you say?"

"Barney! Barney, look at the girl. . . ." Helen's seat came forward, even with mine, her head travelling with it. Her fingers found my forearm and dug in. Her eyes stared over the top of the seat in front of her, towards the door between the passenger space and the pilot's cabin. "Barney. . . ." I could feel each separate fingernail digging through the cloth of my jacket. ". . . Barney, the plane?"

Our stewardess stood in the doorway to the flight cabin, a tall blonde with her hair cut very short. She looked terrified.

3

It was, I hardly have to say, November 22, 1963. It was a few minutes past 1:30. Caribbean time.

There were only nine other passengers on the plane—three couples, two Puerto Rican men in business suits, and a grey-haired woman in some kind of black, religious gown, sitting by herself. From the flight cabin a man pushed out past the stewardess; he looked pale and grim. He stared down the aisle between the seats. His eyes went left, right, met mine and held them for a moment as if he were about to ask my help with something. His mouth worked and his eyes moved off to look the same way at the religious woman; he was in shirt sleeves and black four-in-hand with a tie-clasp. Without a cap, but I was sure he was the pilot.

I spent the war, five years, flying planes or being flown in them by other men, and I knew automatically that if the pilot was out of his seat there was nothing wrong with the plane. But there was something wrong all right.

The pilot came towards us. Helen was rigid beside me. I covered her hand with mine.

"Ladies and gentlemen." The pilot shouted this in a choked way, as if he hadn't already got more of our attention than a man could decently use. I was probably as rigid as Helen by then. I had a clear and unbearable knowledge that he had something to say too solemn for the public address system.

"Ladies and gentlemen. Listen. The President has just been shot in Dallas."

The pilot was heavy-bearded. He had a deeply cleft chin, and thick, dark brows, and his voice wouldn't work very well. He tried to say something more, and shook his head.

I kept staring at him. Then Helen's forehead pressed against my neck, and I heard her whisper:

"Kennedy?" An instant later she tugged at my arm and said, in a soft, fierce voice: "It isn't true, is it?"

One of the businessmen grabbed the pilot's sleeve and asked the same thing: "It's true? It's not true?"

The pilot pulled away. "Wait," he said. "Wait, I'll tell you from the cabin," and hurried forward and away.

We passengers looked at one another. Then we heard the public address system click on and hum. The same voice now, but filtered and faint, with the static of loose wires making it crackle, said: "A sniper. A sniper has shot Jack Kennedy. Right downtown, a little while ago, and escaped. The President is shot in the head, real badly wounded and they've got him in the hospital, but. . . ." The voice stopped. After a moment it went on and said that Mrs. Kennedy was all right, and the Vice-President was all right, and that was all now. They'd had to stop receiving news broadcasts. Because we were making our approach to San Juan airport.

It was a bad dream of news coming, the voice faltering, the speaker volume never up to normal, the story uncertain, unacceptable. . . .

"It must be true, Helen," I said.

She pulled back and looked at me. Then she looked out the window of the plane, but her fingers never stopped digging into my arm. When her eyes came around to mine again they were full of tears and she said:

"What kind of people are we?"

I pressed her hand, looked down at the red plastic folder in my lap and then up, at the stewardess who was still standing in the doorway, pushed back against the bulkhead as the pilot had left her when he passed. I saw green lights start to play on her yellow hair. They came from the sign that said we were to fasten our seat belts and not to smoke.

4

On the fourth day, first semester, that tenth-grade year of day school in St. Louis, I picked up a copy of the school paper from the desk in the corridor where they were stacked, and walked down the hall towards French class, reading a column headed "New Boys."

The class before mine in Room B wasn't over yet. The door was closed. I waited, finishing the column. There were to be eight new boys and of the seventh it said:

> *Doremus, David.* Looks about one-half faun, the other half gargoyle. He whirls about our hallowed halls like a dervish, and seems to have some big bridges for sale in cities like Washington, D. C., New York, N.Y., and Boston, which is in an eastern state your columnist has never learned to spell. We don't see how the United States Senate will get along

without young Dave this year, and are prepared to have him called back. If the Ethiopian crisis worsens, get ready to say, "Abyssinia, Dave."

I knew which new kid was hidden behind that curtain of senior-class prose. It was the long-legged redhead who sat behind me in Solid Geometry, and who had transferred, as we all informed one another, from the Senate Page-Boy School. They said his father knew Senator Truman and maybe F.D.R.

"Hey. Someone's reading over your shoulder," said a crisp voice just behind me, and I turned and looked into a big white grin. "Isn't that nicely put about me, though?"

"Jerry West writes those," I said. "He's a senior. He thinks he's very funny."

"Shall we roll down the corridor laughing?" Doremus asked. "I'm going to Latin."

"I've got French."

"Abyssinia, then," he said, straightfaced.

"Abyssinia," I said, just as solemnly.

We were friends immediately. And, as a matter of fact, though I had best-friend status for some reason, everyone else in that school was Dave's friend, too.

Not mine. I was a fairly snobbish boy, and Dave's pleasure in his popularity used to irritate me a little. My snobbishness wasn't about money or family, areas in which most of the kids in school started out even, but about personal qualities. I couldn't have defined them then; it just seemed to me that some guys were okay, and most weren't worth bothering with. I was probably the best athlete in my class—my sport was baseball—but that didn't necessarily mean that I liked the other athletes. I read hard, but studied poorly except in languages, so my snobbery wasn't intellectual. I had my own, rather pessimistic view of the world, my own slightly surly sense of personal worth, but it didn't mean I approved of showing pessimism and surliness. I'd been taught to keep my grouch private under a screen of pleasant manners which were not insincere but rather another part of the ego, and that seemed to me some kind of minimum standard for the right combination of attitude and behavior.

I suppose all I'm really saying is that the clay of my personality hardened early, good and bad, giving me a kind of knobby essense, sometimes obtuse but firm, that other boys responded to —with liking or dislike, anxiety or even imitation—in an exaggerated way. I would guess that there were two reasons for the strength of their response: one, that I seemed to be indifferent, and the other nothing more than that I'd achieved this inflexibility so young. I was fifteen, and knew exactly what I thought, but I hope all that is not as graceless as it sounds, since I'm afraid nothing has happened to change me very much.

They were wary of me, then, and nuts about Dave; we held school elections that fall, in the style of a Roman republic, and Dave became tribune—the highest office a sophomore could hold, defender of the people against the patrician magistrates and senators in the junior and senior classes.

I said I was surprised. "They've only known you six weeks."

"Why, hell," Dave said, mimicking the accent I used to bring back from summers in the hills. "I believe these old Missouri boys like me pretty good."

"Well, get out there and defend them," I said, and, in a way, he did. I suspected him a little of using his magnetism cynically, to get his way with people, but I was wrong. The charm was not unconscious, but its effect on people simply pleased him, surprised him a little, and his essence was an uncalculating wish to be helpful. He absorbed anyone's problem and made it his own.

"There're ducks on the river," I'd say. "Let's take bikes and binoculars, and go watch them."

And though he liked to go see birds with me, Dave might say: "I've got to help Johnson with tennis," or Perk with Latin, or talk to Tank, who had the first girl trouble in the sophomore class. "That backhand. . . ." Or those irregular verbs. Or support at the time of the crucial phone call.

Often when Dave and I were walking down the hall, some worried boy would come up, demanding attention, and always Dave would stop, nodding for me to go along. If I looked back I'd see them, the other kid talking earnestly, Dave listening with an expression of concern no less total than his great open grin.

Generally, his way of helping was to take whatever he could on himself and minimize the rest.

"Damn coach wants me to play third next spring," I said, early that November. My position, the summer before when I started playing semi-pro, was center field, but I had the arm for the long throw across the infield to first. I would be the only starter on the school team who wasn't a senior or junior, and I was a perfectionist kind of kid; I took looking good at what I did pretty seriously. I was worried about fielding third base, about charging bunts and handling grounders. I didn't want to wait for spring to practice. I needed someone to hit balls to me, and someone else on first to throw to.

"I need some work myself," said Dave, which was ridiculous. He'd be playing tennis in the spring, and had turned out for basketball, which kept him exercised. But late fall and winter days, he'd find us a batter after his own practice, and come out himself with a left-handed first-baseman's mitt though he was right-handed, so I could throw to him. I knew he was tired, but he'd never admit it, and when I spoke of finding someone to relieve him he seemed almost hurt.

Yet he was his own man, poised and wilful, capable of withdrawing when it seemed right to him.

I remember the big boy we called Tank saying once: "I thought we were going to double date again Friday?"

"Sorry Tank," Dave said, "I've changed my mind."

"Come on. Be a good guy, will you Doremus?"

Dave smiled, and shook his head, and he and I walked on.

"Poor Tank," I said. "Trying to talk the whole evening without any help."

"You ought to hear his idea of conversation with girls," Dave said. "He tells one dirty joke after another. The girl he got for me was just so damned uncomfortable. And so was I."

"Why not tell him?"

"You would, wouldn't you? No, I won't make up excuses, but I've got no reason to offend him, either."

Yet Dave would give offense, when the time came, and it came at a school assembly early that December. There was an assembly every day, at which one of the masters would talk about something. Current events, generally, or read an editorial from a newspaper and comment on it. On this day a teacher named Garrison decided we needed a lesson in the manner of Machiavelli, I guess. Mr. Garrison held himself out as a model of cynicism and worldliness. He had bushy brows, a powerful, deep, ironic speaking voice, and a somewhat satanic look, and he made the most of it. He was an English teacher, and his favorite student was Jerry West, who'd written that "New Boys" column.

"Gentlemen," Mr. Garrison said. "I have been reading a most instructive article in the *Reader's Digest* which I commend to the attention of the bleeding hearted and the do-gooders among you. Yes, gentlemen. The title of this article is so suggestive that it sent me to the very source from which the *Digest* digested it—not without a *liberal* dose of bicarbonate of parlor-pink soda, you may be sure. This title, gentlemen, is in Latin: *"Pro Italia,"* and I cannot imagine that there are those in this group of earnest scholars who will fail to be able to translate that ringing phrase. . . ."

And he went on to deliver the rationale for the Italian occupation of Ethiopia, which was a few weeks old by then. We had, I acknowledge, heard several denunciations of Italy and Mussolini from the same platform recently, so perhaps Mr. Garrison was really being an educator in offering his rebuttal. He reminded us that Italy had been on the Allied side in the First World War, had gotten little enough in the way of territory afterwards, had need of room to expand in and skill to offer in developing the country—why shouldn't a strong nation expand? Wouldn't it benefit the weaker one finally?

And so on.

"Gentlemen," he said, and though his impulse may have been an educator's, there was much unpleasantness and condescension in the man. "I am touched to think that some of your noble hearts have bled for your black Ethiopian brothers, with their diseased cattle and their overgrazed wives, but I feel the matter may now have been put in a little better perspective. In the face of these facts, how many humanitarians among you are willing to stand up and be counted as opposing the wave of the future? Eh? No League-of-Nations do-gooders in the crowd?"

Dave, sitting beside me, stood up.

Garrison loved that. "It's Doremus, isn't it?" he said. "Well, now, have you the word for us, Mr. Doremus, from Secretary Hull? Or does it come from Eleanor herself?"

The school laughed. Dave stood soberly, on the aisle, looking up at the speaker and waiting. When the room was almost quiet, he said, very clearly:

"Abyssinia, Mr. Garrison," turned and started out of the room.

The laughter was much louder at that. I could hear Garrison shouting over it, "Doremus. Doremus, this assembly is not dismissed. Doremus, return to your seat."

And at that, I jumped up and yelled, "Abyssinia, Mr. Garrison," and went after Dave. Half the school was gone, crying the magic word, before the headmaster got to the stage and successfully, so I heard, called the timid to order.

We were sent for, of course; Mr. Garrison was there, and Jerry West, too, for some reason. But the Head did all the talking, and when he'd finished about how disappointed he was in us and all that headmaster jargon, he said:

"Very well, Doremus and James. If you are ready to acknowledge that there is a respect due to Mr. Garrison's rank, regardless of your opinion of his views, I wish you to so signify by offering a complete apology."

"Yes, sir." Dave said it very fast, almost enthusiastically. Then he paused, quite a long while, and just as it seemed certain he wouldn't say anything more, he smiled his most winning smile and said: "I do apologize. May I ask, sir, if Mr. Garrison is willing to acknowledge the respect due to the rank of the Secretary of State, sir? And the First Lady?"

The Head had started to return Dave's smile. He finished by swinging around and giving Garrison a long, cold stare.

"Why yes, Doremus. Why yes, of course," said the satanic Mr. Garrison, nervous as a chained dog.

On the first day of Christmas vacation, Dave came to my house and I told him I had to go to Little Rock.

"Why hell," Dave said. "I was hoping we'd get to go spend a cold, cold weekend in that Ozark mountain home of yours."

"Did your folks say you could go?"

"My pappy said to me, 'Son. You kin go up there in the hill country with Barney *Jesse* James, but if you-all hold up any trains, son, I want you to let the U.S. Mail go through.'"

"Doremus," I said. "You and your pappy start talking Tennessee in the Ozark Mountains, you'll get shot for spies. No, I wish I could. I've got to hitchhike down to Little Rock. My stupid brother."

My brother Alex had had a fight by mail with our father and dropped out of college, his freshman year at Chapel Hill. And gone on tour, playing piano in a dance band. I wanted to go tell Alex I was on his side but please come on home for Christmas anyway.

"Want me to go with you?"

"Want to?"

"We could say it's the Ozark weekend, and not mention side trips."

"Listen," I said. "If we can get it running, we can take my car and drive." I had a car, up at the summer place. It was a green, Model A coupe that I'd won in a way that still excited me to think and tell about: the ball team that I'd played with summers had a couple of paid players, but most of us were Argus Town boys who made the Sunday games because we liked to. I was the youngest, and the least typical, since I only stayed near Argus Town three months a year. And I was the one the manager never slipped a five to for doing something especially good, because my family was better off than the rest. But in the eighth inning of our last game, with a lot of local money bet on it, I had a moment. We were a run behind and had two men on base, and as I picked up a bat for my turn I had a strong feeling the manager was about to put himself in as a pinch-hitter. Instead of which he said, goddamn, if I would get a hit he'd give me his car, James, swear to God he would. I hit the first pitch for a triple, a line ball over third. I can still see it rising. And even though I got thrown out trying to go home on a squeeze play, Tim gave me the Model A.

The only trouble was, I had no driver's license.

"You can drive, though?" Dave said.

"Well, I did. All around the woods roads. Into town, too."

"What's wrong with your very famous car?"

"No spark. Why, you know anything about cars?"

"I can't even drive," Dave said. "But I've worked on boat motors. Hear tell they're about the same thing."

"Hear tell," I scoffed. But I surely wanted to drive into Little Rock to see my brother, now that we'd thought of it. Alex was eighteen and making thirty dollars a week, and I wanted now to arrive as a man of substance, my own emissary, not a kid brother off the highway coming down to beg a favor. "The battery's okay. We tested it, and took it indoors in September."

"Got tools?"

"Yep."

That afternoon, Dave talked with a mechanic at the Ford place that fixed his family's Mercury, and got a Model A coil, condenser and a set of points. The next morning we went to Argus Town on the bus, stopped to buy a few groceries from our small, joint hoard of weekend money, and walked the final three miles up the dirt road to the cabin.

I don't suppose there will ever be another car like the Model A, as satisfying for boys to work on. We put the battery back in, connected it, and cranked the car a couple of times; no spark. We put in the new electrical parts and tried again, and Dave yelled because the screwdriver he was holding against the top of one spark plug, to shoot fire across a gap and ground itself against the block, had a split handle.

"Let's not be quite so strong on that crank, Barney J. James," he said.

"We've got spark?"

"That's what we've got."

"It ought to start, shouldn't it?"

"If it happens to have any gas left in the tank."

I slapped my forehead. "We drained it," I said. "Alex said I ought to drain it for the winter."

Dave grinned. "Well, it's downhill into town, isn't it?" He said.

"Sure. Let's eat." I cooked. It was good, greasy depression hamburger—they used to put ground pork and bread crumbs into

it at the country stores, and a little sausage seasoning, and we ate
with our fingers from the skillet because the water was off and
we had no way to wash the dishes.

Then we pushed the little green coupe out of the yard, turned
it around, and got in. It had no top.

"What's that on the wheel?" Dave asked.

"I guess Tim cut his initials," I said. There were letters in the
black bakelite, TW and EE. "Tim Weston. He was the manager.
Maybe the EE was his girl sometime, or something."

"No," Dave said. "I think not. I think it's the name of this
fine car. The Twee. Boats have names . . . drive the Twee, Barney,"
and I released the handbrake and we rolled slowly away, getting
out to push when we had to, till we made the Argus Town Chev-
rolet Garage, and got gas.

As a matter of fact, we rolled a good part of the way to Little
Rock. There were many hills, mountains, and our cash was short,
so whenever we came to the top of something I'd turn the key off,
put the car in neutral and we'd coast down. It was a golden day
when we started, and a silver night we drove into; it got cool, and
we wrapped our shoulders in blankets we'd taken out of the cabin,
and coasted and drove along, under bright stars. Every foot we
could make without gas made us chortle and congratulate the
Twee, and then, at the top of one fine, long, straight hill, with
the concrete pavement shining white in the moonlight, Dave said:

"Now is the time. You must teach me to drive."

"Yes," I said, and got out, swapping seats. "I'll let the brake
off. You steer." From then on, Dave was in charge of coasting.
He took to the steering easily enough, and about one in the
morning I told him to turn the key back on as we drifted into
a flat stretch.

"That's the starter," I said. "Press it with your foot. Push in the
left pedal and hold it in till I tell you." I shifted into first for him,
and he stalled it only once, getting us started. He was a driver by
the time we got to the outskirts of Little Rock, and though I
felt I ought to take it inside the city, it was mostly because I
figured I could stand being caught without a license better than
he could. I'm not sure what I based that on.

It was almost three when we got to the place where Alex's

group was playing. They were a nine-piece swing band, all of them college-age except for the drummer, who was leader, and his wife, who took care of the music and stuff. She didn't sing or anything. She just hung around and looked sulky.

They were playing at a dance hall called White's Garden for a school-kid crowd that seemed enthusiastic but not very big. They weren't, I don't suppose, one of the great little bands, but they were good if still ragged—the drummer was good, they had a fine solo trumpet, and they had Alex.

The drummer told me, "That brother of yours is an interesting piano player, kid. He can arrange, too."

Alex took us to his room when they got done playing; he drove us in the Twee, and told us we were pretty silly guys, driving around without licenses. I stretched out on the floor, with my head on a chair cushion. Dave and Alex were still talking when I went to sleep.

"That's some kid," Alex said to me when we were eating breakfast—spareribs and Dr. Pepper in a diner—about two the next afternoon. Alex wanted to talk about Dave; I wanted to ask Alex about arranging. Alex won.

"Where'd he go on his walk?" I asked, giving up.

"He said he wanted to get the feel of the city," Alex said, and smiled. "He was going to find the state capital buildings, and stuff like that."

"I'd better get the car greased," I said.

"I'm going back to bed. I was going to copy parts, but my eyes are so tired from sitting up I doubt if I could see the lines."

"I'll do the parts for you," I said. "What'd you and Dave talk about?"

"We were comparing fathers," Alex said. "He has so much understanding . . . has he seen a lot of the old man?"

"No. They've met a few times."

"He's really got him pegged. Very sympathetic—he said, 'Your dad's old-fashioned in the right way,' and damned if he didn't have me agreeing along about five this morning."

The rest of the band shared Alex's enthusiasm for Dave; they were pretty nice to me that evening, too. They even let me sit in a little on piano, in Alex's place. I can remember everything we played. I guess it's the only time I ever played with a real, rehearsed orchestra. We played *Thanks for the Memory, Rose Room, I Double Dare You,* and a song called *Bob White,* for a trio of local girls who tried to sing like the Andrews Sisters. They weren't bad, either. And sometime during the evening I had a long solo, on *There'll Be Some Changes Made,* which is easy because it's all in seventh chords (only Alex said, "Don't a lot of those sevenths get to be ninths, Barney?").

Anyway, I played well for me, and thrilled is a perfectly accurate word for how I felt up there.

Alex was tired but rather happy. He played a lot with his eyes closed, and towards the end of the evening he and I alternated sets.

We also got boozed up, which was novel for Dave and me. I stopped, after a few pulls off the quart of Crab Orchard, because I wanted to be able to keep playing. But Dave let them talk and pet him into a pretty good fifteen-year-old-drunk. The drummer's wife did the petting. She kept getting Dave to dance with her, awkward and grinning, on the slow numbers, and I guess rubbed him in ways he hadn't been rubbed before. Neither Dave nor I was precocious about women. I was too absorbed in baseball and Dave, though he'd had a few dates, in his particular way of relating to people.

"Alex," I said to my brother, about as boyish and straight as anyone could be, "I can see why you're bucking Dad. About living this life."

"Yeah? You like it?"

"It's got glamor."

"Where'd you pick up a word like that? That's not your style, kid."

"No. It's Dave's word. He said it."

"Your friend's the one with the glamor," Alex said. "Only he may not quite know it yet."

What the girl was doing with Dave, but she was no girl to us, made me uncomfortable as the evening went on. It was pretty public, and she kept it that way. She was a big-eyed brunette, and she behaved as if there were some kind of competition going on between herself and the rest of the band, with

Dave as the prize. The drummer, her husband, was calm enough about it, but during one of the times when I was up there playing I heard him tell her,

"Let the kid alone, Deedee."

"I like him."

"Yeah? I thought you liked piano players. Go back to four eyes, will you?"

What she went back to was sulking.

Later, in the room, Dave said to Alex: "She was only teasing, wasn't she?"

"Yeah. She does that. Usually he thinks it's funny."

"You know what it's like? It's like meeting the kind of guy who wants to pick fights."

"How do you mean?" Alex said.

"They both get something out of making you hurt."

"Maybe that's right," Alex said. "Cock of the Walk and Chicken . . . Chicken Lick 'Em. Male and female of the same species."

"Hey, Alex?"

"Yeah, Dave? How about some sleep now."

"There's room in the Twee, if you want to ride back to St. Louis. For Christmas."

I'd been having such a big time, I'd about forgotten what the purpose of the trip was. I'd have made my pitch in the morning, I suppose, and got turned down. Dave's timing was better. He'd done it rather casually, at a moment when the sympathy between the two was high, and when tired Alex, who could be difficult, felt like being easy.

"Okay," he said, to my surprise. "I can't let you two little jokers drive around this way without licenses, can I?"

We drove the Twee back up to the cabin, and that is all I think I'll recall about Dave in Missouri, except that at that time he said he wanted to be a journalist. He wrote some for the same school paper in which he'd been described. (And the description wasn't bad, after all. You can see more of the "half-faun" quality in the yearbook picture than you can of the half-gargoyle. It didn't last any longer than anybody else's boyhood delicacy of appearance, but it was replaced as he grew older by something equally engaging and distinctive. Dave's became a friendly, concerned face that crinkled up when it grinned under the red-bronze hair. There were pain lines in it, after the war, but we'll come to that.)

Anyway, he wrote for the school paper. I may not have liked admitting to myself that Dave, at sixteen, for we'd both had birthdays, was that much sharper and more accurate with words than the rest of us. But he was. For example, the summary he wrote of St. Louis was pretty good, though it may have been borrowed or adapted. I don't know. He wrote: "St. Louis is a city of northern business, eastern culture, southern sentiment and western history."

I said I wondered what that made me.

"Why, a northeast southwesterner," Dave said. "An old Missouri boy. An Ozark Kid."

You owe something in this life to the people who help you define yourself.

5

The San Juan terminal building was almost empty, and what people were there when Helen and I came in from the plane were hurrying away, except for one old man. He was out in the middle of the floor with a pushbroom, sweeping and crying. I envied him his broom. It was something in his hands that would push back when he pushed it.

Helen still had my arm in the same place she'd taken hold of when the pilot told us. Each spot where a finger pressed was sore now, and I didn't know how conscious she was of my reaching over to move her hand to a different place on my arm. When she saw the old sweeper, crying and cleaning, she started to cry again, too, but her sobs sounded more nervous than sorrowful.

"Come on," I said. "There must be a radio or TV somewhere."

"Oh please."

I didn't much want to go to the bar. I didn't want myself to want a drink. But it was the most likely public place for news of what was happening, and we started for it, following the two businessmen from the plane.

I wondered if Dave had heard yet. I imagined him out on

the water in a light, fast boat, borrowed or rented, a Star or Lightning. Not knowing. Maybe teaching a sweet girl of a wife, for contrast to his first one, to manage the tiller. Just very happily not knowing. But I thought: no, men in boats will shout across the water.

As I'd guessed, there was a radio in the bar. It was a small, shabby set, standing on the bar itself, out of key with the decor. There were two waitresses and a customer listening, and the bartender on the other side. The two businessmen hurried to join them, and Helen let go of my arm and moved ahead of me, almost running, towards the group. Then she stopped and turned completely around towards me, her mouth open, stricken.

The radio news was in Spanish.

"Sit down," I said. "I may be able to understand." My Spanish is okay, but the broadcast was like a record played too fast. "Come on, Helen," I said. We sat at a little round table. "He's talking about swearing Johnson in."

One of the waitresses turned towards us. She was a trim-looking girl from behind, with shiny black hair, but when she turned around she had a burn scar covering one cheek, so big it pulled her mouth out of shape.

"*Muerto*," she said, looking at Helen. "Is dead now, lady."

"Yes," I said, getting up again, to stand between her and my wife; the girl's scar wasn't any worse than Helen's facial reaction to it. Pardon my wife's flawlessness, señorita—it was as if I could feel hot metal, an iron or a stove top, sear my own cheek.

"Would there be news in English someplace?" I asked her.

"Downtown, maybe. Hotel. We speak Spanish."

I nodded.

"Want drink, mister?"

I shook my head, no; then I looked at Helen and said "Two cognacs, Remy Martin."

"A right-wing lunatic, Barney?" Helen said, as I put the shot glass down in front of her. "Oh God, who would?"

"They don't have anybody yet."

"That beautiful man."

"Drink this, Helen. It's cognac."

She drank, and let me try to listen for a minute or two. "He lived a little while afterwards," I said. "But probably wasn't conscious."

"A Texan. One of those fat-faced men, with short boots and a big stupid hat. . . ."

"The shot came from a building. No one saw the man."

I raised my hand to ask her to be quiet. The announcer's tone had changed. He was saying something about Truman.

"Truman?" Helen caught the word at the end of a Spanish sentence.

"No," I said. "Yes. Just that the last assassination attempt was on Truman."

"But . . . you mean years ago?"

I nodded.

"I don't understand."

"The men who tried to kill Truman were Puerto Ricans. This is Puerto Rico."

"God, Barney."

One of the men who'd made the try on Truman was still alive, he was saying. Oscar Collazo. In prison. What were they going to do? Send a reporter around to ask Señor Collazo his reactions?

"Can you really understand?"

"The governor of Texas was wounded, too," I said. "It's about a lady judge now."

Helen moaned. "A lady judge was shot?" There were tears in her eyes again.

"Please Helen. No," I said. I was trying furiously to solve the announcer's speed and accent. "The judge was crying. Swearing Johnson in, an old friend. . . ."

Gradually, through items that were repeated, I learned and told Helen roughly what had happened. A couple I recognized from the plane had come in and had been standing near us, listening to me try to translate. The man spoke to me:

"We're going to get a cab downtown," he said. "To hear the news. Do you want to join us?"

"Thanks," I said. "We'll stay here."

They left.

"Why didn't we go with them?" Helen asked.

"This is where the planes leave from."

"What time is our plane?"

"I don't know yet."

"Doesn't it say on the ticket?"

I stared at her. Probably I frowned. It hadn't occurred to me that she might be thinking about going on.

She didn't really notice my surprise. "Should we call the children?" She asked. The children were Brad, who was fifteen then, and away at prep school. Goober and Mary Bliss, who were eleven and ten, were the ones with Grandmother Gibson.

"The younger ones are in school now," I said, trying to stay calm, and got transported in a helpless way. I don't mean I just visualized this: I mean that for a second I was palpably there, in a schoolroom. The room was full of straining, tentative human young. Kids have a particular smell when they're anxious, and I could smell it. I was the teacher, and they were listening to the awful news come in. They were looking at me with big, empty kids' eyes. They wanted me to tell them something that would fill those eyes with whatever people were supposed to feel, and I didn't have the time or wit to know my own feelings yet. Teacher, teach thyself.

Helen was twisting her ring back and forth, looking at it, an heirloom emerald. Not too big, not noticeably small.

"Mary Bliss still has her Kennedy button," Helen said. "She says it's her best piece of jewelry."

"Mmm."

"You know what model Goober was making? PT Boat 109. That was Kennedy's. . . ."

"I know," I said.

"They'll be so upset."

"I don't think it would be much help to call them, Helen. We have to be there."

When she didn't answer, I said: "Remember, it's Thanksgiving next week? Brad will be back from school." I tried to say the next thing wryly enough to make Helen smile, but it came out weak: "Chalk one up for Granny Gibson, anyway." As I've said, Helen and I sometimes get away that time of year, but we'd never tried missing the big turkey dinner at her mother's before. There'd been coolness.

"Do we have to decide before we know everything? To go back?"

"We know the President's dead."

"Shouldn't you call Dave?"

"Yes. I'll call."

"Maybe they'll want to go cruising anyway."

"I don't think so," I said. "Dave will be pretty shaken up. He knew Kennedy."

"It's their honeymoon, Barney."

"He didn't know him well. But the Doremus family used to spend their summers on Cape Cod, too. They weren't as important in the government, or rich, but I guess they saw the Kennedys sometimes. Dave resented the Kennedy boys, he says, but then he got to know . . . John Kennedy. A little better. When they were both wounded and both in Chelsea Naval Hospital."

"I know, Barney. I remember that."

"I didn't know whether you did."

"Couldn't we get our plane to the Virgin Islands, anyway? It's only an hour. It would be nicer if we could see them. And Captain Clark. And turn back from there. Could we, Barney?"

"No," I said.

"It's only an hour."

"No," I said. "We can't."

"Don't shout at me."

"Dave and his wife are probably packing. The shock waves from this are going to affect a lot of people who lean on Dave."

"Maybe that would make him want to stay away."

"You don't know Dave very well." I wanted to get to the phone and the ticket counter now, but I was sorry I'd spoken loudly and tried to explain first about what Dave did for a living. He'd got a law degree from Harvard—Helen knew that—but while he drew on it, his career wasn't practicing law. He was a management consultant, a sort of doctor to troubled businesses. But it went beyond that. He was engaged privately, sometimes publicly, in regional development. He'd get himself into trying to help solve the economic problems of whole towns in the area he lived in. I tried to illustrate by telling about a ready-mix concrete firm up around there that called Dave in once for advice on how to grow bigger. Dave went out and talked to their customers, before he signed on, and found out that the concrete people were arrogant and hard to deal with. Having no competition they made deliveries at their own convenience, refused small jobs and special orders, weren't always careful about quality. When Dave went back and told them the place to start would be by improving their present service, as the first condition for growth, the proprietors said no; just figure out how much new capital, how many more trucks, a fool-proof bidding procedure and where to open the next branch. So Dave walked out and started looking for the men who were interested in becoming competition. He even took them to the bank. . . .

Helen said: "Why are we talking about ready-mix concrete?"

"All right," I said. "I'm sorry." But there were fifty stories like that. There was even one with me in it.

"You ought to see Captain Clark, Barney. To be fair."

"The Captain's got my deposit," I said. "Dave's too. The money gets kept when a trip is cancelled."

"But Barney. . . ." The sentence was lost in sobs. I got up and went around the table. This was the most serious crying she'd done. Helen can get fairly hysterical.

I put a hand on her shoulder, pulled her face against me. In about a minute I could feel the wetness from her weeping begin to soak through the thin, blue cloth of my shirt, onto my diaphragm.

"I want to go on, Barney . . . away from . . . Texas. Away . . . on a b-boat. . . ."

My diaphragm was getting damper and damper, and I found myself feeling as if some of the moisture was my own, as if Helen were crying now for two of us or, perhaps, my own tears came out down there, under the blue shirt. I stroked the smooth head. Along with the enormous, national sorrow was a small, particular one for Helen James: boats meant so much to her.

She feels about sailboats, I thought, feeling the thick, live hair under my hand, as a young girl often does about horses. Yearning towards them all, hopelessly attached to any individual

32

one that comes into her life. We oughtn't to be living inland; the coast seems close to me, an hour or so away, but to a boat lover that's transcontinental.

The insensitive husband. I should have known she'd been hooked already by *The Bosun Bird*, even without seeing it. Dave had sent a photograph of the schooner under sail, and that was enough. It really was quite beautiful; after the picture came, I'd looked for it once or twice and couldn't find it. Now I realized it must have been with Helen, in her purse or on her desk, all the time.

I squeezed her shoulder. Helen and I have not always made one another happy, but I know her totally, know why she moves and how she feels whenever I let myself think about it. I don't see how you can know anyone that way and not be sympathetic, unless you hate her. And I've never felt any hate for Helen—or if I did at one time, for a time, it has been long forgotten.

What I felt now was the moisture a dream makes in dissolving, wetting my shirt: a shining leader who loved boats, too, lay dead. It was mixed up in her mind already with nostalgia for something she'd lost, something that was to have been brought out of memory and made alive again by going to a place named, mythically, the Virgin Islands. And sailing out to sea from there, innocent and proud, on a white boat, under white sails.

"Helen," I said, "I'm sorry. I couldn't go cruising now, away from the kids. I don't think you could either."

It wasn't that I imagined that for citizens to return to their homes would do the president any good, or the country. It was just that what had me was stronger than Helen's grip on her vanishing dream, stronger and much older: into the cave. Into the cave, children. Get back against the wall, while I roll the stone up against the door. Something is moving around out there in the night that makes the earth tremble with its weight.

Helen was answering: "You don't know what it is to love a boat," she said, in a flat, prosecuting tone. It sounded strange in those surroundings and that circumstance. It was the voice of a person who has just discovered the bitter and unnatural truth about someone trusted up to now: you don't know what it is to love a boat.

She was wrong there.

In the summer of the valve trombone;

I was best man at Dave Doremus's first wedding, and I walked beside the second wife to his grave. There were three perfect months in my life—his too, I feel quite sure—when we sailed together.

Those were the June, July and August on the Friendship sloop, that started out in Maine when the war was over, and Dave said: "Let the meek inherit the earth now, Ozark James. We'll take the sea."

We had a covenant that said we'd spend some time that way, dated 1941. First we'd gotten out of touch, as boys will, after he left St. Louis. Then I'd done poorly enough in grades at day school so that I needed a postgraduate prep-school year to boost me into college. I had a couple of football letters by then, and was asked to report to the prep school early, which I did, more out of impatience to be there than from any serious interest in playing. Baseball was still my game.

I got there after lunch, was directed to a room where I left my bags, and went on to the gym to draw a uniform. It was a big squad, maybe forty kids, and since I didn't know which of them I might want to know I got dressed quick and was on the field before most of the rest.

The only thing I could do with a football that showed much in the way of skill was throw passes—not the biggest thing in the single wing game. But my arm was in good shape from summer baseball, and I joined the passers, after calisthenics, and started throwing hard and flat, whenever the fat boy up front centered me the ball.

A tall end with a nose guard ran out, cut across, and I figured I'd let him have a good one, full speed that he could drop for the nice coach. He didn't, though the ball made a real clunk when he took it into his stomach; the jerk held it, jogged, cut, jumped up and tossed it back, yelling:

"Come on. Put some steam into it." And it was Dave.

Straight-A Dave; why should he be getting tutored for college? He wasn't, of course. It was just that he'd spent the previous year out of school completely, joining his father in London; and when Mr. Doremus finished the job there, he thought as long as they were over he'd take all his unused and accumulated leave and look around Europe with his boy. The two had been to France and middle Europe, Greece and Yugoslavia, and even spent a week in Nazi Berlin. 1938.

When Germany marched into Poland, 1939, on the third day of our early football practice, Dave didn't turn out. I remember the coach sending me to look for him, and me taking my cleats off, swinging the shoes in one hand and the helmet in the other, climbing the stairs to Dave's room. We hadn't yet managed to change over and room together, though we did that shortly afterwards.

He was sitting on one of the beds, with the radio on, and it's the only time I remember seeing him look pale.

"They've done it, Barney," he said. "Those storm trooping bastards."

"The Poles will give them a fight," I said.

"No. The Poles won't last two weeks."

We talked about whether to quit football. Neither of us liked the game all that much, but there was no fall tennis for Dave. He said:

"You know something? Let's go out and work. It might not be a bad time to stay in shape."

I said it wasn't our war.

Dave would play tennis, I'd play baseball, when we went on to Harvard in the fall, but that didn't work out. Harvard was unimpressed with my day-school grades, and a few A's and B's from prep school weren't enough to change its fair mind. Dave went there, I went to a smaller college, and by the time Dave would have been a sophomore and eligible to play varsity tennis, he was at Parris Island, training with the Marines.

I was told his classmates at Harvard missed him, but were unsurprised. He took the war more seriously than anyone else I knew, and in the summer between freshman and sophomore years, the summer before Pearl Harbor, had written me a note explaining. I got it in some town in northern Missouri where we were playing a series. I'd played a poor game, and was taking a shower at the rooming house we stayed in when a left-handed Indian pitcher named Abe Anniston shouted through the door:

"Barney, there's mail for you."

I guess Abe wanted the shower.

Anyway, I took the letter from him and went up to my room. It was a little attic room, the only single they had, and I lay on the bed in the heat in my underwear to read it; it was written in pencil.

... was sailing a guy's boat for him, down to Block Island, and the breeze was so good I thought I'd go out a little and come in again. Out in the ocean. Anyway, figured it was okay because I didn't have anyone with me. Been supposed to take the owner's kid along for crew, but the kid was a little scared to go out with only two of us. Told him I'd square it with his father, and went alone. Its a thirty-foot cutter, sleeps four, but it's easy as driving the Twee. Anyway, I got out a way and got chased down. The Coast Guard. Real cutter.

They came alongside and a joker with a megaphone yelled to get back over to the Sound, or they'd tow me back. When I got in, they followed over and there was a big mess about regulations and sailing zones, and I don't know. I had my passport, but all I kept thinking was, *The War's Here. It's Here. It Got Here While I Wasn't Looking,* and I can't sail where I want to any more.

You know what they do in Alexandria? The English are sailing wooden boats back and forth to Cypress, with messages and supplies. So I called my father, when the Coast Guard guys let me go, and told him, and then I said was there any way I could get to Alexandria? Dad laughed, and said if I wanted to help with the war, come down there. There were people working to get us to be less neutral, and there were plenty of things I could do to help them. And the next thing, I found myself saying: "Dad, I'm going to join the Marines." Just like that. And now, Barney Jesse Ozark James, I say it to you, too. Only. Not I'm going to, but I have.

Why the hell couldn't I have had the sense to join the

Coast Guard, instead? This way I'm not going to be seeing much pretty water again till we all get out. Yessir, yew tew, I reckon.

What I keep thinking is:

When it's over, let's buy a boat and sail some. Want to?

The reader of that letter had had a lousy day; he'd struck out twice, flied out to left field, got a single to left in the ninth and forced out. Lost it, by five runs. Old Tim, who'd given me the car, was still our manager; though we were playing a tougher kind of ball, we were still theoretical amateurs—when we won Tim would bet each man on the team ten bucks he couldn't jump over the dugout bench. If there was one. When we lost, the bet was for meal money, two dollars. I felt a little bit like taking the two bucks and joining the Marines myself. Or maybe, like my brother Alex, the tank corps, though I wouldn't have had to memorize the vision test, which someone sold him, to do it.

Wrote Dave a card: "Okay shipmate. Yes. I want tew."

2

Captain Dave Doremus, commissioned in the field, won a Silver Star leading his company's advance at Iwo Jima; he was wounded twice in the same day. The second time his shoulder was shattered and he lost part of the use of his right arm. Alex won nothing but his loss was more serious: whether it was sand, or dust, or desert sun, or bad rations, or having his spine jarred, Alex went blind. His eyes had never been much, and I guess Libya—his group was with the British—wasn't the place for them. I won nothing but the automatic ribbons and clusters fighter pilots got for completing zilch number of missions, but I lost nothing either except the same four or five years everybody lost.

I had to go to Washington, right after I got discharged, to see a lawyer. Our father had died, just before I got home, and they were holding up on settling the estate until I was back. The reason I went to Washington, rather than St. Louis, was because Alex was living there. He'd married before he went overseas, and he was living at his wife's home.

I saw the man who was going to represent him at the settlement before I even saw Alex himself; it didn't take long.

"Does Alex know how much Dad left?" I asked.

"Nobody knows precisely, Captain James. There's been some preliminary calculation of course."

"I didn't ask that. I asked if Alex knew."

"No. Not as yet."

"All right," I said.

"If I may advise you sir, you must have your own attorney. It isn't really proper for me to discuss it with you. I could refer you."

"No," I said. "You can do it, and cheaper than two guys. I just want Alex to have whatever there is."

"Excuse me?"

"I've got two eyes and no dependents," I said. "Alex is blind and has a child."

"Your brother's wife has some means, Mr. James," the lawyer said, returning me to civilian life.

That was the point. Tanny had a little money, not much. I wanted my brother to go in with just a little more than she had, and Dad hadn't been a millionaire. Alex might keep some control that way. I liked Tanny all right, and I wanted to keep on liking her. She'd liked Alex enough to want to marry him, and I wanted her to keep on, too. There wasn't anything else I could even try to do about it.

The lawyer sighed and twitched a slightly fussy mustache. "I suppose your brother's not to know that you've signed your share over?"

"You suppose right," I said. "He gets it all, and thinks it's half."

"Very well," he said. "I'll send you some documents to sign. I'd appreciate it if you could show them to some other attorney, to be sure that they are as you wish. I'll represent you both here, Captain. And there'll be no fee except for actual expenses out of this office."

That stopped me. Even so I may have been feeling slightly noble, but when I saw my brother holding the child that was born while he was away, I didn't even feel less guilty. If there'd been a man around who'd known how to give him one of my eyes, Alex could have had it and I might have felt square. A little later they were laughing because Tanny had moved the living room sofa over without thinking, and Alex had sat down in a magazine rack and broken it. She laughed nicely.

As long as I was in Washington anyway, I went to see Dave's father. He didn't have an office at the White House any longer; he wasn't a Truman man. He'd retired from government and was writing a newspaper column of political comment, though it wasn't spectacularly successful.

He was too kind a man, I think, and had too many loyalties to have written things that would get people all excited. He'd asked me to meet him for lunch at the Cosmos Club, and though it was our first meeting since St. Louis, years before, I knew him as soon as I walked in. I knew him because there he was in the lounge, standing, talking, a slight, frail, attractive man with luminous white hair, and he had the same appearance of total attention to another person's problem that Dave projected. I went up without hesitation, when the other man left, and introduced myself.

"I think I would have known you, Barney." He shook hands —an easy, unaffected old man who said warm, simple things that made you feel he took real pleasure in your company. He told me as we ate together that Dave was on Cape Cod; he hoped I'd go on up and find his son.

"He's in damaged health," Mr. Doremus said. "But you'll find nothing wrong with his spirit."

That was it all right. Dave wasn't at the Cape, but I found people in Wonamasset, which was his town, who could send me on to Freeport, Maine.

"Just go down to the shore, and start looking under boats," one man said, and it was as easy as that. My man was under a nice, fat tub of a boat, which was hauled out in a small boatyard at Freeport, painting.

"Barney James!" he cried from under the rudder. "Sir. I'll have your craft ready to sail tomorrow." He wriggled out, pulled a shirt around his shoulders, and came over to me. I'd have hugged him if he hadn't been so full of paint.

"Dave, the Dormouse," I said. "By God. Have you got another brush?"

"What are you doing this lovely summer?"

"No plans," I said.

"Yes you do. Want to hear your plans? We're going to sail this thing out four hundred feet into Casco Bay in the morning, and drop anchor and get half-drunk, and stay that way all summer. Remember your old Missouri post card—had a picture of Champ Clark's statue on it. Champ Clark! And it said, 'Okay shipmate. I want tew.'"

"That's what it said."

"And if you get homesick. . . ." Dave had a way of coming down unexpectedly on some particular and unlikely word or syllable; this time it was *home*. "If you get *home*sick, we'll just take a long tack out past Key West, and come up into the *Mex*ico Gulf, and sail up on the Missis*sippi* River, and pick you up some more of those Champ Clark post cards."

"Tell me where he got the name, and I'll go with you," I said, pointing my finger at him.

"Who, Champ? Why any old Missouri boy knows that. Well, you see, stranger, he was a champeen singer—'You gotta stop kicking my dog around'—but he came up against a champeen or*a*tor in the old convention hall. And when the Democratic party picked Bryan over Clark, they were making the old political error of going with words instead of music—where the hell did he get the name, anyway?"

"Second syllable of his middle name," I said. "James Beauchamp Clark. By rights he should have called himself Chim. I've never been on a sailboat before, Dave. What kind do you call this?"

"It's a Friendship sloop," Dave said.

"Will a thing like that go out in the ocean?"

"We could sail her to England."

"I just came from there," I said. "They might not want me back so soon."

"Take off your shirt and pants and help yourself to a paint brush." Dave tossed his own shirt on a sawhorse, turning slightly away from me, and I saw the scars.

His back was crisscrossed with them, growing deepest around the right shoulder blade where the tissues hadn't yet turned white. This inflamed part was a good two inches across, a diagonal scoop ten inches long and an inch deep.

"Boy," I said. "They used the whole spool of thread on you, didn't they?"

"Does it look bad, Barney? I forget about it. Except I have to paint with my left hand."

"You'll be a first-baseman yet," I said. "How much for the boat?"

"Three hundred, and about a hundred more to the man here for helping me haul and scrape it."

"Can I buy half?"

"Will you sail it with me?"

I'd really been thinking of something else for the summer. I'd been thinking I'd sail for a week and then I'd go get my old view camera, and buy it a couple of lenses, and go up to the Laurentians in Canada to play Ansel Adams. But I said: "Gave you Champ Clark's word on it, didn't I? I've got another mustering out installment coming. . . ."

"Spend it on booze for the voyage," Dave said. "We'll need an ocean of gin to sail this vessel in."

"You're the captain, Captain," I said, and he slapped the rear of my pink officer's pants with a wet paintbrush. Then I had pants fit to paint in.

She was a plain, wide, comfortable boat, that Friendship sloop, and didn't have a name. Oh, she had one: the girl Dave bought her from had named her *Bucky* and we let that stand. But we always called her *The Friendship Sloop*, as if that were a name rather than a kind. The girl had sold her, now that pleasure boats were back in production after the war, because she wanted to race.

Not us. Drifting was more our style. We had a big cabin below, with bunks on either side, and we'd bring the mattresses up into the roomy cockpit, put them one on each side of the tiller and move along slowly, by sail or motor as the mood took us. For about a week we just poked around Casco Bay, going nowhere.

"The idea of a shakedown cruise," Dave said, "is if you start shaking, lie down."

"In about an hour," I'd say, "if I keep moving right along, I should be able to make it from here to the cooler for a beer. If I do, shall I get you one?"

One afternoon we took the girl who'd owned the boat out, quite a nice girl named Marian something.

She'd been to a party the night before, and asked if she could have a drink to steady her.

"Soon," Dave said. "We neither shake nor stir martinis, Maid Marian. We sail them gently around till cool."

When we gave her the drink, she got brisk and started worrying about Dave's future. She didn't seem too worried about mine.

"What *are* you going to do?" she asked, and when Dave smiled and shrugged, I told her:

"We may go into the business of mixing people's martinis for them, if this ocean motion thing catches on."

"It's sure fire," Dave said. "We'll deliver at clubs and docks and moorings . . . slowly."

"That's pretty ambitious," I said.

"It'll be a worldwide fleet of martini boats," Dave said, dreamily. "Barney, could I trouble you to inch your way forward, and do that thing you do with the anchor?"

"Lower it?" I said. "Slowly?"

"Today we'll celebrate," Dave said. "You may drop it slowly."

And at that we sprang into frantic action, for we were at the cocktail hour clam bed, and cocktail hour started, morning or afternoon, when the tide got right. The clam bed was just off a long point; we anchored and leapt overboard in trunks and sneakers. Dave kept a tee-shirt on, because of the scars and having company; Marian sat on deck and watched us splashing around, filling a bucket with the prettiest cherrystones, nothing larger allowed.

We swam them back to the boat. "Quick," Dave cried, and I pulled myself up and reached for the bucket. "The knives, the knives. There's not a moment to lose."

Those tender clams, so fresh from the sea. We sat with our

legs over the side, holding fruit-jar martinis, opening clams for ourselves and the girl, sucking in the clam meat, sea water and all, and scaling the empty shells back into the bay.

It seemed to me that Marian and Dave might have some use for privacy, then; I swam ashore and walked the rocks, counting sanderlings and checking tide pools for an hour or so.

By the time we sailed her back, Marian was so taken with the way we fit her boat, with its scruffy oak decks and its plain, honest gear, that she gave us a new mainsail, one she'd been planning to return.

"That's a nice girl," I said, as we gloated over the big, new spread of cloth.

"That's a lascivious remark," Dave said. "And you could have left out a couple of those tide pools. She loves another. But never mind."

"Are there other fish in the sea, Captain?"

"You are damn well Ozark right," Dave said, and in the morning we sailed northeast, towards Bar Harbor. In the afternoon we stopped at Bath, so Dave could pay a call.

"Fishing season in the sea?" I asked, hopefully, but he said no. These were older people; the man had been a governor of Maine, a friend of Dave's father, and had lost a son in the Pacific.

"Dad seemed to think they'd like to hear about the war out there," Dave said. "I don't know. I'll go, anyway."

"I guess I won't."

"No." Dave was shaving. "Coming ashore, though?"

"I need something to play," I said. "An instrument. Mind if I slip your bunk overboard and put in a small piano?"

Actually, I wouldn't have wanted a piano, even if I'd been staying ashore. I didn't start playing the piano again until I learned that Alex had—and then, for a while, I wanted to play one all the time. For cruising, I thought a clarinet would be nice—I'm bad on any instrument but can play most of them a little.

I went shopping in Bath, didn't find a second-hand clarinet, but someone put me onto the high-school band director and he had cheap instruments. I bought a cornet and, because he had no use for it and wanted only another five dollars, a valve trombone. He even threw in music books, so I could try to teach myself. I'd thought of trying to find Dave a guitar, an instrument he'd spoken of trying to learn, but from the crooked way his right hand held a clam knife it didn't seem like much of an idea.

3

We lay over that night in some little bay. Dave said we might go on towards Bar Harbor in the morning, to pick up passengers, but needn't press on sternly since the passengers didn't know yet they were going to be picked up. How we loved our morning sleep, after too much military service, with the dark cabin warming slowly and the salt from yesterday's ocean bathing making our skin stiff—I don't know how late we would have slept that day if we hadn't heard a powerful outboard motor go by early, very close and noisy, felt something bump us slightly and go off, rocking us with its wake.

"Hell," Dave said. I could see him in the shadow on his side, up on one elbow. "What's he trying to do?"

We tumbled out of the bunks in our underwear, ran on deck and back to the stern. We could see a small boat going away in a straight line for shore.

"Am I really awake this morning?" I said. There was no one in it.

"That is one empty boat," said Dave. For we were high enough above the water so that we could see that nothing was in the dory except for lobstering gear.

Puzzled, we looked back in the direction it had come from. In a minute or two we could hear new sounds.

"There come some more," Dave said. We could see two new boats, coming around a point, headed our way.

"It's the morning of the empty-boat race," I said. But right after that we could see that the new ones had men in them, two in each. We watched them come up and go by, chasing the empty boat, but they didn't come close to us nor did they return our waves.

"Those are lobstermen," Dave said. "Peculiar breed, sir, as of course you know from Missouri."

"Quite," I agreed, and at that we heard something splashing, out by the bow, and a voice called cautiously:

"Hey."

We turned our backs to shore and trotted forward, and there was a fat, muscular looking blond man in the water, hanging onto our anchor line. He was fully dressed.

"Hey, are they gone?" he asked.

Dave looked back. "They're almost to shore. That your empty boat?"

"Yeah. Did it make the beach?"

"Sure did."

"They gotta think I jumped out and ran for the trees."

"You'd better come aboard," Dave said.

The big man looked up soberly, floating by the anchor line and clinging to it, and said:

"I ain't much of a swimmer. I figured I could fight'm better on shore. Then I saw your boat here."

"Fight four of them?"

"I could."

We heaved him up with us, keeping an eye on the men in the other lobster boats who were half a mile away now and on shore, looking at the empty ones. Our man rolled onto the foredeck, putting cabin structure between himself and shore, lay on his back with water pouring out of his clothing, and said:

"Those clamheads cut my pots loose."

"You a lobsterman?" Dave asked.

"Stiggsy Miller," he introduced himself, still lying on his back, he stuck his hand up in the air to be shaken. I kept watching the men on shore. "I get back from the war, how do you like it? They're trying to say I can't trap lobsters in my old place. How do you like it?"

"I don't think I like it," Dave said. "But what'd you do?"

"I went out and found my pots gone, and that took the rag off the bush right there," Stiggsy said. "By God, I started pulling theirs. I got fourteen good lobsters in that boat, let alone a new motor."

"Their lobsters?"

"Yeah."

"You sure the same men cut your pots?"

"I don't know. I get out there, I'm so damn mad I don't care. They're all together, those guys."

"You're in trouble," Dave said.

"I know it." Stiggsy turned on his side, raised up on an elbow, and water started running out from new places under his clothes. "You think I'll ever get dry?"

"We'd better get you out of here," Dave said.

"They'll think I ran. Think I'm up in the woods, like a bear in a cave. Half wish I was, too, I'd claw 'em."

"What do you want to do?"

"I don't know. I just got so mad."

"You'll find a dry shirt below," Dave said. "I don't think any of our pants will fit you."

Stiggsy Miller finished turning over and raised up onto his hands and knees. "I shouldn't have taken their lobsters," he said, and started to crawl towards the cockpit. "That's what I call a stupid trick." He rolled over the combing around the edge of the cockpit, like an infantryman going over an exposed ridge line, landed on his knees and crawled on into the cabin.

Dave smiled at me: "Guys get drowned for it," he said.

Stiggsy's head poked out at us. "I got so mad," he said. "But hell, I'd drown a man stole from my pots too." He got into a crouch and looked up over the stern, towards the beach. "They ain't back yet," he said.

"They may have someone watching your boat, though," Dave guessed.

"Listen, could you . . . are you guys leaving here, or what?"

"You want to go? Come along."

"Would you?"

"What about your new motor?" Dave asked.

Stiggsy grinned. "Aw, hell, it ain't paid for."

"Where do you want to go?"

"Anywhere." He thought and added, "Hell, I been trying to fight the whole town since I got back. Like it was the only town in the world."

"Got family there?"

He shook his head. "Not worth staying for."

"We'll take you Stiggsy. Ever been on Cape Cod?"

"Nope."

"That's where we're apt to wind up. Now you stay inside."

Stiggsy disappeared, and Dave started our motor while I hauled up the anchor. When I got back to the cockpit, Dave was turning the boat towards shore.

"You going in there?" I asked.

"Co-pilot to pilot," Dave said. "Think we better had, sir. They see us turn and take off, they'll pur*sue* us—catch us, too." He was smiling. "Want to tell Stiggsy?"

I went below. Stiggsy was in knee-length army underwear, and one of my shirts, lying on Dave's bunk, quite comfortable. When I explained, he yawned and nodded. His confidence in Dave seemed unlimited.

Dave took us to within twenty or thirty feet of shore. The wind and tide were moving us back out, but when he set the motor to idle we could just hold steady.

Sure enough, as we approached, one of the lobstermen came out of the pines at the edge of the beach where he'd apparently been stationed, watching for the fugitive to try to slip back to his boat.

"Take it, pilot," Dave said, and when I had the tiller he trotted up to the bow and called to the lobsterman:

"Anything wrong?" The man stared back without answering. Dave jumped off, into water waist deep, and waded ashore.

I could hear some of what they said, on the breeze—or what Dave said, asking for information. The other man mostly shook his head. Then there came an exchange of shrugs and they separated, the man going back to his post in the pines, Dave to the abandoned boat. I confess I was a little tense, and wished he'd get back out, now that things were clear. As if he realized my anxiety as I felt it, Dave looked up at me, smiled, held up his left hand and opened and closed it, thumb meeting fingers. Then he leaned into Stiggsy's boat, picked up an empty five-gallon bucket, and judiciously selected six lobsters from the live box. He waded back out with them, past our bow, and came even with where I was sitting at the helm.

"The coolest customer," I said. "Are those things loaded?"

"I offered to buy them. Man said they weren't his to sell, help myself if I didn't mind eating dirty, stolen stuff. Here." He raised up in the water and poured the live lobsters around my feet in the cockpit. "Sic him, boys," Dave cried. "That man wants to eat you."

We went meandering on to Bar Harbor.

Stiggsy Miller made an agreeable passenger. He'd been an army mess sergeant, until six weeks before, and he took over the galley. We protested very little.

He didn't have any money with him, but the first night in Bar Harbor he borrowed ten dollars from each of us, found a poker game and won eighty more. It was the chauffeur's game, he told us; of the different kinds of servants people brought up to their resort homes for the summer, the chauffeurs were the sports.

He paid us each back eighteen dollars; he'd played big-time army poker with company money, and the customary return to lenders, he said, was money back plus 10 percent. I was for just taking what I'd loaned, but Dave shook his head at me:

"Eighteen's right," he said, and I understood this was a matter of honor. After that we were free to accept or decline Stiggsy's standing offer to take our money into the chauffeurs' poker game. I generally declined, so Stiggsy won me a pretty good pair of binoculars one night anyway—I was trying to teach myself sea birds. Dave seemed to like risking something on his man.

"It's better than owning a race horse," he said.

"You not a gambler?" Stiggsy asked me.

"Used to like it. Horses are my vice as a matter of fact, but I never wanted to own one." It was something I'd picked up from ballplayers, summers before the war. Stiggsy said he'd find me the bookie in town, but I really wasn't ready. If I was going to get back into that, I'd want to follow a meeting someplace, read the papers and the forms. "It's funny," I said. "I'd forgotten betting on horses."

I looked at them. Dave was stretched out on deck. Stiggsy was rubbing some kind of ointment around the deep scar. There wasn't really enough for Stiggsy to do aboard the boat, and he mothered us in a gruff way, getting up early after one of his late games to cook breakfast, even shining brass though the Friendship sloop had little enough of it.

"I don't know whether I'll bet horses again," I said. "Guess I might. Sometime. Right now, if you gentlemen can stand it. . . ."

And I closed myself in, down in the cabin, to practice my cornet. Stiggsy and Dave were surprisingly tolerant of the noise I made.

Or maybe they weren't. When I went up, half an hour later, they were gone and so was the dinghy. I decided they must have gone ashore for groceries. The people we'd come to find were away that week, but it was no strain waiting for them— we'd even gotten into an unpremeditated routine, there at our mooring: Stiggsy and Dave would row off on their morning trip. I'd stay aboard, practicing, and then go out on deck and read. In the afternoons we might sail out somewhere to swim, taking people with us, or if there wasn't anyone along, give Stiggsy a lesson. He'd developed a clumsy but enthusiastic way of splashing around, as long as he didn't get too far from the boat. He liked to fish, and sometimes we helped him, though I can't say our catch was spectacular except for the day we got into a run of tinker mackerel and brought in over a hundred to distribute among the people in other boats. We generally had dinner on board at the mooring, and sometimes Dave and I went to parties afterwards while Stiggsy played poker—Dave knew quite a few people in Bar Harbor.

The morning that we talked about horse racing I came up from my practice and saw a dinky little blue and white rowboat bobbing nearby with two large girls in it. The one who faced me from the stern seat was a floppy, friendly looking girl with short, dark, silly, curly hair blowing around—why, hell, a lovable looking girl. The other, whose hair looked pretty similar from behind, was rowing so I couldn't see her face.

The one facing me called, "Ahoy. What was that noise?"

I smiled, and let them row closer before I said: "Who wants to know?"

"I'm Letitia Harris," she said. Nobody ever looked less like her name was Letitia. "I want to know."

"I was drowning cats," I said.

"Wasn't it some kind of trumpet?"

"Cornet."

"You see?" said lovable Letitia to the other girl, who now turned her head up from the oar handles and looked at me. They had to be sisters, if only because of the hair; but this one looked more composed, greener eyed, less floppy.

"A cornet's not a trumpet, is it?" the second one asked.

"May we come aboard?" Letitia had a low-pitched excitable voice; she was, I thought, a cuddly, stuffed-toy of a girl, and I was having a great time looking at her.

"You certainly may." I reached down for the painter, and pulled their funny little blue and white boat in close.

"May I play your cornet?"

The second girl, who was really prettier in a conventional way, said: "She says she can play the trumpet, but I promise you she can't."

I held the boat while they climbed up. They were wearing swimsuits and small, unbuttoned sweaters. Letitia's swimsuit was two piece, and the sight of the skin between made the tips of my fingers tingle.

"How does she go on the valve trombone?" I asked the more composed sister, and Letitia cried, where was it? And the other girl said:

"She's never even heard of a valve trombone before. I'm Vinnie."

Vinnie was shorter than Letitia, compact; she was a little more like her full first name, somehow, which was Lavinia.

"We were named for spinsters," Letitia said. "Do you think we will be? Where's the trombone?" And then, before I could answer: "We're twins. Can you tell which is which? Look."

And I had to laugh, for she was half a head taller than Vinnie, in addition to the other points. I offered a drink, which they accepted giddily—Lavinia no less than the other, now that she was settled. I got the trombone up and oiled the valves. Letitia—Tish—made a lovely show of pouting into it, looking down the bell, rattling it, and finally pressed it to her wide, lip-sticky lips and made it say BLOOP.

"There." She was delighted with herself. "Do you have any olives?"

"She's the worst clown," said Vinnie.

"In my part of the country, clowns don't come pretty like that," I said, and therewith, very likely, settled my hash. If some mountain boy was going to sit around picking out a twin girl to call pretty, Vinnie was going to have something to say about which one. I saw it in the way she suddenly snapped her head back, looked at me, and then purposefully drank off about a quarter of a Mason jar of martini at one, sustained awful gulp.

"Help," said Letitia calmly. "Vinnie's going to be drunk."

"I'm sorry about the olives," I said. "Dave, whose boat you're on. He'll be bringing some back."

"Is Dave the redhead or the fat one?" Vinnie asked, speaking carefully and not at all abashed at letting me know they'd had us under observation. She stood; the gin had really hit her quickly. She swayed, in a dignified way, and said: "Ne'r mind. Nev Er min. D." Tossed her head, smiled. "We will find out. We will be back."

Then she did something which may have been partly unconscious, but was very sexy: she settled her bathing suit. She ran her thumbs around under the edge of the top, under her arms and down her back, and then her index fingers under the elastic from the bottom towards the front of her thighs, wriggling under the garment, getting it in place. And I was caught by the same, strange, girlish looseness, innocent and urgent, that so appealed to me in her twin.

"Come along, Letitia," she said primly, snapped the elastics and bobbed her head at me. "We'll be late to lunch."

I saw Dave and Stiggsy rowing out just then, and pointed at them, promising that olives and gin and even lunch were coming; but the twins pretended that it panicked them, they cried that they hadn't been introduced, and they scrambled into their silly boat, almost swamping it, and rowed away in a heap of giggling, glorious nineteen-year-old flesh.

"Barney, Barney," said Dave, coming alongside. "How could you let them leave?"

"They hadn't been introduced," I said.

"They waved and called, 'Hi, Dave,' and then they rowed away in a panic as if we were chasing them. Who are they?"

"They're twins," I said. "Utterly impossible to tell the difference between them." I sighed happily; I could still see them moving off towards lunch. Vinnie rowed pretty well. "That was quite a little boarding party," I said. "And they'll be back tomorrow for their music lesson."

"Here," said Stiggsy. "Get the box, will you?"

We stayed aboard that night, drinking beer instead of liquor for a change, and listening to Stiggsy talk. The war had been a very different thing for him. He'd been a rear area man, which made it curious for he was far more a fighter in temperament than Dave or me. Or Alex.

"I told them I was a lobsterman, when I got drafted," he said. "Guess they thought that was some kind of a goddamn cook. Anyway, I got sent off to cook and baker school. Hell, boys, I could see right away the thing to be was a mess sergeant, and I bucked hard for it." He had made a lot of money—Stiggsy was being candid—not so much in poker games as in selling food to civilians. "Got close to five thousand bucks," he said. "In postal savings. Listen, I'm going to leave you guys."

"That's sudden," Dave said. "Thought you were coming to Cape Cod?"

"Why, Stiggsy?"

"Aw, I don't know. Listen, there isn't much I can do for you, and . . . well, look. You guys are going to be needing that bunk space. I mean, like them girls this morning."

We both protested, but it was pretty sensitive of old, fat Stiggsy—he seemed many years older, to me, at twenty-nine than we did at twenty-four. Sensitive because I'd been thinking pretty much the same thing. I don't mean I was that sure of the twins, but if not them, then other girls would turn up.

So, of course, I protested harder, but Stiggsy said:

"Look, I gotta get my money. I'll go in when the boats are out, see? And I'll get down and meet you on the Cape, okay? Maybe look around down there a few days. . . ."

"There's not much lobstering around Wonamasset," Dave said. "Of course, there're other towns. . . ."

"I'm getting off the water." Stiggsy sounded vehement. "Sailing around with you guys is one thing, I mean nice. But I want to work warm and dry from now on."

He had a lot of energy and a lot of strength, and I'm sure he'd begun to feel that mothering me and Dave wasn't a sufficient way to use them. Still, it was plain he left reluctantly (and we did try to reassure him), and that he'd have been glad to be Dave's shipmate a while longer.

We rowed him in early next morning, and when we got back we had cold beer and cold lobster for breakfast and lay in the sun a while. About ten I brought up the cornet and said:

"Let me see if I can call some chickens."

"Mmmm." Dave sounded sleepy. "I'll take the Plymouth Rock. You can have the Buff Orpington."

"Don't frighten them," I said. "They're very shy."

I started through, loud and bad, *When the Saints Go Marching In*, which uses only the first five notes of a major scale, and is the brass instrument equivalent of playing *My Country 'Tis of Thee* with one finger on the piano.

I'd half thought they might not come, but it was like magic; I was going through for the fourth time, sounding smoother, when the little blue and white rowboat appeared, rather close at hand, coming around the end of a nearby cabin cruiser. This time Letitia was rowing, and Vinnie, the shorter twin, yelled:

"You're getting better."

"Has Tish been practicing?" I called.

"Don't talk to her. It's her day to row, and she can't talk and row at the same time."

"I can too," cried Tish, and lost an oar. They were close; Dave dived in and retrieved it. Then he caught the prow of their dinghy and swam it over to where I could grab a rope.

"That's Dave," I said. "Dave, Letitia at the oars. Lavinia in the coxswain's seat. But you mustn't expect to be able to tell them apart."

Tish had turned around and was looking at Dave. "Do you always swim with your shirt on?" she asked. He had halfway hauled himself onto deck and he stopped like that, balanced on his hands and stomach muscles, and looked at her rather soberly.

"Oh, I'm sorry," she cried. "Was I terribly pert?" She frowned so, at herself. "Oh, don't be cross."

For as water drained off, the thin cloth of his tee-shirt became stuck to his back, became nearly transparent, and the ridges and scallops of the scarred area were plain as bas relief.

"Who could be cross with you?" Dave said, smiled, and finished coming up. We helped the girls aboard, and the second determining moment was over. If there'd been any question left as to how we'd choose up sides, there wasn't any now. Vinnie'd picked the Ozark Kid—now Tish picked Dave. Would have fair broke my heart, if Vinnie hadn't been so yummy.

What I shall tell next is surely a digression, but it is one of the things I store in memory with real love, getting it out now and then when I'm alone to play through, like a marvelous old dance record:

It is noon the same day, and we have blooped the trombone, drunk the health of Champ Clark (may he rise again) and agreed to go for a sail and swim quite soon now or maybe sometime. I am still excited by Tish's long legs and scatterbrained sweet abandon, but she is fastened to Dave and Vinnie is close beside me, moving right along towards someplace I want to go to. But I do not know at what speed, or how many furlongs: these are gently reared, state-of-Maine girls, recent graduates of a not-unfashionable junior college. That we will kiss, cuddle and sigh is plain, from the way Vinnie's nice firm leg presses mine, thigh to thigh; if I move slightly, she moves too, reestablishing touch. She gives me green-eyed glances, and her lips have nuzzled my neck.

Tish's hand is under Dave's tee-shirt, fingering the scar, and he smiles and removes it.

"Be a good girl and Daddy will let you play with the nice scar later," he says.

"She doesn't have any sense," says Vinnie, pressing a soft, firm thing of hers against my upper arm. "Does she? Did you ever see anybody with less sense?"

Tish jumps up, standing at the edge of the deck, just beside where Dave sits with his legs in the cockpit. "That's all right," she cries, but not spitefully. Not even a taunt—it's a crow, a carol. "Vinnie's a virgin and I'm not."

And she jumps off backwards, holding her nose, into the water with a big, laughing splash. "Take me rowing, Dave," she gurgles down there. "Let's leave the young people alone."

Dave, grinning, hops into their rowboat, hauls Tish in, and they start rowing off.

Vinnie jumps away from me; then she laughs, a pure, hard triumphant laugh and yells across the water at her twin, "Maybe I didn't think Dickie Pritchett was all that nice," and she pulls away the top straps of her one-piece bathing suit and peels it down, baring her bosom to the sun, nipples pointing east and west, and laughing even harder.

Dave is rowing and staring, Tish is pointing back at her sister and me and laughing too hard to reply, and Vinnie doesn't stop. She peels the white lastex on down, baring her stomach, wiggling impatiently as the navel lights up and then curls of pubic hair, lying flat and soft over their hand-sized bulge. Prettiest damn thing I ever saw.

She hops the suit down around her ankles, steps out of it, and I grab her arm.

"Hey, girl."

End of first side. I turn the record over and play the other:

She waves and grins at her gasping audience out there in the rowboat, naked and silly. We're right in the middle of the anchorage, with dozens of other boats around.

"Duck, Vinnie. Come on." I'm frantic for several reasons.

"Where?"

"Below. Get below, before they call the Coast Guard. Or I faint."

"All right."

She promenades into the cabin, which has heated up considerably in the noonday sun, and where we both start giggling and sweating, big drops of healthy young sweat.

Suddenly she turns prim again, sits on a bunk pressing her knees together, hands in her lap and looks at me.

"It's very hot, isn't it?"

"Like an oven," I agree, with idiot enthusiasm, gasping,

sliding my trunks off, relying on pride in my flesh as any male to make me feel more adequate. Her green eyes get round; she stares.

And now it's me who feels a little prim, embarrassed at the adequacy. "It's, uh, not very large, as such things go," I say, in a conversational sort of tone, turning partly away. Anyway, there's equipment to be got from the cabinet overhead.

"It isn't?" She reaches out and just barely touches it with her finger tips as it swings by. Then, in the small firm voice of someone searching for the courteous thing to say to the proprietor of an item not accurately understood: "It's very smooth, isn't it?"

Lips pressed together, she lies back on the bunk, hands at her sides, legs slightly apart, and looks up at the ceiling; a girl waiting for the doctor to make a pelvic examination might have the same expression.

She hasn't asked if this is what the kindly practitioner wished her to do next, and when her eyes move from the ceiling to meet mine, they all but voice the question: *like this?* There is anxiety in the eyes over whether the proprieties are being observed correctly, more than apprehension.

I go onto my knees on the floor beside the low bunk, put my arm across her and my lips against her cheek.

"You're a darling girl," I say, realizing that I've slid completely and helplessly into what Dave calls my Old Missouri Boy accent; I suppose I always do when I'm moved. "Generally we try to work up a little bit to it."

"Oh," she breathes gratefully, seizes my face and commences to kiss the hell out of it. Greedy lips, and then my hands get greedy, finding parts of her to squeeze and probe, and the only other words are when she asks if it's going to hurt. This comes when we have ourselves belly to belly in a tangle of legs and hands, rolling and choking with excitement and slippery with sweat, and I guess the question just makes me sweatier and more excited. Brute male instead of tender, I don't tell her the answer; one thrust, sly and firmly guided, is worth at least a thousand words, and if it does hurt her, it surely can't hurt much from the way she rises. . . .

Dave and Tish didn't get back till late, which was just as well because Vinnie found she wanted to test this thing out pretty thoroughly. You never saw a smugger-looking girl than she was when they did come. Tish and Dave seemed happy, too, if less insufferable than we were: they'd been to the parents' house and Dave had met the mother. And Tish had somehow gotten, if not permission at least resignation to the notion of her and Vinnie sailing down to Cape Cod to visit college friends with nice Captain Doremus on his sailboat. . . .

("Oh, I hope you said 'yacht,'" said Vinnie. "'Yacht' sounds marvelously chaperoned.")

It would be so much better than just having the twins take off hitchhiking, Mummy, and the Captain would probably just sail night and day, and it would be . . . Mrs. Harris, I gathered, had long since given up the idea that she could manage her twins. So Tish had brought bags of clothing. It was Young New England, I guess, rushing back, headstrong and sweet, to wild seed, after many generations and no money left.

We raised anchor and made sail, leaving Bar Harbor and the intention of meeting some people I never saw, with the little blue rowboat bobbing along behind us.

4

We never did sail at night. We lazed down through Penobscot and Casco Bays again, big pieces of water, sailing a little and spending even more time at anchor than on the trip up.

The twins continued to be determinedly, if somehow innocently, wanton. They would throw off their clothes and jump in the water naked any time, often without being dared, and I fondly and distinctly remember Vinnie swimming around the boat on her back in a rather public cove—there were bungalows a hundred feet or so from where we lay at anchor—trying to balance a glass of scotch on her flat, pink stomach.

Tish was getting along pretty well with *The Saints* on the valve trombone. She joined me for practice every morning. And I'd progressed most of the way through *Basin Street Blues*; we could even produce some kind of parody of playing it together.

In spite of being paired off crisscross, Tish and I were effortlessly sympathetic. I felt closer to her, really, than I did to Vinnie. Yet the pairing was working out; Vinnie and I were pretty well committed to one another sensually, something like friendly opponents engaged in an absorbing series of daily matches. Dave and Tish evidently got along fine in the bunk they'd fixed forward and catty-cornered, in the sail locker, too; the tone was probably a little different. Tish's was a more yielding nature than her twin's. Even in our prep-school year and college vacations, his had been the warm, compliant girls, and I sometimes envied the ease with which he found them. My kind of girl, I'm afraid, often seemed to be the nerved up, competitive kind, the kind with whom every ride on the see-saw was a game to see if you could shift your weight at the right time to bump your partner off.

Spines can be malleable, staying as you bend them to fit, or spring wire, which seems to bend a little but snaps back hard.

Sometimes the twins' fancy that they were hard to tell apart came true, but only if you saw one or the other separately. Then you might flop down beside a curly-headed sunbather and kiss her shoulder, and say,

"Know what, Vinnie? You're sweet, but you're salty."

And she'd preen, and say, "Thank you, kind Barney. It's true I'm sweet, but I'm Tish." Maybe I made the mistake on purpose once or twice.

But it was the girls themselves who engineered the Roman comedy identical-twin joke of switching beds one night. Dave had gone down first, and was presumably in bed already, on the sail-locker floor. The girls went down together and I stayed on deck, to finish a drink and think a minute. I was beginning to wonder what I was going to do with myself, and that seemed to require drinking and thinking fairly late some nights.

When I went into the cabin it was dark, which was usual enough. We used lanterns, and liked to save kerosene. I didn't pay any great attention to the naked shoulder and the fluff of hair, dimly seen on the pillow, assuming it was Vinnie.

I dropped my clothes off, slipped in beside her, and got

myself twined around by arms and kissed. And whispered, "Vinnie, let's sleep a while. First to wake up gets to wake the other."

That remark would never have made Lavinia giggle, and when a giggle came, a monstrously welcome possibility suggested itself. My yen for Tish was very strong, and I held tight for a moment, not the least interested in sleep any more; and I quickly decided it was the kind of thing which I'd better not let on I'd guessed, if I had.

But I did want to be sure. It was so damned exciting if I was right. So I whispered:

"Vinnie, honey. Rub my back just a second, would you? In the sore spot, where you did last night?" When she pummelled my back, energetically and impartially, all over, I knew it was Tish, for, of course, I'd described what hadn't happened—and back-rubbing was a little out of Vinnie's character, anyway.

So I went at it very fervently indeed and that, oddly enough, is a record I never play over. But I keep it, I keep it, like the most agonized kind of collector, never willing to expose its perfect grooves to the digging needle of memory, the low-fidelity machine of recreation.

Tish and I were lovely friends, after that night, but then she started falling seriously in love with Dave. I'm pretty sure it was Vinnie, wanting her new experience to take on a little dimension who, with her stronger mind, pushed Tish into switching. And Vinnie continued to like me all right, as I liked her, but she was beginning to sit up late and think what she was going to do with herself next, too.

I really enjoyed myself in Tish's company best. I suppose the foolish seriousness with which she took her valve trombone work had a lot to do with it. She could get a good, big, almost mellow note out of the thing sometimes, though she was likely to break up in laughter after she played one. Anyway, it didn't sound bad, she could do it in several valve combinations, and it worked out nicely for the opening of *Basin Street*. We'd practice in the cabin mornings, and when my lip was about to go, I'd say:

"Brass man, let's take the air."

She'd say, "All right, Bugler. Our public might be ready today."

And up we'd go, often carrying our instruments so that we could blat a note or two at Dave, fishing or splicing rope, and Vinnie sunbathing—or both getting ready for the day's sail, or sometimes, if we weren't going on that day, starting on the pre-lunch drinks that would induce moist, luxurious afternoon naps.

"We brass men are very outgoing, extroverted types," Tish might announce. "We've come to get you passengers over your shyness, so you'll mix and get acquainted."

Then we'd blat a little more *Basin Street,* and inform them, reaching to share their drinks, that we were the holler guys, the spark plugs, the front-line instruments: follow our lead. I might see Vinnie scrootching along towards me, intent on snatching the cornet away, and say, sadly, "Your dedicated brass man is always ahead of his public. But finally, you'll understand. You'll appreciate." And Tish, who had settled down where she could watch Dave, adoringly, do whatever he was doing, might remember to go BLOOP.

Dave had stopped wearing the tee-shirt. A lot of the time he lay on his stomach in the sun, squeezing at a rubber ball with his right hand, and Tish would rest her cheek softly against the terrible scar.

Dave was too nice not to see what was happening and be concerned. "Barney," he told me one day while we were clamming. "She's the dearest creature that ever lived, and I absolutely do not love her. What am I to do?"

He hoped perhaps she'd gradually transfer the attachment to me, and much as I liked the idea I had to say I doubted it would happen. Tish's feelings, as I read them, could only grow stronger as Dave's weakened. I couldn't tell myself Vinnie'd care much, one way or the other, and was glad enough of it.

Late in the summer, Dave left me on the boat one weekend with both girls. We'd been cruising in Nantucket Sound for a time, and he was going to a wedding in the town of Wonamasset, where, as much as anywhere, given the way his family moved, he'd grown up. It was at the wedding that he met Jane Carlsen again, a Wonamasset-Boston girl he'd been to parties with, but never dated, before he left for the war.

Jane had grown up pretty, Dave told me when he got back, and very, very smart. But before he could get back, a couple of things happened. On Sunday morning, my twin, Lavinia, left the Friendship sloop. She didn't give any particular reason, and didn't need to:

"Summer's over," she said. "Say goodbye to Dave for me. You coming 'Titia? No, I don't suppose." And Tish and I rowed her in. They had a classmate who lived in one of those towns, and Vinnie'd probably be welcome to stay a while.

It's funny. After sharing a bunk for six weeks, and with anything but hard feelings at parting, Lavinia gave me her cheek to kiss when I put her in the cab. And then we shook hands.

In the evening, Dave didn't come back. He'd been supposed to arrive by speedboat, courtesy of some wedding guest or other, but didn't make it. There was no reason why he should have let us know, no reason even why he should have tried, but it made Tish unhappy and she got very drunk. She was the only one of us to get really sick and miserable, drunk, all summer long. She and I had a fairly confused, but wildly confidential conversation, before the liquor started coming up, during which she confessed the Roman comedy prank.

"I'm so sorry about it, now," she said. "Oh, I don't mean that to hurt your feelings, I mean, then was different. It was nice. But it made me realize, start to realize, about me and Dave. He wouldn't marry me, anyway . . . would he, Barney? No. I don't mean that, either. Mean, would he have?"

I shook my head. I didn't know. I didn't think so. I put my arm around her, and cradled her dear, dizzy head against my chest, and wondered: if I hadn't called her pretty and brought Vinnie on myself in retribution, or if I'd had the scars, mightn't I have married Tish myself? I never saw, only I heard about, the Harris's big, wandering, decrepit house, where the family had always lived, building on and closing up wings. But I could see, can see, what the old white clapboards look like, and feel the wonderful chilliness of the winter corridor that must go from the kitchen to the barns. Maybe we'd have kept ponies back there; horses when the kids grew bigger.

I put Tish to bed in the sail locker, forward, and myself, after I'd sat out and thought my way around my usual circles, in the cabin.

Dave got back in the morning. He'd had a big time at the wedding, and a tennis date with Jane on Sunday, during which he'd played left-handed and done fairly well. He'd seen Stiggsy, too! Full of mysterious purpose. Liking Wonamasset.

Tish was very hungover, and looked dissolute and drained. It didn't spoil Dave's homecoming to find her so, nor that Vinnie had left, for he assumed what was both logical and suited him —that Tish and I were lovers, now.

That made it easy to do what he wanted, which was bring Jane Carlsen out to the Friendship sloop for supper. There was nothing calculating about it—it was just nice, lucky to have things work out that way.

("Barney Darling James," said Tish, before I could even make the offer I had in mind. "Don't you dare straighten him out. Please don't dare.")

Jane had, Dave told us: a wonderful backhand, for a girl. An indecently big bosom (Tish's was small, smaller than Vinnie's even and softer, too). Jane had her own racing dinghy. And a father who was something pretty good in the Boston financial world.

I'll say for us that Tish and I played it fine for our friend Dave when Jane came to supper. Miss Carlsen, whom we both loathed on sight (though she was the kind of girl I was normally attracted to) couldn't have suspected me and Tish as being anything but an affectionate, illicit couple. Somewhat raffish. The girl kind of a ragamuffin. Young man a kind of college tough. Dave must carry them just to be nice, but really, you should be a little selective whom you're nice to.

Jane was bright all right, as Dave had said, but it was that impenetrable, Ivy-League-girl brightness which can be a veneer for anything. With Jane it covered, very successfully, a cool, firm, ruthless and ungiving nature. She was poised; she produced a splendid show of finding the Friendship sloop charming. She thanked us for piping her and Dave aboard with *Basin Street Blues,* naming the tune correctly. But I felt it was all in the spirit of a duty officer's patronizing inspection of some necessarily grubby part of the base, with which the soldiers have done their best.

In fact, all my images for Jane are military. The most persistent of them, since she really was a stunning girl to look at, blonde with hard blue eyes, is of one of those radiant girls you used to see in newsreel shots of West Point and Annapolis weddings: they were running down under the arch of swords, and you felt that they were smiling for the camera and the groom, but if such a girl should see a speck of rust on the blade of one of those swords on the way under, it would be very bad for the owner's future career.

"Pretty interested in Jane, Dave?" I asked him next day. It hurt me that he could be, but I mean the kind of hurt where your feet tingle when you see a child jump off something high, and land hard.

"Early to say." Dave smiled. "But then what's wrong with saying things early, when the dew's still on them? Come on, Barney Jesse. You and Miss Tish come on." Jane and her father could be seen, even then, on their way towards us in a launch. They'd asked us all for an overnight sail on the Carlsen's boat, which was quite an elegant ketch.

"Thanks," I said. "I might forget to salute. Carlsen's pretty social, are they?"

Moping Tish, pretending to sunbathe with her eyes closed, looked up at that.

Dave laughed. "Social? Are we talking money social or ancestors?" He rumpled Tish's hair; he really didn't know any more than he wanted to know, and she wasn't going to tell him.

"Tish Harris's forebears were messing up Indians and plucking wild turkeys for two hundred years before the first of Janey's grandparents looked to see if his English-Swedish phrase book had the word for dollars in it."

The launch was coming up. I said I'd row Tish in later, when she finished packing to go join Vinnie.

"Please stay if you'd like to, Tish," Dave said. "The boat's yours. You know that."

Tish nodded.

"It's not as if you and the Ozark Kid were utter strangers." Tish shook her head.

Dave raised his glass: "To Champ Clark," he said.

"May he rise again," said Tish, strong as she could, and we three clinked glasses for the final time.

When the launch was gone Tish went down to the cabin. I made a quart pitcher of martinis, and poured a couple of water glasses almost full, and put a dozen olives in hers. She always liked olives.

I took the glasses and went in to her. She was sitting on my bunk, with the valve trombone out of its case beside her.

"Gone?"

"Yes, Tish. Here." I put the big martini on the cabin table.

"Yours is bigger."

"I'm bigger."

"To Champ Clark?" she said, raising the glass.

"May he rise again. Drink it."

"I'm almost packed," and she did drink some. I sat beside her.

"You take your trombone," I said. "And I want you to practice, too."

"Oh, Barney." She leaned against me, cheek against mine. "He's going to, he'll marry her. In June. And go to Harvard Law School, won't he? And never come to Bar Harbor, and. . . ." She began to sob. "It's been such a wonderful, such a summer. . . ."

"Come on, Tish," I said.

"Summer."

"Come on, Letitia Harris. Drink up, now. Come on. Brass men don't cry."

She didn't take the trombone with her, though she'd said she would. The next morning, before Dave came back, I gave it sea burial. I threw the cornet after it.

And there they lie now, I feel quite certain, in two fathoms of Atlantic water, in Nantucket Sound. Sometimes I think of a skindiver happening onto them, think of him seeing the brass shine, green and gentle, up from the sand. I don't think of the instruments as corroded, really, but as softened by the work of salt and wash of waves, so that they still have their shape but the gloss is off their surface. They hardly seem metallic, as I see them, but they are prettier than ever, and useless, with their valves forever stuck. Pretty and useless like one of those bits of sea-soft colored glass you pick up, summers on the beach.

Tag up, tag up.

By two-thirty in the afternoon of November 23, 1963, all the telephone circuits in the world were busy. Our century was off its course and calling for bearings.

I stood in a Puerto Rico phone booth for twenty minutes, trying to get through to Dave in Charlotte Amalie, while Helen finished her second and probably third cognacs at the bar.

"I have a circuit now," the operator said, finally.

"All right."

But when she reached the Doremus's hotel, the room didn't answer. The hotel operator offered to have Dave paged, but I didn't think he and his wife would be sitting in the restaurant or lobby.

Anyway, there seemed to be someone waiting for the phone. I'd had it long enough.

I left word that Mr. and Mrs. James would be turning back, and hung up. I was thinking about the old weeping sweeper we kept seeing around the airport, wondering if he was still going along behind his broom out there, as I pushed the phone booth door back to its pleated position and the fan turned off.

The man who was waiting for the telephone was a tall man —he stepped my way, and wasn't waiting for the telephone at all. He was waiting for me. He was Dave.

"Hey, boy," he said, with a big, unsteady grin—his old one but full of pain today. "Bad times."

"Dave." I gripped his hand. "Yes they are."

"You all right?"

"Just like everybody," I said. I caught sight of my old sweeper, then, and nodded his way. "Just like everybody."

"You getting ready to turn back home?"

"I was just trying to call you to say so."

"Tremendous telephone service they got out here," Dave said. The lines in his face looked deeper than last time I'd seen him, and he needed sun. "Soon as you put your quarter in and said who you wanted, the telephone man caught me and threw me in a little green truck. And brought me over."

"Dave." Yeah, I did want to see him. He was the only person in the world I wanted to see at a time like this, besides my wife and children. It seemed perplexing to me that I should have let the last fifteen years go by without our getting together more than half a dozen times.

"I was a little bit too late to meet your plane. Where's Helen?"

"In the bar."

"You planning to turn back?" he asked again.

"Yes. What about your wife, Dave?" I couldn't think of the new wife's name.

"She's sitting close to a short-wave radio." There was a slight stroke of the voice on the word *short*. "With some *pretty* people that we got to know, over there."

"Connie, isn't it?" They'd come to be married in the Virgin Islands, just the week before. "I wish my wife were sitting by that radio with her."

Dave nodded. "Yes."

"The only broadcast going on here is in Spanish. Helen's about to lose her mind."

What Dave did was simple enough. He gave me a sober look, took a little transistor radio out of his sport shirt pocket, and ran his thumb along a knurled knob. As if he'd done a magic trick, a voice in English said, "*ex-marine Lee Harvey Oswald.*"

"We'll take this to her, then," said Dave.

I carried the set against my ear. While I'd been trying to phone, Oswald had caught a bus, got off it, shot down Patrolman Tippit, run into the Texas Theatre and got himself caught. I heard that very quickly, in the cold-print, you'd-better-believe-it voice of an announcer summarizing.

I asked Dave to take the radio to Helen, while I changed tickets and made new reservations. He hesitated, then he nodded and walked away towards the bar. I watched him, telling myself how great it was that he should be here, and realized it wasn't really so great but couldn't think why.

Halfway to the bar he turned and waved, with what seemed

to be the old, irresistible look of friendly concern, and I decided what was wrong with me was what was wrong with the world: John Kennedy was dead.

I walked to the ticket counter and got into a short, slow line, and thought: nevertheless. Dave looks bad for one thing. Worn, pale and underweight. He looks worse, as a matter of fact, than he did six months ago. And that was in the most fretful part of the divorce, the stupid, ritualistic time when your lawyer is calling her a tramp, and hers is calling you a pervert, and the idea is to see which can lie for the most leverage in working out a money agreement.

He'd looked worn then, but his resignation had a certain low-key sparkle to it, so that the humor in which he took it wasn't altogether unbecoming. But why, I wondered as I stood in the ticket line, wouldn't he seem better now, after a week of Caribbean honeymoon?

Maybe it was because Jane (yes, Carlsen, with the blue steel eyes) had taken the two kids and gone to California, where he'd never see them. Maybe that, and the profound shock of the assassination could account for what was really strange: that what was bright and unmistakable in Dave's appearance, which should have got through my preoccupation in the phone booth, was so dulled that I hadn't been compelled to recognize him, waiting outside. Could that be put down to nothing more than his wearing a new straw hat?

The man ahead of me started talking to the ticket agent. The man behind me said:

"Do you get it? This Oswald's some kind of a Castro nut. You get that? I thought a right-winger."

"Yes," I said, and thought: if Dave's looking poorly, why don't I feel more sympathetic? But my sympathy was mixed up, for some reason. I was upset with Dave.

It was my turn to talk with the ticket agent, before I understood why.

Then it occurred to me ("Terrible day, sir. May we help?") that it wasn't like Dave to have come over to find us at such a time, leaving behind with strangers a woman to whom he'd been married less than a week.

("I have two on a flight at six-twenty. I'm afraid it's not non-stop, sir. And not a jet."

"Okay.")

That wasn't like Dave at all.

2

Perhaps he was never as sensitive to women as he was to men. Neither as sensitive to their feelings nor to their worth.

Women responded to him, to his nice redheaded looks, helpful manner and that easy spill of personal rhetoric which only rarely got thin enough to show depletion in the pool of nervous energy that pushed behind it.

Women liked Dave's size, and confidence and manners, and for some, like Tish Harris, it was nice to have him that way and adore him. It may never have occurred to Dave as a young man that there might be another kind of girl, Jane Carlsen's kind, who might want to drain the pool, once she found how the energy was stored and released, might want to expose the bottom of softness and vulnerability that makes charming men want to be charming.

Dave was a man's man, just as the world of politics towards which he'd always somehow been directed is really a man's world, and he should have had a wife like Tish. She might have just wanted to help, and be fun, and been content to be imperfectly understood as long as she was loved. But Dave loved the one who wanted to tear him up, I'm afraid; maybe we all do. I can't claim I married the nicest girl I ever met, either.

Jane hadn't been willing to marry Dave at all, to start with, so our Friendship sloop prediction about the following June was wrong. Dave finished college and went through law school, wanting Jane pretty steadily. She'd date him when she didn't have anything else going.

In his final year at Harvard Law, Dave gave up some considerable honor (I think it was judge at a mock court) because Jane had got engaged, got thrown over and felt shattered. Dave was given his chance, then, and I guess once it got started she turned him every way but loose. All through the spring, Dave drove out every evening, from Cambridge to Wonamasset, with a basset hound named Roland on the seat beside him, to help Jane get over her broken heart. I made the trip with them once, up there on a visit; Dave asked me to drive on the way back, so he could study by the interior car light, while Roland slept.

In May, I got word that a wedding date was set, and was asked if I'd like to have the dog.

I was married myself by then. Helen was seven months pregnant, carrying Brad, and didn't want to go to a wedding much. She'd met Dave at our own; she said I was to tell the groom that she owed him a kiss, and that we didn't need another dog.

Stiggsy Miller got Roland, the basset.

I never meant to be a major influence in Stiggsy's life, but I was in two ways: one was his choice of hobbies. He'd settled in Wonamasset, as soon as he was certain that Dave meant to live there too, bought himself the most expensive pair of binoculars of anyone I know, and took to watching sea birds. I won't say he became an authority, but in time he made himself into a pretty fair self-taught expert on gulls and terns, scoters and cormorants, and he and that basset hound were a familiar dawn sight on the beaches and marshes and around the ponds.

My other area of influence was corrupt: Stiggsy was now the local bookie. In Wonamasset he promptly became notorious as a man who hung around, had money to spend, and sometimes got into fights. Then he'd put his postal savings and GI loan money together (Dave helped at the bank) and bought out the old man who'd owned Wonamasset's cigar store and newsstand. It had a counter for coffee and soft drinks, and over it, in a modest way, Stiggsy began to take bets. He'd apparently thought he had some sort of tacit approval from Dave since the three of us were able to speak of betting on races as a normal thing. And as a matter of fact all Dave ever said about it was: hell, someone was going to write book around there; it might just as well be Stiggsy, who had strict rules—no kids, no working men unless they were ones Stiggsy knew could afford it. But I don't mean to make him sound like the flower of Knighthood: a lot of white-collar people were eventually somewhat in hock to

Stiggsy, and whatever the central organization is that handles that kind of money controlled Stiggsy's little corner of the operation too.

Betting in Wonamasset became just what Stiggsy had assumed it must be: something that nice people, as distinct from strait-laced people, enjoyed. And Stiggsy himself became a town favorite with some of them. He was the honest ruffian, whom you could hire as a watchman if you needed one, or ask to go along in a tight situation. A good-natured bouncer at parties, source of small loans and credit for the few things he sold. And, along with the rest of it, an almost professional veteran and civic fund man. Poppy drives and the march of dimes used Stiggsy's little store as their chief collection point, and the young businessmen drank their coffee there and read the papers at his counter every morning.

As for the local police, of whom there were four except on holidays, Stiggsy never had to pay them off, so far as I know, because on holidays he was the fifth. Wearing his army field jacket and a policeman's cap, he took tickets at high-school football games, directed traffic around fires, and helped patrol Wonamasset Beach, a cottage area six miles from the town, on summer weekends.

When Dave and Jane's big, well-publicized wedding came along, and the two regular off-duty cops were hired to manage traffic between the church and the Carlsen's home, Stiggsy was supposed to be in uniform, guarding the presents.

"That's something you can't pay me for," Stiggsy said. I was spending the week in Wonamasset, staying with Dave at the beach, getting ready. We'd stopped by the store.

"I'm not paying," Dave said. "Mr. Carlsen is."

"That don't say I have to take his money."

"Why don't you forget the whole thing, Stiggsy," Dave said. "It's just for show anyway. And come to the wedding?"

"I can't do that Dave."

"You've got an invitation. I addressed it myself."

"They just wouldn't like it."

"Who?" I asked. "The Carlsens?"

"Miss Carlsen and her mother," Stiggsy said. "I'll bet they don't know I got an invitation."

"Shall I ask them?" Dave suggested.

"You'll just get them mad at you."

But it was obvious Stiggsy yearned to come.

"You scoundrel. I know you want to see me hung," Dave said.

"I'll just guard the presents," Stiggsy said. "If I show up at that church, you know how people are going to talk. About us being friends."

"Hell, Stiggsy," I said. "You don't think Dave cares."

He shook his head.

"What if we disguise him?" Dave said.

"Would you go that way?" I asked.

Stiggsy said: "What are you guys getting at? I put on a beard and dark glasses, they're still going to know this fat stomach aren't they?"

"No," Dave said, delighted with his idea. "No, listen."

And that was how it came about that the Carlsen-Doremus wedding was attended by a heavily veiled and very fat aunt, who came in on the best man's arm, just a minute or two before the ceremony started.

Dave's father was in on it, and kept a place up front.

"For God's sake, Stiggsy, keep your coat buttoned," I whispered, as an usher came forward to seat him. "Groom's family," I said to the usher, whom I didn't know, and watched old Stiggsy waddle off on the boy's arm, wearing a long, pink, woman's overcoat, the blue hat and veil, and the white nurse's shoes and stockings that were all we'd been able to find to fit him with.

We'd persuaded him not to wear flowers.

It all went fine, too, damn it, until Dave saw fit to take Jane into our confidence—a funny secret, he thought, to keep her gay during the long dull stand in the reception line. The specter of Stiggsy, with his pants rolled up under the skirt, squeezing into those white nurse's shoes, came close to ruining the honeymoon. Jane was so angry she was almost hysterical, right there in the line, and I had to take her out of it for a moment, take her aside and insist that it had all been my doing, Dave hadn't known about it until it was too late to stop us.

It was a good firm step along the way to Jane and my disliking one another. First I'd been the stiff-necked flyboy with the messy young tart on *The Friendship Sloop*. Now I was the man who'd helped an undesirable crash her wedding.

Barney, the thug smuggler.

In the following twelve years, Helen and I visited them once, on our way out to the Cape, and Dave and I had got together a few times in Boston, but only once for an extended time.

As for Helen, she had met my best friend just twice, before he came to our town in the spring of 1963.

3

"We'll be on a plane for home in two hours," I said.

Helen had some unnumbered shot of cognac in front of her. Dave apparently wasn't drinking, but they had a shot waiting for me, and the pocket radio turned low between them.

Dave had a schedule he held up. "We'd gone ahead and figured out the wait," he said. "You want to sit in here and drink?"

"No." But I drank the one they had for me.

"Dave was saying, why not rent a car?"

"Would you like to leave this gloomy little table?"

"We can drive to a beach somewhere and sit," Helen said. She was a bit drunk, mournfully so, not high.

"That sounds better," I said. "Anything new happen?"

"Tell him about Captain Clark," Helen said.

"Captain Kelso Clark." Dave smiled, ruefully. "When the news came some people headed for church, I imagine, and some for a bar, and some just . . . wanted to be home. Like you, Barney. The old skipper made sail on *The Bosun Bird* and took off with his radio, across the Bay."

"Single-handed?"

"Pushes that schooner around like it was a baby-carriage," Dave said. "Shall we?"

Beach and sky and birds soaring between them sounded like

what to look at, all right, but I had to say: "Dave, you've got us set. Isn't there a plane for you, back to St. Thomas?"

I didn't mention his wife. He did: "She's comfortable the way she is. Took something to make her sleep. She—it hasn't been so long since Connie lost her first husband. Don't worry about it, huh? She'll sleep a while."

It hadn't been so long since he'd told me he had left her in good company, listening to the news.

We went to get the car. It was easy. The Hertz company had a whole row of them parked outside, four-wheeled radios, for credit-card boys like us. I don't know why I hadn't thought of renting one myself.

I let Dave drive. The news kept coming in, on the car radio—a lot about Oswald's left affiliations now; and about the Cabinet flying back from Hawaii. But I couldn't get my mind off the new wife. All you ever have to do is tell me not to worry about something to get me good and worried.

4

The reason for Dave's spring visit to us, earlier that year, has to do with the way my business is organized.

The principal ownership is vested in Helen's mother and her brother, Helen's Uncle Troy. I have a small piece, nominally, which comes from the fact that my father dealt in fine woods, and, being friends with Helen's father, an old customer, gave the plant a lot of credit to help through the depression; some of the account was paid off in stock. Actually, my piece was made over long ago, as I've explained, to Alex; it's enough to amount to half a vote, when the board is polled at meetings.

I operate without much supervision; Uncle Troy comes to the office some days, and has charge financially, but he pays so little attention to what I'm doing that I've made it a practice to have an outsider in every third year to look things over. At our winter board meeting, I'd suggested that since things had been left up to me pretty completely since 1959 it was time again for a check.

The other directors—Helen, her mother and uncle, and a couple of cousins—backed off at first. They liked the rate at which the stock was paying, and they remembered that the last management man we'd had in had recommended that we set aside 8 percent more of the gross for plant and contingencies. Cut into their income quite a bit for a while.

Finally, though, they'd agreed to our having a consultant again provided it wasn't the same one—Uncle Troy had cut his 8 percent down to 5 percent and didn't want to have to defend it. Mother Gibson, who is Chairman of the Board, succeeding her late husband, voted her two votes against having a consultant anyway ("Quite unnecessary"). But Uncle Troy's two votes offset hers:

"If Barney wants to be checked up on, he probably ought to be." It was a way for him to come to the office even less—and, as a matter of fact, when he does, he tends to use his secretary and phone, which are charged to Gibson Hardwood Products, to transact personal business in connection with other investments.

So the vote was two to two: Cousin Tully (Troy, Jr.) voted half a vote my way, hoping, I was quite aware, that things might be found that I was doing wrong. Helen went with her mother, half a vote, a perverse half-vote of confidence in me. Her Cousin Beth declined to break the tie, so I did it myself, voting Alex's proxy in favor of our getting someone in.

At the direction of the meeting, Uncle Troy went to his lawyer in Boston for a recommendation, and the management consultant recommended was Dave Doremus. I promptly reconvened the board to say Dave would have to be disqualified, and they all laughed at me; Cousin Beth said I was being prissy.

"After all," Uncle Troy said, "if he's an old friend, and understands that this is something of a formality. . . ."

He didn't finish the sentence, and didn't need to. All of Uncle Troy's sentences end by pointing out that there's money to be saved, if they don't just stop at the implication.

So I phoned Dave's home that evening. The secretary at his office hadn't known where he was, and I hadn't heard from Dave for a while.

Jane answered.

"Well," she said, when I told her who it was. "I'm a little surprised hearing from you."

"You are?"

"Unless, of course, he put you up to it and is sitting right there."

"I'm sorry," I said. "I don't follow that."

"Did you really expect to find your dear friend here?"

"Jane, I don't know what you're talking about."

"Oh my, what a shame. Don't bother trying this again."

"Trying what? What's going on?"

"I'm being divorced, Barney dear. But of course, you didn't know, did you?"

"No. I'm sorry."

"Are you? I am too. I'm sorry it's not a nice big ceremony you can have your racketeer friend dress up for. Let's see, what do you boys call that? Drag?"

"Goodbye, Jane," I said.

I wasn't too sure Dave would want to come down on business with that going on, but when I reached him, next day, he seemed to want to very much. It was a pleasant visit, too, allowing for circumstances. The only thing I remember Dave saying about the divorce was:

"She's got my lock, and she's got my stock, and she's going to barrel my kids away to sunny, sunny California."

He was quick and thorough in his study of the business, felt we needed to do more product research and ought to change the way we were buying wood:

"You let this Ozark manager of yours keep doing it," he told me in my office. "He's going to have you so loaded up with butternut and wild cherry, it'll push you right back into the spindle-bed and rocking-chair business."

I grinned. I like buying wood. Most seriously, he felt we needed to try to program our future; we were okay for now, but should have a clearer idea of where we wanted to be in 1968, and 1973.

Diversification might be part of it, but that was in the area of financial policy and I left him and Uncle Troy with it. Uncle Troy was having a great time getting all sorts of advice from Dave on matters unrelated to Gibson Hardwood, and charging us for Dave's high-priced time.

At home, evenings, we talked of other, future things, and past ones, too. Helen and Dave talked sailing and sailors. Dave borrowed a Sunfish, but Helen beat him in ours in the Sunday race; he didn't know Scott's Lake, where the wind shifts as you get close to shore, and I doubt his mind was really on sailing. Dave and I walked some; we ate and drank well, and he was nice with the kids. About the divorce, Helen surmised that there had been a woman in it.

5

"Did you know him . . . quite well?" Helen asked, sitting on sand in the shade of a palmetto. We were half an hour from the airport.

"Only in the hospital. A couple of wounded men in bathrobes. We used to talk."

"Did you know her, too?"

"No. I haven't seen any of the Kennedys for eight or ten years. Not since the first time Jack ran for the Senate."

"You ran, too."

"For the House. For the other party. 1952. And got beat."

"It must have been exciting, though." Helen looked at me. She was a little drunk, in an involuntary way, from having let the cognac keep arriving at her table without really noticing that she was drinking. Her husband didn't do exciting things, like run for office.

"I don't want to believe it," Dave said. "I just don't." There wasn't anything coming on the radio then, except more sadness as other capitals responded. The sun danced on the water, out in front of us, as if nothing had happened. Dave turned the radio down and talked: "I think I must have sailed against them, as a boy. I'm not sure which ones. They were an unbeatable tribe —the Yankees. The Packers. Montreal. The Celtics, Joe Louis and the Kennedys. That great, doomed family. My father admired Joe Kennedy."

"Even though he worked for him some," I said.

"I think Dad admired him as a family man. A strong father. Dad would have liked a lot of children, too. He used to talk about Joe Kennedy losing his oldest boy, during the war, and his oldest girl right afterwards. I'm sort of glad my father's not around to see this."

"How, Dave?" Helen said.

"Excuse me?"

"The other children. The boy and girl."

"Both flying. Don't you know? Kathleen, who was called Kick, in a private plane. Doesn't everybody know how Joe, Jr., was killed?"

We didn't.

"It's like some . . . grand and terrible movie," Dave said. "With a screen play by Euripides."

Then, as he started to tell us, I did remember. I sat running sand through my fingers, and wondered why I'd never made the connection between the Joe Kennedy who was a Liberator bomber pilot, flying with the British, and the presidential family. I was in England at the time, too, a pilot in a fighter squadron, and now that I thought about it we did say that the man who was killed was a son of the former ambassador.

It had all left my mind, though everyone in England knew the names of the two men at the time: Joe Kennedy, Jr., and Wilford Willey. I found I hadn't forgotten at all—Kennedy had finished two sets of missions and was on orders to go home when the call came for volunteers. We were desperate to knock out V-2 bases, and someone had an idea: why not load up a Liberator from nose to tail with TNT, and rig a set of robot controls? Then a radio plane could fly above it, follow it to the missile base area, and dive it in.

But somebody had to fly the damn thing off the ground first, and make the initial course setting. I didn't understand then, and don't now, why it took two—a pilot and a co-pilot— but then I wasn't a bomber man. And I found myself picturing them not as we looked in our flight boots and crushed hats, but neat and sorrowful, like the heavy-bearded airline pilot who'd brought the news of the assassination four hours earlier.

Kennedy and Willey were supposed to parachute out when they got their big plane levelled off.

I don't imagine they had to keep volunteers for that one away with a firehose. Yet, I can only say there was more volunteering for stuff like that than people today seem to want to believe. A lot of men flew second tours of missions voluntarily. I did myself. Maybe it was stupid.

Willey and Kennedy drew the card. They took the Liberator up all right, and were flying just over the coast when the whole big firecracker went off in mid-air. Twenty-two thousand pounds of TNT.

"Just after that, Kick's husband was killed," Dave said. "In ground action, in France. He was English . . . a lord. I forget his name now. I can't remember the sequence, either, but Kick was home, just before or just after. Not that I knew her, I ought to apologize in a way, for the nickname. But it was at the time I did know Jack, and that's what he called her. God, he was one thin and anguished man."

"And then Kick was killed?" Helen was biting her lip.

"Not for two or three years. Then, flying a private plane."

"I do remember the bomber, and the TNT," I said, and trailed off. I felt suddenly stupid and somehow misled. I didn't want to sit there, thinking and talking of long-ago things, and making fateful Greek connections, as if the President, too, had been dead and enshrined for many years. I turned the radio back up.

"Please, Barney." Helen said.

"Please what?"

"Do we have to listen? Nothing more can happen."

"No," I said. "We don't have to. You want to listen, Dave, or you want to talk?"

He shrugged. "I've heard quite a bit today."

"Okay." I'd turned the set down again. I stood, picking it up. "I'll carry it down the beach," I said, and did.

The others were right. There was nothing new to hear. But listening restored my sense that what was happening was present and urgent.

When the newscast started on the local scene again, I turned it off, and sat by myself a little while looking at the sea.

After these several hours of being concerned with Helen, and meeting Dave, and fussing with airline matters, I wanted to sit still finally and let the news come in and sock me. But by now it was like one of those punches you take, as a boy, in the solar plexus ("Come on. Hard as you can.") with the muscles tensed; when you've set yourself and know the blow is coming, you can't relax and let it hurt.

So I had to get transported again:

I landed at Love Field. *No, boys, never mind the bubble,* I said, and got into the car. I made a joke to Governor Connally's wife. I felt good as we drove along because the crowd at the airport had been big and friendly. I waved and smiled, and thought about some leather-headed dame bopping Adlai with a sign here last week, and couldn't help chuckling because that sort of thing would happen to Adlai. Not to me. The seat was comfortable, the air warm, and we were coming to an underpass where I could relax, stop sitting straight and smiling for a moment, rest my back. . . . I let this play until I could feel the appalling betrayal, the bullets tearing into the back of my head.

When I joined Dave and Helen again, she said: "Barney, Dave still wants to go sailing."

"Okay," I said.

"It wouldn't help anything for me and Connie to turn back now," Dave said. "Nothing to turn back to for her. I think we might do best to carry the big shock out to sea."

"Sure."

Dave hesitated. Then he said: "I'll be more candid. I don't think Connie's altogether sure yet, about having married me. I think going on as planned might help that. I don't presume to know what would meet your needs and Helen's, Barney. But . . . wishing isn't like presuming, but it may be more persuasive."

I just looked at him. That was Dave talking all right, but the meaning didn't seem to connect with him until I realized what extraordinary thing was happening: he was asking me to do something for him.

Helen drove the nail home: "Will you go on with Captain Clark, even if we don't?"

"I hate to answer that," Dave said. "No. I don't think Connie'd do it."

"I wish Barney's country didn't need him quite so much," Helen said. She's quite good at making me feel pompous.

"You know, it doesn't have to be in a pleasure-mad kind of spirit," Dave said slowly. "May I tell you about our little Yacht Club? Things like this can sound silly, but two years ago one of the past Commodores died. Big, burned-out old yachtsman. And by God, we sailed the ashes out to sea. Eight little boats, sailing a close haul. All very solemn and fitting and very moving finally. Not silly. I keep thinking that Kennedy was a sailor, Barney."

That got to Little Miss Helen, and she started to cry again. "If we called the children?" she said through sobs. "And mother says they're all right?"

"If you just won't rush," Dave said. "Come over for the night, and see how you feel. There'll still be room on the Virgin Islands plane. There's a hotel room waiting. You can talk to your children from there this evening, and in the morning make whatever move you want to make. . . ."

"Please?" said Helen. "Oh, Barney, it doesn't even make sense. We wouldn't be back in time to see the kids before morning."

"No." I said it loud and stiff. "I can't be cut off on a boat. How do you know it's over?"

"If it isn't," Dave said quietly, "I guess I'd just as soon be cut off."

Helen stopped crying and looked at him adoringly. Helen is always looking to fall in love a little, and every now and then she manages. Keep them together for a little while. Go and meet the five-day bride. It might pass. Take her away from here, as I was going to, and it wouldn't pass, not for a while.

"Barney, am I a monster?" Helen said. "Am I supposed to be an unnatural mother, if I don't feel these great big patriotic necessities of yours?"

It would help her, of course, to stay over. To see the boat and meet its captain and Dave's wife, and not be taken so abruptly from the thing she'd counted on.

"I'm sorry, Dave." Stiffer than ever. "I'm sorry, Helen. Come on." I was standing. Dave stood. "I don't want to miss that plane."

"That makes one of us." Helen sat where she was.

"You're welcome to go on with Dave, and his wife. You can go cruising without me."

She looked up at Dave. I can't say his face lighted up. She stopped being mournful, and lost her temper.

"Oh, Christ." She jumped up. "The martyred husband. No thank you, Barney dear."

"Then come on," I said.

Dave looked at his watch. "There's no great hurry," he said, pleasantly, and knelt to tie his shoe.

I can't wear a wristwatch; they don't keep time for me. I'll carry a watch in my pocket, when I get old. Dave knew that, of course.

I went for Helen's wrist, and had it before she could move her arm away. It took a moment to read the tricky little no-number face.

"Twenty-five minutes," I yelled. "It took us longer than that to get out here."

I rushed them to the car. I drove on the way back. Return space would be getting tighter and tighter. I drove very fast, and none of us spoke.

After a while I turned on the car radio, and we heard of the preparations for taking Kennedy's body out of Texas, back to Washington. How the new President looked, and Mrs. Kennedy. At least I heard it. Helen was probably too resentful of me by then to listen to the same words.

As for Dave, I couldn't think of anything to say to him, and kept pushing away the realization of how deep his personal trouble must be.

6

Sometime on the long flight home, while Helen slept the dreamless sleep of seconal beside me, I found myself remembering that I was in the air when the news came that Roosevelt had died. Flying a Mustang, not even on a mission; I was test-flying some new modification that had reached us. I was senior pilot by then, executive officer, and would have been the next C.O., if I'd been willing to stay on. But the European war was almost over. The Japanese war, where our group might go, was far away and I would never see it; it was a different war, a different place, and I read of their landings and their bombings as I might have followed war between Saturn and Mars.

My ground crew and some others were waiting when I brought the plane in. I supposed they were interested in hearing what I'd have to say about the test, until I saw, as I braked, that Jones, the chief, was going to be the first to reach me.

It was unlike Jones, a sly and scornful man, whose pose would have been to make it plain that he was only waiting on the field because he was required to.

"Mr. James, the President's dead," Jones called out, as I started to unbuckle, and I could see tears on the man's face.

I sat in the plane, overwhelmed. Roosevelt had always been President—except, long before, when I was a child in grammar school, and the President was a chubby, cleft-chinned man named Herber Toover, who kept Wicked Al Smith from putting the Pope and the bootleggers in the White House.

That Roosevelt should die was like losing an august, infuriating, immortal relative, on whom we grudgingly relied. So that my father's continuous anger with him had no more force or credibility than one of the running radio jokes in which rival comedians were supposed to be feuding.

While I fly/ Presidents die, went my jangling mind. Keep James on the ground / And your country sound—the rhymes started to come up like hiccups, hard to turn off as a bad song that hums, up in the nasal area between the roof of your mouth and your eyebrows. Stop. Just stop.

Roosevelt's death had brought an hour of sadness for an old hero, gone to rest. We were ready for it, even if we didn't know we were. But I am no more ready for Jack Kennedy's death, I thought, than I am for my own.

I recalled voting for Roosevelt. My first ballot. Breaking away from home into the hominess of war, making the classic reversal of my father's politics—I mailed that ballot in from England. It was a vote for the war to be over successfully, and for home to be unchanged when we got back.

Only whole-hearted ballot that I ever cast.

Went for Dewey in '48, persuaded it was time for a change,

but I could tell how little I'd liked my man when I woke next morning and found myself tickled to learn that Truman had beat him.

Had a lousy time in the next election. I always do, in a way. I never can understand, in the closing weeks, how the people I talk to can be so certain of their choices. I haven't seen the election yet where I couldn't argue against both sides with damn near equal conviction; the bad guy isn't ever that bad, is he? Or the good guy that good?

In 1952, I voted for the General—I didn't like generals, but the brilliance and beauty of Stevenson were too much of a wonder for me. It was a wise-guy vote on my part, choosing mediocrity over the possibility of greatness with my cynical eyes open to both. I told myself it wasn't a wonder the country needed, but a chance to rest our wings. I was wrong.

So next time I went against the General, and was wrong again because I'd started liking him all right. I just wanted to pay my disrespects to that funny, sewing-circle kind of government they had going. Eisenhower seemed harmless and genial as a television father, but there was Granny Dulles, and Auntie Wilson, and Nixon as the young housewife, sewing and chatting and doing appalling, vindictive things sometimes—all that and McCarthy, too, as the bride with her own shotgun. I could vote against that, and I would have, too—except that I spent election day in the woods, trying to photograph woodcock, and didn't get back in time to vote.

The airplane window framed my sleeping wife's clear profile. Caribbean winter night was falling, brighter than New England day. If there were no dreams in seconal, couldn't the pill boys invent an additive? Pick a pill, choose a dream: The Great Minuet, Landing a Big One, Hold Me Tighter. And for Helen James tonight, White Sails.

I voted for you, Mr. Kennedy. Sir. My usual disgruntled vote. Didn't like the choice. Didn't trust you. Trusted the young housewife less. But towards the end of the campaign, I was a little less disgruntled. American politics came to life for me, or maybe I was old enough, for the first time, to have a vote. Because for the first time I felt I was considering men I knew about. I started, even, to like Nixon some. But voted for you, Jack, and in the three years since I haven't been disgruntled. I've cared, quite a lot—outraged at some of what you did, cheering for other things—but caring more about what you've said, and thought, and done, than I would ever have thought possible.

7

Long after midnight we got home to Scott's Fort. The sky was beginning to lighten over the lake, which is all the sea we have. I found myself looking, as we drove along it, for the little boats of summer, canoes and rowboats on the beach and at the moorings, but they were put away of course. And the sun-burned boys and girls who played on them were pale again, and back at school. My own children among them.

When we went to get them in the morning, Mary Bliss and and Goober seemed rather puzzled that we'd come back. Not displeased, but in no great apparent need of us either.

Mary Bliss wanted me to drive by the Post Office to see the flag at half mast, and I did.

I was in the house late Sunday morning, and the TV, heard continuously since breakfast, was finally, mercifully off.

It was a pretty fall day, and I was sitting on the sunporch, changing a camera lens. There was some fungus out in the woods I wanted to photograph in color, in the hope that some-time someone could identify it for me from the picture.

Helen was sleeping again. She had a little complex of shocks and disappointments to sleep off, before she'd start to function much again. There were more dishes waiting to be washed than the dishwasher could hold at once. And I didn't feel especially like picking out a load, but I thought I would before she woke.

Mary Bliss was bicycling with a friend.

I could hear Goober in the kitchen close the refrigerator door, and thought I'd take him to the woods with me. I called.

"Goober. Hey, Goob." His name is Gibson, for his mother's family; Mary Bliss is named for my mother, Brad for Helen's father.

Goober came charging in, his mouth full of bread and jelly, the rest of the sandwich in his hand. He went bouncing right past me, as a matter of fact, and skidded to a stop by the television set. He turned it on, for no reason except that it was off. It's a reflex.

"Goober!" He was going to get yelled at for that.

Then a voice came up saying something about Oswald and the Dallas jail.

I thought: okay. Let's do have one more look at the boyish face, with the Mona Lisa smirk. Born October, 1939. A month after Germany invaded Poland. Dave and I were playing football at school. Jack Kennedy was swimming at Harvard. A lot of men our age were already in uniform: the first war baby grows up.

But what was happening on the screen was curious. There were Oswald and two cops. Then a back blocking the camera. And a scuffle, and a shot.

A shot?

Noise, disorder. An announcer's voice saying the unbelievable:

"He's been shot. He's been shot. Lee Oswald has been shot."

I sat there sick, idiotic, incredulous.

Once, the summer I was seventeen, playing ball in Missouri, I saw a fan throw a beer bottle at an umpire and hit him in the head, hard. I had a lead off second base, and the ump, lying on the ground now, with blood running down his face, had just called our batter out on strikes. My first feeling then was idiotic, too. I felt I must tag up. I felt I should run back, tag up, be safe on second, though it passed before I did any such thing. Before I ran in, like the other players, to help hold off the rest of the fans, making a circle around the stricken man, while a half-drunk doctor fixed his head.

It was the same feeling now: that if we left the set on, the game would have to continue; there'd be a commercial, and then the announcer would say that the part of Lee Harvey Oswald had been played by. . . .

What kind of people were we?

Goober turned from the set and looked at me. His mouth was quivering, and he said:

"Dad?"

I raised my arm to him, and he came, two steps towards me and threw himself, my big, eleven-year-old baby, into my lap. All knees and elbows, face against my throat. I gathered in the limbs and held my son tight, knowing now why I'd come home. Goober had to tag up, in that incredible moment of his life, had to touch something magic to feel safe, and I was second base.

But suppose a time came like that, as I guess it had for Dave Doremus, when you look to reach your foot back there, and you do, and there is no second base?

ii

A salesman calls.

I didn't hear it directly from Dave, but a machinery salesman, who came through a couple of times a year and who lived
in their town, told me for sure that Dave and Connie hadn't
taken the cruise.

"They were back the day after the assassination," the salesman said. He'd seen them at the beach and tennis club to which
they all belonged; people noticed, he said, that they were back
because there was a lot of local interest in the match.

"What's the new wife like?"

"You knew Jane?"

"Sure."

"Connie's the opposite in every way."

"Is she?"

"Big and awkward looking, and a little bit shy. Kind to dogs
and children. At least she's tall enough for him."

"I hadn't imagined her that way," I said. "Let's see the new
price list." This salesman was a gossip—it goes with selling—
and I found I didn't want to hear any more.

"Connie has a lovely figure, as a matter of fact." His name
was Russ, Russ Fisher. "Awkward's not the right word exactly.
It's more, you feel as if she doesn't realize, about the figure."

"Yeah," I said. "Well, I imagine I'll be meeting her." I got
up and went to the bookshelf behind my desk. "There are a couple of little things in your catalogue I want to go into. You're
going to have to do some fierce discounting, I have an idea."
Russ had the New England territory for a tool-making firm in
Michigan, and I favored their stuff. But the shipping made it
higher than buying equivalent things from his competitors, who
were in Providence, so that finding a net price was always an
interesting kind of skirmish.

"Weren't you in business with Dave once?"

"No," I said.

"I swear he told me something like that."

"Mahogany plywood," I said. "For panelling. We thought about it, a long time ago." I decided to try to dispose of the topic. "Dave had a client in high-grade home construction—he was making market studies. He thought they might be able to use enough of it to make the plywood worth producing."

"You were going to make it here?"

"Good God no," I said. "We were talking about buying a plant and moving it down to Guatemala, where the wood is. I took a trip down there to see it, and talk to local people."

"What happened?"

"I fell in love with the jungle," I said.

"But the plant?"

"Dave found his client a better deal, among other things. You'd probably know him if I could think of his name." I opened the catalogue.

Russ thought of a couple of names, but none of them sounded right. Then he said, "I guess a lot of us made false starts after the war." I let that go by. I wasn't going to get into it with him. Probably I liked the figures and fine print better than he did; I'm not an engineer but I can see our whole procedure, from cost to price, clearly enough so that I trust myself to decide on production investments without much help. It was one of the things I enjoyed doing.

So Russ said: "I was in the ski troops. I was going to operate a school, and a tow. Heck, I used my GI loan to buy into it." He laughed. "Mildest winter they'd had in years. Try skiing without snow. Well, it wasn't a big bundle like your friend Dave's, but it was plenty for a kid."

"When did Dave lose a bundle?" I couldn't help asking.

"Before the divorce, during the divorce, after the divorce," said Russ. "Just to name three times."

He was a man who liked to bring bad news, I thought, and I could disregard it. I knew that Dave had had some setbacks; but I also remembered one of our conversations in Boston, when he told me that his earnings had doubled each of his first four years in business, starting at $6,000 the first year. That meant he should have levelled out at $45 to $50 thousand, if he wasn't exaggerating, which is enough income to cover some pretty fair setbacks.

"Want to sell machinery?"

"You know Dave's business went to hell, don't you?" Russ said. "He wasn't minding the old store. Other things on his mind." I must have managed a pretty convincing frown. The man actually interrupted himself. "Oh, well," he said with a puppy-dog smile. "Dave danced his way out of it. Lucky he went to dancing school, I guess."

"What's that supposed to mean?"

"Let me sell you some machinery."

"Say it, Russ."

"Just if, if I had an interest in a widow with a nice hunk of insurance, I don't think I'd leave her lying around where Dave could find her."

I threw his catalogue across the desk. "Take it and get out, Russ."

"Come on, Barney. What are you getting hot about? I used to worship Dave. Our whole town did."

I stared at the man.

"Look, Barney. You're a customer and I'm a peddler. If you want me to get down on my knees and write 'Dave Doremus is a square shooter' with my nose, in the dust, I'll have to do it. But, listen, the . . . the big fall hard, huh? Maybe you don't know."

"Maybe you'd better tell me."

"Not if you're going to get sore."

"I'm sore already. Tell me."

"About Connie?"

"I'll figure that out myself. Tell about the big loss."

"I'm not sure I've got all of that straight."

"Get it as straight as you can. Just the business part, Russ."

"Well." Russ thought a moment. Then he spoke very carefully: "It's a firm called Southport and General Electronic Timers, Incorporated. It had Boston money behind it, and it was doing a helluva good business, making these timers on license from the patent holder. For automation, you know?"

"Yeah. Out here in the backwoods we've heard of that."

"You want me to tell it?"

"I want you to tell it."

"Okay. There's a beef with the patent holder, and he decides to cancel the license. They got some kind of dumb contract that will let him do it."

"What'd they do? Try to hold back royalties?"

"No. I don't know. I don't know what the beef was exactly. Maybe it was made up. But anyway, here's this plant, all built and the building paid for by the town of Southport. A work force trained, plant in production, and all of a sudden they aren't going to be allowed to make what they're set up to make. They been selling hard, got a lot of orders for these timers with nice penalty clauses if they can't fill the orders on time."

"It sounds rigged," I said.

"You're being a little smarter than the boys that got strung up. Of course it was rigged."

"I'm being smarter because I know the end of the story," I said. "What's the middle?"

"The Boston money was after a killing," Russ Fisher said. "All this old family dough up here. You know as well as I do, it works together. Not even by collusion, either. One guy's lawyer is on this board of directors, and his partner's on that one, and the private bank across the street might just as well be in the same office when it all gets going—word gets dropped here and there. Very clubby, if you're in. Pretty soon everybody's pulling together, all over New England, without anything ever being written down or even said, that you could point to."

"I'd have thought Dave would know about something like that."

Russ shook his head. "Why don't you hope he didn't? Maybe they left him out because he and Jane were having trouble. Or maybe he knew, but . . . anyway, here was the idea: they'd bankrupt SPAGETI. . . ."

"What?" I said it rather sharply.

"What's the matter? SPAGETI—Southport and General Electronic Timers, Inc. The initials, see? That's what everybody called it."

"I've heard of it," I said, starting to feel a little grim. You don't forget hearing the name of a firm everybody calls spaghetti. "Come on, Russ. Run it through for me."

"All right. SPAGETI's got to go out of business. That's a good tax write off, especially since the land's not paid for and the town of Southport went for the building. The land and building revert. The machinery gets auctioned. The patent holder gets his license back, to go somewhere else—and SPAGETI has already developed his customers for him. But remember those penalty clauses? SPAGETI's got a lovely big cash reserve; they haven't even been paying rent—their lease said not for the first three years. They can cancel their material orders. So all that cash will get distributed to the customer companies, as pure, sweet penalties. Money for nothing. Imagine being in on both ends of that? You get a tax loss on something that has no real value for one pocket, and nice fresh cash capital gain to put in the other."

"Pretty," I said. "Where does Dave come in?"

"He's the patsy, if you want to look at it that way. Or he helped rig it, if you want to look at it the other."

"But if he helped rig it, he'd have made a bundle, wouldn't he?" I said. "Instead of lost it?" It was hard to imagine Dave as patsy. "What's the rest?"

"The Boston boys had Dave working on it from the beginning," Russ said. "He romanced the town for the building, and helped organize. Except on the legal end, I guess. People wonder how he could have been kept out of that, but—well, to be fair. He didn't have any reason to get into it. He's a business consultant, not a legal advisor. Anyway, when the license beef started, Boston fired the management and asked Dave to take over."

"He was supposed to make it look like someone was trying?"

"You got the idea. He was going to be canvassing, trying to find other stuff they could make with the same machinery and work force. Get the operation going in another direction."

"I'm with you," I said. "That would make it look good to the town, but it would turn out he couldn't swing it."

"Right. Okay. Here's where Dave pulls the gun. When he takes over, they're on 90-day notice to cease making and delivering timers. But of course they'll fill what orders they can, to avoid as many penalties as possible. From there on, its arithmetic: he figures what's time and a half worth, and what's double time worth—and if you operate three shifts, 24 hours a day, and spend up that cash reserve, you've got 270 days of production instead of just 90. And if you work the same three shifts for 11 Sundays, you got 33 more days. That's 303—you're getting on towards a year. If you add a little to your crew, and pay incentives for speed so everybody pushes, you can fill all those orders. It'll cost like hell, there'll be some net loss—but nothing like the loss from shutting down and paying off the penalties. This way there'll be some cash coming back for every timer delivered."

"Sure."

"I think there were some orders Dave figured he had leeway to raise price on a little, too. Hell, two hours with the adding machine, and it looked like he could whip it. He'd close temporarily after ninety days, if he had to, but he'd have a chance to try to get SPAGETI licensed for something else, with that kind of production record."

"Might even get the original license renewed?" I said. "If he beat the scheme?"

Russ nodded. "Southport was delighted. Boston has to pretend that it's delighted, too. But they quick cut off his credit for materials—just by letting it be known that the license has been lost, see? And they tell him he can't spend the cash reserve, they're sorry; it's gotta be protected, in case he doesn't accomplish all that production. So what's the answer? Easy—just raise new money for SPAGETI, when everybody in New England knows it's going broke.

"My opinion is," said Russ, but I suspect it was an opinion he arrived at just that moment, "that Dave figured it, and really meant to beat them. By a kind of reverse con; you can't cheat an honest man. I think he started going to all the larcenous old guys who'd heard about the first part of the scheme, and wished they were in on it. So now he offered to let them in, maybe without saying that he was going to try to pull the firm out. He'd use their own dough to beat them, see?"

"Why isn't that right? What else could he have been up to?" I asked.

"He was putting in his own money," Russ said. "Using personal credit. Taking small money, from Southport. That looks like a patsy. Or: he had a way of trying to re-rig it, for himself, that either didn't work, or hasn't come out yet."

"Let's keep it simple," I said. "Why couldn't he work his 303-day production program, Russ?"

"You kidding? They aren't going to let him do that. They got labor connections, too. All they got to do is pull a strike. . . ."

"Yeah."

"The materials he bought, with the new dough. They're probably sitting there in the empty plant. Maybe that's where he gets his own money back sometime, and some to boot. I don't know. Or maybe he just went off his head—you know about the divorce. The girl?"

"That's enough, Russ," I said. "You can put the lid back on the garbage can now."

"Now wait. That's where you were getting sore at me. You going to let me explain or not?"

"No," I said. "I've got it, now."

"But about Connie's dough. That's all. See what I'm trying to say? Where would you go for sixty grand with no tax on it if you need it fast? And to buy a house if you didn't have one left? A widow with life insurance. . . ."

"Is that your opinion, Russ? Or is that just what they say around, what the hell's the name of that town? Wonamasset."

"You know how small towns talk, Barney."

"Yeah, I live in one. Excuse me, will you?" I got up.

"Come on, Barney."

"Sit still for a minute, will you please? Excuse me."

"You still sore?"

I left him without answering that, and went out of my office. First I went to Uncle Troy's. I knew he was in. He'd sent his secretary earlier to boost a couple of Dictaphone records of mine. He was using the machine when I opened the door, and I waited for him to look up at me. After a moment he did, turned the Dictaphone off, and said:

"Yes? Hello, there, Barney."

"About a year ago," I said. "When Dave Doremus was here?"

"Why yes."

"You and he were chuckling about something called SPA-GETI. A nice dish of spaghetti, I think you called it."

"Ah, Barney." Uncle Troy looked martyred. He's a chipper, bald-headed vest-wearer, with a watch chain and a Phi Beta key for decoration. He affects little-old-New-England-bookkeeper spectacles, square and rimless. God knows where he gets them. His expression now said that the world was very hard on upright men. "Ah yes. I'm afraid your friend didn't serve me very well in that matter."

"How much did you drop?" I asked.

"Now, now," he said. "That's personal. Nothing at all to do with Gibson Hardwood, does it? I'm just writing to the fiberglass people again. . . ." There'd been talk, from time to time, of our going into fiberglass canoes, since we sold other marine stuff. But I doubted that we would, and I doubted Uncle Troy was really writing letters about it. I nodded and closed the door.

I didn't care how badly Uncle Troy got took, as long as it wasn't company money. The takers are there to be taken, and that's as it should be. But this particular small shark was my relative and business associate. That was how Dave knew him. It seemed to me you didn't work that way, through friends.

It also seemed to me that some of what Russ Fisher had to tell must be true. I'd had enough to do with Russ, now, to last me the rest of my life, but I wanted to be fair. So the next office I went to was Tully's—Troy Gibson, Jr.'s.

Tully has an engineering degree from M.I.T. and is plant manager.

"Tully," I said. "You got a lunch date?"

He looked up from some graph paper he was studying. Tully works pretty hard. "No. Aren't you having lunch with that salesman?"

"Come on a minute, will you?"

Tully'd been wanting to talk hard with Russ Fisher for quite a while. He put on his jacket, straightened his tie, and came with me.

We came to my office door, and I moved Tully in.

"Russ Fisher," I said. "This is Troy Gibson, Jr. Our plant manager. I think you've met?"

"Sure. Hi, Tully." Russ got up, nervous.

"I believe both of you are free for lunch. Russ, if you'll pick up your catalogues and price lists?"

"Huh?" Russ Fisher said.

"Tully, I'll leave the files on this and the competition on your desk."

Tully went to Yale before M.I.T. He knows how to pick up a cue. "Okay, Barney. Fine."

"You'll be seeing Tully when you come through town from now on, Russ," I said. "Good luck with him. Watch your shipping costs, Tully."

Tully'd been wanting to take over buying our machinery ever since he came to work.

I went out, leaving them, and walked onto the floor of my plant. Everything was running, making the racket that woodworking machines make, but the racket soothed me, the molders and planers and sanders, lathes and drills and different sorts of saws.

2

So I stood there, trying not to mind that I'd just given away a piece of my control of this little complex I'd built up to Tully Gibson. I listened to the blades, tearing into wood and shaping it, and played another of my records.

This is a marred record though; I have to keep lifting the needle and filling in, and even so I don't really like it, particularly not the first side:

September, 1950. I've been married just over three years.

Helen's family and mine were distant friends but cordial. I went to Scott's Fort for the first time in spring vacation, my final, veteran's year in college. To see what sort of plant it was of which I'd given a piece to my brother Alex. Met the Gibsons, met the daughter Helen, Widow Gibson's girl. And Beth, Uncle Troy Gibson's. Dated them both. Married Helen ten weeks later, and sometimes wonder why it happened so fast—I don't know that there's any better explanation than to call it history, nudging away on its lowest level. 1947 was the year of the marriages, except for Dave's; I went everywhere to weddings that year, just as my friends came to mine and Helen's. As if getting married were the final, delayed, but inevitable part of being discharged from the war.

Brad is a year old. About me and the plant: I'm running it now.

First, after college, I took Helen west and worked for the Forest Service. I thought I might take a degree somewhere in forestry, or zoology. That kind of thing, and try it for a career. But the Forest Service (and the graduate schools, as well) were too damn much like the Air Force in the way men were structured. And I quit. Thought about taking pictures for a living, but that field comes down, doesn't it, to public relations? I hate public relations. Troy Gibson, senior, wanted me at the plant. Tully was still in school, and the old Uncle had a strong sense of there being something sacred in its being a family firm. I could feel that, now that Helen was pregnant. I went in as plant manager, like Tully now, and sales manager too. And got excited over some of the things we might be able to do. Started on them, and then got in a real, mean fight with Uncle Troy, who didn't want the pay scale raised. Quit. Went over to Hartford, and took a selling job. That was all I could find, in January, 1950.

If Gibson Hardwood needed me, it was going to have to be my firm, not a place with jobs in it for grateful sons-in-law.

Helen was hurt and puzzled with me about that; it wasn't anything quick and hot like a quarrel. It was something cool that went on as long as I kept selling someone else's stuff in Hartford, and I couldn't let myself care much.

Helen and I drank a lot evenings, more than before or since, when I'd get back from work. We did our drinking with a quiet undercurrent of mutual defiance. We also did our drinking generally with other couples, and especially some friends called Dick and Dottie Tracy. Dick was one of those guys who takes a life-long kidding about his name, of course, but they were quite nice people. We were all just short of thirty, and Dottie, like Helen, had her first child raised to playpen age.

Put the needle back on: I'm playing the piano. Dottie's sitting by me, on the piano bench; almost sitting on me, as a matter of fact. We should all have called it an evening two hours ago; instead, we're pulling off a jug of drugstore bourbon.

Helen says: "Play something Dick and I can dance to, Barney," and for a time I do. Dottie drums on the edge of the music rack—it was an upright, then; Dottie couldn't keep time with a watch. So after a while, as much to suppress my rhythm section as anything, I start playing moody, left-hand chords and with my right I alternate between the treble and the top of Dottie's nylons. She has chubby thighs. Moist.

"Come on, Dick. This orchestra's terr'ble. Let's go dance at your house," Helen says. They take off. Dottie and I are extremely, drunkenly pleased to see them go. We move unhesitatingly into a sloppy clinch and grope, there on the piano bench. She is small and cute, as well as chubby in certain areas; pretty soon she jumps up, pulls her pants around straight, and says:

"My goodness. Doesn't this house have bedrooms in it?"

She is a girl who feels that, when the time comes, it's uncivilized just to keep on, wherever you are; you go to a bed, take off your clothes and fold them, and do your wiggling under a sheet. We follow that protocol. Some of the fine, horny impulse has left me with Dottie's insistence on observing these proprieties. I get detached enough, as she pulls the sheet under her dimpled chin and smiles, so that I could stop this, but I think of Dick Tracy and his girl Helen, have another drink and dive in anyway, alcoholically enthusiastic again. Helen spends the night at the Tracy house.

That, as a matter of fact, isn't the part of the first side of the record that I mind so much; I accept it now, as I did then, with a shrug, as something that happened and was bound to happen —if not with Dick and Dottie, then with others, somewhere along the line. At a party perhaps.

And the next time, as a matter of fact, it is at a party, ten days later. And it's Dottie Tracy again who goes home with me; Helen is off with a man I don't even know. About four A.M., this time, Dottie says, sitting up, in a hungover, exhausted kind of voice: "Oh, Barney. We've got to stop this." I try to conceal the pleasure and relief with which I hear her say it. I get dressed and take her home. Helen doesn't get in at all, and in the morning I take Brad over to Granny Gibson's for the day, with some kind of headache explanation. I sit there with Helen's mother, speaking of her daughter as if she were home in bed ("Better not disturb her this morning. Needs sleep."). Listening to Mrs. Gibson rearrange her day so that she can take care of the grandchild. I go back to my house, leave a note for Helen explaining where the baby is and what the story, and go on to Hartford. Late for work.

After that flareup, it all died down, not in shame particularly but in an unvoiced agreement to dismiss it, as you may want to dismiss drunken thefts and insults; false steps; sorry, but you know? Yes, it's all right. We acted, not as if it hadn't happened, but as if it hadn't counted—except for poor Dick Tracy, who didn't seem to know what had hit him. He used to yearn after Helen, and she used to lead him on as long as it amused her, and then squash him like a bug. I was sorry for Dick, but chiefly I was just relieved we all hadn't turned it into a real mess.

One night when I got back from my Hartford job late, about eight, I found Uncle Troy waiting for me with Helen. He asked me, quite humbly, if I'd come back to the plant.

"No, sir," I said.

"The new pay scale's in, Barney."

"Good."

"I want to be much less active."

"You've said that before, sir."

"I'll give up my office, Barney. The manager's office."

"Are you offering me full management?"

"If you'll take it."

I said I would. I'd missed it. I had more ideas of what to do and how than ever.

I started really working hard then. I flew the plane around, getting orders. Signed a contract to remodel the factory interior, but kept the old yellow brick structure outside with its lawns and the original bronze signs. Set up to make quite a few new things. I made Uncle Troy and Helen's mother put in quite a lot of new capital, and I flew myself to Washington to get Tanny, my brother's wife, to put enough more in so that our holding would stay in proportion. I had a stock accumulation deal in my new job and, as I told Tanny, it would all go to Alex as I earned it, and she could take her money out as mine went in. I don't mind saying that I was pretty effective, then; in six more months I wanted to be ready to start buying a house. I felt as if my feet were under me and I could start using my strength on things I cared about. My family; my factory.

It figured, too, that the tension ought to be over between me and Helen, and it was over, on my side. I was joining her family, on my terms; good enough compromise. Or maybe I didn't have any energy left over from work to keep tension going. I couldn't say, in that particular time, what Helen felt; I wasn't noticing. But I know, of course, what she did.

I'd hired a man named Jeff O'Neill to take over sales. He was good, a big, smart young guy with a big hooked nose, bright eyes and a lot of drive. We had a lot going on, building, planning, and Jeff spent many evenings at our house talking and working or relaxing sometimes. We had a pretty good time together, given that neither of us, personally, was really the other's sort of man. Jeff found me rigid about things—I thought he was a corner-cutter; Jeff's idea of a good time was a big steak dinner and a night club afterwards, no matter how far you had to drive—stuff like that seems a waste of money to me, unless there's something interesting to eat, or some music you can't hear otherwise.

He had a wife and a home over in Litchfield, but I only met her once; make-up over mousiness, if that's not too irritating a way to dismiss someone.

In any case, Jeff and I got along all right, until I had to realize that he'd become Helen's new lover; then, I'm afraid, it wasn't all right at all. He was a crude guy, who came into my house as an associate, not a guest, and didn't understand that those were circumstances that would make me friendlier and more solicitous towards him, especially when my local friends were around and might have been a little slighting to him.

Snobbery again, on my part? Maybe so, but Helen's taste offended me. I went to bed early one night, as often happened those days, leaving them together. I got up an hour later, and walked noisily into the dark living room, confirming what I'd decided about them, though they acted as if they didn't realize they'd been caught. I excused myself, took a jug of whiskey up to bed and stoned myself to sleep.

Got up the next morning, polite to Helen at breakfast, and went down to fire Jeff. He wasn't the strongest guy around, and I was just going to do it, if I could, without getting violent or offering explanations, though I was in a pretty nasty mood. When he didn't show, I remembered that he'd told me he was going to spend the day in New Haven, calling on accounts. And now the needle goes on again:

Helen is dressed up, when I arrive home from work.

"Barney. Hi, sweetie. I've been trying to call you."

"You have?"

"Yes. Lucky me. Jeff's been in New Haven. . . ."

"I know."

"He phoned. He got two tickets for *Mr. Roberts!* Such an absurd man—he's driving all the way up here to get me, and take me down to it! If you don't mind?"

"That's what he's doing, huh? Big Jeff."

"Do you want a drink, Barney? I'll fix it for you."

"No. Not now thanks."

"I'm having one. Come on. You don't mind, do you?" She and Jeff have gone one place or another before when I was tired. "I didn't call a sitter. I thought you'd probably be staying in, and listen: if it gets late, I can stay with Pammy Allen. I talked to her already. In Branford. And come back in the morning, but could you take Brad to mother's if I'm late?"

"No," I say. "I don't think I could do that."

"Well. Well, I'll get back then."

"You'd better get yourself a sitter, Helen."

"Oh. I thought you'd be tired."

"No. No, I'm not tired. Call your sitter."

"But Barney. I mean, he's only got two tickets. . . ."

"Oh," I shake my head. "I'm not going with you, if that's what you mean."

"Do you have something else? I didn't know."

"You'd better start working on that sitter, Helen, if you're going out."

"I don't understand. It might be too late. . . ."

"Yes, it might be," I say. "Goddamn. Wouldn't that be a shame?"

"Barney?"

"You can work it out, Helen," I say. "Just give it the big try. *Mr. Roberts*, won't that be fun? If only you can get a sitter. . . ."

And I turn and leave the house. See? No violence, no explanations. Except that Jeff pulls in as I walk towards the driveway. First, I'm just going to let him go on by to the house, nodding to return his greeting. Then I think, what the hell, stop, make myself grin, beckon to him, and when he comes over deck the son of a bitch.

It didn't make me feel any better about myself that I'd hit a guy like that, and the next thing I did was pretty mean, too. We had two cars, and I was paying for both of them—a little car I drove to work, and the station wagon we called Helen's. I decided I preferred the station wagon, and as Jeff O'Neill was picking himself up, I tossed Helen's stuff—gloves and Kleenex and glasses she used to drive with—out of the glove compartment, onto the gravel.

As I was getting in, Jeff called:

"Hey, Barney. What the hell?"

I poked my head out the window and said, "That was just to wish you every happiness, Big Jeff," and drove away.

No violence, no explanations.

The other side of the record has fairly jumbled stuff on it, but Dave gets to blow some. I'd never thought he would; it was as if ever since we'd met as boys, he'd been waiting patiently for me to need some help, and I'd been making myself harder and harder to do anything for. I suppose sufficiency was part of my pride, just as being of use was part of Dave's. But finally, after five or six days of driving around New England, calling a few people to make appointments I didn't keep, eating and drinking and trying to think what came next, I gave in. I turned towards Wonamasset, got as far as Providence. I sold the station wagon, so as to have some cash, and called Dave up.

Needle for the second side:

"Hold yourself, Ozark Wonder. Hang on and stay one-third

sober. I'll cancel my appointments and be right there."

He arrives with cold lobsters in a paper bag. Comes into my hotel room with a soft frown of concern that turns into a grin that turns into a handful of some new kind of fountain pen a client has given him that he thinks may entertain me. Leads me to the window and points to a "No Parking" area, along the curb, where I see his car, a gleaming Lincoln Continental, guarded by Stiggsy Miller who is simultaneously attached to a panel truck in front of the Lincoln.

"Why the truck?" I ask.

"Here, eat this." He has peeled me a lobster tail. "I thought you might like Stiggsy to make a run to Scott's Fort, for gear."

"Helen would shoot him."

"I don't think so."

"You've talked to her?"

"She called me," Dave said. "I heard all about you. Off the chain, baying in the woods. Knocking over garbage cans and running rabbits. Sounds like fun."

The lobster tail tasted great. "She tell you I'd sent her a card?"

"Shall I quote it? 'Just have your mother and uncle look around for a sitter for their business, too.' Beautiful card. No picture. Why don't you give her a call?"

"Just like that?"

"If you feel like it."

And I do. But by the time I do, Dave's told me about the mahogany, so when Helen asks what I want to do, I say:

"I want to go to Central America."

"Where?"

"Central America. On business."

"Well, it's . . . it's nice that you speak Spanish, isn't it?" Pause. "You don't feel that you have a business, Barney?"

"I really don't know what I feel," I say. And I ask her to let Stiggsy get the clothes, and the cameras, and binoculars.

"Yes, Barney," says the fiery, the untamable Mrs. James, and I wonder what on earth Dave can have said to her. "Please call again when you want to?"

Dave whips me off to Wonamasset in his Continental, telling me all sorts of exuberant things about life, love and how to rehabilitate your oyster industry. We get to the pretty house that he's started buying for himself and Miss Jane and Master Peter, one year old and walking; the house is white brick, the lawn is green grass, and Miss Jane is all smiles. Glad to welcome our old friend Barney, and here's your room, darling. I know everything will straighten out for you.

"Nothing paid for," Dave says. "And a circus around here all the time—phones ringing, people waiting to see me in various rooms, a dozen things going on at the office. Barney, I love it. You know what I like?"

He sits on the bed, grinning and watching me get ready to take a shower, and I don't know how he managed to get such a thing while carrying a suitcase, hugging his boy, and showing me up here, but there's a drink ready for me, too.

"What do you like, Dave?"

"I like a day with fifteen crises in it. Domestic, commercial and personal. Fifteen different people and situations, all as unlike each other as possible. And seeing how many times I can shift, think fast, reassure and put the crisis away. All done. See? There wasn't any crisis after all."

"Sounds restful."

He laughed. "I thrive on it."

"So does Jane."

"She manages to produce my favorite crises," Dave said. "Really dependable that way."

He had her in hand all right, and he did seem thriving. Big and tanned and healthy looking. And those favorite days he was describing—I spent a string of them with him, and it looked like he was managing to have maybe ten such favorite days a week. He operated not only at home and at his office—but the office really was more message center than a headquarters—he operated out of that very distinctive car. Everybody in ten towns waved when Dave went by in the car, and all day long and into the night Dave would be getting people into the car, and driving off somewhere, to eat, or drink coffee, or to the beach to sit in the car and talk. It was rather magical; some harassed man would be put into that comfortable front seat, Dave would let himself in the other door and drive away, smooth and careful as an old lady's chauffeur. The car would do the soothing, the scene he picked to visit would be one where a problem could be placed in gentle perspective, and the feeling of being there, enclosed, in the front seat—just you and Dave—gave a kind of privacy and detachment to the discussion that let you move towards solutions as easily and smoothly as the automobile rode.

I know. We set up the plywood investigation for me in the car. There was work for me to do, of course, with Dave's client —a man named Schnieder—with figures and references. That we did in Danny Schnieder's office, generally without Dave. But it was Dave who shaped the relationship, getting us together, solving our disagreements, knowing whom to call when we needed more information. It was hard to believe that he had a dozen other balls in the air, for other people and combinations of people—hard because his attention to us seemed total, and the time he had for it always sufficient. But I know he had the other dozen going as well, along with things at home; I saw enough of it, while I stayed with him and Jane to know that.

The fourth day I decided that I'd move over to a hotel. Jane continued being as cordial as she could, but she and I weren't really ever going to be friends.

"Dave," I said. "It's been wonderful. Danny Schnieder and I are going pretty good. I think I'd do better off by myself. . . ."

"I've got the place for you," Dave said. "Little hotel on the beach. Off season, but comfortable. Cheap, I whisper to you. Decent restaurant across the street, and Stiggsy says there's a good bird marsh right there."

"The hotel's open?"

He smiled. "I went by yesterday, and asked them to open it for you."

I liked it there. He'd known I would. Away from the dazzling display of energy he put on, I could get my preparation for the plywood operation really firm in my mind. Mornings I'd go out with Stiggsy, early, to see the migrating birds come through. The fat scoundrel had learned a lot. He could even do fall warblers. I went to bed early, too. Stopped drinking, just out of general dissatisfaction with myself.

I talked with Helen a couple more times. She told me Jeff

O'Neill had left and Uncle Troy was half out of his mind. I'd begun to see that it was going to be a little harder than I thought to leave Scott's Fort. And Gibson Hardwood. There was the deal I'd made with my sister-in-law, Tanny, for one thing. But I told Helen:

"Look, I'm not sore. In fact, I'm very sorry I hit Jeff, and took your car. But I'm not very sure about anything, Helen. Are you?"

"I'll write you," she said, but, actually, she didn't. Being Helen, the longer I was away, the less she thought about me. I understand she started fooling around with Dick Tracy again, and perhaps with someone else. It was Cousin Beth who wanted to tell me all about it, later on, but I'd never allow her to.

I made a fascinating visit to Texas. There wasn't any deal yet, about the plywood. We'd gone as far as my agreeing I would make the trip, do the checking, and pay a third of my own expenses. What I went to see in Texas was a whole, small factory for making plywood, crated and standing on a railroad siding. The firm that owned it had expanded, replacing every single piece of equipment, though it wasn't old. That was how they'd spent their wartime excess profits, instead of paying nine-tenths to the government in special taxes. To complete the play, they wanted to sell the equipment they'd replaced as a unit, for use abroad. Foreign-aid sort of deal. So we were offered the whole thing, with performance and condition guarantees, for $44,000 as I recall it— over a hundred thousand bucks worth of stuff, if we'd had to buy it at market price. Decent terms, and they were throwing in dismantling, cleaning, crating, and the loan of a man to help us set up.

I couldn't see anything wrong with that. In fact, my chief reason for stopping off was to look into what shipping arrangements would have to be made, and I remember leaving that Texas town with an almost dreamy feeling that I'd return, in a month or two, to see the whole thing put on freight cars and then ride down with them, watching over our stuff—a long, slow, marvelous train ride through all of Mexico.

Nothing was wrong in Guatemala, either. The local people were eager. We'd have a couple of them on our board, and they'd already found me a Guatemalan mechanical engineer, with a degree from Texas Tech, who convinced me he could get the factory up and operating under the direction that had been promised as part of our purchase. The only slight set-back I can remember was learning that we'd have to import corrugated metal for our shed roofs, but that was almost entertaining when you stopped to realize that the wooden parts would all be solid mahogany.

So everything was smooth. I phoned Dave, to say so, and went on down to the jungle. The rain forest. To see the wood. I was flown in by light plane, and left off at the headquarters of the loggers with whom we'd be tied in. And then: wet weather started. It was unseasonal, much too early, but it started anyway. There was heavy fog over the rain forest every morning, and every afternoon we'd watch to see if enough of it might clear for the plane to come back in for me. The other way out, by truck, was closed just then, while they rebuilt part of their road.

I wanted to be stuck like that.

The balance of my record, and I start to like it very much, is a kind of tone poem about the jungle.

I walk the roads and trails and sometimes, if I feel adventurous, the watercourses. The growth is much too thick for walking off them. But as I learn how to go quietly, in the first light and the last, I begin to see toucans and hummingbirds; I see ocellated wild turkeys feeding, and huge crested guan. I see birds I will never identify, extraordinarily colored. I see agouti, and javelina once, and little jungle deer and foxes, and, quite regularly, an old tapir who hangs around a water hole.

The company manager offers me a rifle, a 30-30, but I don't want to shoot. I'd like, or half-like, to have a light shotgun, I suppose, to collect some birds—not for sport but to make study skins for the man at college who taught me ornithology. But the only shotgun's a twelve gauge, the only shells are buckshot, and I don't mind passing that up, either.

I have a long lens for my camera, and some color film, and I spend hours of time taking bird pictures, and insect pictures, foliage, an animal or two. Sometimes I see jaguar tracks. I make a few field notes. I wonder, all over again, if I ought not to go back to graduate school and become a naturalist.

We eat venison and wild turkey, chachalaca and guan (which they call pheasant). We drink excellent bottled beer, warm. When the clear day comes, and the plane gets in, I'm really quite sorry. And I don't want to make plywood here. I don't want to do anything noisy, anything disruptive. It'll get done, of course, but I'd rather it wasn't me, invading the peace of the toucans, and the old tapir, and the great crested guan they call a pheasant.

I don't want it to change, ever, and of course it won't, not all of it. It will be there, I think as we fly away, over the grey spars of chicle trees, sticking up from the green sea of vine and philodendron leaves. And I'll be back, whenever I can, and not bring anything along that makes a noise.

"Dave," I say, on the phone from Guatemala City. "I guess everything checks out down here but me. I seem to love that old factory in Connecticut, after all, and the things I was going to do there. This will be easy here, for somebody, but it's easy in the wrong way for me. I'd miss the competition."

"Sure you would," Dave says.

"And, I miss that boy baby. I even miss my wretched wife, I guess."

I don't say: it's all part of the United States, good and bad, and so am I, good and bad, but I feel that kind of thing, too. And so my record ends in a small crescendo of minor patriotic chords.

Dave said it was okay, about the plywood deal. "As a matter of fact," he said. "It was going to have to be just you and me. I had to decide my other boy'd get spread too thin. And maybe you and I would, too. But tell your Guatemalan friends there's another way to work it out, new people, okay?"

"Good, Dave," I said. "Very good."

"May I tell Helen?"

"No. I'm going to take another week or two," I said. "As long as I'm here. I'm going to move by stages down to Panama, and see an alligator, ride a boat through the canal one time if I can. Then I'll call her probably. I probably will."

And it seemed to me, after I rode that boat, and spent a day photographing pelicans, diving after fish, and drank a bit with some old colonial gentlemen I met, that Scott's Fort was too far into me for me to leave the game.

When I got back I about cried, holding Brad again. He'd grown a lot in two months. Helen was wary, quiet, enigmatic —for twenty-four hours. She was a needle poised on the arc between resentful and submissive. I had nothing to say that wasn't plain from the fact that I'd come back, and I was young but not so young as to want to elaborate on that. Maybe what went on was a wordless quarrel about my wordlessness. If that was it, I won, because by the middle of the second day Helen simply slipped back into being her pretty, snippy self again, often exasperating but far from dull.

Uncle Troy was ready to give up everything in the way of control of Gibson Hardwood but what my common sense said he ought to keep. I picked up my romance with the old plant.

There's machinery there sixty years old, and a machinist to match who can keep it going. There's some extraordinary new stuff working right beside it, and a world full of Russ Fishers, I suppose, who, if they can't keep it going, can certainly hustle up the replacement parts it needs to sell you when it fails.

I put my jungle record away, and stood there thinking that I probably loved that plant the way a farmer loves his farm. Russ and Tully went walking off to lunch behind me, but I didn't turn to acknowledge them. The foreman was turning off the line for noon. Men were going to their lockers for lunch buckets, cleaning the sawdust off their clothes with air hoses. I walked into the middle of the floor, now abruptly quiet.

My dream would be to own it all, outright, I thought, and the building, and the real estate it stands on. That would put me and Karl Marx toe-to-toe, wouldn't it? I want to own the means of production Karl, and pay labor to operate it. And direct the labor—yeah, Karl. Me, personally. What a monster, huh?

I want to make, say, Pitman rods—you know what they are Karl? Over there, stacked for shipping. You better get a wooden one from me, not a steel one, if you farm where it's rocky, Karl. See, it's a connecting rod for, say, a mower, but it also operates like the shear pin in an outboard motor. It's the thing that breaks, when something has to. But it's got to work as well as steel, till you hit the rock; we use white oak.

I like making things, supplying things, that other people are really going to want or need. The homelier the better, unless it's something genuinely fine. Strong and homely. Dreary of me, huh New York? I could not stand to make and sell things people neither want nor need. BBe Damned and Offal. That's the way I feel. I don't give a goddamn if I'm loved, but I don't want the world feeling it could get along just as well without me.

That's the kind of pride and pleasure I can find in my plant. Which can never, of course, be mine. Which, in a way, I'd just lost a little piece of. Turned over a little bit of control.

Well, Tully wanted it bad enough, and I didn't want to have to see Russ Fisher any more. And it wouldn't have been fair, just to drop him.

3

Have I left the impression that Helen and I were evermore faithful to one another? We were not, but each of us had learned that when you make a mess, there's no need of rubbing the other's nose in it.

Nor have I been back to the rain forest, though I yearn to go sometimes. I have thirty-eight good prints from there. The colors have changed a little, over the years, but when I get them out to look at, now and then, they still please me and excite me. Especially one of some enormous butterflies—I don't know what kind—settled over a bush, like flowers.

The battle with Betty Beep.

On the borrowed stationery, the address was crossed out, like this:

PAINTER'S MARINA
Texaco Marine Products
Charlotte Amalie
St. Thomas, V.I.

The letter followed, in a strong, insultingly legible hand. The writer was taking no chances on being misread by dolts:

P.O. Box 14B
Feb. 18, 1964

Dear Mr. James:

Thank you for your letter about the deposit check for the charter cruise which was cancelled out last November.

If it might yet happen that you and Mrs. James will wish to sail with me this season, I will be glad to keep the check, as you suggest.

However, I did have a substitute charter party first thing, in the week which you had reserved, and so lost very little income by your cancelling. Actually, it has been a very busy and prosperous winter. Actually, I did not expect it to be so, and would have thought more time would have been spent in mourning.

Many, many people, in wild sports shirts and rope-soled shoes, staying and spending here this winter. Ladies in small, tight bathing costumes, which seem unhealthy, as they must impede circulation of the blood.

114

*If you are not planning to come down here after all,
I will return 5/8ths of the sum you remitted, keeping
3/8ths as a pro rata deposit for the three cruising days
actually missed on my part. I will contribute the sum
retained to the Kennedy Memorial Foundation, if this
meets with your approval, in our names jointly.*

*By this mail I have offered the same alternatives to
Dave and Mrs. Doremus, though of course I hope that
you will all four be able to come here, after all.*

Faithfully yours,

Kelso M. Clark

"Here. From the captain of *The Bosun Bird*." I handed the letter to Helen across the breakfast table.

"Can I have the stamp?" Goober asked.

"*May* I," Helen corrected, reaching a round white arm out of her dressing gown to take the letter.

"I want it," said Mary Bliss.

I told them it was a U.S. stamp, and Goober claimed to know that. He said he wanted the whole envelope, for the postmark. Mary Bliss, who has no stamp collection, said she wanted it, too. It was Saturday.

Outside it was snowing for the fifth straight morning.

If it followed the pattern of the other mornings, the snow would stop before noon, the day would warm up and be cloudy, and the snow turn wet.

The kids already had four different snowmen falling around in the yard. With this kind of snow, about all they could do would be to make a fifth—or have a snowball fight. And I wasn't sure which would be harder on them, that or the old Betty Boop and Mouse cartoons from the 1930's, that would start on Saturday-morning television any minute now.

Betty Boop is a sort of flapper figure, I suppose, with bangs, curls, a bodice like the top of a valentine, and a wee, bonnie, irritating voice in which she says: "Boop-boop a doop."

When she says this, my kids shout back at her, "Beep-beep a deep." It seems to please them.

How do you like your blue-eyed, centerfielder now? Playing in a league in which he feels he goes to bat every Saturday morning for his children's souls, against the electronic shadow, relentlessly pitched into his home for the turning on of a switch, of a piece of cuteness that got stale and died thirty years ago?

There was an owl. He was a great horned owl, in grey plumage now, and I knew what dead branch of what grey tree he'd probably sit on for an hour this afternoon. Suppose I could climb the tree and nail a bracket to it for my Nikon F. Then I'd focus on his branch, stop down and use a slow shutter for depth, and then climb down, stringing a long cable for remote release. I could make a little blind somewhere, then, and wait out the owl—and suppose there were grey sky and nearly white snow on the hill behind the tree? Setting up for that, with a thermos of cocoa and some sandwiches, might do for fighting the battle with Betty Boop on Goober's behalf. Or on Mary Bliss's, if Helen would fix the zipper on her down jacket. But I couldn't believe the two would enjoy it together.

"It's an odd letter," Helen said. "He must be an odd man. And nice."

Goober put salt on Mary Bliss's cereal. Mary Bliss yelled. I sent Goober away.

"Makes you want to sail with the old guy, doesn't it?" I said.

"I'd have to check my shoe soles very carefully for rope," Helen said. "And my sport shirts for wildness."

"And your small, tight, unhealthy bathing costume?"

"Are you going sailing again, Dad?" Goober asked, poking his head around the doorway from the living room.

"Bring your sister another bowl of oatmeal," Helen said. "And you can come back to the table."

"*May,*" said Mary Bliss.

"Take Goober's oatmeal," said Helen. "He hasn't touched it."

There's a small victory for New England, that oatmeal that Helen cooks, every winter morning. I could go ham and biscuits better, or salt pork which I never see—sometimes I feel New England cooks to match the sky. Well, nuts. Push some weight onto the feet, press a little energy from them back up into the ankles, through the knees; tense those flanks, babe, let it gather in the trunk, chest, shoulders, and by God up we bounce:

"Come on, kids," I cried. "We are going to tear the walls off the playroom."

I didn't ask them if they wanted to. I yelled that we were going to, rah, let's go. If they so much as mentioned the damn cartoons, according to my secret rules I'd be licked, I'd give up and go out by myself to try the owl.

But good old Goober whooped: "Tear them off?"

And Mary Bliss forgot her sticky oatmeal: "How, Dad?"

"With crowbars and hammers and banging and whamming, and big mean screwdrivers," I said. "Put on some jeans, Mary Bliss, honey."

"Can I really? Bang the walls?" And off she ran upstairs to change.

"Will Mom help too?" Goober asked me, but expected Helen to answer.

"Tear down the house?" Helen said. "Wait, I'll run downtown and get some dynamite. What on earth for?" But Helen knew, of course. The playroom, with its white wallboard and nursery pictures of seals and circus horses she had cut, we'd fixed for little children, long before. It wasn't suitable for these big stamp-collectors we had on hand now. I've remodelled my whole house (sometimes with Helen's help), room by room, through the years —starting each room with a desperate invocation of energy, in response to any sort of unpredictable stimulus. It can be a hangover, a quarrel, or good news, I suppose, as easily as Betty Boop. Or Beep.

It happens maybe once a year. When it starts I get possessed, I keep going, almost insensibly, till I'm done.

"Goober. Now. Down in the shed are some boards, packed in boxes. Solid walnut, Goob. I bought that tree in Iowa seven years ago, right under the nose of the skunk who was going to turn it into veneer. A tree like that! I paid in cash, boy, hired a farmer with a chain saw to help me cut my tree down there and then. . . ."

"Who used the chain saw, Dad?" Goober asked.

"The farmer, dear," said Helen.

"All right," I said. "I'm an axe man, myself. I trimmed the tree, and we hauled it out to the road with the farmer's tractor. I gave him two more bucks to guard it from the veneer man, and went down to the local sawmill and got them to come back with me, with a jammer, and pick it up. I stood in the mill, and watched that they quarter sawed it and packed it right. Rented a truck and drove it here myself. Stacked it at the plant, air dried for six years, and last year I finally finished all those boards myself. And tongued them, and grooved them, and primed them with varnish."

"Save your breath, dear," Helen said. "You'll need every scrap."

"Are you really going to get dynamite, Mom?" Goober asked.

"No, but I might as well. It's going to be hell around here this Saturday and Sunday," Helen said. "While you and your father tear off wallboard and put up his panelling."

"Are you going to help, too, Mom?" Mary Bliss asked, bustling into the room, trying to get her jeans to close around her stomach.

"I think I'll make a door-to-door canvass for discarded sherry," Helen said. She was still holding Kelso Clark's letter. "Until about four A.M. tomorrow morning. When your father will lie down on the playroom daybed, exhausted, and pull the nail apron up under his chin for warmth."

"Me too," Goober said. "Can we work all night, Dad?"

"Oh, boy," said Mary Bliss.

I sent them for tools to the basement, poured another cup of coffee and went in to look over the playroom. After a moment Helen followed me in.

"It will be nice in walnut, Barney," she said quietly. "We could put the hi-fi in here, couldn't we?"

"I think I'll build it in," I said. "And one of those little bar refrigerators, too. Pop for kids' parties, ice for grown up ones...."

I started moving furniture away from walls. I felt fine about it, even about the exhaustion Helen had predicted, late tonight and again tomorrow evening.

Goober and Mary Bliss came running in with hammers and the crowbar, which Goob dropped on the floor.

"Can we really hit holes in the wall?" Mary Bliss's eyes were damn near bulging.

"Where should we start, Dad?"

"Pick a wall and whack it," I said.

Helen leaned down and got the crowbar. "What might I do with this?" she asked, and, handing me Kelso Clark's letter: "Do you think we could go? Is there any way at all?"

Tap. Mary Bliss bounced her hammer off Betty Beep's Boop. Whang. Goober put his hammer right through Popeye's spinach.

"Get 'em," I yelled, and I wished the fat-faced man who calls himself Colonel Bob, who shows the Saturday cartoons and their commercials, could have seen the enthusiasm with which they were forgetting him.

"I'd like to, Helen. Very much indeed."

"But could we?"

We were trapped in the little overheated station called Southern New England, Late Winter, waiting for Spring when the excursion trains could start coming through again.

"Be pretty expensive by ourselves," I said. "I wonder who'd be free to go? The Graces?"

"But couldn't we ask Dave, and what'shername? Doremus."

I hadn't told Helen, about Dave and her Uncle Troy and SPAGETI. I didn't want to tell her. "I don't know," I said. "It's pretty doubtful, Miss Sweets. Things in the plant, just now . . ."

"Can't Tully do them?"

Wham. Mary Bliss was through a piece of wallboard, too, and laughing.

"I'm sorry," I said.

Helen handed me the crowbar, took the letter, and left us to our work.

The only time I stopped, all weekend, except to eat and sleep, was when Mary Bliss—who'd left us for a while—came in to report one of her tropical fish dead. We took an hour off to dissect it, and look at sections through Goober's little Japanese microscope.

2

The old ram had boosted his stationery from somewhere

else this time, but the handwriting and the substituted heading were as before:

Air Conditioned——Fresh Water Pool——Internat'l Cuisine

GRAND OVERLOOK HOTEL
Charlotte Amalie, St. Thomas, V. I.

P.O. Box 14B
March 18, 1964

Dear Mr. James:

Here is a proposal which might interest you and your wife, as well as Mr. and Mrs. Doremus.

In the second half of April I must sail The Bosun Bird *from here to Long Island. I plan to sail up to Nassau, which is about 1000 miles, and rest there a day or two. Then I will sail across the Gulf Stream, to the coast of Florida, and enter the inland waterway to proceed north under power for summer chartering in Long Island Sound.*

I have not been in the waterway before, generally preferring to sail outside, but have heard it is an interesting passage.

I will need a crew to help sail the boat, and could not afford a paid crew, except for the boy who is already helping me on the boat here this winter (a fine young man from Dartmouth named Artur LaBranche, who is called Art. My passengers seem to find him agreeable, though I must tell you in all candor that his ways may have been a bit too wild for Dartmouth).

If you could find time to make this cruise with us, and would enjoy doing so, there would of course, be no charge to you since you would be helping me very greatly. In fact, I will include in this proposal your food and liquor, within reason (though I do not use the latter myself while at sea, it certainly enhances the pleasure for many). So that should you be able to accept, there would be no expense involved for you, other than that of your transportation down here.

This will take place beginning about the end of April, and should require approximately three weeks. At this season we would not anticipate severe storms.

There has already been some movement of birds out of the Islands, but am not a birdwatcher so cannot tell you which ones or where they are going.

I recall your saying in a letter last fall that you do not have much sailing experience. However, I do not think you would find the helm of a larger boat very different from that of a small one, and in any case Dave Doremus is quite expert, should he be free to come. In addition, I realize that both his wife and yours have sailed considerably, and though of course nothing would be required of them, have noted that today's ladies often seem to like to aid in the work of a watch in clement weather.

I hope I may ask you to let me know at your convenience whether this proposal has appeal for you.

Sincerely yours,
Kelso M. Clark

Goober asked for the stamp. Mary Bliss said he had got the last one.

Helen looked at me from her end of the breakfast table, as pleading as if she could read what the letter said through its back.

I tossed it to her. The walnut panelling was all in place and looked fine. I still had the bar refrigerator to build in, the hi-fi to finish, and was wondering if I could manage a glass door on the upstairs shower. It was going to be a slushy weekend, and the color of the sky hadn't improved much in a month.

The letter made it hard to think of glass doors, suddenly, and teaching Goober to solder phonograph connections. The letter, I swear, hummed and curled like a sea-shell. Sun shone from the page in Helen's hand; salt wafted; waves swelled. No wonder my life looked pleading.

I glanced out the window, and probably looked pleading too.

"Oh, Barney," Helen said. The phone rang.

"Yeah," I said. "Yes, Miss Sweets. I know."

The phone rang. Mary Bliss went to answer it.

"Look at the weather," Helen said.

"I looked."

The phone rang. Goober dashed off after Mary Bliss, saying he would get it.

"It's not really us he wants, though," Helen said. "It's Dave, isn't it?"

"Except in clement weather," I said. "When today's ladies might do very well . . . ."

With Goober trailing, Mary Bliss came back into the room, smug at having won the telephone race. "It's for Daddy," she announced. "Mr. Do-*ray*-muss."

"Mr. Dormouse," Goober yelled, jumping up and down. "Dormouse. Dormouse calling Daddy . . . squeak, squeak-squeak, squeak-squeak . . . ." and, of course, shoving Mary Bliss around by the shoulder.

"Mama. Make Goober stop squeaking me," Mary Bliss said.

"Quiet, will you please kids?" I said, and went into the next room. Smiling. They'd hit on a rather fond old name, for Dave the Dormouse.

"Hello, Dave," I said. "Our mail must come at the same time."

"I think we have synchronized mailmen," Dave said. "What do you think, Barney *Jesse* James? Or shall I say first?"

"Go ahead."

"I think it would be rather wonderful."

"Helen's in a sea swoon," I said. "Your wife?"

"She doesn't swoon so good," Dave said. "But . . . what about you, Barney?"

"Dave, I . . . I honest to God don't know."

"Would Champ Clark have hesitated?"

"No. No, he'd have gone right out and bought a Sou'wester. No, listen Dave. I'd better say this: there's something you and I'd have to get past first."

"Is there, Barney? I didn't realize . . . is now the time to say it?"

"No. What I just said doesn't make the chimes ring, huh?"

"Guess not, Barney. But, if you say they should. Well, bong, I guess."

"I'd like to get past this, Dave."

"Could you and Helen come up? Actually, that's what I was going to ask if you could do anyway."

"Why, Dave?"

"Connie's got her doubts, too. Enough so that I can't offer to have us come to your house."

"Well."

"I think if you could make it for a weekend, we might see how much stuff we could all get past."

"I guess we could," I said.

"It's a favor, Barney. I'd like it very much if you could."

"Okay, Dave," I said. "I don't think I'll bring Helen though. What weekend?"

"Next. Or any other one that suits you better."

"Just a second," I said. "Don't count on me for the Caribbean. But let me see if I can get as far as Wonamasset, anyway."

I spoke to Helen, who had got up from the dining table and was standing in the doorway now, openly watching and listening. "Am I clear to go up next weekend, to go up and talk about this with Dave?"

She nodded, urgently, and I saw how the pinch of winter was beginning to draw the small mouth smaller, towards the brows, and pull the cheeks in. And I thought: poor, pretty face. Ought to be allowed to launch one ship, anyway. And I said, into the phone:

"Okay, Dave. I'll be there."

And, hanging up, feeling suddenly exuberant, caught Goober in the nick: "Don't touch that teevee trigger, partner. Hey. Get down to the cellar and bring us up the soldering iron, will you?"

Our highways are haunted.

If this weren't a criss-cross world, Helen would have made the trip. Helen, I'd say, had more reason to want to see Dave Doremus, to size up and reassure his wife, than I did. Helen could have found out about the SPAGETI thing just as easily, and probably would have enjoyed the whole prospect. I didn't, especially, once the exuberance wore off. So I might have stayed home, for another round with Betty B., which I'd have preferred —but we're rather conventional people, it seems to me. Most of the time. Not invariably and compulsively, but more often than not, we do the expected thing.

Mothers are expected to stay home with the children. Fathers are supposed to go forth and investigate, negotiate. Take action.

So this father was driving to the Cape, a little bit reluctantly, in some misty state of mind that matched the look of things along the road. The father was going a steady sixty-five, and thinking improving thoughts. (*Stop at a bar for one, or wait till Wonamasset?*) when the P-51 D Mustang levelled off and let him have it.

Huh?

It was foggy, and the plane really loomed.

Its wing guns swept the car window as I went by, and my foot went to the brake, full weight and muscle, in something like an emergency stop.

I skidded along the shoulder, flung a wild glance into the rearview mirror, saw nothing coming on the road, and couldn't have gone into reverse any faster if I'd seen a Messerschmitt coming the other way.

I sent the station wagon scrambling back, and in a moment, I saw, at my right, the unforgettable shape again. In another moment, I was stopped in front of it: a P-51 in the fog, on a patch of grass, with a circle of white-painted rocks around the patch.

And I could hear the voice of my crew chief, Jonesy, with

the whine of eastern Wisconsin in it: "Looks like a pregnant sea cow."

Jonesy and two mechanics, Pifer and the new boy who got caught in London in an air raid and killed, on his first weekend pass. Before I even learned his name. Jones called him "The Dummy."

The three were standing on the field together, watching us bring Mustangs in from Africa; so the ferry pilots weren't going to pick them up after Christmas and fly them over to us, after all. Because we'd gone for them ourselves. (Tony was a thirty-two-year-old brigadier, and I was with him in the office when he said, in his peculiar, violently respectful way, to the major general: "Sir, I can't wait for the Ferry Command to enjoy Christmas, sir. I've got pilots. What we need is transport for my pilots to Africa, sir, to get those planes. Hey Barney. Tell the General if you can find your way back here with about two dozen P-51's. Can you? Or would you rather get your Christmas presents late?")

Christmas, 1943.

(And I said: "I believe we can find the way, General.")

I sat there in the car, looking at that shape, and thinking how we'd got them. Half my pilots were still drunk from Algiers, Christmas eve, because I'd turn them out at dawn on Christmas day. But they were men who could fly drunk. Or boys, as I see things now, nineteen and twenty. I was twenty-two myself; senior.

We went in tight formation across the Mediterranean, with the sun rising over Corsica, and violated a little Spanish air space, too, for a short cut. I knew we were supposed to have the range to go around, but I wasn't taking any chances.

I guess I nearly got Tony busted back to lieutenant colonel, too, by crossing Spain, but we lived through the chewing, and we'd brought the planes in. We'd landed in formation and in love—what planes they were. I rolled up to Jonesy and Pifer and the boy that was going to get air-raided, and rolled back the cowling—you couldn't see behind you, when you flew that model, but they fixed it later—and I said:

"Here's a Mustang, boys." We'd all seen them in the air, and some of us had qualified in them, over on an R.A.F. field earlier. But these were the first on our field. I could see our other pilots starting to come out in jeeps, to see.

Jonesy called all officers Mister, except Tony whom he admired. He liked me well enough, but didn't admire me. He thought I was the world's damndest fool, still flying when I could have been home. And he said—I got out of my Pontiac station wagon to hear him say it again, because I could stand there and look at the plane, in its circle of white rocks, and see it about the way Jonesy first saw it: "Mustang, hell, Mr. James. It looks like a pregnant sea cow."

I never liked Jones, as a matter of fact. The other guys decided to take him as a salty, colorful character; I read selfish for salty, and don't much care for unpleasant colors. When he said exactly and without reflection those things which his disagreeable nature suggested to him, you could laugh if you wanted. I'd as soon have busted him in the mouth, but in almost three years of daily association, I managed never to let him know that. I didn't laugh much either, though.

Actually, I think it surprised him when others seemed to find him witty, but he could see the advantage in it so he was always trying, in an overbearing way. He was a superb mechanic, when he had a careful man or two under him to sweat the close work.

That Christmas day was as close as I ever came to letting Jones know I thought he was a bore; I loved that plane I'd just brought in, and the Algerian drunks who'd flown behind and on my wings. Jones wasn't entitled to badmouth it, or them— but hell, it was Christmas.

He patted the air-scoop bulge, underneath the fuselage, and tried to improve on his poor joke: "How about it, Captain?" Giving me my rank this time was supposed to set me up, I guess. "Shall I have the Dummy paint it pink for a girl sea cow, or blue for a boy?"

"I think we'll go easy on the decoration this time, Jones," I said. I kept my voice even. ("What about it? When you've got bars and the other man stripes?" Alex had said. I'd seen my brother in London, six weeks before, on leave from the hospital and deeply tanned from the desert. He was a corporal, and his eyes were about gone. "How do you keep your attitude to yourself, Barney. Some of the scum this army gets?" "You just smile and shut up, Alex," I said. "About all you can do. I wish I were about a well-paid sergeant." It wasn't certain that he'd lose his sight but I'd talked to the medical officers, and they didn't like his chances. "Don't expect me to be one of those philosophical son-of-a-bitches, if it does happen," Alex said. "I'm going to hate it like death, Barney.")

I stood in the park, on the way to Cape Cod, a little more than twenty years later, and rested my hand against the Mustang, finally able to make my reply to Jones's joke: what color should he have his Dummy paint the air scoop? "Why don't you have the kid paint you brown, Sergeant Jones, for a dull fool?" The boy he called dumb had already shown he could paint very nicely.

Part of the park plane's body had been cut away, on each side, a couple of steps installed with rails and a walkway up the wing, so that kids could climb in, and sit in the seat. The controls and instruments were gone.

Who talks to airplanes? I did. "It's all right, baby," I said.

Sergeant Jones had his little act of defiance. I wouldn't name the plane, or let them paint it up. But Jonesy told the new boy, the Dummy, to paint initials on the fuselage, below the insignia, small and fancy, pink-blue-pink: *P S C*. I'd have simply told the crew to paint it out again, except that the kid said to me:

"I don't think of those letters as meaning Pregnant Sea Cow, Captain James. I think of them meaning . . ." He was from Oklahoma, I think, or Texas. And he said in the voice of a country singer: "Pretty Star Climber."

So I told him it was a good job, and that weekend he stepped under a German bomb, and a day or two later it was New Year's, 1944. So I let the letters stay, since they were what he'd left for the world to remember him by.

Now I glanced at the place, on the body of the Mustang in front of me, but it had nothing written on it, of course. It was a different model, anyway.

There were the brown stems of last year's rye grass and alta fescue around the wheel chocks. And metal cables, hooked to concrete blocks, to keep the wind from moving it. A piece of playground equipment. I'd seen old fire trucks used that way, and once a locomotive engine. Never a plane before.

I was glad it wasn't the time of year for kids to be here, romping over stuff.

I put my hand against the cold metal. I took my driving glove off to feel it. "It's all right, baby," I said again, looking out through the fog, across the road, and then behind me, into the rest of the little park. I could see sandboxes and the standards on which see-saws would be balanced, come spring. Soon now. Slides and swings and empty picnic tables, and then, way out beyond them, by what must be another entrance to the park, a second plane.

Oh no. The old double body, lovely and beloved, the first plane I ever flew in combat. A P-38. A damn Lightning.

I took a step backwards. The Lightning was barely visible in the fog, but it was there. For sure. Just like the Mustang.

Both ready. Okay? It's all right, babies. Are the Heinkels coming? Let the siren sound, and wouldn't these two old planes cough, and rev, and break these cables? Crack the cement that held their tail wheels down, and into the sky, steeply soaring, firing a round or two as they rose to clear their guns. Pretty Star Climbers. Oh yes.

2

I began seeing signs that told the distances to places on the Cape, and John Kennedy rode with me, off and on, because all the signs included Hyannis and Hyannis Port.

They about made me miss my turn, as if those towns were at the end of some magnetic route I couldn't leave. But I did. I got off the four-lane road, onto blacktop, and then bumped in, over some construction and was in Wonamasset.

I stopped at a service station to ask where Starr Street was. The guy at the service station had four little streaks of grease on his forehead. He said he'd lived in Wonamasset all his life, and never heard of Starr Street. So there wasn't any.

I didn't ask if he knew of Dave, or Stiggsy. I could have

128

driven straight to Dave's old house, where he'd lived with Jane. I thought it wouldn't hurt to phone the new house, anyway, to say that I was here, and get directions.

"Barney James calling," I said. "Is that Mrs. Doremus?"

"Yes." There are a dozen low tones on the clarinet, warm but not without fragility. The *chalimaux* register. Barney Bigard used to play in it sometimes. He could have played the way she said *yes* over the telephone. "I know you," she said. "But you don't know me."

"Should I?"

"No. No, but you were a very important villain of my girlhood." Doctor, you could take her pulse from her voice, it was connected so directly with the way her heart pumped blood.

"I was?"

"You, Barney James. On May 19th, 1939, you ruined my brother's no-hitter."

"Buddy Marlow?" I asked. "Are you Buddy Marlow's sister? He was the best schoolboy pitcher in New England."

"Yes."

"That's right," I said. "I got a double off Buddy when he was going good. In a late inning, in a play-off game."

"You were a ringer, that's what you were. A professional baseball player, from Missouri."

"Did Buddy think that?"

"No, but all the rest of us believed it. Of course, Buddy'd pitched under a Spanish name in Cuba for a month the winter before, but you can see that's different, can't you?"

"I wouldn't have remembered the date of that play-off game," I said.

"I'll never forget it," she said. "It was my birthday. My fourteenth."

"No!" I said. "He was pitching it for you."

She laughed: "If he was pitching it for anyone, it was a scout from the Red Sox. And a skinny eighteen-year-old blonde named Susan Halstead. Barney, can you find our house?"

I told her the filling station didn't know, and she gave me directions. Dave was still at work, she said, but I was to come right up. She might give me a drink, in spite of my poor behavior in 1939.

"Oh, Barney, wait. We're having a ghost band," she said.

"Excuse me?"

"At the club tonight—oh, never mind. I don't know why I keep talking to you on the phone, when you can come up here and be talked to just as well."

"I'll be right along," I said.

"Barney?"

"Yes?"

"Who won the game? I've been trying to remember."

"Buddy did," I said. "He shut us out. I went to third on a fly-ball, after that double, and I'm still there."

She laughed. "Hurry up," she said. "You see?"

"See what, Connie?"

"There wasn't any sense in you getting that hit. It didn't do a bit of good."

"Goodbye," I said. "Listen, it wasn't Buddy's fault. He had major league stuff that day. He got a bad call, from his catcher."

"He got what?"

"I could never hit the curve ball," I said. "Buddy had good control of his curve, for a kid, and he'd struck me out twice with it. What did his catcher want to call a fast ball for?"

"Uh-huh." Connie pondered. "Why would a catcher do that, do you suppose?"

And we finally hung up.

It wasn't until I was back in the car that I finished remembering who Buddy was, and thus got Connie placed: Connie Marlow. Their father was one of the great old New England schoolmasters. Dr. Dan Marlow. I wondered if there were men like that any more, and thought, as I drove, that if there were— the country was so big. The business of education such a giant business. It would be unlikely for some new-breed Daniel Marlow to have anything more than a local reputation. Anyway, I doubted it about the new breed; the field was so big, the total money handle in American education now so vast, that there must be an enormously complicated number of people reaching for it—not just teachers, but suppliers, builders, maintainers, publicizers, administrators; students, too, generally finding support from the industry, the way I heard it. They had to buy their students, like a plant buys raw material? No wonder it was turning into something that had less to do with training youngsters than it did with increasing and perpetuating itself.

The St. Louis sorehead—I was blowing off, to myself, because I'd tried to hire a guy a couple of weeks before who was about to graduate from Harvard Business School, fairly well up in his class but not among the very best. And found I couldn't compete for him against five or six colleges who wanted him to teach for more money and more free time than he could have been worth to us without ten years' experience.

Connie Marlow (Ferguson, I remembered) Doremus, looked as fine to me when she opened the door as her voice sounded on the telephone. It never occurred to me that I might be disappointed, so it's a wonder that I wasn't.

She was a big, healthy, youthful woman, almost my height (which is five-ten), with square shoulders and a deep bosom. Round-limbed; somewhat thickly built, I'd have to say, but in no way fleshy; and with shiny brown eyes, like melting chocolate.

You thought of a splendid, playful mare, till you looked at the eyes a second time; then you thought of a doe.

She smiled like an old friend. Then she caught her lower lip in her teeth for just a second, in a little parody of wariness, and then, with nothing left on her face but a look of joyful impulse, she reached out, held me by the wrist, and said in that irresistible voice:

"Spoiling a person's no-hitter!"

"All right," I said. "I give up. What's a ghost band?"

3

That night, at the Doremus's club, the ghost band was Gary Rodger's Happylanders.

"How *can* it be the Happylanders?" said Ozark James, quaint, dumb and straight as a board. "Gary Rodgers got himself killed."

I remembered reading that vividly, because of the way the news came—the bandleader was one of the casualties in the big Coconut Grove fire in Boston in the fall of 1942. We waited in England for the list of dead to appear in the *Stars and Stripes,* after the first big radio flash stories about the disaster.

There were a number of us with Boston connections—me because I'd gone to college in northern New England, others with much closer ties. We had friends around there, we knew girls who sometimes went to the Coconut Grove. But the only familiar name to me, when the list finally did come out, was that of Gary Rodgers—and not that his band was playing there, either. He'd gone by on a night off to hear a different band, the newspaper said. After which, with the war on and talent short, the Happylanders—who were named for a big Cape Cod amusement park—broke up. Or so I'd thought.

But here were these guys, some much too young, playing an arrangement of a song called *Hurry Home,* a swing arrangement thirty-odd years out of style, and I recognized it as authentic, without question. My brother owns that record.

"It's not possible," I insisted. "Gary Rodgers is a long time gone."

"That's how it can be a ghost band," Connie said. "We've had quite a few."

"The Glenn Miller Band," Dave grinned. "The Jimmy Dorsey."

"That Glenn Miller band sounds for real," Mr. Bistrek said. He and his wife had just been introduced and sat down with us. Mr. Bistrek owned large commercial bakeries, and was branching now into home development. In fact, Dave and Connie lived in one of his houses.

"If it were Shaw or Goodman," Dave said. "A leader who was still around, then for him to appear would mean he was introducing a new band, wouldn't it? With all those risks and challenges. But once the man with the name is gone, and there's a sideman left who can get the book, all you need is guys in the other chairs who can read."

"And you don't improve a single note," said Connie, sternly.

"It's for the nostalgia crowd," said Dave.

"That's us." It was Mr. Bistrek speaking again, and I realized, looking out on the floor where people were dancing, that they were nearly all around my age. Only a few were kid couples, very young kid couples, accompanying their parents. Mr. Bistrek put his arm around his wife: "I went to junior college, you know? CPA school. We had the Happylanders for commencement. The year before us had the Casa Loma. Big nights. Big nights, hey Mary?"

Dave saluted somebody. I didn't think the man returned it, and Connie, noticing too, made an encouraging face at her tall husband. I remembered my talk with Russ Fisher, the salesman, and thought: yes, they're still being watched. People here are guarded towards Dave. It made me like the hell out of Jerry Bistrek, who'd come to join us; at the same time, I thought, I'm probably taking more notice, feeling it more, than Dave is. Things slide off Dave, and people come back to him.

Anyway, Jerry was a nice man, bald but trim; he wore a small mustache and a rather loud but not unbecoming sports coat. His wife, who seemed pleasant, was one of the few women there who looked her age. She was plump and wore glasses, and had the laced-in look of the women who play bridge in communities where their contemporaries swim or sail or play golf. Her make-up was smooth; you felt she looked as well as she could, and that he liked her—but on the floor, the other forty-year-old dancers in the rosy light, impelled by the recreated music, were college boys and girls again.

The Bistreks got up to dance.

"It's the fountain of youth," said Dave.

The Happylanders were in the final chorus of *Hurry Home*. It was amazing how accurately they had the sound—something less massively harmonized and sweet than the Miller reeds-plus-trombone sound; less driving and less soloistic than Goodman. The Happylanders sound had a hardness to it, an edge, but so precise and well-drilled that the first impression one of their arrangements gave was of some kind of delicacy.

I wondered who the arranger had been, what had become of him. Then I stopped wondering because of the girl who came wandering in from the back, from behind the bandstand, and slouched up onto it.

She wore a green evening gown with loose, thin straps, that

slid on her fragile shoulders in directions contrary to the way the shoulders moved. The dress fit only here and there, as if she'd started to make it herself and was wearing it before it was finished. Her hair was pale blonde, and as she climbed to reach the band, they played a few bars, stylized, of *Sunny* (". . . for shocking the town / Is all that you do . . .") and then modulated into an introduction: *Keep on Doin' What You're Doin'*.

Things seemed a little slack at our table. I made an announcement: "That is not Nina Connolly," I said. "It isn't Nina Connolly's ghost, either."

"Look at Barney James." Dave was still on his fountain of youth theme. "That man's forty-two? I'd say a dissipated twenty-eight, wouldn't you, Connie?"

"Well-preserved for twenty-eight," Connie said.

"She is altogether different," I said. "That girl couldn't have been born when Nina Connolly recorded *Keep on Doin' What You're Doin'*. Remember? It was banned from the air waves." It had been a pretty suggestive recording.

Dave started to say something more, but I said: "Hey, let me look. Let me listen." And I turned my eyes to the bandstand. Nina Connolly, the Happylanders' original girl vocalist, had been dark-haired, full-bodied. She'd chortled and swung, when she sang, and even bumped her hips a little, as if half-involuntarily, half out of good-natured sensuality.

This girl slumped. "I saw Nina Connolly once with the Happylanders in New York. At the Commodore," I informed my somewhat distracted audience, and turned towards the singer again.

"Her name is Sunny Brown," I heard Connie say.

Then Sunny Brown began to sing, and it was kind of incredible. Her voice was big, throaty, more like Nina Connolly's than ought reasonably to have been produced by a slender frame like that one. It was like a thin little girl appearing to sing on film, with an old torchy voice dubbed onto the soundtrack. You could close your eyes and think of Nina (or Ivy Anderson, Ella, Anita O'Day) if you wanted, but keeping your eyes open and on this child was even wilder. There was just nothing big there to match the voice except the breasts, which moved around loosely, and the eyes which stared.

The body quivered, the voice throbbed out of the slim throat, as if the girl were inhabited by it, rather than having free use. Nina Connolly—I was letting her stand for all the girl vocalists of the swing age—had had something easy-going but controlled about her; it seemed to say that female warmth was something that she thought about, didn't mind, rather liked, might get generous with. This blonde stick of a girl, this Sunny Brown whose chest jumped around illogically, was battered by her female quality. It was the thing that whipped her and wouldn't let her be.

So that the song, and it really is suggestive, of course, had said, the way Nina Connolly sang it: *Hey. Keep on. This is fine, fine, fine.* But with Sunny singing it, it said, *Keep on. If you stop I'll scream.*

But I wasn't sure the eyes had that much life to them.

There was applause when she finished, and then, as the band got up for a break, shuffling and scraping. The dynamo of club members' voices hummed and gained.

The Bistreks, coming back from the dance floor, stopped to talk to people at another table, and beckoned Dave to join them. Dave excused himself.

"The same night that I heard Nina Connolly in New York, we heard Goodman, too. With Peggy Lee," I said to Connie. "Christmas vacation. 1941."

Connie smiled. "Very important evening." She was teasing, but so gently.

"Very important date," I said. "But what was her name?"

"Gee, I don't remember," Connie said.

I took a guess: "Elaine."

Connie laughed at me. Then she said, "The Happylanders started right around here."

I remembered the billing. " 'The big band from Boston.' "

"Gary Rodgers was an Italian boy. I can't remember his real name—Dave would."

"Ruggieri?"

"It may have been. His father used to have a shore restaurant, that made pizza. Before there was any such thing as pizza."

"You must have come here summers." She nodded, smiling a little. I could remember that, and I said: "Driving along the Massachusetts shore, down from college in the spring. Knowing if we could find a place that cooked Neapolitan, we could get this wonderful tomato pie. If we could think of the name of it."

Abruptly, Connie said: "Barney, I'd better tell you. The singer. Sunny Brown. She was Dave's girl."

"Oh?" I said, or maybe, "Uh?" And what made the nice lady want to share a thing like that, just when the evening was settling into a fine, boozy glow?

"I'm sorry. I just thought you'd better know. Now that I've told you, I'm not sure why I did."

"I was calling attention to her pretty hard," I said. "Hey, everybody, look. Look! I suppose I was wondering in my stupid way why the rest of you wanted to change the subject."

Connie said: "I don't mean he's seeing her. I don't think he **is**. I don't know."

"Yeah."

"In a way, I don't even care."

I nodded. Or shook my head. Or both.

"She was in the divorce with Jane. Then she left town, and people said she'd left the band and gone to New York. I don't think Dave would have brought us here tonight, if he'd known Sunny was back."

"No. Of course." Helpful. Articulate.

"Or maybe he would have. I can't tell about Dave."

What I wanted to do was to touch Connie, at that moment, press my hand against her arm or shoulder in some comforting way. And since the band was coming back—without Sunny just now—I asked Connie to dance.

I knew it was a mistake the moment we got up and moved close to one another. It was altogether pleasant and not a bit comforting—not for me, and I was fairly sure she felt the same, indecorous glow. Candescence.

We quit dancing with no need for consultation, after the first tune—it was fast, fortunately for boozy Barney, *Shanty in Old Shanty Town*, swung hard. God knows what kind of ass

I'd have made of myself if they'd played *Deep Purple*. As it went, I was able to back off from that firm, friendly body and do some absurd, schoolboy steps, grinning and putting the energy from the glow into it. I used to pass for a good dancer—I could truck, shag and Lindy (What, Gramps?), and when there was a Big Apple, and they made the circle and yelled "Shine, Barney," I, uh, could . . . sure. Have some more of this geriatric applesauce, old boy.

Connie indulged me; we even had a gallery by the end of the tune. I guess I went so hard because I felt so completely unlike doing it, trying to counter a mood that wasn't light-hearted at all. People clapped, for Christ's sake.

As we faced one another, before starting back to the table again, the girl was getting ready to sing some more, and Connie said: "I shouldn't have told you about her, Barney. I'm sorry."

"I imagine everybody else in this room knows it," I said, but I didn't mind having been told any longer.

"Are we going to help Captain Clark with his boat?"

"That was the idea, wasn't it? To see if you'd feel like taking a cruise with Helen and me."

"Maybe it was. I didn't think I wanted to go, and now I do. Is Dave Doremus that smart?"

"He's a smart man," I said.

"Are we going?"

"I don't know yet, till I've talked to Dave."

"What's Helen like?"

"She wants to go sailing very much. . . ." There we were, standing in the middle of the dance floor, unable to stop talking to one another again. Couples began to move by. "Connie— something I was going to ask Dave—don't answer if you don't want to?"

"Can't force a wife to testify, can you?" Connie said, moving her foot towards mine. "Go ahead."

"After the assassination. When Dave came to Puerto Rico, to try to get us. What was happening?"

"Dave was being kind, I think. I'd . . . already thought about begging off the cruise, Barney. With strangers." She smiled at that. "Bride's jitters, and me such a dewy young bride."

We started to turn back for the table, with my arm lightly around her waist, guiding, and stopped to let a graceful fat man jitterbug by, with a thin, pretty partner. And Connie said:

"Poor Dave. When the news came about Kennedy, I shut myself in the hotel room and asked him to stay out. It was bad of me, but the news made me want to think about Joe. Joe Ferguson. My—my husband. I hoped Dave would understand."

(And Dave hoped, then, that if Helen and I would come, Connie'd appear? Nothing wrong with that, I suppose. Okay.)

"He died of Addison's disease, Barney. And the more pain he was in, the sweeter he got. What's happening to us, Barney?"

"Some of our bunch are dying already," I said, as lightly as I could. The graceful fat man was still jumping in front of us. His partner was clapping in time.

"Comes naturally to us?"

"Sure. Dance with me?" We danced, five steps. We had to stop; the tune was slow, an introduction to something I didn't recognize.

"I hope we do go cruising." She was against me, standing still, very lightly. "Is that improper influence?"

"It sure is," I said, and we started again, back towards the table slowly, through the intent dancers. The girl was singing again, a song I'd never heard but won't forget, called *When Sunny Gets Blue*. Or maybe it's spelled "Sonny" in the title. I don't know.

Then, while we were still making our slow way back, the band turned it into a two-song medley, going into one that sometimes breaks me up though it's lively enough: *Don't Be That Way*. As we sat down at our table I noticed that Sunny Brown, whose vocal part was over, was singing this one anyway, sitting on someone's trumpet case, snapping her fingers on the first and third beats inaudibly, singing it to herself. You couldn't hear it, but since I'd known the lyrics once, I could come pretty close to reading her lips.

I saw Jerry and Mrs. Bistrek, too, on their way back to our table, waiting for the dancers between steps just as we had, and Connie asked in a quick whisper:

"Barney, is it money between you and Dave?"

138

"Only in a way," I said. "Not really. Never mind, Connie."

"I just have to say—because it might make a difference. Jerry Bistrek's going to help. Dave's business was just about gone. He got into a local firm too deeply. . . ."

"Yes. I know."

"But then he got to help Jerry reorganize the bakeries. And Jerry, who's a fine businessman, was impressed." The fine businessman was pretty close now, and she finished in a rush: "So he's going to put new money in Dave's firm, because what I had is mostly all gone. For the house, and bills. . . ."

"Secrets?" said Jerry Bistrek, affably.

"No. I'm being pushy," Connie said. "Telling Barney things he doesn't really want to know."

"Sure I do, Connie," I said, standing for Mary Bistrek, and reaching over to pat Connie's hand. "Of course I do."

And Sunny Brown stood up again to sing. Every singer has particular songs, if she has any individual quality at all, which best express it. The one which came closest to distilling the weird essence of Sunny Brown was the one she did now, *Dancing on the Ceiling*. It's generally played as a polite little piece of hotel music, lilting and not even especially wistful. I've heard it played with a lot of velocity, too, as a modern jazz instrumental. Sunny changed it into something else again, something quite depraved, or if not that, then innocent because of madness:

> It's a first-person song, and in the first eight bars the girl tells us that she lies in bed every night, and sees her lover dancing on the ceiling.

And Sunny Brown watched the ceiling while she sang the first eight, stared at it, motionless except for her hands. They were very white, thin, long-fingered hands, and they jumped; you wondered if she knew they were jumping.

> In the next eight, she sings of trying to hide from the overhead lover, trying to hide deep under the bedclothes . . .

where the hands were. The eyes still searched the ceiling, but her face showed something like shame, or being ashamed, at the way those hands moved, up and down along her sides, in towards her stomach.

> In the release she asks that her lover go away, saying it isn't fair.

139

Sunny Brown demanded this, but fearfully, in no hope of being obeyed. And by the end of the middle part her hips were moving and an excited smile had come onto her face. She admitted. She was glad that her lover was still there. Yes.

And finally the mad girl makes her true confession, that it is really the ceiling itself that she loves, more and more and more, in the rhythm of sweet release—I've seen burlesque and heard the dirty songs that are sung by men and armies, but I never encountered anything as seriously, and somehow touchingly, obscene, as Sunny Brown singing *Dancing on the Ceiling.*

And with all that she managed to give me, and, I suspect, each other person who listened carefully, a feeling of its all being confidential, a secret about her that only I could understand and somehow find exciting too.

"Barney?"

"Hi, Connie."

"Was it good news, what I told you?"

I smiled at her. The evening was getting to be too much for me, with the drinks and music and the gathering information. Maybe the band thought they'd let me off now, by playing a nice bright tune like *Skylark,* but even that had special associations for me.

I drank off what was left of a drink I hardly needed, watching the deft way—I realized I had been watching it—that Dave was moving around, getting himself greeted, talked to. People I felt certain hadn't waved when we came in were beckoning him over now. Damned if I know how he'd warmed them up; Connie'd told me that was the first time they'd been there, at that particular club, in a long while.

I got up, then, and lurched over to where Dave was standing, in the carpeted area in front of the check room, just done talking with a man in a dinner jacket.

I moved over with *Skylark* pushing behind me, a real country boy complete with wet eyes and catching throat, dizzy head, shuffling walk and plowboy manners, meaning to shake Dave by the hand and tell him he was the best old Dormouse in the world. And other such lang syne.

Instead of a handshake, though, there came a naughty

moment for our simple-hearted, rustic hero. As I reached Dave, I saw his eyes leave me and go to something back behind my right shoulder. Stopped in front of him and turned my big thick head to look where he was looking, and here comes that crazy thin blonde singer, towards us off the bandstand in her wandering way.

I gawked at the strange, pendulous bosom, moving loosely under the incomplete dress; and assured myself she wasn't as far gone as she let on. No sir. Must be part of the act.

"Do you mind meeting her?" Dave asked.

We couldn't have moved, by then, without its being obvious that we were avoiding her.

"Me mind?" Visions of Cape Cod sugarplums danced through my Ozark head, though I did manage two footnotes to myself: hey little buddy, this is a family visit. And: be sure Connie sees you're with them.

The girl was within a shambling step or two of us, her hand went out a little way towards Dave, and the fingers began to snap in the way I'd noticed.

"Hello, Sunny," Dave said. "Sunny, this is Barney James."

The fingers kept going, in obscure rhythm. She looked at Dave, not me. She said, or sang. Or incanted:

> "Three. Three."
> Snap. Snap. Snap.
> "Three.
> Three bees."
> Snap.
> "Honey bee.
> Bumble bee."
> Snap. Snap.
> "Useta be."

With which she started to go by us, snapping. Then she checked herself, and looked back over her shoulder at Dave again, and her face got all screwed up like a little girl's about to cry:

"Sailor?" she said.

Her head turned away again, dropped, and she shuffled off,

skirt trailing, looking down at her feet. I watched the slatty buttocks flap along, under green cloth, and it was about as pitiful and sexy a sight as you could want to see—if we assume that you, like our rude-natured but upright hero, have such steel strings on the guitar of your country heart as will start making chords with the notion of inflicting sex on an object of pity.

"She's very high," Dave said. "On pills."

"Pills?"

"She'll stay awake forever. Dancing by herself to, . . . to strange records."

"What records?"

"*Jungle Drums of Borneo. Primitive Jazz of French West Africa. Ceremonial Music of the Quiché Maya.* Anthropologist's records. Someone gave them to her. She has one of sports car engines, racing. Antique locomotive sounds, for God's sake. She dances to those, too."

"You know her pretty well," I said.

I felt Dave's hand lightly on my shoulder, and looked up at him. "No one knows this but you, Barney," he said. "I was married to her."

Night in Wonamasset.

Empty glasses crowded our table. There were three more people sitting with us now: the man in the dinner jacket and his wife, and a handsome, chesty woman around thirty who sat back smiling with her bust raised nearly to her chin. Her husband, I understood, was out of town and it was clear that she was proud to have people see her sitting there as a guest at the Doremus's table.

Jerry Bistrek was asking Dave about his election campaign. I'd never really heard it before, so I listened, too.

"How can you say you struck out?" Jerry asked. "That was just the first pitch. You've hit everything you ever went for since. Voted for you myself, and I'm in the other party."

Dave said: "School Board. City Council. Sure. Thanks for your support."

"Try Congress again, when you get ready," Jerry said. "There's men I know who'll leave our party to work for you."

Dave smiled. "Quite a few in my party," he said. His party was Republican. "Who might leave to work against me, Jerry. But I won't pretend I'm resigned about it. National office is too old a dream, you know? I'll try again. Maybe I'll even jump the fence, if anybody wants me to."

"Your old dream, Dave?" I asked. Because when Dave was younger, he hadn't talked about politics—yet we always assumed that was his direction, for some reason.

"I wouldn't have said it, even to you. Boy's superstition: it's a jinx to say out loud the name of what you really want. Anyway, it was partly my father's dream for me. You always rear back against that a little, don't you?"

The man in the dinner jacket asked about Dave's father. Jerry wanted to know, too, and Dave explained. Then he said: "Those like him who were a new kind of man in government because they had New Deal religion—they ran things, but they were in awe of men who could win elections. Sometimes pretty grubby men, too. I don't mean in awe of their power. Dad was as good as anybody at whipping Congressmen, in committee hearings. But he felt inferior, at the same time, because they could go to the people, when the time came, and win."

"Maybe that was part of the loyalty to Roosevelt," Jerry Bistrek said. "He could go to the people with what men like your Dad were trying to do."

"Damn right," Dave said. "He wasn't just the Chief. He was the Champ, too."

"Why'd you go Republican?" Jerry asked. "You'd have won with my boys."

"John F. Kennedy," Dave said, and let that lie around on the table for a moment. Then he said: "It's complicated. I'd have told you I was a Democrat any time in my life, up to a couple of days before I became a Republican candidate."

The man in the dinner jacket wanted to sign for a round of drinks. Connie and Mrs. Bistrek and the lady with the proud bosom were having their own conversation. It was intermission now. No more music for the next half hour or so.

"My father worked under Joe Kennedy, senior," Dave reminded us. "Not for long, not all that close, but close enough so that he knew a man who believed in his sons. And Dad took pride in his son, too. Joe Kennedy wasn't the most popular man in the New Deal, and he had, oh, rivals I guess. A level or two above Dad. Who got some pleasure out of having Dad show me off. When I was in Page-Boy school, they used to like to have him bring me around to their offices, to talk to them about different senators—not pumping for information but because they liked to test my understanding of what those men were like. Bilbo. Vandenberg. Lehman. Borah. It tickled the executive branch men to hear me talk about the big politicians wisely; it even tickled my father's friends that I felt I ought to be discreet about some of the personal things. Habits. Tastes. 'Boy knows how to get to all of them, and how to keep his mouth shut, too, Carl,' I remember one man saying. An assistant secretary. And he chuckled about it. 'He'll be majority leader over there on the hill, one of these days.'"

"It sounds pretty innocent on your father's part," I said.

"Were you really supposed to be compared to the Kennedy boys?"

"Oh no," said Dave. "Nothing that direct. Washington's full of people's favorite, precocious kids, and I was one of them. That's all. I did know the children in that family collectively, I guess, but never well enough to think of them as individuals. There was some direct rivalry in the summer sailing. And envy of the money. But I think the thing I minded most, and I'm not sure why I picked Mr. Kennedy to mind it about, was that I always thought my father was as able as any of them. I wanted him to have his own show to run, an agency or a bureau. And he was never—oh, say, more than a colonel. With four kinds of generals over him." He thought a moment and drank. "Probably I was wrong," he said. "My father was a good administrator, but he wasn't a tough one. You know the difference, Jerry. You're a tough administrator. So's Barney. If you weren't, there'd need to be one over you, wouldn't there?"

Jerry nodded. I'd never thought about it, and didn't know.

"It was sort of magical meeting a Kennedy in the hospital. They'd always been glamorous people to me, and here was one getting bossed around by Navy nurses, just like me. He had one of the worst cases of malaria they'd ever seen—I don't think he weighed 130 pounds, and he was a tall, big-shouldered man.

"I'd probably be inventing if I tried to quote anything he said directly, but we did talk a lot. In spite of the hospital gown and the thinness, he was starting to have the great, magnetic self-assurance of a kind of American Prince of Wales. He was very sure of a lot of things, and I thought he was wronger than hell about some of them—we used to argue. European politics. What to do with Germany. I was impressed by him, and attracted to him . . . I don't think it's wrong to say that he thought pretty well of me. He must have because I stopped feeling challenged by him, and I wouldn't have if there'd been anything patronizing in the way he talked to me."

"I don't see it," Jerry said. "Why wouldn't that make you a double-dip Democrat with hot fudge sauce?"

Dave shook his head. "I said it was complicated. I don't even know how much was practical and how much idealistic. The practical part of it was a standoff. Representative Kennedy was running for the Senate. I'd started getting into things around here enough so that I heard what a lot of bright young men were being allowed to know in Massachusetts—that I might get to go to Washington, if he won. Be a congressional committee counsel, that kind of thing. Which might have been a pretty good way to start chasing a democratic congressional nomination for myself. But they had an incumbent to run; I couldn't have that nomination yet. Maybe I was impatient, but I don't think so. I'd had an awful lot of Washington, growing up. I liked what I was starting to do here."

He looked around, smiling, and shrugged. We were all listening.

"Well, I didn't want to just get a job down there. And maybe I didn't want to wait my turn. Kennedy was going to win his Senate seat without me, of course; but suppose he didn't? It was going to be a big Eisenhower sweep nationally. That was pretty clear. So call the practical thing a standoff—wait my turn with the Democrats, and build some local strength. Or try it with Ike, and hope he'd carry me in."

"That makes enough sense," said the dinner-jacket man.

"So I think the idealistic part's what tipped it," Dave said. "At least, I'd like to think so. There were a lot of men I admired personally in the Massachusetts Republican party—Saltonstall. Lodge. Men like that, who'd made theirs a reform party. But you don't base political choices on admiration, do you? It's finally a very emotional thing, and I got emotional. I think I became a Republican most consciously because of a Republican I hated. Joe McCarthy. He wouldn't come up here and campaign against Kennedy. Kennedy people said it was because he was scared. The men who were talking to me said it was a deal."

"I always thought it was a deal," Jerry Bistrek said. "And I was working for Kennedy that time, too."

"The whole thing of Irish, conservative, Catholic power. Democratic city machines. I didn't know if the Prince of Wales I'd liked in the hospital was its victim. Or even a new-style leader of all that, a sort of potential, Madison Avenue, big-time McCarthy. With the manners and plausibility and smile to lull the scrupulous. Unlimited money. Tremendous political ability.

"He could be a monster. Maybe what the Republicans had for me—we were talking. They were looking for war records, still, and I wasn't unknown. Maybe what they had for me was a white horse, and a suit of armor to put on . . . hell, that's enough of that," Dave said. "If that's what they had, I got the iron pants beat off me."

I knew he hadn't been beaten that badly. It was a way of closing the subject. But a minute later it turned out that Dave wasn't quite through. He was through only in wanting to say the next thing to me, not to Jerry and the other man, who'd started talking with the wives now.

"I would have won that time, Barney. At least, the people who worked with me thought so. The pros. If I'd been willing to tone down the stuff I was saying about McCarthy. But I made it my campaign, my issue, against all the advice, and I had a crazy reason: I thought I could take him."

"McCarthy?" I asked, a little puzzled. "Or your worthy opponent?"

"Kennedy," Dave said.

Probably I stared. Dave looked wry.

"I was going to be on record, strong, even if it meant losing. And then—I was getting into my thirties. I'd started thinking, as a kind of American afterthought, that I ought to make some money. And, when the time came to run again, I'd spend big and win big. And then in six years, or twelve, I wanted to go up against him. Personally. I thought I could take him."

He grinned, and drank, abashed.

"You were wrong about him, weren't you? The Madison Avenue McCarthy stuff?"

"I'm not sure I was," Dave said, and thought, "I could have been right at the time, you know. We're never willing to acknowledge that there's growth in this country, after adolescence. I think he grew and grew and grew, like Roosevelt. I think that . . . persistent growing's what it takes to make a great man. There isn't enough time to grow up great in your teens, or your twenties, or your thirties even. You couldn't be any better than brilliant. You've got to keep growing. In your forties, your fifties.

That's what makes a great man different. And I'll bet it hurts, all the way. You going to see Stiggsy?"

"Yeah." I'd told Dave earlier I wanted to go down to the cigar store during intermission. "He's going to be disgusted with me."

"He is, huh?"

"I got a two-horse parlay." I felt pretty sly. "A parlay's a sucker bet, but this one might just not be. They're both good horses. The odds will be short is the only trouble, but it could work."

I'd been following the Gulfstream Park meeting all week, starting as soon as I'd known that I was coming up here. I wanted to have a couple of Saturday afternoon horses picked, to bet Friday night. I didn't do a lot of betting, but sometimes would follow the races, somewhere, in the papers. If I was in a city where I could get my money down, without too much furtive nonsense. And I always tried to have some kind of bet in mind to write with Stiggsy when I saw him, through the years. For old time's sake—no. Because I like to.

Some winter I'd like to take a couple of thousand bucks to Florida, and go every day, from one to another of those lovely tracks down there. And go broke, and then watch the major leaguers, in spring training. See the new kids, and the old stars who'll be younger men by then than I. But maybe Musial and Schoendienst will be around, managing, coaching batters—Williams, DiMaggio, or Whitey Ford, who beat us in the series. And someday I'd like to go to Africa, to see the birds there, and to Paraguay and to Australia; they've got wonderful birds in Australia.

2

I asked Dave if he wanted to come watch me bet my parlay, but he declined. Still other people were coming over to see him.

"Take the car," he said. "Want to go with him, Connie?"

"It's your chance to be a big-time gambler's moll," I said.

Connie smiled, and said her evening purse was too small for my big gun, would I mind taking the little one tonight?

It was a damp, mild evening, and when we went out of the

club it was actually raining a little, and everything looked pretty and shiny in the parking lot lights.

"Spring has every intention. . . ." I said, putting her in the car.

Two or three other cars were pulling out as we did, but I didn't suppose they were all going to Stiggsy's to get their bets down for tomorrow. They were the people who'd said, "We'll stay till intermission," and hadn't had anything happen at the dance to change their minds.

One car did come along after us, following each of the turns that Connie directed me to make, and when we stopped it did, too. This was right in the middle of town. Stiggsy's cigar store stood on the square, which was more of a triangle, too small to have anything but a traffic signal and some "Keep Right" signs in the center. Across from Stiggsy's was the moving picture theater, included as part of a small office building. On the third side of the triangle were a bar and a restaurant, and, coming back to Stiggsy's, a couple of other little stores. His was the only thing open, aside from the bar and theater, as we drove up and the other car stopped behind us; I could see Stiggsy in there, his stomach pushed against the counter, reading a magazine.

I imagine he was waiting for the movie to let out, so that he could sell some pop or coffee, visit a little, and then close up. Most of his bets came in by phone, or over coffee in the mornings.

As Connie and I got to the door, Stiggsy saw us and yelled, "Hey. Barney. Hey, come in out of the rain."

He met us as we cleared the door, wrung my hand, grinned at Connie and said I was just the man he wanted to see. Was it possible there could be meadow larks back already, or did I think the ones he'd seen were some that had wintered there?

I said if anyone would know, he would, and Stiggsy beamed and said he thought they were back. It was going to be an early spring for birds, and boy he was glad we'd come in.

"How's Dave, Mrs. Doremus? Fine, I bet."

"You probably saw him this morning," Connie said. "Didn't you?"

And Stiggsy grinned some more, and sold me some Easter

seals. "You don't have to buy them Barney. Probably you get yours at home, but just if you want them. . . ."

I gave him a couple of dollars for the seals, and asked if he was ready to take a big bet. The dog—it was Roland III by then—got up and scratched at the word "bet," and Stiggsy said: "You see that? He's the bookie. You think he'd ever wake up to help me sell seals or something? Hey, I got an office now, Barney."

"You do?"

"Across the street. Just today. In the theater building. The phone rings here and there too. Why don't you come in in the morning?"

I said I didn't mind if Connie watched me betting, and old, straggle-haired Stiggsy, beaming and looking stronger and fatter than ever, said: "All right. All right. I just thought maybe you didn't want her to know what a big loser you were."

We kidded about that a while, and I told him my horses: one was called Ship's Cook and the other Daylight Savings, and I wanted a fifty-dollar win parlay.

"It's a sucker bet, Mrs. Doremus." Stiggsy couldn't have been happier than he was to have us there. "I just hate to take his money."

"Just be glad I don't have a third horse that good, Stiggsy," I said. "I'd win this store away from you."

He was writing the ticket, and laughing, and I heard the door open. Abruptly, Stiggsy stopped laughing and said to me: "I'll see if I can order some of those, sir. Would you try something else for now?"

Quite smoothly he handed me a half dozen cigars, up from under the counter. He slipped his other big hand over my money, and the bet slip, and had them all crumpled together out of sight almost without visible movement. I glanced back to see that two men were standing in the doorway, and realized I'd been wondering for five minutes, half-consciously, why no one had followed us in at first.

"Thank you," I said, and took the cigars.

"How you doing, Stiggsy?" one of the men said.

He was taller than Stiggsy, but not as heavy, a good, sizable man with a pallid face, a smashed-in nose, and dark blond, slicked-down hair.

"You want something, Buster?" Stiggsy's voice was hostile.

The man behind Buster didn't say anything or look very interested. They were both wearing raincoats.

"Selling a lot of cigars?"

Stiggsy just looked at him.

Buster nodded at me: "I don't know him."

"He don't know you, either," Stiggsy said. "You want something?"

"No." Buster waited till Stiggsy started to speak again, and then smiled: "Just happened to be in town. Thought we'd fall by."

"Go ahead," said Stiggsy. "Fall."

"I want a candy bar," Buster said. "Gimme an O. Henry."

Stiggsy reached behind him, picked out the candy bar without looking, and moved up behind the counter, away from Connie and me. He put the bar down, and said: "A dime."

"You want a candy?" Buster asked his companion.

"Let's go," the other man said.

Buster paid his dime, and tore the wrapper off the candy. "Look at that," he said. "It costs a dime, and they still put less stuff in than when it cost a nickel."

"Some law says you have to buy it?" Stiggsy asked.

For a moment I thought Buster was going to throw the candy bar on the floor, but suddenly, smiling his pale smile again, he dropped the wrapper and put the whole thing in his mouth at once.

"How 'bout you, lady?" he said to Connie, with his mouth full. "You want one, too?"

"Get out of here, Buster," Stiggsy yelled, furious, and started around the counter. Buster backed out of the store, laughing. The other man turned and followed.

Stiggsy went to the doorway, no further, and shouted: "There's other places that sell candy, slob." Then he turned back to us, and said: "I'm sorry. I'm sorry, Mrs. Doremus."

"That's all right," Connie said. "Who are they, Stiggsy? Policemen?"

"No." He started to recover himself. His cheeks, which had been bright red a moment before, got pink again. "No, Mrs. Doremus. Oh, one of them was once."

"I thought so, because you didn't want them to see Barney betting."

"They know I'm a bookie," Stiggsy said. "It ain't any of their business who my customers are."

"You're not in trouble?" I asked.

"With those guys? That Buster? That's Mr. Blowhard," Stiggsy said. He finished writing my ticket for the parlay. I put the cigars he'd handed me back on the counter.

"I don't think I've seen him before," Connie said. "Is he from around here, Stiggsy?"

"I don't know him," Stiggsy said. "I don't know where he's from. He just comes in here sometimes and blows off, see? But I don't know him at all, Mrs. Doremus. No kidding. Here you go, Barney. Boy, I hope they come in for you."

"Maybe I better put the ticket in the night box at the bank," I said. "It's as good as money, isn't it?"

We said goodnight and went out, and I had just closed the door of the car on Connie's side when I heard Stiggsy call.

"Hey, Barney." He was standing in the doorway. "Hey, come back a minute, will you? I wrote your ticket wrong."

I went back into the store.

"Did they follow you, or what?" Stiggsy asked, in a low voice.

"You mean Buster?"

"Yeah. Buster Brown and his rat."

"I guess they did," I said. "From the Shore Club."

"That's Dave's car you got."

"Right," I said. "What's going on?"

"I don't know," said Stiggsy. "Nothing. I didn't want to get her worried."

"You do know Buster. What about his being a cop?"

"Just probationary. Up in Boston, a long time ago. Hell, they threw him off the force. He was trying to clip people before he even got his badge."

"What is he now?"

"A fathead," Stiggsy said, violently. "Listen, don't worry. He's not even working around here."

"Working at what?"

"Collecting. Juke-box money and stuff. But not in this town. This ain't his area."

"For the same people that bank you?" I asked.

"You don't want to know nothing about it, Barney," Stiggsy said, very sincerely.

"Okay."

"Buster don't scare me any."

"I don't think the man's been born yet who could scare you, has he, Stiggsy?"

"You staying at Dave's?"

"Yes."

"Barney, look. The thing is, that's his sister."

"Who?"

"Buster Brown. That's his sister, that Sunny. That sings with the band."

3

Back at the club, when we got there, Dave and the Bistreks were having a good time.

There was a little gallery of people standing or sitting around their table, and Dave was goodhumoredly playing straight man while Jerry Bistrek clowned.

They'd convened a meeting of the PTA. Dave was chairman, and Jerry was a new member, speaking from the floor:

"You see my point, Mr. Chairman?"

"I don't believe I do, sir. About the typing teacher?"

"That's right! That's right. If we're going to have parents and teachers associated, I want to get associated with the typing teacher."

"I don't believe you quite understand the function of this organization, sir," Dave said. "You see, we're concerned with children."

"So who's not concerned with children? I'd be very concerned. I wouldn't want to have children with her, Mr. Chairman."

"I should hope not," said the chairman.

"I mean I'd be very careful. Besides, I already got children."

"Ah. Very commendable. And they're in school?"

"This time of night? I hope not."

"Really, sir. Calm yourself. I didn't mean. . . ."

"They're keeping them after school till eleven, twelve at night?"

"Please, Mr. Bistrek."

"Please? Please what? Those poor kids. What'd they do that's so bad they've got to stay in after school all night long?"

"You don't understand. The building's closed at night."

"Oh no. Lights off. No heat. Shivering there in the dark, maybe, poor little things, for what? Passing a note in class? And here we are, sitting around like a bunny club with typing teachers. . . ."

People were laughing. They'd go home and tell each other Jerry Bistrek should have been a comedian, and perhaps be partly right. His timing was good, and he improvised his lines with a screwball earnestness that was pretty effective. But I'd seen Dave bring people out like that too many times not to realize how much of it came, somehow, from him. That some of his lines even suggested the replies. If they were a comic and a straight man, so, I thought, were a jester and his king.

The band played. The PTA meeting was adjourned. But the people stayed around the table, wanting to talk to Dave, wanting, I was sure by now, to be seen talking to him. And Dave had all the old ease and attention for each of them.

He was in good shape, I thought, and credited Connie. I relaxed about Dave, and barely remembered to hope that he'd be able to clear up the matter between him and me, as we danced and drank and hammed our way through the rest of a gay evening.

We left about one, and drove home. Connie went up to bed. Dave was wide awake; he'd agreed to go across the street to Jerry's house, where some of the others were gathered for a final drink. He didn't take his coat off.

"Want to come?" Dave asked me. I was tired. The drive

was catching up with me. I said I thought I'd had enough evening.

"Anything on your mind, Barney? That we ought to talk about tonight?"

"Right now my mind's a big ball of bourbon-colored fuzz," I said.

"We'll wait till morning, huh?"

"Yeah," I said. "Only, Dave, I couldn't have heard you right. You weren't married to that girl, the singer?"

Dave nodded. "Yes. For about ten days."

"How can you be married to somebody for ten days?"

"I admit, you've got to be pretty stupid to arrange a thing like that," Dave said, and smiled. "What else, Barney?"

My head was a little clearer. Might as well, and wake up in the morning with everything else clear, too. "Spaghetti," I said. "SPAGETI, and my goddamn Uncle Troy by goddamn marriage."

Dave looked surprised. "What did Mr. Gibson tell you?"

"I gathered he felt he'd been bilked," I said. "I mean he's a larcenous old guy. He's got it coming. But, Dave, what the hell?"

Dave shook his head. "Barney, can you remember what he said? Exactly?"

I tried. "Yeah. That you served him badly. Or didn't serve him well."

He'd been standing by the door, ready to go back out. Now he came into the main part of the house. "For God's sake," he said. "Have a drink, Barney Jesse. I can't tell you how happy I am, if that's what's been bothering."

"Happy, huh?" I said. Stupidly.

"I didn't serve him well." Dave was beginning to grin. Hell, he was about to start turning cartwheels of joy. "Here, old Ozark gismo." He led me to a little wheeled bar in the living room; ceremoniously, he mixed me a drink, and another for himself. Pretty big ones. "Damn, I should have made you spill it earlier. It wouldn't have been eating on me all evening, would it?" And he drank off his drink, while I sipped at mine. "You lick up that corn juice," he said. "I'll be right back."

In a moment he returned, with a letter in his hand. "This is just a carbon," he said. "A pretty, pretty carbon. Set it to country music, boy, I'll sing it for you. Look. To your Uncle by marriage." He handed it to me. "You're damn right I didn't serve him very well. He was begging to get in, and look here, Barney. I wouldn't let him. I wouldn't serve him at all."

> ... as I explained, because of my personal relationship with Barney James, which goes back many years. And in addition, that I have been engaged by your firm as a consultant and, in that way, had access to your books and to the privilege of meeting you. For these reasons I do not feel that I can ethically accept your offer to invest in a high-risk enterprise like Southport and General Electronic Timers, Inc., since I am myself involved in the firm.

"Well, I'll be damned," I said. "I'll be double damned."

"Okay, what else? You want to know about the SPAGETI deal itself?"

"No," I said. "I don't care, Dave. I really don't."

"I want you to," Dave said. "I want you to do something for me."

"You got it," I said.

"Will you talk to Jerry Bistrek, and ask him what went on?"

"Sure," I said. "Sure, I will."

"Will you believe Jerry?"

"I believe you, Dave," I said. "And no more explanations requested. I feel like an ass."

"Mule," he said. "You know where from, too. No, listen, talk to Jerry. He knows the story as well as anyone. Come on, you want to see him now?"

"No." I begged off. "In the morning, okay? Jerry might not be in a mood for business stories."

"Here I go then," Dave said. "Sure you don't want to come?"

"No, but . . . boy, I'll go to bed contented. If I weren't so sleepy, I swear I'd call Helen and wake her up."

"A-sailing we will go!" Dave shouted, opening the door.

"Damn right. Damn right," I called after him, pretty drunk with the new drink. I went to the door, opened it and waved. I nearly called after him to wait for me, after all, but I was really enjoying leaning against the door stop, watching him dance across the street, light-hearted in the rain.

4

And then I couldn't sleep. Sometimes drinking works like that, if things have been disturbing me. And it's uncomfortable, with my mind going 16 rpm's, stuck in a 33 rpm microgroove.

This time I didn't even know what notes I was stuck on, because I felt I ought to be reassured about everything. Pleased. Maybe it was just a habit of worry. Maybe I was too tired to sleep. Anyway, when I got up again, in fifteen or twenty minutes I felt half sober, and that wouldn't do at all. A stiff one, then, to knock our weary worrier off for eight—long, deep and dreamless.

I put my pants and shirt back on, found some slippers, and went quietly into the living room, where the bar was. I mixed the drink, and I took note of the furniture, Connie's antiques I guessed, some of which were lovely. She'd done the best she could with them, in that plaster walled, over-carpeted, $30,000 development house. You couldn't make a house like that look warm, but you could use it as a gallery for warm things.

I started thinking, then, about Dave talking about Kennedy.

I wondered if I hadn't minded it, for some reason—begrudged Dave's having known him.

While I thought that I started to whistle, and when I heard myself, I realized it was *Skylark*.

Tommy Angus.

Tall Tommy, hell, that was it. That was it: I knew Kennedy. We all knew Kennedy, didn't we? He went to college and the war with all of us. Tommy Angus.

Skylark.

There was a pretty little spinet piano, with a nice soft tone. I knew about the tone. Acrosonic. I'd already tried it.

I sat down and put my foot on the damper pedal, to make it even quieter. And I started to play *Skylark*, but the words in my head went:

Wasn't Kennedy the particular upperclassman in the fraternity, poised and cool but not unfriendly? It was the poise that made a freshman 'feel uncomfortably awed by him; and the grooming. What'd the guy own, a barbershop? His jackets were never too short this year, because he'd grown in the last six months. And his ties had no spots, and his sweaters—in college you didn't stop. Or stoop. To think the petty thought: that look is bought, with money, starting young and rich with orthodontists and saltwater summers, to build what goes under the cashmeres and the camelshairs. You were better in college for not thinking things like that.

Second chorus: Wasn't Kennedy the upperclassman about whom you asked yourself, does he know I'm here? And so, trying to imitate the quickness and accuracy with which he could keep the senior table laughing when he wanted to, you tried some of your own, jejeune stuff on him once. And he didn't even cut you down, in reply, just frowned for a second and then smiled and went on with his interrupted conversation, kind enough to ignore you. He could sting your tail, that boy, paddling at initiation time. Powerful. But seldom showed up to take part in those inane activities. Yeah, but when he did, whack, and would say something as he struck to make you want to laugh. Which didn't particularly relieve the sting, but did something for the mild humiliation of bending over to get hurt.

Skylark. Third chorus. He was what you hated in the fraternity and the college, coming east from St. Nowhere on the Mississippi, with your baseball glove and your old taped spikes, everything you hated when you hated it. And everything you liked, eastern, when you liked it. Everything you loved and hated in New England. Fair; always fair, when you could get his attention. Once or twice, when you happened to be sitting near, he might be briefly interested in you, and could look right past you the next day. Yeah, you were ignored again, but there was no intention to belittle. Really no attitude towards you at all. You never thought in terms of having him on your side, only of being permitted to be on his.

Maybe younger kids at Harvard had felt a little that way about Dave. I played a run, some chords, got into another key and back to the melody, up tempo.

Skylark. Tommy Angus's solo. The Dean comes to the house

in person, sign of a really serious infraction. Town girls. Drunkenness. A college night-watchman thrown bodily out of the house, into the snow. Letting off winter steam, but the watchman, called Big Jim, never again affectionately, reported it. Eight weeks, now, since Pearl Harbor.

"I know it didn't involve every member of this group," the Dean says to the house meeting. "I don't want to punish every member, but I shall be forced to, unless the house president will submit a list to me of those students actually involved. These men will be put on academic *and* social probation, for the remainder of the year. I want the list in my office no later than two this afternoon."

Academic pro meant no class cuts. Social pro, no party dates, no team trips. Untwinkling for once, the pink little Dean leaves the house. The meeting is silent for a moment, waiting for a tone to take.

And Tommy breaks the silence: "Mr. House President," he says to his closest friend, in a deep, droll voice, just loud enough to be firm. "I move that you put my name on that big, bad list."

I feel deprived, having been away from the house last night, that I can't be on the list with him.

I went back to the original key, and slower, quite softly now, and extended the chords where I knew how. Ninths and elevenths.

My solo. It's spring house party now, their last for Tommy Angus's Class. '42. My last, too, till after the war, for I will enlist right after commencement—but I don't know it yet, and tell myself that the only reason I'm taking flying at college is because I want to know how to fly.

Tommy's class are all enrolled in stuff—V-12, Air Force, Army or Marine Reserve. Scrupulous about their probation, they see the house party only briefly, not dressed up, coming by to talk a minute or get things they need for class. Tommy comes in, sometime during the second evening, to ask one of the chaperones to get a book he wants, from his room—inhabited now by other members' dates.

While the chaperone is away, looking, someone says: "Play the piano, Tommy."

"Play *Skylark*."

Tommy smiles. This is both a familiar and an odd request: Tommy has been heard to play the song occasionally, and does now—with feeling, and full bass, and an ornament or two in the treble. Odd, because he cannot play the piano, really. This is his only number; odd because he does it so well. I know about this, because it was I who taught him, finger by finger, just after Christmas vacation.

"I cannot play the piano, Barney James," he'd said. "But there is a smallish blonde girl, just five feet nine, weighing 144 pounds?"

"Yes," I'd said. "Smallish." Kind of a beauty. Big enough to look well dancing with Tommy. Most girls weren't.

"This tiny creature likes a song called *Skylark*. I would play it for her if I could."

I happened to have learned it. I showed off.

"Yes. Teach me to play *Sky*- first, Barney James. If it please you. And then, perhaps, *-lark?*"

Of course it pleased me, and, impossible though it was, I did it. *Sky*- and *lark* and *have* and *you* and *anything. . . .*

We worked on it five or six afternoons, an hour or so each time, and he wouldn't let me simplify it for him. By the second week Tommy had it, by rote. Could play it through without a stumble, though he had to watch the keyboard. Then came the evening when they pitched Big Jim, the watchman, into the February snow, and with that the time would never come for which he'd learned the song: the moment when the lovely blonde girl would be at the spring house party with him, and would mention that she liked the song. And Tommy, dressed for the formal dance perhaps, would smile, and set down his glass of Scotch, sit, pretend some brief confusion, and then smoothly play it through for her. . . .

It is not technical awkwardness, then, that makes him change the tempo this last spring house party, May, 1942. He is wearing a tan sweater, instead of a tail coat, and a cap. He is waiting for the chaperone to bring the book he requested so that he can leave us to the party he's forbidden to attend, and we all say:

"Play it, Tommy. Play *Skylark*."

160

Last chorus. Half tempo. Clarinets, trombones. A flugel-horn, why not?

We have our arms around girls, most of us, and he is playing for us. But of course he is playing for himself, too, and for the girl who isn't there. He changes the bright, melodious little song, with its occasional minor passages, into something I never taught him, slow and melancholy and graceful, with impeccable rhythm. It is going to haunt me, played like that, all through the war at odd moments. I will hear it when I'm flying alone sometimes, maybe when I land and cut the motor, or late at night after a mission when I'm last man at the bar at the Officer's Club and the record player has stopped.

It is slow, sweet and surprising . . . like the blue sequence in a movie musical when the lovers' happy song is reprised at some sad turn of the plot, quietly, in the background. Slow. They did it with the Kern and Berlin tunes, in the Astaire-Rogers pictures, I'm quite sure: *Isn't This a Lovely Day?*, *Who's Got the Last Laugh Now?* Fred, dancing, shuffling, a hurt look on his wry face. Ginger pensive. *Top Hat? Swingtime? Follow the Fleet?*

I know how we listened to Tommy, arms around the girls of 1942. I know the war was next for all of us. I heard the war was what came next, even for Tommy Angus's Skylark herself— I heard it long afterwards, that the smallish blonde girl, five feet nine, had gone overseas with the Red Cross. And become an alcoholic, somewhere along the doughnut line.

"Barney. Trouble sleeping?"

5

It was Connie Doremus, coming into the living room, waiting until she heard the song end to speak.

"I'm sorry," I said. "I really didn't think you could hear this piano."

"I couldn't. I didn't know you were playing until I walked into the room."

"Then it's you who's having trouble sleeping."

"I wasn't even trying," she said. "I was, kind of, waiting for Dave."

She was wearing a knee-length robe, over her nightgown,

and bare feet. She had scrubbed what make-up she wore off her face and tied back her hair for the night. She looked pleasant and anxious.

"Worried about him?"

"No. Just to say good night, nice evening. And let's go sailing with Barney. And all of that can wait for morning. You?"

"I was thinking back," I said. "Tonight's been full of ghosts. Not just your band."

She hesitated, and then said: "It's been ghosts all the way, Barney. Ever since the assassination, hasn't it? What were you playing?"

"That song? *Skylark.*"

"It was?"

"They played it at the club tonight, but up-tempo. This way." I played a few bars, restoring the time.

"Of course. But I like the way you play it. I, as a matter of fact, I stood outside the door, just now. Listening."

I smiled. "A man named Tommy Angus taught me to play it that way. I was thinking about Tommy. I haven't seen him since college. He's in the Foreign Service, I think, and doing well. Ambassador to a small country, I can't think which."

"You hear from him?"

"Oh, no. We weren't even close friends. I was two years behind him."

"Hero worshipper." She smiled so warmly that her saying that was evidence of pure attunement.

"Sure," I said. "Like you and your one-hit brother, Buddy."

"The right honorable Buddy," Connie said.

"Why? What's Buddy done?"

"Pitched his arm out in service baseball. A lovely case of bursitis. So he signed with the Harvard Laws instead of the Red Sox, after all. He and Dave were classmates there."

"Lawyer," I said. "Old counsellor Buddy."

"Judge," said Connie. "His old honor Buddy. He's one of the Federal circuit judges in the South, Barney. Married a Carolina girl and lives down there. People have thrown bombs at their house. Tough man."

"He was always good on the three-two count," I said. "With men on base. Imagine Buddy ending up an umpire."

"Imagine," Connie said. "All of you. The boys I knew, so marvelous and irresponsible." She sipped her drink. "Five years ago it used to make me feel wonderful and smug to see you taking over."

"Now?"

"Joe died. Kennedy. Dave, in a way, but maybe he'll be back. One of those bombs could have got Buddy. I guess it's when you get to be king of the mountain that the danger starts."

"Buddy's special to you, isn't he? I like to hear you talk about him."

"He always was," Connie said. "Of course, he's called William now. And I mean, as long as I don't see him *all* the time, and get too familiar . . . what am I trying to say?"

"We were talking about hero worship."

"Yes. Barney, this is going to be silly, but . . . whenever I hear Dave talk about having known Kennedy, I think of growing up with Buddy."

I looked at her and knew exactly what she meant. I shook my head, and finished my drink and said: "I have a rather slow mind. It's taken all evening to get to the same general place. It was Dave talking about Kennedy that eventually started me thinking about Tommy Angus."

"Let me fix you another drink," Connie said. "And me one, too. I mean, if you feel like sitting up and talking a little?"

"That's what I feel like."

I followed her to the kitchen and watched her put more ice in the bucket. When she spoke it was almost to herself.

"So we've all known Kennedy," she said.

"I'd have thought you were a little young."

"Right on the edge," she said. We went back to the living room, where the bottles were, and on the way she said: "I was ten years younger than John F. Kennedy. You going to throw me out of the game?"

"I knew a British flying officer," I said. "A man just nineteen years old, younger than me. Only he commanded quite a big bunch of kids fourteen and fifteen, who were flying Spitfires under him. When I say half of them were in love with him, I'm not exaggerating much." We sat down, Connie on the sofa, me in a big chair. "Those pilots were too young to think about girls when they got down from flying. The older kid absorbed an awful lot of emotion from his boy fliers. And they were out, flying interception two and three times a day. Getting killed. Defending England. The younger ones were your age. The older one was their Kennedy, of course, but he didn't survive the war. I imagine those of the others who did, think of him that way. I'm a sentimental man, Connie, I guess. Is that all right?"

"Oh, I think so," she said. "Yes."

We talked then, Connie and I, for three hours. Or four. I don't know just what time it was when it started. We were like two terribly sincere adolescents, suddenly glib from finding someone in the other with whom shyness could be overcome. It was a night of sheer communicating, of a kind I hadn't known since boyhood, when Alex and I sometimes used to talk that way, and sometimes Dave and I. It was a pleasure all the more incredible for being so totally unexpected—who expects to open up that way, with anyone, after his family is started, his hostages given?

There is not much that Connie and I said to one another that needs to be quoted. But she did at one point tell me a story I found necessary to hear. We had come back in our conversation—we kept doing it—to the assassination, and I said:

"Connie, I sit here and think of those two sick crumbs, with their guns, and it makes me want to tear down curtains and break furniture."

"Oswald and Ruby?"

"Yeah."

"Not my little walnut end table?"

"All right."

"The more you think about it, the harder it is to take," Connie said. "Oh, go ahead. Get the walnut table."

I smiled.

"I can't understand it, really. I can Ruby, I guess. He's a familiar kind of crackpot, with a cause and a sense of righteousness, isn't he?"

"Yes, but not on the grand scale," I said. "Not like John Wilkes Booth or John Brown. A sort of operator-crackpot. That's twentieth century, isn't it? Something new."

"I wonder if I ever knew a boy like Oswald?" Connie said.

"Women don't. The Oswalds don't date girls or show up at school dances. Don't mean to belittle you, Connie, but you'd have had to be a social worker to know a boy like Oswald."

"No, wait."

"Not just by being a girl."

"Wait. Don't say anything for just a moment." She frowned over her thought. "Girls were," she said. "We were. Innocently. Not knowing what we were doing, of course. And very bad at it, too. Social workers. Terrible, amateur social workers. . . ."

"Girls?"

"Isn't that what the war pressed us to be, sometimes? Not that we knew it—it pressed you into being soldiers, but you were better at it finally. And it made us clumsy social workers, every time we'd say yes, all right, I'll go to the U.S.O. dance Thursday. Oh, how I used to promise myself I'd never go again."

"Weren't you a little young?"

"Sixteen. There was a boy. I'm starting to remember him so very well. A bitter boy. His name was Greek, I think."

"You were sixteen?"

"Older than your Spitfire pilots, anyway. I probably looked older, because I was big. I don't think I was very pretty, but sometimes boys seemed to take me for a nice, soft boy to wrestle with. Nothing more romantic. Anyway, this Greek. He only came to the U.S.O. once, at least when I was there. Mostly soldiers would come in with friends, and then they could kid one another into asking us to dance. But the ones who came in alone were the problem. The lady who ran it all, was she called the director? Mrs. Malone. She'd give us talks about that: 'Girls, the ones who come in alone are the bashful boys. The ones you have to ask. Now go ahead, tonight. It won't hurt any of you to ask a boy to dance once, and you'll probably never see him again.'

"I only got my own courage up enough one time to do that, and then it had to be this boy. He was sitting by himself at the club, with a book, scowling at it. I mean right at a little table near the juke box, so we could see him, but scowling at the book.

"I was dancing with a sergeant, jitterbugging as a matter of fact. The sergeant was fairly good, but an exhibitionist. He wasn't really dancing with me, he was dancing around me, and I kept looking away at the soldier who'd come in alone, with his book."

"Where was this?" I asked.

"New Hampshire. Durham, New Hampshire. Sometime in '44. So I was almost seventeen. Barney, that boy never turned a page, all the time I watched him. He wasn't reading, he was sitting there, and I decided he must be fiercely shy. Pretending to read, and dying for some nice girl to ask him to dance. So, oh Barney, I was so scared I nearly shook my dress off. Big clumsy me. I went up to this boy, shaking, and asked him if he wouldn't come dance the next one.

"And he looked up from his book and said, 'Don't do me any favors.'

"I stood there, shaking, with my mouth open. He closed the book and said, 'You really want to dance with me?'

"I nodded my big dumb head.

"'Okay, Kid,' he said. 'I got five left feet, one after another for you. Let's dance.'

"I was bad, but he was even worse. He kicked my left ankle just about black and blue and never knew it. And right after we started, he started talking. A streak. A mean streak. I'd never heard anybody talk like that before. I mean use those words, for one thing. Little New Hampshire girls don't hear words like, well, even words like *crap*, except by accident, or they didn't then, and he used all the other ones, too.

"The thing that started him, was me looking around for something, anything, to say, and asking if he knew the sergeant I'd been dancing with. And the boy said:

"'Lindsay? I'm going to cut the liver out of him one of these dark nights, and sew it in his mouth. You can tell him that for me.'

"I didn't even try to answer. Would Mrs. Malone have been proud of me, the way I'd drawn him into conversation? One awkward, girlish question, and the chute was open. The filth and abuse poured out—yet I wasn't offended. Isn't that odd. I was a little scared, but I wasn't offended."

"I'm offended," I said. "For you, twenty years late."

"But what he said was so bitter and so unreal. It couldn't mean anything. It was just coming out of him like, oh, like sweat. Something he couldn't help, so I told myself it wasn't his fault, you see?

"Then after that dance, I thanked him and he wanted to dance the next. I couldn't refuse, and no one came to cut in, and well, I wanted to. A little bit. I'd never met anyone like that. But then the next dance, he was much more personal. He wanted to know where I lived, and how old I was, and did I go steady with some 4-F character? Did I like to neck? Mostly I didn't even answer, but—I don't know. It wasn't like a boy talking to a girl, or a man to a woman. It was something terrible and self-conscious, and it scared me quite a lot more. When the dance was over, I said I had to go to the rest room, and he said:

" 'What's the matter with me? You don't like me, do you?' I said, of course I did, and he said: 'Tell me why you don't like me. Are you scared?'

"That was fairly bright and less self-conscious, I guess. To guess that he'd scared me. So of course, I had to say I wasn't, and start to dance with him again. But the music was fast. Sergeant Lindsay wanted to jitterbug and cut in.

"My Greek went back and sat down, and scowled at us, and as soon as the record was over I ran off to the ladies' room. I hid there a little while, quite upset, and when I came out there was the Greek, blocking the way. And he said: 'I'm sorry. I'm spoiling your good time.'

"Good time! I hadn't wanted to go to the U.S.O. that night anyway. I never really liked going. Probably I gaped at him, and he said:

" 'I hate myself for what I'm doing. Should I go away and kill myself? Would that make you happy? That's what I ought to do, isn't it, Connie?'

"And I—he sounded so serious—I said, 'Oh, no.'

"I guess he saw he'd got to me a little with that, because he started going on about it. He said he knew where there were some live hand grenades, not just dummies for training. The supply room had some live ones, and he could get the key because the supply sergeant was a drunk, and would be sleeping it off. So this boy said he'd steal the keys, and get a grenade. And then, he said, he'd go out on the company street, and pull out the pin and fall on the grenade, and how many pieces did I guess it would blow him into? And how his blood and organs would be all over the buildings on both sides, and of course it would be a nuisance for some detail to have to clean up, but nobody else could be hurt that way, and nobody'd care.

"I remember he said, 'I suppose the guy'd be sore who had to climb up and get my ears off the roof, huh?' But he said the others would all be glad about it, and he guessed I'd be glad, too, when I heard.

"I nearly broke out into tears. Not because I believed him very much, but because I'd started feeling he was persecuting me. But he misunderstood; I guess a tear was rolling down my cheek. I was feeling sorry for my gawky self, but he thought he'd convinced me and I was weeping for him. He smiled a mean smile; and then he stepped close to me as if we were going to start dancing. I sort of automatically, stupidly, raised my arms, and he put his hands on me. It probably looked as if we were really about to begin dancing, but he didn't raise his arms. He grabbed my bottom and pulled me against him, and I started squirming away.

"And then he did the craziest thing of all. He said, 'Come on, Connie, what's wrong?' and I kept backing away, and he burst out laughing. He laughed at me, and he said, 'What are you scared of? I'm impotent.'

"I ran, Barney. That was the last I ever saw of him, but I was upset over it for a year. I had to grow up quite a lot before I realized that he wasn't really impotent . . . that it was said to outrage me. . . ."

"You got outraged," I said, and about then we remembered we were grownups, reminiscing—not kids talking seriously, after all—and we both laughed.

"Connie," I said. "I'm sorry. Doubting you on Oswald. I think you're closer to him, after all, than I could come. Did you know a Ruby, too?"

"No," Connie said. "He seemed easier at first, but he isn't."

"I thought of my crew chief," I said. "But that doesn't get it. Jonesy would never have tried to sacrifice himself."

"Barney?"

"Yeah?"

"It's four o'clock, and Dave still hasn't come home."

"I'll go look," I said.

"Yes, please." She walked to the door with me. "I told you before, Barney. I don't get my feelings hurt or anything. I'm just concerned. Dave doesn't drink very well these days."

"Okay," I said. Dave never did drink very well when he was under pressure, but there wasn't any particular point in saying so.

6

I hoped it was just a matter of walking across the street, to the Bistreks' house, but I hoped wrong. The lights were off there. The door was open and I went in; I could see by the street light, coming through the window, that the living room had been picked up. Somewhere, Jerry was snoring strong, and I wondered if his wife would have any luck if she turned him over. But she was probably plowed, too, and didn't need to.

I found their phone book, switched on a vestibule light, and looked up Sunny Brown. She wasn't listed in Wonamasset. I wished I could have thought of anything else to try, but couldn't, so I dialed information. They had her in Wonamasset Beach, the resort part of the area five or six miles off. The operator asked if my party lived at 319 Commercial Street, which didn't sound hard to find, and remarked that it was a new listing.

I thought about phoning, and decided to drive out; went along, found my turn. It seemed to me I recognized the road, and that we'd travelled it earlier, going back and forth to the Club.

Commercial was the only street with a name in Wonamasset Beach. It ran parallel to the shore; shore on the left, Commercial with its long row of bungalows on the right. I drove slowly, trying to see house numbers, but I saw a lighted front porch first. There was a man stretched out on it, and even as I stopped the car I had an awful, prescient feeling that it would be Dave, and that there'd be blood on his head. I think I had that feeling first; it was confirmed so quickly that I can't be sure.

He lay there, left cheek up, face towards the house, and the blood was there but not running. Clotted. There was a sound coming from inside the house, a funny, grating noise with peeps and squawks, like the calls shore birds make in flight.

I lifted Dave's head, and he groaned and exhaled, but he wasn't conscious. There were bloody furrows on the top of his head, and his nose was very swollen. And the cheek turned downwards was pulp. I tried his arms and legs gently; at first I thought there was nothing broken, but moving the right arm made him groan again, and I decided he probably had a broken collar bone—rebroken. It was the side where his shoulder had been damaged once before, by war wounds. He'd been hit with something, it looked like, a number of times and hard.

There was a porch swing with a cushion on it. I laid Dave out straight on his back and put the cushion under his head. The noise from the house sounded like gulls crying now. The screen door was hooked from the inside. I wrenched it open, and went in.

Sunny was dancing in a little living room that was almost bare of furniture. She was leaning forward oddly, as if her stomach were cramped, but her legs moved freely and her head went up and down in rhythm. She still had on the loose green gown, but it was torn from hem to knee along one leg. She was barefoot. The noise now was of terns, and suddenly I realized that she was dancing to a birdcall record, highly amplified.

There were two boys in there, both with beards, both in shorts and sandals and stripped to the waist. One was asleep on the floor. The other might as well have been; he was sitting in a dilapidated wicker chair against the wall, with a half-gallon wine jug in his stupid lap. I took it away from him, rougher than I needed to be, and said:

"Come on. Where's the phone here?"

170

Beard shook his head and reached for the jug. "No. I don' know that."

"Where's the phone?" I shook his shoulder.

"I don' know that."

I pushed the jug back at him. I picked up the record arm, cutting off a Franklin's gull. Beard laughed loudly, and said:

"Hey. That's better." When I looked at him, he quieted down though, and went back into his shrewd defense: "I don' know that."

Sunny wheeled past me, hunchbacked. I don't know if she realized that the record was off. I caught her arm.

"Sunny."

"Don't touch," Beard said. "Don't touch Sunny."

"Shut up," I said.

"Buster'll get you. Okay."

"What?"

"Buster's got a stick."

"Who's Buster?" I asked. Then I remembered.

"Sister. I mean brother."

"Yeah," I said. "The one that was a cop." I could see that big pale face, closing around the O. Henry bar. I had a sick feeling of what Dave must have been beaten with. I shook the girl: "Sunny. The telephone, damn it."

She only stared at me.

"Dave." I said. "Dave's on the porch, hurt."

"On the porch?" That made Beard leap up. "Right here?" And he ran out the door. If I'd supposed it was to see what had happened, I'd have supposed wrong. Beard was getting out of there.

"Sailor?" Sunny finally spoke. "Man with sailor?"

"Yes," I said. "Dave the Sailor. Hurt, Sunny."

She began to cry. "Buster took Sailor home."

"Buster took Sailor out and beat him up," I said. "And left him on your porch."

"Hurt?"

"Where is the telephone, Sunny?"

She shook her head. Then she put it on my shoulder. Her

hair was full of the smell of marijuana smoke, and her breath reeked wine.

How could I have thought this mess appealing? I led her to a daybed, and pushed her onto it. I looked for the telephone, not sure who to call. What doctor, what ambulance? Not Connie, I thought, if I can help it. Stiggsy, of course. Stiggsy was part cop. Stiggsy had a panel truck, if we needed it. Stiggsy'd know what doctor could decide if it was possible to by-pass the hospital, and patch Dave up without this getting public.

I found the phone on the floor, under one end of the daybed on which Sunny was slumping. I lifted the receiver, meaning to get information for Stiggsy's number. There was no dial tone.

"Sunny's phone split," the girl said, woefully helpful. "Nothing . . . works without nickels. Where's Sailor?"

"Sit still," I said, and went back out to Dave with a swab of wet paper towels to sponge him off. He was still out, or out again. I began to wonder if there might be a bad concussion. When I lifted his head and started to sponge the temples, the one eye that wasn't swollen shut opened and recognized me. He spoke. He even tried to smile.

"Barney. See the little pendula? Swim." Then he amended it and said, "Swing."

"Hold on Dave," I said. The head bleeding didn't try to start again. I let the head down and opened his shirt. There were welts on his body. I went in and pulled a blanket out from under Sunny. I didn't dare move him now. There might be a rib busted. I covered him up. I decided I'd have to drive off and get Stiggsy. I was thinking about the engineering. If we backed the panel truck into the yard and right up to the edge of the porch, with the rear doors open, and could slide Dave onto something—a table top? A piece of plywood? No, the mattress from the daybed inside.

Then we could slide the thing into the truck with Dave on it, and get to a doctor without a public ambulance call. I knew there were doctors who were friends of Dave's. Hell, he'd got a clinic built for some guys to start group practice. Stiggsy'd know. I turned out the porch light.

I'd leave it to the doctor friend, whether we could avoid a

hospital. I figured there were several things riding on getting Dave away from here quietly—maybe we could even bring a doctor back to help us—things like what was left of a reputation, and starting in again of a career. And maybe a marriage.

Then, as I straightened up, and glanced in the door to see that Sunny was still where I'd left her, there was the sound of a car on the street. Lights. I moved, to put my body between whoever might be passing and Dave, but the lights turned in, a red one was flashing, and the car stopped by the curb.

I walked towards it, knowing it was a police car.

A cop got out. "What are you doing, mister?" He asked.

"Taking care of a friend." I kept moving towards him, and across the porch, to try to lead his eyes away.

"This one of your friends, too?" My young buddy Beard was sitting in the back, arms pressed against his sides, looking pitifully young.

"Picked him up running down the street," the cop said, coming to the bottom of the short flight of porch steps. "He was yelling the sea gulls were after him . . . hey, what's that?"

He'd caught sight of Dave. He came up. He turned on a flashlight. He stared, and said in a slightly awed voice:

"My God. It's Dave Doremus."

"Do your wretched duty, officer," I muttered, but he was too excited to take notice. When I said I thought Dave might appreciate it if we could get Stiggsy Miller here, before we did anything more, I got a pretty good idea of how things had been going for Dave around his community. He might be rehabilitated, or on the way, with the Shore Club people, but downtown things were on some slim point of balance. Not gone to hell, but wobbling. Because the cop didn't say that would be all right, to get Stiggsy; and he didn't run me in. He told me to watch that stuff, mister.

While he was telling me that, Beard scrambled out of the police car and ran, and wouldn't stop when the cop yelled after him.

7

It made the Boston papers.

Helen even heard it on the midday TV news, down in Connecticut. When I phoned Sunday afternoon, after Connie and I were back from the hospital, Helen said:

"Barney, what's really happened? I've been trying to call."

"So have five hundred reporters. What'd it sound like?"

"Like scandal. Prominent young political figure. Racketeers, sex, beatniks, marijuana. Hints like that. They said severely beaten, and summer cottage of a girl with a dope record. What's it about?"

"Racketeers, beatniks, sex and marijuana, I guess . . . I don't know, Helen. I'm too tired to think."

"Haven't you been to bed at all?"

"I went to sleep in the lobby of the hospital, for an hour. While they set some bones."

"Will he be all right?"

"Can't see him. Doctor's vague."

"Were you with him, Barney?"

"No. I found him afterwards."

"I was worried."

"I should have called."

"What about his wife, Barney? Connie?"

"I just now got her to take a sedative," I said. "She's asleep. I'm going to leave the phone off the hook after I talk to you."

"Maybe you should take a sedative too, Barney."

"I got one in my hand, Miss Sweets," I said. "Sour mash sedative. It tastes like hell by now, but I'm going to drink it and fall on a sofa."

Helen wondered about putting the kids with her mother and coming up, but I thought not. I said I'd call again when I knew more.

I didn't sleep long actually. I didn't know what I could do, but whatever it was I wanted to get started doing it, so I woke at eight P.M., four hours later. I decided to go see Stiggsy, and drove down to the store. There was a thin kid there, minding the counter; he phoned the office Stiggsy'd mentioned, and then said I could go up, pointing to the theater building.

I walked across Wonamasset Square. The rain had stopped, and the temperature had dropped some. The Sunday night show had started; it was a revival of *Warlock*, a big western. I could hear muffled shouts and hoofbeats. On the left side of the lobby was a door leading to the upstairs part of the building. It opened, but the lights were out beyond.

I felt my way up the steps, went past the first-story landing and on up to the second. At the end of the short corridor, there were lights showing through a pane of frosted glass. The door opened, and Stiggsy peered out.

"Barney?"

"Yeah."

"Come on down."

The office had a desk in it, a phone and a cot. There were Audubon prints on the wall, in ornate, expensive frames.

"An auction I went to," Stiggsy said, seeing me look. "I'm not supposed to sleep here, but I do a lot. How is he? I keep calling the hospital."

"What do they say?"

Stiggsy shrugged, and I said I didn't know anything new. "What's happening, Stiggsy?"

He shook his big head. "Nothing so far. They got the girl, but they'll turn her loose. They say she didn't witness nothing."

"How about the beard kids?"

"They got one of them. Material. He says he was passed out."

"Yeah. He was. They didn't find the one that ran?"

"No. All them beard kids look alike. The one they got says he don't know the other one."

"How about Buster?"

"I got a call in to find out," Stiggsy said. "I got the guys here to say they'll hold the girl, till Dave wakes up. That'll give us a way to reach Buster, if Dave wants to make charges. But he won't."

"Why not, Stiggsy?"

He shrugged, and the phone rang.

Stiggsy answered by giving his number. "Yeah, wait," he said, and looked for a pencil. "Yeah?"

He wrote things down for a minute. Then he hung up and looked at me. "Your parlay came in," he said. "You got a hundred and twenty-six bucks coming."

"Give me credit for it. I'll put it on something, sometime."

He nodded, and the phone rang again. He answered with his number.

"No," he said. "I don't want to see him." And then, "Tell him tomorrow, will you?"

He hung up. The phone rang.

"Yeah?" And listened attentively. Finally, "That's what I figured. Thanks, Doug."

He hung up and looked at me. "Buster's in Boston."

"Did he do it?"

"I guess we knew that, Barney."

"By himself?"

"No, not Buster."

"How do you think they did it, Stiggsy? Without Sunny and the kids knowing?"

"I figure they took him down the beach, and worked him over. And dragged him back on the porch."

"Why drag him back?"

"They're not dumb, Barney. On Sunny's porch, to do the most harm."

"What's in it, Stiggsy? Besides Buster telling Dave to stay away from his sister?"

"Nothing. Buster's people don't care if Dave gets hurt, but they got no reason to want him hurt, either."

"But they wouldn't stop Buster?"

The phone rang, and Stiggsy wrote some more things down. When he finished he said:

"I told them to keep Buster away from here. I was surprised to see him last night, tell you the truth Barney. Oh, he'll be in a little trouble at home. Taking a chance for something personal. Not bad trouble."

"Why won't Dave press charges?"

"He wouldn't do anything to hurt that Sunny," Stiggsy said. "He goes off his head about her. He's not the only one, either. Listen, Buster might have made an all-right cop. That's what I hear. But even when she was just a teen-ager, and she wanted to be a singer. Buster figured that's gotta be better than a hophead and a whore. And she's gotta have clothes. Fancy stuff, to sing in. That's when they say he started taking."

"And taking didn't work out so well," I said.

Stiggsy spoke to me as to a child: "The older cops, Barney. They don't like a rookie to be in a hurry. Like in the sales business, he's supposed to work up his own contacts."

The phone rang. I got up while he was talking. I heard him thank the man called Doug again.

"That Doug. Found him a house here last summer. Took his kids clamming."

I asked him where I could find him if anything came up. "You going to sleep here?"

He hesitated. Then he said.

"I'm going to take the mutt and go sleep on the beach tonight. In the truck. C'mere Roland."

"Birds?" I was a little surprised.

"Maybe. Maybe about dawn," he said.

I left and went to Jerry Bistrek's house.

Jerry was home. I don't know where his wife was.

I hadn't noticed the room we were in, when I'd gone through at four A.M. It was just like Dave and Connie's living room across the street, except that the Bistreks had new furniture instead of old. It made me think of Connie, though I didn't know it was so, moving out of some tall, cool wooden house, with a big shaggy lawn around it probably, old lilac bushes and a swing from an elm limb—except that she and Joe Ferguson hadn't had children—into one of these brick and glass places. But the last thing I needed was to be led into any more sympathy and admiration for Connie.

Jerry wasn't sure he needed a drink. He poured one for me, lit a cigar, and said it was terrible.

"Is there anything we can do, Jerry?"

"You tell me. Dave's in a personal reputation business. I think the harm's done. Done all over again, Barney. It was bad enough before."

"How are his finances?"

"Terrible," Jerry said, and then his phone rang. I was batting zero on uninterrupted conversations.

"Hello," I heard him say. "Yes, Jerry Bistrek . . ." He looked at me from the vestibule, and said "It's a person to person from La Jolla, California. I don't know any persons." Then, into the phone: "Hello . . . yes, this is him. . . . Yes. . . . Yes, Dave's had some trouble. . . . No, I'm not his partner, Miss." He listened a moment, and then he said: "No, I don't know about a lawyer. Maybe Dave represents himself. I don't know . . . Look, you want to talk to somebody knows you? Mr. James? . . . Yes, he's here. . . . He's here with me. . . ."

He laid the phone down. "She wants to talk to you, Barney."

"Who does?"

"Mrs. Doremus, from California."

"Huh?"

"Jane Doremus. The first wife, isn't she?"

"Oh boy," I said. "You don't know her?"

He shook his head, and covered the mouthpiece with his hand. "That was before Dave and I got associated."

"What's she calling about?"

"What you were just asking. Finances. Some nice kind friend called her—Dave got hurt. She's worried about a check that's due. She heard I was his partner. Says the check can't be delayed. Nice. You want to talk to her, or do I hang it up?"

"I don't want to talk to her," I said, getting up. "But I guess I will."

I took the phone, and said: "Hello, Jane. This is Barney James."

"Just what I need to help me," said the unmistakable voice. It managed to be gushy and sarcastic at the same time. "When can I talk to Dave?"

"He's not even conscious yet. He's badly injured."

"Yes, I heard. Fighting for his country again. I may send a medal."

"I'll give him a message if you like."

"I can't get through to the hospital," Jane said. "Or the house either. How come I get a busy signal at the house?"

"Connie's asleep. I took the phone off the hook."

"I want her to call me," Jane said.

"All right."

"She's a friend of mine, believe it or not."

"All right."

"Now she knows what all us ex-wives know. Messing around with that singing thing!"

"Now she knows."

"Are you going to stand there at four dollars a minute, just repeating what I say?"

"What is it you want me to do, Jane?"

"I want you to tell Mr. Helpful that I'll accept no excuse for delaying my check. Tell him I've got tuition bills for the children."

"I imagine he knows that."

"Another Mr. Helpful. Were you along on the big party, too? Did he let you have a turn with Sunny? I know how you boys like to share. Oh, it must have been nice."

"What party was that, Jane?" I said.

"Oh hell. I want to talk to Connie. Listen, give me Bistrek back, will you?"

"What for?"

"Maybe I can trust him to tell Connie to call me. Collect, if she wants."

"I'll tell her that."

"Maybe she can write the tuition check. Before she starts on whatever *she's* going to get out of him."

"Same old pleasant Jane," I said. "I don't really know anything about it, but if I were you I'd see if I couldn't scrape up that tuition out there somewhere."

"Just what do you mean by that?"

"I have a feeling your patch is out of turnips, Jane."

"He can go to work, can't he?" Jane said, furiously. "Tell him to get a job and take care of his responsibilities, or he's going to be talking to the judge again."

"That's a charming message, Jane," I said. "That's the nicest get-well card a man could have."

She replied with one, clearly enunciated, Radcliffe-accented, obscenity, cold and sweet. So I hung up. Then I put Jerry's phone off the hook, too—looking at him for permission to do it.

"You never knew her," I said. "Congratulations."

"I've heard about her," Jerry said. "That was one messy divorce. Dave was going along with everything the way I hear, without the detectives and the flash pictures and that junk. She just did it for fun, and charged it to him, anyway."

"What about Dave's bankbook?"

Jerry shook his head. "Jane took the house, two cars, the sailboat. Sold them all. Took the investments with her. He saved some of the cash, I guess."

"How much do you think?"

"Several thousand," Jerry said. "Dave told me once he took what he had out of personal checking, and just carried it around in a manila envelope in his coat pocket for two weeks."

"It went into SPAGETI?"

"You know about that?"

"Not very much," I said. "Dave thought you might tell me."

"It was a beautiful thing," Jerry said. "Beautiful."

I was somewhat astonished. "You serious?"

"That's how I met Dave, really. Oh, I'd known him around. But one day he comes into my office at the main bakery. I say, 'I'm flattered to see you, Mr. Doremus. But I know what you want. You're raising money.'

"'Not from you,' he says. 'You're Bill Holtz's brother-in-law.' My brother-in-law was in SPAGETI; he was supposed to take the dive, but they hadn't bothered to tell him that. To Dave, a business is a man, and an idea, and if those two things are right the business oughta go. He liked Bill; he told me he was going to try to save SPAGETI, and he was going to go to the money boys who were mad because they thought they'd got left out. 'I'm going to let them all in, now,' Dave said. 'All they want. I'm telling them exactly what I plan to do. If they want to take it that I really mean the opposite, that's up to them.' He smiled that big smile of his, Barney, and he said: 'The fact is, they might even wind up with a piece of something pretty decent, if I can make this work. A nice, normal, slow return instead of robbery.'

"All he wanted me to do was keep Bill Holtz cool—poor Bill didn't know who to believe. You can't blame him. Anyway, it was so beautiful, what he was trying to do. Like a double negative. For Bill and the company. Finally I said, 'Dave I can sell a lot more bread in Southport if that plant keeps running. Now that I know the whole thing, will you let me in anyway? Just for a long-shot bet?'

"And Dave said: 'I'm betting my own money that way, sir. Sure. If you want to jump in. The water's cold as hell.'

"We shook hands on it; the only way I ever do business is on handshakes, Barney. Not that I was going in very big."

"You get it back?"

"Some stuff was left to sell," Jerry said. "I got some back. Dave didn't get any of his. He put himself last. Maybe my brother-in-law and I were the only ones who knew that. Anyway, after that, and after he married Connie, I'd do anything for Dave. That house. They got it at cost. And that came back wine instead of water too—Dave turned around and did me a hell of a job on this building operation. You ever see Dave work?"

"Long ago."

"Fourteen, sixteen hours a day are nothing to him. And still going, strong and easy at the end as when he started. Ideas, surprises, supervision, everything."

"But he's out of dough now?"

"Been making current expenses, probably. He's got a ton of paper at the bank, though."

"Are you going to back him, Jerry?"

"I've been thinking and thinking about it," Jerry said. His cigar had gone out. He lit it again. "No."

He gave me a steady look. I returned it, I think.

"No, Dave can't make it here after this, Barney. You don't know about before. Jane isn't altogether wrong, I'm afraid. He acted like a madman. It was, 'Do anything to me, but don't touch the girl.' I didn't know him then, but that's where his cash went. And the first of what he borrowed. And I used to hear. Really crazy stuff about him. Then, somehow, he got away from her, after the divorce. And into the SPAGETI thing, and married Connie. You know the rest."

"Last night he turned into Mr. Hyde again, huh?"

"That's what they'll say. I don't know. I don't understand

about it. I was going to pick up his notes at the bank, nearly twenty grand. Let him pay me the interest as he could, and call the rest investment in his firm. I'll still do the first part. As a matter of fact, I'll buy the house back from him, and give him a profit on it. For a stake."

"If?"

"I'm not going to try to run Dave's life, but he oughta leave here now. Him and Connie. Maybe all the way out of New England. Maybe practice law somewhere, or find a place that needs a real good executive. He's still a restless, ambitious man if he gets himself together. He's got the right wife. He could still make a fortune, or be a governor someplace. If things went right for him."

"Say you're right," I said. "But what if he stays?"

"I'll do everything I can."

"All right," I said. "Either way, put me down for half."

He gave me the steady look again, and asked the ungentlemanly question; I loved him for it. "You got money, Barney?"

"I got credit."

"Let me take care of the money. There's other things you can do for Dave that no one else can."

I remembered what he'd said, and shook his hand on that.

I went back across the street to check on Connie. She was deeply asleep. I called Helen again.

"No news yet. Nothing new," I said.

"I'm afraid there is here."

"The kids?"

"No. They're all right. It's . . . Rosey's in jail. For drunk driving."

"Rosey is?" Rosey Rudenquist was our sales manager.

"Yes. He ran right into a State Policeman's car."

"Hurt?"

"No. But apparently Rosey stepped out from behind the wheel laughing, and tried to give the trooper some money. You know how he would."

"Yeah," I said. "He sure would."

"Anyway, Tully's been trying to reach you. Frantically. Can you call him?"

"Sure," I said. "But what about it?"

"Rosey was in the company car."

"Oh," I said. "Oh yeah. I see." Because if Rosey was driving the company car on Saturday night, when he should have been using his own, we were in it a lot of ways. Our insurance, for one thing, was issued on a no-personal-use basis. Did we stand behind our man or throw him to the wolves? "Tell Tully we help Rosey till he's out of the jam. Get him a lawyer. Back him up. But when it's over, Rosey goes."

"I don't think that's what Tully wants to do, Barney. He says you need Rosey on the job. Can you come down?"

I hesitated over that. I'd shaken Jerry Bistrek's hand.

"Barney? Can you come down?"

"No," I said. "I can't Helen. Tell Tully—tell Tully it's his. He's in charge till I get back. Tell him to do whatever his best judgment says he ought to do."

"Should I tell him what you said first? About letting Rosey go?"

"No. Please don't. Don't tie his hands. Tell him he's got it, Helen. I'm not there. I won't second guess him. He's got it."

And I went to bed. I don't know how I managed to wake up. I certainly hadn't thought of doing it, but I did. About four-fifteen.

For a minute I lay there thinking that maybe it was because just twenty-four hours earlier, I'd found Dave on the porch. Then it went: porch-house, house-beach, beach-Stiggsy, and I pushed myself out and into my clothes again.

Stiggsy, on the beach, at dawn, *watching birds*? We come slow, from Missouri, but we don't come totally dumb, every time.

I trotted to the kitchen, and found some left-over coffee to warm. While I was drinking it, Connie came in in her dressing gown. I asked her how she felt, and she smiled and bummed half my coffee and said okay, but she wondered how Dave felt.

"I'll bet he hurts," I said. "A lot of places."

Connie's mouth pulled down; she nodded. Then she said: "I'm glad you're here."

"Me too." I said. "Me too, Connie."

"I put the phone back on the hook. But thanks for leaving it off."

I said there was a chance she'd have to endure a call from Jane; she smiled and said she didn't mind.

"What do you mind, Connie?"

"Nothing. Just that Dave's hurt." I liked the way her face showed thought, sometimes, before she spoke. She said: "After all, I didn't manage to get . . . the past all cleared away. For my new marriage either, did I?"

I told her I was going out for a while. Connie said:

"Wherever you're going, be careful."

8

The sun wasn't up yet when I found Stiggsy's truck on the beach.

I'd followed the road most of the way to Sunny's cottage. When I saw a sand road going left showing tire tracks, I went that way, too. The truck was parked in some brush, just short of where the dunes started. I pulled my car in behind it. I didn't know how concerned to be with looking casual, but I took a pair of binoculars with me and walked down to where the tide had left the sand packed down, impersonating a birdwatcher.

Only I was one. I didn't want to enjoy it, as I walked the wet edge—sea sound, and the sea smell, the piping and twittering of life waking up, and the little crabs running in the pre-dawn air. But I put the glasses on a purple sandpiper. That was an unexpected bird—a European bird, that makes our beaches sometimes in the winter. Nuts, I hadn't come out to get new birds for my life list. It was too beautiful out there.

Then, like a damn hunter, I saw tracks. Man and dog tracks, so it must be that Stiggsy and Roland III had gone this way since high tide.

"Clearly a basset hound, gentlemen," I muttered. "The basset spoor is unmistakable to the trained eye." In the silly, euphoric mood that the salt-water morning was easing me into, the tracks made me miss my own dog, at home. He's a springer, named Baby-Face Nelson, who helps me photograph woodcock in flight because he can find them in the woods better than I can. I whistled, just loud enough for the sound to reach my own ears: *Do Nothin' Till You Hear from Me.* My older boy, Brad, does the dog naming: Baby-Face was by Machine Gun Kelly, out of Ma Barker. Kelly'd been a good dog, too.

I saw a match lit, over in the bushes.

I went to it. There was enough light, as I came up, for me to see that it was Stiggsy, with his glasses up, his back to the sea. He was kneeling, and partly concealed from the side where the road was.

"How'd you know it was me lit the match, Barney?" He was chiding.

"Roland," I said. "How'd you know it was me, to light the match for?"

"Binoculars. I didn't know if you'd come."

"I didn't know if you wanted me."

"I thought about it after, that you'd probably figure out. Barney, he's there."

"Who?"

"Buster. And two guys."

"In Sunny's house?" I looked through my own binoculars. We could see past a curve, where the highway turned to follow the shore, the row of cottages, three deep. The street lights had gone off, and none of the houses showed lights. But at the one I thought was Sunny's, a sedan was parked. I stared through my glasses at it, but all I could have said was, it looked like a Buick.

"Shouldn't there be a cop there?" I asked. "That's not a cop car."

"He left when they came," Stiggsy said. "Twenty minutes ago. He'll be back when they leave."

"That's nice. What are they doing?"

Just then I saw a man come out on the porch with his arms full of dresses, and another following, carrying the phonograph. Neither one was Buster.

"Cleaning out," Stiggsy said.

"Apparently."

"It ain't the clothes and stuff he got sent for. What I hear, there's a state man coming this morning. They want to make sure the place is clean."

"I always liked neat housekeepers," I said.

"They're looking for her dope."

"Oh."

"You want to?"

"What?"

"Go talk to Buster."

I looked at him. "I'm not the man I once was, Stiggsy. And I left my Tommy gun in the car. But sure. If you want to."

"Leave your binoculars," Stiggsy said. "There won't be no trouble. Not unless we start it."

Roland got up. Stiggsy told him to stay, and he got down again.

"Buster's move was last night," Stiggsy said. "It's not his turn, you know, Barney? And he's got them on his back in Boston, without trying any more with us."

"Okay." But I wasn't all that reassured.

"See, they told him: 'You made a mess. You clean it up.'"

"Okay."

"And there's a lawyer coming with habeas corpus for the girl today. That's another thing. That comes out of Buster's pay."

"I hadn't thought about dope," I said.

"I got no question about that part. If they didn't come to get it out of there, I was gonna look myself. But I knew they'd come. Marijuana, probably, and pills."

We'd covered half the distance to the bungalow. I thought: I would like to turn around now, and resume my pleasant walk along the shore. I said, softly: "I saw a purple sandpiper just now Stiggsy."

He smiled. "Did you? For sure? I saw him too, earlier, but I wasn't sure."

We walked more quickly. Then I heard Stiggsy's breath starting to shorten, and we slowed a little.

When we reached the sedan, there was already a man behind the wheel. The other had apparently gone back inside.

"Hey!" he said as we went by and turned into the yard. "Where do you think you're going?"

Stiggsy didn't bother to answer, so I didn't either. The man was out of the car by the time we'd climbed the steps to the porch, but we kept right on. He didn't seem to want to shout.

We went straight in. It was darker inside; the hook I'd pulled out hadn't been repaired. A flashlight caught me in the eyes.

"Who's that?" a voice said.

"It's me, Buster," said Stiggsy, and turned on the lights. "Who the hell do you think?"

"My name's James," I said. "If anybody cares. Barney James."

The man with the flashlight turned it off. He'd been using it to throw woman's underwear and stuff into a small suitcase.

Buster was sitting in the broken-down wicker chair against the wall, in about the same position the beard kid had been in the night before. He didn't get up.

"What do you want, Stiggsy?" he asked, and his voice astonished me. It wasn't hostile, or frightened, or inquisitive. It was mournful.

"I came to bring you a candy bar, what do you think?" Stiggsy said. "God, you're stupid."

"What do you mean?"

"You take all her clothes out of here, the state man won't know there's somebody been here?"

"What do you know about the state man?"

"He's got something, Buster," said the man who was packing.

"Yeah? Then leave some stuff. Some of the old stuff. Maybe you better get a coupla dresses back from the car, huh?" Then he looked at me. "Who's he?"

"I'm a friend of Dave Doremus," I said.

Buster hitched himself up. He really was pretty big, but paler than ever.

"I didn't mean to hurt him like that," he said.

"Is that right?"

The other man was watching us warily. "Go on about your business, creep," Stiggsy told him. "We ain't gonna tear the slob's arms off. Not right now."

The other man looked to Buster. "Go on," Buster said. "Fix the stuff up, like I told you. Listen mister. I was just trying to take him home, see? He was drunk."

"Where'd they bury the last guy you took home, Buster?" Stiggsy said. "You'll be lucky if you get off with ten years."

I could see by now that Stiggsy was right. There wasn't any fight in a man who bowed his head like Buster did. For the first time, I let myself look carefully at the other man, and decided I might have been able to handle him. I didn't know about the one outside, and I was sure I was no match for Buster. But Stiggsy would have been a match for anyone. He spoke:

"Why'd you follow Mr. Doremus's car around?"

"Look," Buster said. "After I was in your store, I went away. I wasn't looking for him. Then later, I came in here, and he's bugging Sunny."

"So you were just gonna ride him home," Stiggsy said. "And all of a sudden, a bunch of bears and Chinamen jumped out of the bushes at you."

"He tried to fight me," Buster said. "I couldn't help that. He swung on me."

"Did he?" I said.

"That's right, mister. No kidding, I'm buddies with Dave. I wouldn't want to hurt Dave. Look, I had his arm over my shoulder, you know, like this?" He put his own big hand behind the back of his powerful neck. "He caught me. A hell of a shot. He can punch, and I guess I lost my head. . . ."

"What are you lying for?" I said.

"It's no lie."

"Dave Doremus's right arm hasn't raised high enough to go around your shoulder for twenty years," I said. "Not since the war. So you had his left arm, friend. If you had either one. And he couldn't hit a fly with his right, hard enough to break its wing. That arm doesn't work."

Buster looked down at his feet. It was hard to believe in the kind of shame he was showing.

"Tough Buster, the cripple beater," Stiggsy said.

"Go ahead, goddamn," Buster yelled, suddenly at the other man. "Finish up, will you? Finish up."

Then he got up. He seemed a little more self-possessed. "All right, Stiggsy," he said. "What do you want with me? I got trouble in Boston, I got trouble with Sunny. Dave's not gonna press charges, huh?" He asked the last of me. "Listen, willya tell him I'm sorry?"

"Tell Dave you're sorry?"

"Oh, hell." He said. "I always liked Dave. I always did."

"What do you do to people you don't like, Buster?" I asked. We looked at one another. He looked away, and Stiggsy said: "You got the place clean, stupid?"

"Take a look."

"We will. And it better be. We watched the cop take off. It was Arnold Turner, wasn't it? My buddy Arnold. So if Mr. James decides to tell the state man who he saw leave, and who he saw come, it's gonna be pretty isn't it? Along with the charges that might get made?"

"What do you want from me, Stiggsy? Say it." And yet it still wasn't a man cornered; it was an agonized man speaking, a mourning man. I felt that very strongly. And we all knew there'd be no charges, to keep the newspaper story alive.

"This is my town, Buster," Stiggsy said, not too loudly. "Stay out of it. Whoever you know, I know too. And I ain't in any trouble with them, and ain't gonna be. They'll tell you, and I'm telling you. This is my town, Stiggsy Miller."

After a moment Buster said: "I didn't know about his arm. Honest. I was in Korea. I didn't know about his arm."

"You probably had your creeps holding him for you," Stiggsy said. "So how could you know? Go on, Buster." The other two were done now, and were outside. "Go on. They're waiting for you."

Buster shifted his feet. "I said . . . won't you guys believe it? I was . . . I didn't mean to. I was out of my head, huh?"

"You're a slob, Buster," Stiggsy said. "I wouldn't care how bad I got hurt, hurting you. Get out of my town, slob."

And after Buster left: "We ain't got it all yet, Barney."

"He's still lying, isn't he?" I said.

9

Early in the afternoon, Connie and I got to see Dave, but we couldn't see much of him. He was wrapped in bandages like one of those traction patients that cartoonists draw. He was going to be two or three weeks in the hospital, and I guessed it would drain whatever Connie had left in the way of money.

"You get those things off in time for the cruise, Captain." I said. Dave said he would, and I left them alone for a while.

Then, when Connie came out, I asked if I could talk to Dave a little by myself, and she said of course.

"Look, Connie. Way back. Just after the war. Dave and I spent a summer on a Friendship sloop we bought."

"So I've heard," Connie said. "At some length."

"I was supposed to pay for half the boat, but I couldn't. And Dave's never let me pay him back for my share."

She looked at me. I don't know if she believed it or not.

"So don't tell Dave," I said. "Let him think it was something you had in the sugar bowl, if he wonders." And I gave her a check.

She nodded seriously. Then she looked at the check and laughed.

"All right, buddy," I said. "What's so funny?"

"You're such a terrible liar," she said. "Half a Friendship sloop in 1947 couldn't have cost anywhere near five hundred dollars."

"Haven't you ever heard of interest?" I asked indignantly. "Anyway, it was a very fancy sloop. Come on, Connie. I don't want you and Dave to miss the cruise."

I hoped it wouldn't come too soon for him, or be too much. It could be just the right convalescence.

"All right," Connie said. "All right, dear friend and sweet man. If we need it for passage, I'll use it. And I expect we will."

Then we said goodbye; I was going to leave from there for home, unless something turned up for me to do. Connie was going out to get things Dave would need, and come back.

I went into Dave's room.

"Feel like talking?"

"Softly," he said. "This jaw doesn't waggle well enough for loud."

"You got any idea of charges?"

"No. I can imagine what's being said. Let's let it die."

"That's what Buster expects."

"Okay."

"Anything I can do?"

"Is Connie . . . all right?"

"She's fine."

"Isn't she, Barney?"

He asked about Sunny, and I told him about the Boston people, and the lawyer coming to spring her. It seemed to satisfy him.

"I loved her, Barney," he said. "I really did, in some . . . imponderable? Some imponderable way."

"I guess you did."

"I wasn't going to try to make love to her last night."

"Night before last," I said. I didn't say he owed me no explanation. It was so, but the way Dave and I had known one another, it didn't need to be said. Nor had I any reason to doubt what he was telling me; I'm sure it was almost the whole truth.

"I just wanted to see if she was all right," Dave said. "I get such a feeling of responsibility for Sunny. Fact is, even in the little time we were married. We never slept together much. A few times, before and after, but she's . . . very unresponsive that way. It just, doesn't seem to matter to her. And she was sick a lot, and still would or not, and . . . I stopped wanting to. I really did. Seeing her in the club, I just, I don't know. Wanted to take care of her again, I guess. Like, like being fixed on having to take care of a particular child. I couldn't have made love to her last night. Night before last. It's as if we've gotten way past that, into something else."

"You want to save it, Dave?" I asked. "And tell me some other time—on the cruise, or sometime?"

"No. Marriage can be ridiculous. Pointless. You know?"

"Yeah," I said. "I've had my times of thinking so."

"It's the dope partly," he said. "That's another thing that's way past sex, I guess."

"So I hear."

"When I first started seeing Sunny. When Jane and I were married. I knew Sunny took pills and blew pot sometimes, for kicks. I didn't know she was high every day. And I guess I loved her a little more normally, then. Hooked myself on her kind of looseness."

"Jane was pretty tight," I said.

"Then, I found out. That Sunny used that stuff constantly. I should have been disgusted, but I wasn't. I was anguished. I wanted to help her more than anything else I could think of."

"So you married her?"

"In due time, Old Missouri Boy. In due time."

"That's probably enough talking Dave," I said, but he wanted to go on:

"She used to tell me about her brother. She was frightened of him, and maybe if I married her . . . well, Sunny was nineteen then. She said she'd been paroled to Buster, from a marijuana sentence."

"Marijuana?"

"She hardly ever tells the truth. When Sunny and I went to see the family, I learned it wasn't prison she was paroled from, though she'd been there, too. It was the State Mental Hospital. Sunny'd been in and out of it since childhood. Think that was enough for me?"

"I think it should have been."

"I wasn't a rational man just then, Barney."

"So I've been hearing."

"Her family had no use for her. Except Buster who was very possessive. He was still hoping to be reinstated to the police force then. He and I had long, serious, crazy talks . . . I think of him sitting at the kitchen table, in his uniform, worrying with me over Sunny. The annulment was his idea. He said he thought it would be wrong for Sunny to have children, and I had to agree. I wouldn't have wanted to. The parents were just indifferent, unless that was to cover their despair. God, I kept wanting to do something, to bring that girl to life. It wasn't as if she was my woman any more. I hardly thought about her that way, but my feeling was . . . so deep. As if she were my child, drowning. Helpless. Only me between her and . . . I don't know what. Prostitution. Insanity. Death. All right, I was in bad shape, Barney, but when you are, when you really are, you don't know it about yourself. And Buster's idea of taking care of her was to give in to . . . anything she wanted . . . I ran away with her from him, and tried to bring her here. We had a cottage, and the landlord came . . . with court officers to throw us out. That scared her. So, so I took her back to Boston. Suddenly that's what she wanted. She wanted Buster again."

So it had all been settled Buster's way, Dave said. Buster'd been especially indignant about the flash pictures, taken of Dave and Sunny during the divorce proceedings. And the name in the papers. He felt that continued public association with Dave would hurt his sister's career. Buster and Sunny both believed in her singing career, Dave said, to the point of its being another kind of nuttiness.

"Could there be anything to it, Barney?"

"She's got some talent," I said. "It doesn't sound as if she's built to last, though, Dave. Talent's pretty cheap without that."

It's strange, talking to a man with his face bandaged. You can't watch his expression, so I had no way of knowing how he took the things I said.

"Buster has to believe in Sunny's career," he said, finally. "Either that or admit that she's been a lost girl since she was —five or six years old. So I agreed: annulment. Eight months in a private hospital for Sunny, with special care. That's where my money went. And a new car for the parents so they'd go along with us."

"With you?"

"I wanted to keep her and care for her," Dave said. "I felt like some kind of traitor, watching her go off. But she . . . she seemed pretty certain, in her lucid times. Barney, she can tear me up like paper."

I had no answer for him there.

"I tell myself the things she does just aren't her fault. Because she's crazy. So I figured to forget her, and jumped into the SPAGETI thing. And married Connie. And look, ma . . ." His hand moved up to the top swath of bandages. "No head."

"I'm going back to Connecticut, Dave," I said. "But I want to finish telling you about what's happened." I told him about Jerry, and about Stiggsy and Buster. Then I said: "Dave, what did he hit you with?"

"A nightstick, souvenir of the force," Dave said. "He keeps it in his car."

"Did he have guys holding you?"

"I was pretty drunk."

"All right," I said. "Never mind. Connie'll call if you want me back, huh?"

I got up.

"Wait a minute, Barney. She was there."

"Sunny? When they beat you up?"

"I think she was. When I arrived, she was very loving," Dave said. "There were some boys there, and another girl, and Sunny told them I was her husband. Then she stopped being loving and got shrill, and told them I was her husband from the merchant marine. She said, 'Now we want to so bad, after him being out at sea, you might all have to watch.' She was laughing, and very excited, and it drove most of the others away. And that made her sad. I can't resist her when she's sad. I was trying to comfort her; she was weeping, and saying I didn't love her enough. So. I tried to tell her I was married again. That was the only reason, I said, why I couldn't stay with her, and she got . . . very hurt and bitchy. And then angry. Buster came in the middle of that. She was hitting me with a shoe, as a matter of fact. Funny scene."

"Yeah," I said.

"It stopped being. Buster grabbed me, and understood whatever he wanted to understand. He and another man. I guess one of them knocked me out, and I don't remember much after that. But we were on the beach, Barney, and I was being pounded. With the stick. And yelling. And it seems to me Buster was saying, 'Quit it. Quit now. You want to go back to the hospital?' And pulling her away. She might have been . . . whacking me . . . or lying on me, kissing me? . . . I don't know now. I really don't."

"I wish you did, Dave. I'd guess, both?"

"It's all such a nightmare," he said. "I don't know dream from real."

I wondered if there was anything left, dream or real, I didn't know.

It was late afternoon when I started back home, and the sun would have been in my eyes a lot, going straight west. I went southwest, more or less, along the shore through Massachusetts and Rhode Island, taking back roads when I could that would keep me in sight of the water.

The only other thing I can bring to mind about the drive back was that some of the roads I used were bumpy. I went slowly, and in one stretch where I was by myself, I began to hear alarming, high-pitched, metallic sounds. For a minute or two, I thought my car had developed quite a bad new squeak, but then I realized that Stiggsy was right, there were meadowlarks back already, making the noise, singing from the fence wires strung beside the road.

iii

The cigarette age.

It happens that I quit smoking, during the five weeks between the time of my visit to Dave and our next meeting in St. Thomas.

I thought it would be hard to do, but that I'd be quite pleased with myself if I could manage. Instead, it was easy, and what I felt, strongly and strangely, was regret. Cigarettes, it turned out, hadn't been a habit or a twitch or a stimulant for me; they were a romance.

I missed, not a taste or a sensation, but the physical link to a lot of memories. One of the first, in time, was of me and Dave, sitting on a dock on the Mississippi in the spring of our sixteenth year, gravely smoking cigarettes. We had hitchhiked to Hannibal, because Dave felt he had to see Mark Twain's town before he left Missouri for the East. There was a tearoom there, I think—or perhaps I remember it from later visits. In either case, the house it occupies is said to have been the model for Judge Thatcher's house, where Tom's girl, Becky, lived. A less pretentious one, but also built of wood and painted white, is supposed to have been the Sawyers', right across the street. Huck Finn's shanty, wherever it may have been along the river, is not among the monuments.

Oddly enough, the house he gave the Thatchers in his book is the one Mark Twain really grew up in, and it was his father who was the judge. (Dave said: "That's a nice name for a judge, Clemens. But I wonder why Mark Twain didn't want to make Tom's family quite as respectable as his own?" We spoke confidently of just two writers, then, Mark Twain and Ernest Hemingway. There were others whom we read, but those were the two who made it possible for boys like us to be unashamedly literary. Maybe Dashiell Hammett made three.)

Aside from those remarks about the two houses, what I remember most clearly are the cigarettes. They came in a brown pack, and were called Wings. We had bought them, along with a loaf of bread, a little jar of peanut butter and two apples. We'd made our lunch there, on the dock, and I recall that Dave opened the pack, afterwards, showing me how to get the first cigarette out without tearing its paper. Wings were a new thing, to meet the depression, a ten-cent cigarette when the established brands all cost fifteen.

"I love your big river, Mr. James," Dave said. "I'm going to put it in my pocket, and take it back east, and let it flow through Washington."

"Your friend Mr. Ickes will like that," I said. Dave's father was being loaned, again, this time to the Department of the Interior. "Couldn't you and he arrange to enjoy it here?"

"I wish we could," Dave said. His father had already left St. Louis. Dave and his mother would be following as soon as school was out. Ten more days.

"Next weekend," I said. "There's one more river—the Current River. We can take the Twee, and I'll arrange to borrow a boat. We'll float down, and get someone to drive the Twee down, and sleep overnight on the way, on a bank. . . ."

"Yes, sir." Dave said. "Would you arrange that?" And then: "I don't know, Barney. Mother's apt to declare she needs me."

"If she does, then I'll come help you pack."

In this mood, each of us lit his Wing, and we sat there quietly, watching the broad water through smoke, for solace.

It was some part of the continuity of times like that I was giving up—not a tired, yellow taste in the mouth, and a throat sensation less interesting than sneezing.

So the physical part of quitting didn't need more than a motive, and I had three: Brad, Goober, Mary Bliss. With the righteousness of children, the younger two listened to Brad, when he was home for Christmas, expound the cancers, the heart damage and the emphysema, and watched me smoke reproachfully. They were quite right, of course, nor have I ever been indifferent to the example that I set my kids. I hope they will think enough of me to want to imitate me in some ways, and I try to restrict myself to the vices I can practice after the young have gone to bed.

I didn't try to quit cold turkey, but the way I found was what made it easy: I went to a pipe for about six weeks.

"Do you like your pipe, Dad?" Mary Bliss asked me, after five of them.

"It gives me drouth in the mouth, and an ache in the trache," I said. "Not to mention goat throat, brain pain, and my stomach doesn't always feel just wonderful, either."

"You better stop before it reaches your legs, Dad," Goober said.

"Daddy's knees will turn to cheese," cried Mary Bliss.

They were right. Pipe-smoking friends said I ought not to inhale, but it seemed to me just as easy to learn not smoking as to learn a new way of doing it. I gave the pipes away, to men at the plant, and tapered off on chewing gum which I learned to dislike pretty easily, too.

So I didn't smoke, but I dreamed.

In the dreams there were cigarettes, slim and white and impossibly fragrant. And somebody said they were all right. Or I just knew it was all right, after all; or perhaps there wasn't any question of all rightness. Just a normal, not unreasonable wish, and gratification, as I lit the thing. My smoking dreams were like sex dreams, just as simple. Just as convincing. Just as disturbing and sometimes disappointing to wake up from.

If it is a fair-sized crime against oneself to smoke, then it is a lesser one, but still a crime, to extinguish memories: what about the ten-minute break, in basic training, when a cigarette seemed the real purpose of it?

Sharing one with a girl. "Consider yourself kissed," she might say, handing it back to you again.

Driving, and having her light two, and pass you one.

Landing after a flight; feeling of feet on the ground and smoke in your throat, both at once. Lighting one in the lobby, after a movie.

Robert Taylor. There was a year when Robert Taylor, Tyrone Power and Don Ameche (I think) were the new young stars, all introduced at once. . . . Taylor, though. I wonder what the movie was? He's lying in a small room, still dressed, on a bed. Has been, I think, rejected somehow. Turns out the lamp and lights a cigarette. We see him in profile, silhouetted against a window, exhaling the smoke, reflective. The cigarette seems more than benign; it seems a tool of philosophy.

No, I couldn't hate cigarettes. I loved the damn things. There were too many times when they were the company I wanted, alone, say, in the woods with a camera. Waiting. A cigarette was something to do, something pleasant that gave the waiting minutes value.

"I'll have a smoke."

That was a way of taking time out, sometimes, whatever the game was. John Garfield. There was an actor who could smoke a cigarette, and look the way you felt when you were smoking one. The cigarette was misused by actors who let it hang, made it part of their toughness. The picture with cigarettes was tenderness, reflection, pause. Consolation.

A cigarette in a long holder, tilted upwards, was the optimism of Franklin Roosevelt.

A cigarette watched, as if its smoke might resolve into a pattern, was the humanity of Ed Murrow.

There was someone, but this is shadowy—was it Heywood Broun, or Alexander Woollcott, or Robert Benchley? — someone whose cigarette seemed to me a working partner to his wit. . . .

If I loved the sin that I gave up, I could think of sinners to hate: to have made smoking a romance was innocently harmful. To try to perpetuate it, after the bad news is in, seems to me the sickest of all Madison Avenue's perversions. This is selling someone not merely what he shouldn't want and doesn't need but what will poison him, and bring pain at his death . . . sure, Barney. Giving up whiskey next, are you?

All right. But in another century, if the world lives to see one, people will say of us over their cocktails: "Do you realize that a hundred years ago, people did this stupid thing called smoking? It actually dirtied their lungs and weakened their hearts. And they knew it! Thought they were enlightened, apparently, and had this billion-dollar slow-death industry, that came from someplace called Medicine Avenue, wouldn't you know it? Turned their teeth brown and made them stink, and whole regions of the country grew the junk, that could have been productive, and even presidents smoked, first ladies. . . ."

Like other primitive matters, our smoking will be misunderstood, I suppose. Where was the pleasure and the elegance in taking snuff, when all the dandies did it? We can't understand; they won't understand. That in our brief, fuming age, a cigarette was what you asked for, if the firing squad was sympathetic, instead of a blindfold. What you lit for a wounded friend and put in his mouth, and he puffed on it and grinned. What you offered a dark lady, and her eyes glowed at you in the matchlight. . . .

For quite a time, after I quit, when I drank to a certain point, the wild thing that I did was not to pinch a fanny but a cigarette, feeling wicked and defiant when I lit the silly thing.

2

Dave and Connie got to the Virgin Islands two days earlier than we did. They met us at the airport about noon, in a big old taxi. The boy named Art LaBranche was with them; he seemed pleasant and polite, though his manners were a little more elaborate, careful maybe, than those I think of when someone says "Ivy League." He seemed quite close to Dave and Connie already.

Art made himself agreeable and useful with suitcases and baggage checks, and I took only brief notice of him. The changes in Dave's appearance were so striking, it was hard to look at anyone else, even Connie.

The most surprising change in Dave was his hair. It had all been shaved off, I guess, so that his scalp wounds could be treated, and instead of red it had grown in silky and white. It was like his father's hair had been now.

They'd gotten his nose back almost straight, but it had been a small straight nose; now it was thicker and a little crooked. There was a small, new scar on the left side of his forehead, but it was well-healed already, and the most poignant thing to me was that he had a rubber ball again, after twenty years, to squeeze on with his right hand.

Other than that, the doctors and Connie had done a good job of feeding and grooming him; he looked rather distinguished, no older than his age, and the Caribbean sun had started to give him a nice, healthy color.

Mrs. Helen James, my well-known wife, thought he looked okay, too. *Flash*, went her largest smile, like a big sign turning on. *Flash, Here I Am.* And when he reached for her hand in greeting, *Flash, Mr. Dave. You Take My Breath Away.*

Then off, letter-by-letter, until there was nothing left but afterglow and a warm hand.

Art LaBranche got the junior whammy, appropriate to his youth and curly-haired good looks. It had been a long winter for Helen in Scott's Fort.

It had been a long five weeks for me at the plant, too, but I can't say I was altogether glad to get away. There were after-effects of the sales manager's drunk-driving difficulty, and about the time those were cleared up, we had, believe it or not, mumps. A couple of guys who were neighbors brought them to work; three more came down, and after that it was a general scare. We didn't have that many actual cases, but one week there were as many as fifteen men staying home, fretting about symptoms— mumps is that kind of disease. So we had production to make up, right along, and Tully chose that as the time to put a new floor plan he'd been working on up to me. It was pretty good, too. He was impatient to start rearranging; I thought we ought to get caught up, first. Uncle Troy'd been feeling the spring of the year and had revived the fiberglass-canoe idea pretty energetically; glass people and tool people had been up several times, and the board was likely to go for it. Tully especially, was pushing hard, and my uneasiness about him was growing, if not very logically.

My feeling about Tully was that he didn't, essentially, care about the plant, or the men, or the product—and not really about money, either. He was grasping in a way I'd never seen. What Tully cared about was bigness; what would suit him would be to have the initials GH stand as exclusively for Gibson Hardwood, in the business world, as GE and GM stand exclusively for those little enterprises.

Nothing radical was going to happen in three weeks, while I was gone—it was just that it didn't feel like vacation time to me, with all that going on. But there was Helen, and there was Dave—and there was Connie, who was looking wonderful, now that I looked. Big, and wonderful, and not tough enough.

We got in the cab to go to the hotel for lunch, and I couldn't be sorry I'd come.

What was on Helen's mind, now that we were there, was the boat of course.

"When will we meet Captain Clark?" she asked Dave, first thing, and Dave said that we would go down after lunch.

We'd been in St. Thomas four hours, though, before we left the hotel for the dock. Art LaBranche had declined Connie's invitation to lunch with us; he had a lunch date, he said, at one of the houses on the hill above town. After it he was supposed to get some of the provisions for the trip.

"They want to leave tomorrow afternoon," Dave said, while we ate. "Though if you'd like to stay right here a day or two, I think the Skipper'd be agreeable."

"Oh, no," Helen said. "Let's tell him we're ready, Barney. All right?"

"Fine with me."

"Is the Captain staying here, at the hotel?"

"He and Art sleep on the boat," Connie said.

"He sleeps on the boat, and Art keeps his clothes there, anyway," Dave said, wryly. Connie smiled at that, and said the Captain had left word that he'd be glad to see Helen and me at the dock any time after two.

So we got Dave's cab driver—characteristically, he had a particular man attached to him already—and drove on down about three. But when we got there, *The Bosun Bird* was gone.

The dock was a long series of duckboards, floated on oil drums, stretching out in a series of walkways with the main one starting just below the solid, piled wharf on which we stood.

"*The Bosun Bird* was over there, wasn't it Con?" Dave said, pointing along a particular boardwalk.

"Other side of the green yawl," Connie said, and there was an empty space out there.

"Do you suppose he's gone to get fuel?"

But there was only a cabin cruiser in the marina area where the fuel pumps were.

"But aren't they all lovely?" Helen said. "Let's walk out."

There were all sorts of pleasure boats strung along, a couple of hundred anyway, but Helen didn't mean the deep-sea fishing boats and launches, or the cruisers and motor sailers—not even the two big, million-dollar motor yachts, too big to dock, moored out in the harbor, pitching mildly in the blue swell.

Helen was looking where Dave had pointed, past where class boats and day sailers were tied up—Stars and Snipes and miscellaneous small sailboats—to a brief row of sailing yachts: the beautiful little green yawl they'd pointed to—a honeymooner, from its size, which is what Helen, and for all I know other sailing people, call a boat that sleeps just two. There were two cutters, a white one and one that shone softly with spar varnish over the warm, natural color of its lapstrake wooden hull. There was a big white sloop, and another yawl—each between thirty and forty feet long, as far as I could judge, but there was nothing like a two-masted schooner, fifty-two feet at the waterline.

"He may have left a message with someone," Dave said. He sounded quite perplexed.

"Oh, it doesn't matter," said Helen, to whom, of course, it did. "Let's do go walk around and see the boats, though."

"He's such a reliable man," Dave said, leading the way down a companionway. "A real, New England rock."

Single file, we reached the duckboards, floating eight or ten inches above the water.

"Wait," Helen said, and put a hand on my shoulder, so that she could pull her shoes off. The heels would have gone through the spaces between the boards. Very sensible wife. Very pretty legs. Dave politely turned his eyes away.

The dock swayed under us as we started out along it. The sun shone, and felt as good as only sun can feel, after a long damp winter. The water and the boats were so alluring, down here at their own level, that I could hardly believe that I'd be privileged to get aboard one, and sail out, an overnight insider in this special world. Feeling that, I began to share the disappointment Dave and Connie showed on our behalf, that the schooner wasn't there to see.

Way up over us, floating in air currents, was one of the race for which *The Bosun Bird* was christened—that's a vernacular name for a long-tailed soarer, the tropic bird, one of the loveliest things that flies.

Connie saw it, too.

"Is that our boat up there?" she asked. "I think the old enchanter turned it back into a bird, and set it free."

"It must be something like that," Dave said, smiling, pleased with his wife. It was the first time I'd ever had a sense of Dave's having any kind of husband's pride in her, and it made some little area of visceral tissue that had been tight in me for a long time relax. I could feel it let go.

We followed them out along the row of sailboats, and came to the green yawl. Beside it was the empty slip. There were narrower, board walkways on each side of it. For no good reason we went on out, along the one we would have used to board *The Bosun Bird,* and stood there in a foolish line, looking into the empty rectangle of water, with the green boat just behind us. A foot under the surface, where we looked, suspended in turquoise, was a piece of paper, an indecipherable label. I stared at it, and a fuzzy voice spoke, just behind us:

"Mister Dave, sir. Did you lose a boat?"

I jumped. I think the others were just as startled. We all turned in the direction from which the sound came, and there was no one there.

"What size of a boat, Mister Dave? 'Bout fifty-two feet?" The voice located itself, now that we were looking in the right direction. It came from the cockpit of the spotless green yawl, in which, now, Art LaBranche sat up.

He had his shirt off and I noticed, as I hadn't before, what a muscular kid he was. The rippling chest, for some reason, made the silly, youthful mustache that he wore rather endearing. His hair was curly brown and his eyes bright blue. He was about twenty, I guessed, and wore khaki pants, torn off above the knees, and a pair of sandals.

"Art! What are you doing in there?" Dave said.

"Drifting and dreaming, Mrs. Dave." He sounded amused with himself, us, everything. He sounded drunk, too, or high anyway. "What are you doing out there?" He stood up, and said, ceremoniously: "Come aboard. Come aboard."

"You know the owner of that boat?" Dave asked. Young Art grinned confidentially, and shook his shaggy head; the curls went down his neck and around his ears. I saw that there was a box of groceries with him, and a bag too, which had split. There were tomatoes and lettuce, spilled sugar and assorted cans all around him in the otherwise spotless cockpit. "They'll keel-haul you, boy. Come on, hop out and let's pick up."

"No, no. I'm the owner," Art declared, grinning. "Right of marine salvage. Here it is—abandoned. Deserted. Masts broken . . . holes in the sails—must have washed in here in the big storm." Connie looked concerned for the boy. Dave smiled to reassure her, and Art said, lugubriously: "All hands lost, I imagine."

"Where's *The Bosun Bird*, Art?" Connie asked. "And Captain Clark?"

Art stepped up onto a strip of the deck beside the cockpit, balancing, a little closer to us, and said: "My shipmates. Mr. and Mrs. Shipmate James." He said it fondly and politely, with a smile that was almost shy. Then he shouted, suddenly: "Sailing under CAPTAIN KELSO CLARK. R.N. Not Royal Navy. Registered . . ." He tottered towards us, caught himself, and straightened up. "Registered Nurse. And handsome . . . curly-headed, Art LaBranche. Your ablest-bodied sailor. For an ocean trip." He bowed. His eyes softened and looked at me, and he shook his head. "Mr. Able-bodied Barney."

"Sounds like a great crew," I said.

"That must have been quite a lunch date that you had," Helen said, smiling at him.

Art looked at her, and nodded. "Hello, Mrs. Barney," he said.

"Where's the boat, Art?" Connie asked again.

"Skinhead the Goat has taken the boat."

"Captain Clark?"

"Yes, the rascal. Claims it's his, by right of marine salvage."

"What's wrong, Art?" Dave stepped across and onto the deck of the yawl with him. "You're not drunk . . . ?"

"Out of my skull," Art yelled. "Believe I've got the lepsy. That's a seizure, take your pick. You know, there's cata-, and there's nympho-, and there's epi-lepsy. Hey! Take an overdose of soft drinks, what've you got? Pepsilepsy."

I had a curious feeling of having heard that voice, or the rhythm, or the intonation—something—before.

Dave got down now into the yawl's cockpit, and started tossing loose canned goods over to me. "You on pills, Art?" he asked, matter of factly.

And of course I knew then what the recollection was: Sunny Brown, as I'd first seen her at the club, snapping her fingers and chanting. Different later, at the cottage. . . .

"A pepsileptic fit! Great seizure's ghost," Art cried. Dave threw me a large can of pineapple.

"You on pills, babe?"

"Won't be on them long. My pills got marine-salvaged."

"I don't get you."

"Skinhead the Goat, put out to sea, with all my . . . deximillity. Dave, Connie, shipmates, you should have seen me. Pounding along the dock here. A box of groceries. Two bags. And one, one went into the briny deep, briny, when I turned the corner. It was one of the great runs, Dave, you should have seen me. Flapping and mumping and whooping along, and there went Kelso, casting off, his noble head gleaming in the sun, heading into the bay with all my . . . dear, little pills."

Suddenly Dave started to laugh. "Art, Art boy," he said, choking a little, then throwing back his head to laugh again. "Is that why he's gone? To put some water between you and your deximil supply?"

Art laughed too. "He saw me uptown," he said. "He doesn't like me to turn on, but he'd never say so. So he, he ran down, and got his boat, and took off. Didn't he? Oh Captain, my Captain. . . ." He stopped abruptly and a look of pure hurt came over the friendly young face. " 'The fearful trip . . .' " he said, and stared at me again. "You were coming," he said. "You were coming here. Las' November, and Lee Harvey got . . . Johnny Fitz." He gave me a wild, almost frightened look. Then his face lost expression. "Yes, you were," he muttered. "I gotta pint here . . . two more dexies . . . ." And would have pitched off the yawl if Dave hadn't reached up and steadied him. The pained look went, and he crowed: "I was running. Yelling. Pounding. Shouting. And Skinhead the Goat was steaming. He was putting. Motoring. Zooming . . . ." And Art gave a leap, zoomed across the two feet of water between boat and dock, and landed with his arms flapping. I grabbed to help him keep his feet and lost one of two tall cans of tomato juice Dave had just tossed me. It rolled off the dock, and floated for a moment at about the same level as the paper label I had seen, and could now identify as having come off a tenth of Dewar's scotch.

Even as I looked, Art dropped flat, in a surprising display of coordination, catching himself on one hand, and scooping up the can of juice with the other before it could go down further. He turned over on his back, and lay there, looking up at us, holding the tomato juice.

"Come back to the hotel with us, Art," Connie said.

He sat up. "No. Better wait. Guard supplies, and wait for Skinhead," he said. "How about that, Mrs. James? How about it?"

"I take it Captain Clark is bald?" Helen said in a voice that was dry but not disinterested.

"Not all that bald," Connie said.

"A cool, cool head." Art nodded, hauling another tenth of scotch out of his hip pocket. "Would you save me from myself, shipmates? Drink it. Drink it. Anybody? You know what?" Now he'd turned sad again. "I didn't mean to get this way. But I was having lunch with . . . with sticky people. And you were coming, again. . . . That was Dave's friend. Johnny Fitz. One time, one time inna Boston Garden, Mrs. Barney. . . ."

"Yes." Helen was being pleasant and kind. "Yes, Art?"

"It was schoolboy hockey. Played for champs inna Boston Garden, and I was MVP. Most Valuable . . . anything. Anything you want. Imagine that? And he was senator, I guess. And pinned a medal on most valuable me. . . ."

Helen knelt beside the boy and put a hand on his shoulder. "Then you saw him," she said.

"Did you ever?"

"I don't know."

"You did?"

"When I was a little girl," Helen said. "I went to a dance as the guest of a little boy who was just starting in at Choate. And somewhere in the mountaintops there was a boy named Kennedy, a senior, who was pointed out to me. So I might have seen him. But I never knew whether the senior that I saw was John or Joe. Or maybe even another boy named Kennedy who happened to go to that school . . ."

"You could . . . ask the little boy?"

"Oh, yes." She stood up, and she tugged and Art raised up, too. "Come with us," she said. "Yes. Come on. Yes, I could ask the little boy."

I was pretty certain which little boy she meant, Roger Penny. Her first love. But it would be a few more years before she could ask Roger; he was in Federal prison, where he was due to sit a while longer for his share in some kind of stock-rigging scheme.

3

"The liquor prices are low, but so's French perfume," Connie was telling us. "Ladies can't lose."

We four were at dinner in the hotel. Art had sobered up and gone back out again, long before.

"I may spend thousands," Helen said complacently.

"I wish I were a real perfume buff. They've got so many that I'm sure I should have heard of."

"The only way to try them is to buy a half dozen of each," Helen said. She was planning what she'd do with her few hours of free-port shopping time in the morning. She had it about set, when a man came into the dining room, looked around and headed for our table.

It wasn't hard to guess that he was Kelso Clark; and Connie was right. He wasn't all that bald.

He was a medium tall man, and spare, with a powerful set of shoulders on him, sloping like a boxer's. He had the weathery, blue-eyed look that you'd expect, and you hoped your gut would be as hard and your back as strong when you hit sixty-four. He was an intelligent-looking man, whatever it is I mean by that—I guess I mean that there were certain details, like wrinkles around his eyes, the high dome of the head where the hair was thin and the skull-skin freckled, a long upper lip where a vain man would have grown a mustache—that I associate with intelligence in my personal stereotype. It checked out, in Kelso's case. He was a very bright man, not opinionated but something of a thinker in the old, individualistic New England way. Like Thoreau, I learned, he played a flute sometimes to help himself think, and since he wasn't a writing man, there were times when he relished a certain kind of almost boyish, abstract conversation.

By now I've stated quite a few things about him I didn't know till later.

He came to the table. Dave and I rose.

"Skipper." Dave made the introductions. "Have you come to eat with us?"

"No. No, thank you, Dave, I opened up some cans on board."

"A nice fattening dessert? We're about ready to skip it, and we could all watch you."

"I'm very well-fed, thank you."

"A drink?" Dave said. We were having a pretty wet dinner, cocktails and now wine, and highballs in prospect. After the brandy, that is.

"Sailor's last night ashore," Connie said.

"Come on, Captain Kelso."

Kelso Clark said: "You know, Dave, I only drink ashore." Then, having set forth the principle: "Certainly, thank you. I'd enjoy s-something." He spoke with a slight, almost noticeable stutter. "But then, I'm here to ask one of you to come away."

"We all will," Dave cried, signaling to the waiter. "What'll it be?"

"Canadian C-Club?" he said tentatively. "That's considered quite good, isn't it?" He didn't sound like the world's biggest lush, even ashore. We all sat down.

"Where to?" said Dave.

"Well, it's A-Art LaBranche, I'm afraid."

"Is something wrong?" said Connie.

"Nothing, probably," Kelso said. "I'm just being old and fussy, I'm quite sure. And I don't want to behave like the boy's keeper. But I, uh, would like him to be in condition to sail tomorrow, so I thought perhaps we should, well, if one of you would help. Find him and see if he won't turn in. That is, I suppose it's my job, but, I haven't always managed to be very persuasive with Art."

"Do you know where he is?" I asked.

"No. At a bar, possibly. But more likely someone's party. He's very much sought after—we could, oh, move around and inquire."

"I'm your man," Dave said. "Or maybe Barney wants to?"

"Whatever you like, Dave," I said. "Bar-to-bar with Captain Clark, or stay here and drink with the ladies. I like both prospects."

"Maybe you ought to let Barney go," Connie said. Dave grinned. "My nice steady grown man here is such a good influence on a boy like Art LaBranche."

"Straighten him right out," Dave said.

"Night before last, Dave strolled out to bring Art home about eleven. At four-thirty they were in the hall outside the door of our hotel room, singing."

"Any lady likes a serenade," Dave said.

"Sure," said Connie. "Especially when it's a song your husband keeps telling his young friend he learned in the First World War: *That's the Wrong Way to Tickle Mary.*"

"I wonder why Barney doesn't know that one?" Helen said. "He was in the First World War, too."

"All right," I said. "I'll be the good influence tonight. Or do you want to go, Dave?"

"Old shipmate of my youth," Dave said. "Leaving me drink with these perfume buyers? Go shine, good deed. I think you'll find the world naughty enough."

"Am I to be allowed to finish my drink, Dave?" Captain Clark asked mildly.

"Ancient Mariner," said Dave. "Wherefore stoppest thou thee with one?"

"I'm terribly fond of young LaBranche, Mr. James," Captain Clark said, as we walked along. "It's probably what makes me so fussy. He's a Dartmouth man, you know."

"I think you said so in your letter."

"But perhaps not really." It was important to Kelso Clark that things be truthfully set forth. "He was sent to Dartmouth, by an alumnus, I think, to play hockey. But he only stayed a year."

"I see."

"I found him in Florida. He was what is called a beach bum."

"He's got the curls for it," I said.

"I met him through a client, and persuaded him to sail with us. Now I don't know what I'd do without him."

"That good a hand?"

"No. There's a lot he'll never learn about sailing. He doesn't really care to. But he gets on well with people. When you're chartering, you know, it's important to, oh, m-mix drinks and have cheerful conversations. You must keep the customers jolly, and the boat a happy one, you see? I'm not always comfortable at that part of it, unless the people just happen to be my sort."

"And all people are Art's sort?" I said. "I can understand that. Even when he's out of his head, he's pretty likable."

"He does drink on the boat," Captain Clark said. "Which is quite all right, if he's going to sleep a while afterwards. Before going on watch, that is. But you may be reassured to know that I've asked him not to use those pills, when we're under way."

"And does he?" I asked.

"No. He gives them to me to put in the safe. That was his own idea. He said, then when he started acting silly, I'd know it was his natural silliness."

It wasn't hard to track our boy. In the second bar we visited there was an acquaintance of Kelso's who could tell us where the party was. Up the hill, he said, in a house that looked like a castle. Kelso and I walked on up, talking of this and that, and by the time we got within a block of the party we could hear it.

"I'll wait. Or perhaps just leave you here, if you don't mind?"

Kelso said. "These people have chartered with me, and they're likely to be quite insistent that I stay."

"I see. Shall I try to bring Art out to you?"

"Oh, no. No, I think I'll really go along back to the boat. Just—if you'll be sure he's all right? And keep an eye on him, perhaps? But of course I don't mean to restrict him, or you. . . ."

I said fine. I told myself I'd get the kid out of there soon. I also told myself that I could use another drink before I did. To Kelso Clark I said:

"See you tomorrow, Skipper." Fond of him already.

Then I went into the party.

It was big, so big I couldn't find Art in the growth of sports shirts and neat, nautical blouses. It was Art, after a few minutes, speaking with his head at the level of Bermuda shorts and tailored waistbands, who saw me:

"Hey, Barney. Mr. James."

He was sitting in a big chair in the third roomful of people I went into. There was a girl sitting on the arm of the chair, a pretty one, and another equally pretty but twenty years older sitting on his lap. He moved her aside and squeezed past, onto his feet, stocky and smiling.

"The man I've got to see," I heard him explain, and then he reached me. "Let's move, Mr. James," he said. "Okay? Unless you want to meet mother and daughter . . . ?"

"No," I said. "I don't think they'd see it as a fair trade."

"Would you like a drink?" He was leaning towards me and speaking low, as if our conversation were a very urgent one.

"That's what I'd like," I said.

We went back into one of the rooms I'd just come through, turned and took a room that would get us past the one he'd just been in. As we went, people kept clutching Art's arm, slowing him down, speaking to him. He'd been there all winter, and was one of them.

He smiled and ducked, grinned, replied, twisted away, and I followed as best I could and nearly made it through a swinging door, where a tall girl with a lot of cleavage showing swayed his way as he went through. Missing Art, her sway caught me, her arm went across to hold me and all that nice cleavage was distributed on both sides of my right shoulder. It was as if a soft tree had fallen on me. She was so tall that even leaning forward at a sixty-degree angle, her mouth was on my temple when she spoke.

"Hello."

"Hello," I said, turning slightly to face her. I thought it would be easier if I could see more branches and less trunk. Even so, I wouldn't have had far to lean to chew on an apple, if I'd wanted to.

"You a friend of Art LaBranche?"

"Yes." I did feel pretty friendly towards Art by then.

"Get him . . . for me?"

"No," I said. "I doubt it."

It wasn't just people pressing this tree-girl against me, thigh to stomach, stomach to chest, cleavage like a collar, as if we were dancing in a dark room and wanted to be close. She was doing the pressing, and I was surprised. I don't often have the feeling these days that I'm what a girl in her twenties is looking to find at a party.

"Art's bes' friend?"

I liked the way she felt against me, and there was some kind of nice, musky scent on her bosom.

"No," I said. "I barely know him." And I followed Art into the kitchen.

"There was a barboy earlier," Art said. He was standing by a vast table, along with other people, with the damnedest array of bottles on it I've ever seen. Free port and cheap liquor, okay, but there was still five hundred bucks' worth of high-grade booze there. I mean, if you were a Scotch drinker, you didn't just reach for Scotch, you reached for your brand: assuming it was Ambassador, Dewar's, King's Ransom, Grant's, Johnnie Walker Black, J&B, or Haig's Pinch. They were there in quantity, and there were single bottles of half a dozen other brands as well. There were Bisquit and Remy Martin, among the cognacs, along with the more expected Martell, Courvoisier and Hennessy. There was the whole line of Harvey sherries; there were Wild Turkey, Jack Daniels, Old Crow, and Old Granddad for starters on the bourbon; and in the refrigerator were stacks of champagne. Guy ran out of imagination there. Only one brand. Piper Hiedsieck. What it was like, more than anything, was a grownup's version of a kid's fantasy: what I'd buy for me and my gang from the candy store, if everything cost a penny and I had a million of 'em.

"A barboy?" I said. "What happened? He run out of stuff to pour?"

"One of the guests punched him out," Art said. "Did he leave in a huff? No, he left on his bicycle. But oh, God, it was funny, Mr. James."

He picked up a fresh bottle of Bushmill's Irish and opened it for himself, indicating that I was to make my own choice. I decided on Bisquit. Always did like the stuff, and we strolled off together with our bottles, looking for a quiet spot.

"Call me Barney," I said.

"Our host has two children," Art went on. "And an athletic wife. So there were three other bikes at the door, and these people went running out to chase the poor old barboy, who was making off with a little champagne. Someone yelled 'Stop, thief,' and drunks were jumping on bicycles, or jumping on other drunks to try to get bikes away from them. One stud went screaming down the hill, imitating a siren, and he must have thought the bike had coaster brakes. Didn't seem to know about the handbrake, and he went into the side of a parked car about twenty miles an hour. I ran down the hill to pick him up, and here came a girl after me, on a boy's bike, with her skirt blown back completely around her face. I mean, she couldn't see a thing, but I see *you*, baby. She went onto her side, laughing and shrieking, and the third bike went over her wheels. Not over her, thank heavens. Oh, there were pretty sights and sounds out there. Banging and screaming and scraping, and off goes the barboy with his two magnums, pedalling steadily into the night."

"You speak as the sober observer," I said.

"I'm sorry about on the boat."

We'd reached a pantry, or some such little room, off the kitchen. We hadn't turned the light on, but there was light coming in through the door, and no people.

"Did I sound like I wanted an apology?"

"Were you looking for me for something?"

"Kelso Clark asked me to come in, and see if you were okay."

"Bless the old Skipper. Yeah. The pills wore off."

"What the hell, Art," I said. "Does everyone twenty years old get on pills, now, instead of booze?"

"I don't know," Art said. "It's like all those bottles out there. Now one, now another—pills, pot, acid, booze. Whatever you feel like, and can get. How about that?"

"Doesn't bother me much," I said, hesitated, and amended my report. "Yeah. It does. I ran into a girl six weeks ago. About your age. It bothered me quite a bit." I didn't say where, or with whom, of course, but I described the scene at Sunny Brown's bungalow, with Sunny hunched over, dancing to the birdcall record. "Violent things had just happened," I said. "And she seemed to have forgotten. But she recognized me, though she'd met me and appeared not to acknowledge it, only once. Hours earlier."

"Hunched over?"

"That's right."

"How did her voice sound?" Art asked. "Dry and scratchy?"

I thought about that. I nodded. "She's a singer," I said. "And her voice sounded real good, earlier. But at the bungalow, it was a hoarse croak."

"She was on horse, then," Art said. "That's what it sounds like."

"Horse?"

"Yes."

"That means heroin?"

"The Puerto Rican peddlers in New York go through the streets calling, 'Caballo, Caballo.'"

"And when you feel like it, and can get it . . . ?"

"No. No, that's hard stuff. I wouldn't do it, Barney. I might cocaine, or opium. Something exotic once, to find out. But not horse."

"Now, that's what I call exquisite discrimination," I said. "Why not horse, just once, to find out?"

"Horse is dirty," Art said. "You might as well try rattlesnakes."

It was then that mother and daughter found us bad boys hiding, as mother put it. Daughter looked petulant. They'd sailed with Captain Kelso and Art LaBranche. That gave them a claim prior to mine, they felt, and they meant to exercise it. And when I began to gather that Art didn't have much objection to daughter—and not really all that much to mother, either, though she's what he'd have been generous to me with—I slid on out of the pantry.

I felt their claim to me was pretty weak. Art acknowledged that, as I left, with a wink and a salute.

And it was quite a party, after all. And quite a bottle of Bisquit. I talked to someone here, and someone else there, and moved to another room, and came upon the tree-girl again, swaying. She looked a little melancholy up there, with the wind moving through her branches. I thought I'd give her a chance to cheer up and sway into me again, if she wanted, and she did.

"I'm sorry," she said. It was a big night for the junior set to apologize to me.

"Me, too," I tried. "What are we sorry about?"

"Saying for you to get Art." She sounded deeply serious. "Very sorry."

"Terrible behavior," I said. "But I forgive you."

But she was full of meanings, by then, and had to be allowed to declare them all. I let her. She was still nice to smell, and nice to have spilling around my shoulder, and after a while I managed to stop myself from wondering if I reminded her of her damn father or something, and wondered instead what sort of tree she was. At first I picked a willow. Then I thought, no, something with smoother bark. An aspen. One of the ones that grows away from water, a little out of place, by itself, in a grove of oak and hickory. Protected from the wind, and in soil that lets its roots grow deep, an aspen can get quite tall and graceful, growing in a long, smooth curve, generally, up and out of sight among the more durable trees.

The leaves rustled in my aspen's branches, and seemed to say, "I need a drink."

I thought that might very well be so, in so dry a time and place, and handed over the bottle. What I thought very little about was Helen James, and how she might be improving her last hours ashore. With Dave? That would be a man of low susceptibility, just now, nor does Helen move with blazing speed in such matters, if she was due to move at all. Anyway, if that kind of possibility came into my mind at all, it was out again in the time it took to swallow the next drink. It may have been there long enough to remind me what a fine, free, untrammelled, twenty-two-year-old swashbuckler of the boudoir I was; the cognac carried much the same message.

The aspen swayed back and looked at me. I don't know if she bent a little at the knee or not, to bring us eye-to-eye.

I gazed, then, deep into her big brown sunglasses. I believe I pointed out that since it was now a little past midnight, the glare of the sun wasn't too intense. It seems to me she laughed, and said we should go out and check.

Irish LaBranche saw us going towards the door, and chanted: "O'James McBarney, the Pride of Killarney."

"Scots," I corrected him. "Wha' hae wi' Wallace bled." I tried to think of Wallace's first name, but all I could come up with was Henry, which didn't sound quite right.

The next place we were was on what she pleased to call a yacht. I'd have said it was a fair-sized cabin cruiser, down in the general docking area where we'd been in the afternoon. The docks were lighted, and enough came in through the portholes so that I could see the girl still had those sunglasses on. Being a wily fellow, I suggested she remove them. She laughed at the notion, and started undoing her sweater instead. It opened down the front. It that what you call a cardigan? No, it looked more like a great big pair of matched cardigans.

She pitched exuberantly backwards onto one of the bunks, laughing again, and the laugh stabbed me in some old way that had to do with bunks and cabins and exuberance—was it Tish or Vinnie, and was I Barney, the Ozark brass man, once again?

No, but this tree girl was a great laugher. Her knees went up, as she lay on her back, in a way that would have been highly indecorous if she'd still had her skirt on. She clapped her bare feet together and giggled, and the feet made a muffled, applause-like sound, which may have been a tribute to the grace with which I was trying to take my pants off without undoing the zipper. She had a nice giggle, as a matter of fact, but it wasn't up to her laugh; the laugh was happy hail in the branches.

How on earth it could have happened, I don't know—tripped over my pants finally, or something, but where I landed was right there on the bunk beside her, and it was plain, even to a silly drunk like me, that there wasn't room for two people to lie side-by-side on so narrow a bed. That was my bold deduction, my witty and scientific conclusion (and did I manage to keep wistful recollection out of it, for a Friendship sloop?); I rolled up and over. It was very much more comfortable that way.

Then there were squeaks and thrashing below, grunts and pushes above, and a mutual exchange of so-there smiles, after what was possibly two minutes. It couldn't have been longer.

She stayed, sprawled and naked, smiling up at me as I dressed, but concealing her eyes modestly behind the sunglasses again. She must have kept them in her hand.

I walked away along the dock, thinking of nothing in particular, not as completely guiltless as I thought I was entitled to feel. Hoping, I suppose, that by the time I got to the hotel, things would be quiet and I could quietly go to sleep.

And I passed a two-masted schooner, white in the Caribbean moonlight, and didn't need to look to learn its name. I knew it from its picture, which had been tacked to the wall in our kitchen all winter, along with calendars and reminder cards and children's art from school. A pin-up boat.

I wondered if Kelso Clark, the painstaker, and Art LaBranche, the jingle-maker, were asleep in there, and supposing that they were made me feel easier, for some reason, better-humored with myself; and I thought, very well, *jongleurs*, but only Barney can make a tree.

If I got back to our room smiling, though, it was with older memories; this evening's wasn't a record I'd expect to play much, rarely as those things happened any more.

6

Helen never shows hangovers. She has up mornings and down mornings instead, which don't always correlate with what she had to drink the night before. She was up and bright the next day.

I show hangovers, and feel them, but I might not have had one if I'd gone straight to sleep when I got in. Instead I'd sat and drank from a bottle, watching Helen sleep, thinking long, lachrymose, befuddled thoughts—like what the hell my life had become. Or anybody else's who was forty-four.

Helen woke me at seven, but I didn't want to get up. She called for coffee, and said they'd sat up fairly late talking, and asked if it was a good party.

"From the shade of your eyes, I'd say quite good," she said. "They're not scarlet, but they're a good, warm pink."

"Nothing wrong," I said. "That closing them won't help."

"Don't you want to jump up and see town with me and Connie?"

I took the question as rhetorical, and went back to sleep. When I woke again at ten, I'd had enough rest to be as cheerful as everybody else seemed to be. Dave had slept late, too; we met in the dining room, and had breakfast, while our wives shopped.

"I guess we go down to the boat," I said. "And help get ready?"

"You're not too bad for a man who went to a party with Art LaBranche."

"What a boy for punishment," I said. "Does he find one of those every night?"

"I guess there's one to find. He hardly needs it, though. Kid has the best time with himself of any two people I ever knew. I get the feeling he'd stay high with or without the liquor and the other junk."

"That's pretty much what Kelso said." I wondered if I should tell Dave Art's conclusion about Sunny and the heroin, but I was pretty sure that if it were so, Dave knew it and had kept it from me. As why shouldn't he? So I said: "I don't gather Art's the world's finest seaman. Sort of surprised me, since he's an athlete."

"You could be a hell of an athlete and not much at riding horseback, if you couldn't feel the horse," Dave said.

"What happened at Dartmouth?"

"He left after freshman hockey season," Dave said. "Went to Florida on one of those spring-vacation migrations, and didn't see any reason to go back when vacation ended. That was last year. But he's Kelso's brand from the burning because of having been at Dartmouth at all. College man, you know. A little wild but he'll straighten out."

"Where's Art from?" I asked.

"It's no secret. Slums of Toronto. Then his father got a factory job in Lewiston, Maine, got laid off, moved to Boston and put the family on relief. He sits there grinning, telling Kelso all that, and Kelso nods and smiles, and thinks, yes, Dartmouth. Good school. Wild oats. Straighten out. Of course, Kelso's just as much a stereotype to Art."

"New England sea captain?"

"There must be someone who walks in the strange little room called the captain's walk, on top of the big frame house you pass on your way to school," Dave said.

I smiled. "Someone exacting, but not unkind," I said.

"Who calls the household to evening prayer on a gong from the China seas." Dave smiled back.

It was nice to talk to him again. I'd been wanting to ask him what he knew about fiberglass and boats, because of Uncle Troy's interest; Dave told me a lot, much of it reassuring.

We talked about Tish and Vinnie. He told me that the Scots' Wallace was Sir William.

We decided the date was around 1300, and we got a third pot of coffee, and thought of things to laugh about. We saw Helen and Connie come into the lobby and go by with parcels without looking into the dining room, and knew this break would be over now, very shortly, and something new would start up.

"Want a cigarette?" said Dave, who had congratulated me on quitting when he lighted one, just a little earlier.

I grinned. I realized that I hadn't, even in my drunk the night before, smoked any. "Sure," I said. "I'll have one with you."

I lit the thing, and enjoyed it, every drag. It was a Lucky Strike, the American cigarette, somehow, that foreign civilians particularly wanted overseas, during the war. It brought a premium, I've been told, on the black market. I smoked that one

223

down till I could feel heat from the lit end on my finger tips, and I was quietly sorry when it was time to put it out.

It's the last I shall ever smoke, I feel quite sure, unless I judge myself too kindly.

St. Thomas to first fish.

Kelso Clark said we would sail at 3:10, when the tide turned.

I hadn't believed we could be ready. I underestimated the Skipper. At 3:05 he had us under way, moving out from the dock by motor, sails ready to raise as soon as we got clear of the moorings.

He had managed somehow to get us organized so completely that we were all sitting in or standing near the cockpit, while Kelso took us out, with nothing left to do. Yet there'd been no sense of rush and effort about the final preparations; it wasn't, I thought, so much that he'd organized us, after all, as that he'd quietly done so many things himself.

In spite of her length and the proud height of her masts, it was striking that *The Bosun Bird* rode no higher from the sea than many of the smaller sailboats, and a good bit lower than the power jobs. You could lie down at the edge of the deck in the middle of the boat, stretch down and touch water.

Below, in the cabins, everything was in place: the food in chests and lockers, ice enough to last four days and fresh meat and milk to go as long as the ice did. The milk was for Kelso, who confessed to an ulcer, and I found myself smiling, remembering that just before we actually cast off, Art had said: "All right if I have a glass of your milk, Skipper? Growing boy, you know," and almost tricked Kelso into giving him serious reasons why he'd prefer not.

At the forward end of the cockpit of *The Bosun Bird* were two steps down, through a varnished door which was generally fastened open. This put you in the galley with the food. Going on forward, you got to the main cabin in the widest part of the boat, which had a table and four bunks, then into another cabin with two bunks over the sail lockers. Helen and Connie had moved their things up there; the head, and I shall forgive myself the nautical language, was up in the bow, past their bunks.

The four males would sleep in the main cabin; there was one

more sleeping place, but it was very cramped, to the rear of the galley and beside the diesel engine; you had to crawl to get to it. Art and Kelso had used it in turn when they were chartering, but then there'd been gear that could be left behind. Now we had everything with us and the crewman's bunk had been hooked up, out of the way, to make space for stowage.

Personal things were all unpacked, put into long, narrow drawers and in nets over the beds. So we sat and stood, unhurried, watching Kelso at the wheel, and Dave said:

"We are, in the medieval meaning of the word, a motley crew."

"Oh?" said Helen. "Jesters?"

"Jokers," I said.

"I was thinking of costume, more than function," Dave said, and smiled. So did Kelso, and it was true. We all wore bright colors, except for the Skipper himself, whose sea clothes were khaki and a nicely fitted blue cotton work shirt, washed until white thread showed through. He'd rolled the sleeves up, and I saw all over again how hard and ropy this old guy was, and how lean. He wore a white nautical cap, to protect his skull from the sun. He had style, dressed that way.

Dave had style of his own, white ducks and a red short-sleeved shirt, and that still surprising white hair over the skin that was showing tan already. As for Art, his shirt today was bottle green with a continental collar and a waist band—I don't know where you get shirts like that—bare feet and brief, bright trunks. A bit exotic, with the long, curly hair, but not unacceptable, once you got used to him. You noticed that his muscles were thick and bulging, rather than long like Kelso Clark's; Art had skater's muscles, I supposed, though the square shoulders and big legs and arms would have fit a weight-lifter just as well.

The three of them made me feel pale and soft, as if I must look my early middle age, and I thought I would pull heavy on the ropes and drink light on the booze, stay in the sun and out of the shadow of anxiety, and I'd take a little of the physical motleyness out of this crew.

I looked at the wives in bright shorts and halters, then, and decided that Helen's prettiness kept her looking younger than that big, soft, handsome quality kept Connie, but neither of them had really started aging yet in looks. It was just that Helen had some girlishness left; Connie looked mature. When they did begin to age, Connie might look better if she watched her weight —maybe the weight wouldn't even matter, too much. Helen wasn't ever going to have to watch her weight, in a painful way, but her complexion would go; she'd shrink up. Hell, they both looked younger and better than I did. But not necessarily younger and better than I'd begun to feel, now that we were leaving shore behind.

Kelso asked about watches: "I'd suggest four hours on and eight off," he said. "In pairs."

"Two at a time will do it?" Dave asked.

"Oh, yes, as long as we're not in a hurry."

Helen smiled at him, her big smile, and the Skipper said: "Unless you'd prefer to sail hard?"

"We aren't racing to Nassau," Dave said.

"I never like to push a boat. Ocean racing shakes a boat up so."

"As many as you've been on," Dave said.

"Only to help friends. I wouldn't do it to a boat of my own, and I try to make that clear. Are you up on navigation, Dave?"

"I think I'm okay."

"Mr. James?"

"Barney," I said. "I can navigate an airplane over land. Theoretically. I'll be glad to learn if you'll teach me."

"We might all three check each other," Kelso said.

"I'll check you all, and then we'll know who's right," Art said. "When it comes to navigation, Logarithm LaBranche is your natural best man for the job."

"He's the only man going," Dave said, "so he tells me, who can take a star fix in the Caribbean, figure out the tables and show you that you're really in the Indian Ocean."

"That's the new navigation," Art said. We were still motoring among moored boats, heading for channel markers some distance away. "I got us in the North Sea, once, down towards Barbados. Everybody was breaking out parkas and woolly gloves."

"The temperature was ninety-three that evening," Kelso said, with dry indulgence. "It gave our passengers a lot of confidence. How shall we divide for watches?"

"I'll take the midshipman here, if you like," Dave said, nodding at Art.

"Perhaps I'd better," Kelso said. "There's some work Art and I can do together."

"He means I go to sleep," Art said reproachfully. "That was only once, Captain Skipper, sir. I was just seeing if I could steer with my eyes closed, and my head on my knees. . . ."

"Nevertheless," Kelso said, apparently at the line now to which he'd let Art push him, "I'll have to continue to take the responsibility of trying to make a sailor out of you. I can't ask one of our guests." I'd half-expected Kelso to pick me for his watch mate, and I wouldn't have minded. It seemed to me I could have learned a lot that way.

There was one thing no one could have learned from Kelso Clark, though, because it was clear he didn't know himself—that was how to ask the next question. He looked at Art for help, then at Dave and me, avoided looking at the wives, and finally addressed the door of the companionway, directly in front of him. "Would you, uh, p-prefer to have husbands and wives as watch mates? Or, that is . . . ?"

Helen answered, our authority on mixed cruising: "It's like seating people at dinner," she said, and smiled—not at me, Dave, Art or Kelso, but at Connie.

"Barney and I have kept each other up before," Connie said. With that the great Ozark mind saw what all these mixed-cruisers knew so plainly: that during the day, we'd all pretty much be milling around the fifty-two linear feet of deck space, hatch-covers and cockpit, seldom out of range of one another's voices, never out of sight except in the rather public sleeping rooms below. But the night watches would bring a curious solitude. For four hours out of each twenty-four, Connie and I would sit alone in the Caribbean dark, while the others slept, down under our feet. As, for four hours, would Helen and Dave.

I said it was fine with me. Connie said: "Be warned. I'm a compulsive volunteer for dawn watches."

"Let's apply," I said.

Kelso said we'd change watches at two, six and ten. This was so that he and Art could do certain daylight maintenance jobs in the cool part of the day, from six to ten each morning. And they would be in charge, too, from six to ten in the evening, the dinner hour, when the rest of us might like to have a drink or two while getting ready to eat.

"I don't know how Barney can last till six," Helen said. She and Dave would take the middle watches of the day and night, for sunbathing and star-gazing. "In Scott's Fort they set watches by Barney's first drink. Five-thirty, every day."

It was true, in a way. I've got a bloodstream full of jazzy little antibodies, that sleep all day till 5:28. Then it's up and get the beat going, corpuscles swinging, juices ready to blow, everything waiting for the alky to come down—"Maybe I'll put my antibodies on ice for a while," I said.

"Oh, no," Helen said. "We'll just make six o'clock attractive to you, dear. Little organized parties, I think. Captain Clark, would you mind going back to a stationery store so I can buy some printed invitations—you know, the cute kind with funny drawings?"

"That'll melt his old Missouri heart," Dave said.

"I'm afraid I shan't be able to attend," said Kelso, getting into the ride-Barney spirit of things. "But I'll watch with pleasure."

"But Art will come, won't you?" said Helen, going aft, to where Art was standing, out of the conversation. He was watching St. Thomas recede. He'd had quite a winter there, a lot of good times, I guess. With people some of whom may have come to mean something, that he wasn't likely to see again. Helen drew him in, with her smile and a hand on his arm: "Can we count on you?"

He pulled his eyes back across the bay, into the boat, and looked at us all. "I'm a secret drinker, Mrs. Barney," he said in an earnest voice. "I'm the only real alcoholic anonymous there is. When I drink I won't tell anybody my name."

"Stand by, gentlemen," said Kelso just then, and headed *The Bosun Bird* into the wind. Art slipped over to cut down on the motor speed till it was just enough to keep us from drifting. "Mrs. Doremus, would you take the helm?"

I don't know if Helen felt slighted or not, but she watched cheerfully, a little mockingly, I suppose, while Connie held steady and the four of us raised the heavy sails. It seemed marvelous to me, as I put my back into hauling on a halyard with Art, to think that Kelso Clark could do this all alone.

It was my watch to start with, mine and Connie's, but Kelso thought he'd take the helm until he had us out of the harbor. He sat back with the wheel, turned us slowly downwind; the sails filled, and Art cut the motor. It coughed, and died, and there began a wonderful silence that I hadn't heard in twenty years.

It was a silence of small sounds. A little slap of water against the sides; a hum of wind in the stays. Helen James in the cockpit, sighing as she stretched and shook her hair back, eyes on Kelso Clark; a light, steady hiss as the hull cut water.

They were the relevant little things you never hear, with all the noise irrelevance makes in this world. Every light creak and whisper came from ourselves and our being in motion, as surely as Dave's voice on the wind from thirty feet away, asking Art for a look at the harbor book. The only sounds there were in our environment as shore blurred were those we made, and our boat made, as the sea and the wind rolled, unobstructed by anything but dinky islands, all the way from South America, with nothing to sound against except ourselves.

The Bosun Bird seemed to rise a little, as the motor left off, to skim, sailing the surface of the sea as the wind did, not pushing its way through any longer. We were buoyant; waterborne. Airplanes don't fly; sailboats do.

"Oh, Barney," Connie said, and I turned to see my watch mate standing just behind me. "Barney, isn't it?" She had no word.

"Yeah," I said. "It really is."

2

I'd been a little worried as to how long it might take before I could manage the helm of something the size of *The Bosun*

Bird. Anything else I'd ever sailed had a tiller, not a wheel. But it seemed to me the big schooner was easier to hold on course than some of the smaller things. Like a big plane, I remembered (or thought I did), holds easier than a light one.

Kelso Clark turned her over to me as soon as we were past the last channel marker. He knew, for I'd been careful to tell him, how green I was. His response was to seat me by the wheel anyway, tell me the compass course, see to the trim of the sails, and walk away.

Connie smiled encouragingly, and sat nearby.

"Watch me," I said. "That I don't have us going back towards town right away."

But as a matter of fact, I wasn't bad. When Kelso came back in ten minutes, and made a suggestion or two, I had already found that I could sense how far the push of each wave at the stern wanted to move us off the heading, and could have us on it still as the bow rose. There wasn't much easing back to do, in the light sea that followed us, and the feeling of control without effort was lovely.

Connie was better than I, of course, and by the time our first watch had ended, I felt that she and I would do all right.

But if I was finding it easy and natural, I learned the morning of the second day that Dave, who'd been helmsman for big ocean races many times, was rather erratic. Helen told me that, during Art and Kelso's early watch.

Dave was eating breakfast below. Connie was still asleep— I should have been, too, I guess, but hadn't yet persuaded myself that seven in the morning was bedtime. So I was sitting on the foredeck, running fishline through my fingers, checking it for worn spots and knots, coiling it as I did.

"Barney."

"Hello, Miss Sweets," I said. "You're looking pretty naked there, in that sunsuit."

"Barney, is Dave all right?"

"Just barely," I said. "I considered clobbering the man when he woke me at two A.M. to go on watch. But I remembered he was just a tool in the hands of higher powers."

"He gets very abstracted, Barney. We were talking. It was

a little after midnight, and of course we'd been on watch quite a while."

"Something happen?"

"He doesn't let me take very long turns at the wheel. As if he ought to have the endurance to hold it for four hours straight himself. But I looked at the compass, and we were ten to twelve degrees off, and I think we had been for quite a while."

"Well," I said. "We got all kinds of navigators aboard. Including one, I guess, who can prove we're in Istanbul. What'd you do? Tell him?"

"Oh, I got up," Helen said. "And walked around and came back, and said could I have a turn, and what was the darn course, anyway? As if I'd forgotten."

"Man was fooled?"

"No, he laughed. And gave the wheel a twitch and said we'd better put the first team back in. But then later, he did it again."

"How was he, talking to you? Abstracted, too?"

"He seemed to have his mind on the conversation—whatever it was we talked about . . . Uncle Troy, partly. I was telling Uncle Troy stories. No, it was as if he could think of two things —what we were saying and whatever else was on his mind. But not the boat, too."

"Maybe you shouldn't talk so interestingly," I said. "A little duller there with the conversation, Miss Sweets."

"I can promise I wasn't being interesting the second time," she said. "I was in the galley, making coffee. It seemed as if we were losing way, and I stuck my head out of the galley, and heard the sails start to flap just a little. Not a real flap, but— well, a little noise they make when you're too close to the wind. It was all very quick because he heard it, too, and corrected right away, but I could see his face by the light from the binnacle. It looked strange."

"Faces do," I said. Faces do, because only the neck and chin and mouth are lit, by that glow from the source that lets you read your compass at night, down below eye level.

"I think it woke Kelso."

"He get up?"

"No, but I pulled my head back quick, so Dave wouldn't see I'd been alarmed. And then I glanced in to where you and Art were sleeping, and I think Kelso was up on one elbow."

"Well," I said. "The longer we're away, the less we'll feel pressed by . . . whatever goes on at home. Nice fish for supper, lady?"

"Is it fresh?"

It was so fresh it hadn't been caught yet.

Art and I rigged the lines, two of them, each a couple of hundred feet long with big yellow feathered jigs on the ends. They weren't for sport; fresh food was the object, and the lines were ninety pound test. We tied them to cleats, on each side of the cockpit, and let them out all the way. We ran each rig through a clothespin, up on the lifeline. Each clothespin was tied with a separate piece of string. When a fish struck one of the trolled jigs, way out behind us, Art explained, the pressure would straighten the slack sharply and the clothespin would be snapped off the lifeline. We'd hear it. But even if we didn't, whenever we noticed that one of the pins was no longer holding fishline and lifeline together, but dangling free on its separate string, we'd know something should be on the hook.

There was no reason to let Helen worry it, but I asked Connie about Dave's state of mind, sometime between two and three next morning. She had the wheel. I was sitting on deck, a couple of feet away, with my feet in the cockpit, watching behind. The sky and sea were bright with darkness, and for a minute or two, after we came to a pause in whatever we'd been talking about, I watched phosphorescence in the wake shine and disappear. There wasn't any way to be but abrupt, so I said:

"How's Dave been, Connie?"

"Sad and jumpy. If it were anyone but Dave I'd say confused."

"Anything new, since I was up there?"

"No." She was quiet a minute, and then said: "Dave's always been in trouble, Barney, ever since I knew him more than casually. A little deeper all the time. Since the divorce, really deep, hardly ever coming up. . . . I find him, well, very attractive and appealing. Everybody does. But it breaks my heart to be married to Dave."

"Sure, Connie."

"I wish I'd known him before. Before he got troubled."

"I wish you had."

"Remember the night when we were doing Oswald? All that?"

"Your Greek boy. I can't forget him."

"I don't think of the soldier any more, when I think of Oswald, Barney. I think of that girl."

"Sunny?" That puzzled me longer than it should have. By the time she started to explain herself, I knew what she was going to say. I even knew that I'd agree.

"Sunny's the same age as Oswald and just as crazy. Just as much in need of a good man to destroy. As if she were born to do it. Maybe I'm being stupid, but I feel as if she's shot Dave down. Just like Oswald."

"Connie."

"Be sorry for Dave, Barney. Not for me."

I shook my head. Don't be sorry for Connie, no matter how much you happen to like her. One husband dead, another damaged, but don't be sorry for Connie.

"Barney, it's no torture being married to Dave. Nothing like that. He is just as absolutely nice and loving to me as he can make himself be. Even if it's a fight for him, every minute of the time."

I looked at her in the starlight, liking that outline of a woman—there was honest bone for you, firmly fleshed, and muscle. I said: "If you're going to sit there and tell me wild lies like that, I'm not going to be able to trust you with the wheel."

She laughed. "I didn't mean to say that I repelled him all the time. I don't know Barney. . . . Some of the time I think . . . maybe there ought to be a ceremony where two people could get pronounced brother and sister . . . ."

I wasn't sure I wanted to hear what she was telling me; as a matter of fact, it seemed to me she wasn't sure she wanted to have told it. So we both tried to change the subject at the same moment. I said, *"Blurt,"* meaning to ask something like when had she last sailed the Caribbean? And Connie said, *"Blurt,"* right along with me in the moonlight.

It was funny, so we both laughed.

The extent of simultaneous feeling I had with this Mrs. Constance Marlow (Ferguson) Doremus was a little alarming. If it went on like this, not only could either one of us tell the other one anything at all, but given that four-hour watch together every night, we probably would.

3

Guess who I ran into next day? Dave Doremus.

Think of a house, fifty-two feet long, with four low, semi-submarine rooms and bath. The bath tapers down to no width at all, and even the middle room isn't more than nine feet wide. The rooms are full of apparatus for eating, sleeping and moving the house around, so there's hardly any free floor space in the interior. You spend your waking time on the roof, but much of that is occupied by cleats and blocks and hatch covers and ventilators; by coils of line and the bottoms of spars and a dory. There are six people living here, on dovetailed schedules, so it isn't all that easy to contrive to see one of them alone, if you're not paired with him.

But I did manage to happen on Dave, up by the intersection of Port Street and Starboard Avenue—if he'd gone any farther forward he'd have been dangling from the bowsprit.

It was his and Helen's watch. I'd been asleep from the time we were relieved by Art and Kelso at six, until after eleven. Dave was leaving Helen with the helm, when I got up on deck with a cup of coffee in my hand. Dave was standing up there on the foredeck, about where I'd been coiling fishline the day before. But Dave wasn't coiling anything. He was just up there. Connie and Art were starting to cook lunch, and Kelso was busy below at his chart table.

We were altogether out of sight of land, of course, and had been now for long enough so that I couldn't have said how long—a day and a night, at least. The sea was running a little higher than it had been, and I went carefully, swaying with the motion, not wanting to see the coffee that I held splash onto the scrubbed teak of the deck.

"Dave."

"Hi Barney. I've been wanting to ask you something."

That was my line he'd just said. "Okay, what?"

"I'm worried about that kid. LaBranche. Do you trust him?"

That wasn't my line, though. Hell, that wasn't anybody's line. "I hadn't thought about it," I said. "I like him. I thought you did?"

"Skip it, then," he said. "How do you feel about cruising now?"

"Real well," I said. "Real well. The loudest telephone in the world could ring till it shook its black self to bits, and I couldn't hear it, could I?"

"Not as long as you keep your head off the hook," Dave said, and smiled. That was worth noticing. He hadn't been smiling all that much.

"Ask you something?"

He nodded, and sat on his heels. "Have a seat," he said.

"What became of Sunny Brown, Dave?"

"I guess you've got as much reason to be curious as anyone."

"She's been on my mind some."

"There's something you don't know about Sunny. And you don't need to use your accent on me."

"Huh?"

"The Old Missouri Boy drawl, that comes out when you're feeling awkward."

"Sorry."

"It's okay. Sometimes I wish I had a drawl myself."

"What don't I know?"

"Sunny's an addict, Barney. Heroin. She wasn't when I first knew her, but she . . . picked it up. She's been cured once, but it isn't apt to last."

"I guessed it," I said. "Or rather Art did." Dave looked at me sharply, and I said: "From something I said about her voice and posture, Dave. I didn't say where'd I'd seen a girl like that, of course."

Dave's laugh was a little strained: "That's where it started," he said. "Art was referring to that conversation, I suppose. Only

236

he didn't say where he'd had a conversation like that." He paused, and then said: "She left, Barney. Buster took her away. I don't know where. I hope I never find out."

"You saw Buster?"

"He came to the hospital to ask for dough."

"You give him any?"

"A couple of hundred, Jesse James. My last. Connie found some tucked away, for the trip. Now look, you ask me everything you feel you've got to know, right now. Okay? And then let's sail farther and farther away from that black telephone, and think less and less about it, all the time."

"I got it all now, Dave," I said. "I hope she's really gone."

"God knows, I do too."

"You figured out what you're going to do?"

"Go back to Wonamasset. Build my business up."

"There'll be a job at my place, if this new fiberglass expansion goes in. A fair-sized job."

"It's for Tully, isn't it?"

"No. He likes the way my chair swivels. He wouldn't settle just for a division."

"I hope that I won't have to either, Barney," Dave said. "But thanks. I know how Tully'd feel, and how you feel, too. About being first man, in your own shop."

It was hot now, on the foredeck, sailing steadily north on the rock-a-bye sea. "Things'll work out, Dave," I said. "That's a statement that comes from the way the sun makes me feel. Makes old dogs feel that way, too."

"Barney, don't ever kid yourself that you think worse of me than I do of myself."

"You wanted to sail away from it. Let's do."

"One thing more. Okay?"

"It isn't anything I asked."

"About Connie."

"Well."

"Barney, you're a betting man. I never was much. But I put it all on marrying Joe Ferguson's widow, Connie."

"I like the odds."

"You get to be forty, and you've learned how to work from

a kind of . . . emotional set. Some men have to learn to work out of their pain. Most of us function out of a sense of well-being, a reasonable amount of personal happiness."

"Yeah. Sure."

"Don't be impatient. What I'm trying to say is a little difficult."

"Sorry."

"Suppose you're one of those who works well out of being happy, you're used to that, and you louse things up? Your kids are gone, your marriage, your dough. The springboard you were going to make a real, world champion dive from cracks, and down you go, smack on your belly and sprain your back. I just hadn't learned how to be an unhappy man."

I nodded.

"I hadn't been the silliest optimist around about abstract things, but the personal stuff was always pretty much okay. So . . . if I called on courage, it was just nerve courage. For taking a risk, something like that. But I'd never found myself having to, oh, kick myself in the ass continuously, all day long. Tell myself to straighten up and hang in there, no matter what was hurting. That kind of courage. Didn't know about that. All the time. Every day. Being . . . unhappy takes a lot of energy. Boy, I admire those guys that function out of pain."

"All right."

"I was trying to learn to do it, too, with Sunny on my back, desperate about the kids being taken away. . . . We'd always known the Fergusons. Joe was a sailing friend and . . . everybody loved Connie. I didn't think of it at first, when Joe died, but after a while I did. It seemed to me that marrying Connie might be my only chance to recoup. . . . Don't be a jerk, Barney. . . ."

For I'd stood up, in some disgust, thinking: Good God, you don't marry someone like Connie to recoup. You marry her because you have the enormous good fortune to find someone like Connie.

Dave stood, too.

"I'm not talking about recouping financially, jerk. Whatever your salesman buddy may have said. Or what the hell did you think I meant, anyway?"

I looked at him.

"What have I been talking about?" He asked recovering a certain patience. "Recouping emotionally. Being able to function. Barney, I'll tell you exactly what I said when I proposed to Connie, may I?"

"If it isn't anything she'd mind your telling."

"I assure you I wouldn't offer to if I thought she'd mind."

"All right. Sorry if I'm being dumb."

"I'm talking about a bet, goddamn it. You ought to be able to understand this. I said: 'Connie, I've felt since Joe died . . . and everyone I know feels this. That any man in his right mind would marry you, if he could. I'm not in my right mind, but could I? Anyway. And maybe my right mind will come back.' "

"Irresistible," I said. "Romantic."

"It was a bet I offered, and she took, Barney."

"I don't like the odds any more."

"Okay, ask your watch partner how she felt about them, will you? Maybe I wasn't the only one who was desperate."

I didn't have to ask her. Connie and Joe Ferguson had been childless, and you didn't have to do much more than look at her to be convinced she was the kind of woman who'd have had all the children health and reason allowed. If she could have. She'd been thirty-six when she and Dave were married. That'd be the last chance. And the old Dormouse, whatever his other faults and virtues, was a proved stud.

Punched the man on the arm, lightly, schoolboy style. Gave him a nod.

Big of me.

4

I never asked Connie about the children she didn't have, but there wasn't anything else we didn't talk about. We even got back to Jack Ruby, one night, finishing our very first long conversation that had started a couple of months before. Not that we got any closer to finding the real-life analogy in our pooled experience. The assassination was six months past, by then. The Warren Commission report hadn't come out to fill things in.

"He's a quarreller," I said. "A barroom fight picker. Maybe something in him of the kind of guy who goes out to beat up queers, or beatniks, or pickets."

"But he went alone," Connie said. "And his grief was real."

"It wasn't his grief."

"Wasn't it everybody's?"

"There's a difference between grief and grievance."

"Of course. Oswald had a grievance. Against anything. Anyone. For all the things he lacked, or couldn't be, and it didn't matter who he killed. It just had to be somebody important. But Jack Ruby probably would have lived out his life without killing anybody at all, if he hadn't been out of his head with grief."

"I never knew a murderer," I said. "Maybe that's why I can't do Ruby." And then, after a moment: "Except me. Only it was more like Oswald, probably."

"Barney James, steer the boat. What in the world are you talking about?"

"Oh," I said, taking her place at the wheel. "Nothing deep and dark. Matter of public record—matter of fact, I believe I got an oak leaf cluster for it. No, it . . . it's because I was twenty-three, and something happened that made me feel mortal for the first time. Worse than mortal, old."

And I told her. It was no buried story. In fact, it's one I've probably told too often—once I remember trying to tell it to my oldest boy Brad, and that I couldn't make him see its particular meaning to me. Brad must have been eight or nine at the time.

The war was damn near over, and we were so certainly going to win that I really had stopped flying missions. Been a long time since I was required to. I was staying on, doing a little instructing. I was acting C.O., I guess, and had made captain. There were kid fliers coming in, and I didn't altogether feel like leaving it to them. Maybe I was ducking certain home responsibilities, like trying to do something for a blind brother. Anyway, what happened was that the Luftwaffe started flying jets. The ME-262 jet, the first one ever operational, and the fliers coming back from escort missions over Germany said they were incredible. I wanted to see one, stupid as that may sound. Does sound. So every day or two, if the mission was going into a 262 area, and if someone were on sick call so that I could use a plane, I'd go along.

The first couple of times, no luck. The third, we ran into a dozen of them. I was in somebody's Mustang when the 262's came down and through the bombers. I made a turn to follow one, and before my turn was finished, he was gone. I started after another, and it went away so fast I had the feeling that my beautiful, my speedy, Mustang had simply stopped, in the air. I didn't even fire a gun.

I felt a hundred years old, bewildered, lost. I remember staring at the instrument panel, expecting everything to be shut off. My big Merlin engine didn't roar anymore; it whined, like a sewing machine, and if I touched my triggers marshmallows would float out. Just then I saw one of those amazing jets in trouble, in a limping glide. I think one of the bomber gunners must have hit it. It was on its way down, for sure though I could see the pilot trying to fly. I went after it; so did two other Mustangs, and the three of us pounded rounds into it, senseless and furious, almost down to the ground until we blew it up.

("That's the way to get 'em, Dad," Brad had shouted.)

"Of course you felt old," Connie said, and then she laughed at me, which was always her privilege: "Shooting marshmallows from a sewing machine. What do you expect?"

I'm not sure what we talked about after that. I was looking at her, more than listening, because it was dawn just then, half an hour before sunrise. The sky was pearl grey and pink behind her; she stood, looking at or past me, and the sight made me squeeze the spokes of the wheel I held. I wished for a camera, and some better color film than anyone's invented yet, and the luck to hit the one, right exposure that would pick up the way the glow came from behind as if the light were blown through her hair so that it shifted and moved, all around her face.

No one could take that picture. Only the mind can hold it, printed and unfading, showing for the first time and the hundredth how square her shoulders were, and what a sense they gave of framework, proper and proportioned to the structural needs of the fine bosom the woman carried, and the long waist. It shows a line, strong as it was straight, from hip to ankle without a bulge. It shows the features, lovely for their honorable plainness, surrounded by that translucent hair. It shows her thoughtful, serious, then smiling at her own seriousness just before she gasped and said:

"Oh, Barney!"

I looked. She was pointing past me, and out the boat, and I saw a great shelled back, slowly sinking. A giant sea turtle, big as a car, that must have been basking in our path, was lowering himself gently out of sight.

Connie sprang across the cockpit, going down on one knee to watch until it was submerged. Then she turned to me, delighted, and found her face a foot away from mine. We looked at one another, holding our breath, suddenly, and there is no question that what I thought to do was her thought, too. It was the thought of kissing, and I have no question that each of us wanted to.

But I had been waiting for that moment, thinking about that moment, because it was so evidently bound to come. If I am not faithful to my wife, it is nevertheless not because I think every pair of people's problems can be solved by coming physically together each time it seems it might be gratifying.

I think, in fact, that while it may help some combinations of two, there are quite a few others whose problems can be made unbearable that way. So I won't say that I hadn't thought about the confines of the boat, and how a thing like that might be managed, even there, if a pair found themselves full of hunger and complicity. It was not impossible. But at this moment, when it might so very easily have started off for Connie and me, I was applying one of the few things I think I know: that all any of us has and lives on is an idea of himself. And I judged that it might be as important to Connie's idea of herself that she didn't do those things as it was, say, to Helen's that she did them as and when she pleased.

So I said: "Turtle lover."

And she hesitated, and then said: "You'd have loved him too, if you'd seen his big, hooked nose." Then she moved away, facing east now, and after a while she got a half smile working with which to watch the sunrise.

"The sun doesn't come up like thunder, does it?" She said, after the silence.

"Doesn't come up like much of anything."

"It doesn't even come up, does it Barney? We spin slowly and meet the sun."

"Yeah," I said. "It's just been sitting back there, waiting for us."

5

It was the same day, mid-afternoon, that the cruise ship went by, not that that was a big thing in itself but it was what started Art talking about magic mushrooms. He was at the helm. Dave and I had just gone through the navigation procedure, with me using Kelso's sextant; now the skipper himself was repeating what we'd just gone through. Helen was sunbathing, her halter straps undone, a foot away from Art, and Connie was below watching Kelso work the tables and the chart.

"Ship ahoy," Dave said, suddenly, and I looked back to see a white steamer coming up astern. I don't know why none of us had noticed it earlier. It tooted at us; Kelso and Connie came up to see, and the passengers up there above us all came running to the rail to look down and wave.

We waved back, all feeling pretty lordly I suppose except Helen who said her privacy was being invaded.

"I can't raise up and look," she laughed.

"If you did, they'd all come swan-diving down," I said. "To share the trip."

When the boat had gone by and started dwindling, Helen said to Art: "You might have reached over and buttoned me, helmsman."

"Duty of the watch," Connie agreed.

"Will you next time, Angel?"

Art's reaction to being discomfitted was to talk: "What Barney said. About sharing a trip. Once I did in a way, down in Oaxaca, Mexico. Mrs. Barney. On a magic mushroom."

"You aren't even changing the subject very nicely."

"Narcotic mushrooms?" I asked, helping out.

"They give hallucinations. I never expected to. It's the only time I've ever been in Mexico, but I went with a friend who'd done it before. Just, just really to try the mushrooms. That was all we went for. We got construction jobs to earn the money for it and then flew straight to Oaxaca."

He had our attention, all but Kelso's, who was below again at the chart table.

"What do you do?" I asked. "Walk into a bar and say 'give me a shot of tequila and a mushroom chaser'?"

"It's a kind of ritual thing for those Indians down there," Art said. "They don't use the mushrooms all the time. It's something special, maybe once every year or two, when the crops have been especially good. Or bad. That's what my friend said. Then the Indian will take four or five days, and go to a mushroom woman's house. That's what we did."

"What sort of house does a mushroom woman keep?" Connie asked.

"Dirt floors," Art said. "It was kind of a sloppy hut, not like most of the Indians live in. She was a real crone, too, and she put a couple of blankets on the floor for us. Serapes. We lay there, waiting, for a couple of hours while she cooked the things into a broth, and talked to us. Only I couldn't understand it, and my friend Jerry couldn't very much, either. He claimed a lot of the words were Zapotec. I don't know. She was talking about trips. Then she brought us the broth to drink in old china cups, like you get at the dime store."

"Pretty tasty?" I asked.

"I don't know what she put in it, besides mushrooms," Art said. "It was bitter. But not bad, not like peyote."

Dave said: "Tried that too, have you?"

Art nodded. "Sure. We lay there on the floor, for a couple of days. One thing that was strange is, I started feeling I could understand what she was saying, where she said we were going. And then Jerry and I started going those places. Mexico City. Montreal. Heaven. Each of us making his own trip, but when Jerry'd get to something good, or I would, we could share it. Imagine that? Join the other guy. Take the other one along for a while. It was wild, and wonderful, except there was pain, all the time. In the legs. Jerry said the same thing afterwards; no matter how beautiful the trips were, you were always conscious that your legs were aching.

"The old woman kept bringing the broth, and we kept travelling until some kind of exhaustion. Then we slept, overnight there, and in the morning we went back to the city. It was a terrible morning for us, all dislocated and nervous. I was convinced that there was—excrement—on my face. And everyone could see it, and couldn't look at me. And I'd keep wiping my face, and going into places with mirrors to look at myself and wipe it."

"How dreadful," Connie said.

"Would you go back again and do it?" Helen asked.

Art thought a moment, and said: "Yes. I guess I would."

"If he had a good crop year," Connie said. "Or a bad one."

Dave turned, without saying anything, and went below. There was some quality in the way he did it that made me follow him. I went by Kelso, still working with his chart, and into the main cabin. Dave was sitting on the bunk.

"Now do you believe me, Barney?" he said.

"Believe what?"

"Not so loud, huh? That kid's smuggling dope on this boat. Heroin, or cocaine. I'm sure of it."

"For God's sake, Dave."

"I'm damned if I'll be a party to it," Dave said. "We've got to find it."

"Calm down, babe," I said. "Calm down."

He was very upset and very convinced. Connie said on watch that Dave had told her too. Art asked me the next morning what was wrong with Dave.

"He'll barely speak to me," the boy said. "But he watches me. All the time. Have I done something to piss him off?"

"No," I said. "Of course not. Dave isn't really well yet."

Connie said it would pass, quickly she hoped, but during our afternoon watch that day, Art came up and said:

"Barney, he's got my clothes all turned out of my suitcase, on the bed."

"What'd he say, Art?"

"I asked him what he was doing, and he said, 'That's all right about what I'm doing, kiddo.' What is it, Barney?"

"He's got it in his head you're running dope," I said. "You got any—supplies on board?"

"Some benzedrine. I gave it to the Skipper to lock up."

"Why don't you get the Skipper, Art?" I said. Kelso and Helen were up on the foredeck. I'm not sure what they were doing—counting flying fish, maybe, or Helen was drawing the old boy out and admiring his knowledge on the subject of jibs. Something like that. "Connie, want to take the wheel?"

Art went forward. "Maybe I should go to Dave," Connie said.

"Whatever you think."

Just then Dave came up. Connie went to him and said, "Dave!" and Kelso arrived, Art and Helen right behind him.

Dave turned away from Connie to the Skipper, and said grimly: "Sir, permission to search this boat?"

Kelso was very mild: "What's the trouble, Dave?" he asked.

"Sir, I have reason to believe there may be illegal cargo aboard."

"You don't mean Art's little pills?"

"I suspect it's worse than that, Skipper. Commercial quantities."

"Why, Dave?"

I don't know if Dave had an answer, but Art said: "May I have the key to the desk, Skipper?"

Kelso said, "All right. Surely." And handed him a key.

Art said: "Dave, you want to see what I've got locked away?"

Dave stood there stiffly, while Art went below.

Art said: "Coming down?" Quite pleasantly, but Dave still stood there, in the cockpit as Art left. I tried to remember to watch the compass. That was when Kelso said, very gravely:

"Dave, I want you to drop this matter. I'll vouch for young Art. You have my word on him. Will that be satisfactory?"

And with that, Dave seemed suddenly confused. The stiffness

melted; he sat on the edge of the cockpit and said: "Oh, yes. Yes, of course, Kelso. If you say."

And Art came up, with a couple of plastic drugstore bottles in his hand, smiled at Dave, and threw them into the sea.

"That's to turn on Davy Jones," he said.

"I'm sorry, Art," Dave said. "You didn't need to do that. I'm sorry."

Helen wanted to know, later, what it was all about, but she didn't want to know very badly. Mrs. Live-a-little, Love-a-little James was having too nice a time, with three fine men to work on, to want my opinions or information about any of them in much detail.

I didn't know what kind of intensities and diversions might be going on between her and Dave on their night watches, and didn't think about it much. On Kelso she practiced flattering admiration, which made the old sea goat puff up and do hornpipes. Art she plain teased hell out of.

There were many variations of the sunbath-with-straps-undone caper. There was one that evening, while Dave was sleeping his suspicions off, and Kelso had the wheel.

The sun was still bright at 6:30. Connie and I were having gin and limes, and Helen was making something pretty cute out of how to raise up high enough to sip at hers without her nipples showing.

We were moving through some sort of weedy area—something like the Sargasso Sea, I suppose, but not as large. And we were in a different latitude. But there was quite a lot of growth, floating at the surface, and there were seabirds feeding over it. We couldn't have been too far off some shore: the Dominican Republic was a couple of hundred miles to the west. Anyway, I was watching the birds through binoculars, sharing them with Connie and wondering what they were. Gannets? I didn't know.

Helen asked Art if he would be an angel and rub just a little suntan oil on her back.

Art looked at me with his brows up, and I said: "Go ahead, Angel. Oil the lady's back. She's left her maid at home."

Art grinned and I grinned, and there was a snapping sound.

"Fish!" Art yelled, put down the bottle of oil and scrambled over to one of our fishlines. I could see the clothespin we'd rigged hanging loose; I slung the binoculars and went back to where Art was.

Kelso turned the boat into the wind a little, to cut our speed, and said: "Here Barney. Use these."

He tossed me a pair of canvas gloves, which I shoved on. Art could do very little more than hold the line, barehanded; I took it from him, and tried to pull in. Whatever was back there, several hundred feet, was heavy to start with. The drag of the line and our forward speed made a feeling of extraordinary weight. I got my back into it and started to heave, and Art to catch the line, and wind it on a cleat. After a while, we traded, Art putting on the gloves. It took us twenty minutes to get the fish to the boat, and heave it up on deck.

It was a beautiful fish, though we didn't know exactly what kind—"One of the tuna family," Kelso said. I'd guess it went thirty pounds or so, blue-black with a castellated ridge along its back. A long, sleek fish; Art hit it on the head with something that looked like a blackjack, when we had it landed. I wondered at it. I'd never seen a fish like that.

"Poor Barney," Helen said. "He can't name it, so it doesn't exist."

But I could follow my own slovenly field procedure, and I did: I took a picture or two, to show someone who'd know, sometime.

Art brought up a big sharp knife from the galley, and said, "This is going to be so good."

He cut a big slab off each side of the fish—eight or ten pounds, I guess—flipped them over and sliced off the skin.

"Two fillets of unknown fish," he said. We dumped the carcass back into the sea, pulled up a pail of water to sluice the deck, carried the fillets to the galley and broiled them. We used just a little oil, and cooked them fast—ten minutes on each side—and Art was right: that sea flesh, so fresh there might almost have been some muscular quiver left in it when it started to cook, tasted like nothing I'd ever had before. A deep-ocean taste, untainted by exposure to the weak, warm winds of land. Its texture seemed almost crisp, more vegetable somehow than meat—like a perfect cucumber or a melon, but hot and tender.

"Golly," Helen said, tasting it. "Whoever caught this fish gets a hero's reward."

"Art," I said. "He rigged the line."

"Barney," said Art. "Barney pulled it in."

"As a matter of fact," said Kelso, who was at the wheel still. We were all eating in and around the cockpit, and he had a plate in his lap, too. "As a matter of fact, I caught the fish."

"Captain Skipper, sir!" Art said, reproachfully.

"I saw the birds feeding," Kelso said. "And I went quite a way off course to run through the area where they were." He was smiling. He was being quite loquacious, though I noticed he wasn't eating much. "Where the birds feed are little fish. Where the little fish are, you find big ones."

"You see," Helen said to Art. "You might just as well have oiled me. Captain Kelso didn't need your help nearly as much as I did."

Dave said the fish was good. He had a drink and, I believe, apologized privately, first to Art, then to Kelso. When he and Helen took the boat over at ten, he seemed himself again. His new, wounded and resting, self, turned inward because of the wounds, resting while his strength gathered. He was sorry enough, it seemed to me, but not deeply; deeply, I guessed, he was driven into indifference by what had happened. Pretty hard on a man like Dave Doremus, to have to make himself indifferent.

To Guanahani.

At six next morning I turned the wheel over to Connie and went through the galley into the main cabin to wake our relief. It was the first time that I'd needed to, and I was a little surprised. Generally Kelso would appear, brisk and ready to go, fifteen or twenty minutes before his morning watch started. Then Connie and I would invent some new silly way of waking Art, who slept as heavily as any boy. One morning Connie would tell him, in a mother voice, that he had to get up this instant or he'd be late to school; once she whispered in his ear, "Artie, the movie's over. Please wake up and take me home." And another I yelled, "Time's up, LaBranche. Get out of the penalty box and show me something."

I walked through the galley trying to invent today's gag. I wondered if Kelso'd mind my trying *Reveille* on his flute. But when I got through the door and into the cabin, I saw that Art was already up and dressed.

It was Kelso who was still in bed, turned towards the wall.

"Who's your lazy friend, Art?" I asked.

"Barney, the skipper's sick."

"He's sick?" That indestructible man? I'd been coming to think of him as being made of the same scrubbed teak—hard, pale, unvarnished—as his own boat's deck. What could attack a man like that? Then I remembered: "The ulcer?"

"Partly. And some kind of malaria or something, that hits along with it. He really can't get up."

"Happen before?"

"Last fall. Off Florida."

"Let's go in the galley," I said.

"It doesn't matter," Art said. "He's so weak, he probably can't understand us. We better wake Dave."

"I'm awake." Dave sat up.

On the other side of the cabin, Kelso moaned and turned towards us. He was shivering, but his eyes were closed. "We've

250

got to keep him covered," Art said. "When he wakes up, there's some quinine stuff."

"How long will it last?" Dave asked. "Any idea?"

"A couple of days, last time," Art said. "We were sailing south, to pick up a charter at Key West. He'd got the flu, I guess. Something to start it all off."

"You bring the boat in, by yourself?"

"We were only a day out, and sailing coastwise. So I could see where we were. I just got the sails down, in a terrible mess and crept back up the coast till I found the harbor, under power."

"Good, Art," Dave said. Suddenly he sounded fine. "With three of us maybe we can keep the sails up." He slid onto his feet. Like Art and me, he slept in his pants, so getting dressed was just a matter of putting on sneakers and a shirt.

"The bad time's when he starts to get better." Art grinned. "I brought a big piece of rope down into the cabin, about three inches thick, and said I was going to tie him in the bunk. We were already back at the marina, though, and I'd wired the charter party."

"What'd Kelso do?"

"Laughed, and went to sleep for twenty-four hours. He was okay when he woke up. Hey, Dave, it's my watch. I can hang onto the course while you finish sleeping."

"Sure," said Dave, grinning. "And which one of you hotshots is going to decide what course to hang onto?"

"Same one we've been on," Art said. One of the things I was having to get used to about ocean cruising was that there was hardly any tacking. Changing tacks took a lot of calculation out there; mostly we sailed long, straight lines, for hours at a time. "Been on it two days."

"But we haven't. Remember we went off it last night? To go through the weeds, and catch the fish."

"That's right," Art said.

"Kelso didn't give me a new heading when I went on watch," Dave said. "It was hazy, and he couldn't get a star. Neither could I. We were waiting for the sun this morning."

"Let's go," I said. And we headed for the chart table at the rear of the galley, where the sextants were kept.

Art said he'd try to get some medicine into Kelso. Dave and I went up on deck.

"Neither of you looks a thing like my relief," Connie said.

"Art'll be up in a minute, chief," I told her, and Dave said:

"Ma'am, we aim to navigate this vessel."

"What did you do with Kelso?"

"Mutiny," I said.

"Check the keel," Dave suggested. "I believe you'll find him down there being hauled."

"All this morning wit," Connie said. "And me too sleepy to keep up with it."

Art appeared then, took the wheel and told her what had happened.

"Men are wonderful," Connie said. "Someone's sick and delirious in a little cabin that I walk through twenty times a day, but men are going to make patronizing jokes, and I won't realize anything is wrong."

"Good night, Constance," I said, fiddling with the sextant.

"Sweet dreams, ma'am," said Dave.

Dave was far better than I with figures. We had our sights taken, agreed on a reading, and went below at the same time. But he'd worked through the tables and had our position figured five minutes before I did. At least I came out in the same spot, and without cribbing from him. I was pleased with myself.

"There," I said. "Now I think if we go up on deck, there'll be a nice black X in the water, where we're just crossing over."

Though Art protested he was perfectly able to stay at the helm four hours at a time, and had been doing it all winter, Dave and I extended our watches to shorten his. When one of us wasn't with him, Connie or Helen generally was.

Helen was alarmed by the situation for perhaps ten minutes; then, when she saw how firmly Dave was taking charge, she seemed almost pleased. In a way we all were, not that we ever ceased to pull for Kelso to be up and with us; but it was really heartening to see the change in Dave. By the end of that day he was handling everything, not just the sextant and the helm and sails, but his funny crew as well, with good-humored deftness and charm that went beyond tact. He started being like the old Dave, seeing to it that we all had a good time.

On the second day of his illness, the Skipper was rational and able to eat; he and Dave had a long consultation, and after it Kelso agreed not to get up until his fever'd been normal for twelve hours. "Since you're here, Dave," he said, I doubt if there were many amateurs around Kelso would have felt that way about.

Helen fussed over him. "I tell the children twenty-four."

"You put them to bed earlier than I go to bed, too," Kelso said.

"Well, it isn't normal yet." Helen read the thermometer. "So don't start counting hours."

That afternoon, there was a second conference, with Kelso, Dave, Art and me. We went over a number of things, some of which meant very little to me. When we'd done, Dave said:

"All right if us Skippers have a private chat, mates?"

"It's my watch," I said. "I'm on my way."

"I want to pull the fish lines in," Art said. "And make sure we've still got lures."

About fifteen minutes later Dave came up, smiling, and said to me and Connie: "We're going to run a little more before the wind," and gave us a new bearing to follow, a little more north-west than the north-north-west we'd been going in since we'd left St. Thomas, seven days before.

"Humph," I said, trying to visualize the chart as it looked when we'd done our navigation exercise earlier.

"Got the Skipper's permission to navigate alone for a couple of days, Ozark Lad," Dave said. "Will you mind?"

"Lock the chart away?"

Dave grinned and showed me the key. Then he put it in his pocket.

"You look smug and mysterious, sir," Connie said.

"Your smug, mysterious servant, ma'am."

"Let's infuriate him, and pretend we don't notice," Connie said.

"Dave," said Helen, interrupting her perpetual sunbath. "What are you going to do with us?"

"Take advantage of the Captain's illness," Dave said. "To sail this craft away to where I've always dreamed of sailing."

Art, still busy with the fishlines, said: "It's like the movies. We'll never be heard of again."

"Notes in bottles," Helen said. "We must save all our bottles from now on."

"If there are wild goats," Connie said, "I shall learn to milk them."

"We'll make cheese," said Helen. "And rum from wild sugar cane for Barney."

Dave waited patiently for someone to speak the cue. It was Connie who said, curiously: "Where is it that you've always dreamed of sailing, Dave?"

He smiled: "Guanahani," he said, and on the eighth day out, from St. Thomas in the Virgin Islands, we reached it.

It was great, the way he had us all excited and puzzled. Neither he nor Kelso ever gave a hint, beyond that name.

It was just a little after five in the morning. The sun was low and bright behind us, and the day calm. I was at the helm, when Dave came up, looking at his watch.

"See anything before sunrise?" he asked.

"A freighter, about 3:30," I told him.

"No other lights?"

"Were we meant to?" Connie asked.

"No. Not for another half an hour."

"You're going to make a landfall in precisely half an hour?" I asked. It was all very well to navigate, but to time the first sight of land, after seven days at sea, would be a touch miraculous. In the old days Dave could produce little miracles like that. I was hoping for it harder than I'd have cared to admit out loud.

"At five-forty-five," Dave said. "Steady as she goes, Barney, if it's all right with you. May I get Helen up for this?"

"If I knew what it was, I could say whether she'd slug you for waking her, or slug you for not."

At five-forty, he had everyone on deck.

Kelso came up, too, bundled by Art into sweaters and a dressing gown. We'd been seeing birds from time to time, and the color of the water was changing. But it was Kelso who knew at just what moment it could be said for sure that the vague bulk detaching itself from the horizon was no cloud.

"Land ho," he said quietly. "Congratulations, Dave."

It was an island, and we were sailing obliquely by it.

"May I break out the spinnaker, Skipper, and turn in?"

"Oh yes. By all means, Dave."

"What is it?" Helen asked.

"We've reached the Bahamas. That's . . . Guanahani."

"Is there really a Bahama Island called Guanahani?" Art asked. "I sneaked a look at your chart, and no such thing."

"Yes, there is," Kelso said.

"Guanahani was the Carib Indian name," Dave said, "for the island that the Spaniards called San Salvador."

"Columbus!" Connie cried. We all stared, and Art said softly that he would be damned. The rising sun behind us seemed to catch the island, and it gleamed.

Kelso said: "As far as anyone can tell, Dave's made the same landfall that Columbus made." After a moment he went on: "Land doesn't change that much in five hundred years. We're seeing it now about as the crew of the *Santa Maria* saw it. When we put the spinnaker up, it will be . . . very much the same course, I should think."

"Let's get it up," Art cried, and I was right after him.

With the big sail riding high and full in front of us, and our main all the way out, we made a stately run, then, for an hour, towards San Salvador, watching the hills separate out and become an outline, seeing it emerge towards definition.

Kelso Clark never took his eyes off it. "I wonder why I never thought of doing this?" he said, at one point.

Then there came the time when Dave said, "All right, Skipper. Thanks."

And Kelso, "Thank you, Dave. Want to get the main sheet?" And took his boat's helm back. I went up to the foredeck to help Art get in the spinnaker, and when we got back to the cockpit, Kelso said: "Want to take it, Art? 342's your heading now."

And we were sailing north again.

Helen asked me, as she and I and Connie all went below to go to bed, why I supposed Dave hadn't gone in any closer.

"We had to make the turn," I said, "before we could get close enough to see boats or buildings, didn't we?"

"Sorry," Helen said. "Dumb of me. What a man you married, Connie."

2

Someday, I promised myself, we would charter—with Kelso, if he were still sailing these waters—and we'd bring my three American children here, just this way. They should see Guanahani, I thought, as Dave had shown it to us, coming to it silently out of the sun, with only the wind for power. It was the same wind that the Genoan used. It brought the *Niña*, the *Pinta*, the *Santa Maria* and *The Bosun Bird*. It was an old wind blowing out of Africa and Europe, the trade wind.

I would want to turn the kids away, too, as Dave had us, because there would be no gentle Indians on shore to greet them, with wonder and with gifts—only the descendants of the Africans and Europeans, like ourselves, who'd been blown there and stayed. Land doesn't change much in five hundred years, but the tribes of man do; the Carib Indians are long extinct, in one of history's interminable genocides.

I didn't know as I lay in my bunk, thinking of San Salvador, lying to port now and starting to fade back, whether the kids would be moved as I was, but they ought to have a chance to be. I was grateful to Dave: after you're through your twenties, there isn't much left in the way of good experience that's really a new kind for you. Life becomes a matter of repeating, as you can, familiar pleasures, and excitements you have known before.

As I went to sleep, I was thinking it was fine that Kelso was well again. And hoping Dave was, too.

We got back, that day, to our regular scheme of watches with Kelso up. We were sailing into the outer banks of the Bahamas now, over shoal water sometimes that was beautifully blue. We were catching so many fish we finally took the lines in—barracuda, a dolphin, and what I think were bonito. I took color pictures, so we could find out for sure. We began to think about an anchorage, where we could rest a day, swimming and exploring and lying on the sand before we went on in to Nassau and city things. We all told one another Kelso needed it, but of course we'd all begun to need it.

In the earliest hours of the day on which we found our name-less, uninhabited cay, Connie and I had one of our more intense times on watch. I won't say that it went on for four whole hours that way. No one over the age of seventeen could take that much intensity without breaking up. But it got pretty strong, between laughs.

It was a watch that started strangely, too. Helen came to wake me—usually she was tired at two in the morning. I go to sleep hard, but I wake easy, so all she'd have to do was touch my arm in passing, and say,

"Time, Barney." That would be enough.

This time though she hesitated after she said it, instead of going on forward to wake Connie and fall in bed.

"Can I get you some coffee, Barney?" she asked softly. I was sitting up by then, trying to remember which goes on first, the shoe or the sock. I was somewhat surprised at her offer, but it sounded nice.

"That's a kind thought," I said. "Yes. Coffee, please."

Helen went back to the galley. By the time she came with a cup of black I was ready to go on deck.

"You're a kind woman, Miss Sweets," I said, but Helen replied in her most serious tone:

"I wish I were." She sat opposite me, on Dave's empty bunk—he was up on deck, hanging onto the wheel till I arrived. She watched me drink part of the coffee, rise up and start for the galley door. She watched and didn't move.

"Night, Helen," I said. "Thanks."

"Would you wake me for the sunrise?"

"Really?"

"Please. I liked seeing it yesterday morning."

"Sure," I said. "I sure will."

Dave sat very still at the wheel when I came up. While we'd been moving towards Guanahani, we'd gotten into a little pattern of clowning about changing over ("James Beauchamp Clark, reporting, Mr. Bryan." "They shall not crossify you on a cruce of silver, Champ."). This time, he just sat, almost as Helen had, watching me come up. When I sat by him and took the spokes, he said:

"Trip's about done."

"We'll still have the Gulf stream, after Nassau. And the waterway."

"Won't need so many hands for that."

"We won't have Helen," I said. She'd planned to fly back to the children when we reached Nassau. "Well. Swimming and beach tomorrow, anyway. This morning, rather."

"Yes. Looking forward to land?"

"Isn't everyone?"

"Barney, does Kelso mean to lie over tonight at the beach?"

"Yeah. He wants to sail into Nassau harbor by daylight."

Dave stood, sighed and stretched. He stepped to the edge of the cockpit and looked back at the bright wake we trailed. Then he turned back towards me, and said:

"Man gets pretty impatient, I guess. To get along and meet his fate. What do you do when you get there, gentlemen? Say, 'Hi, Fate. Glad to meet you'? Steady as she goes, Barney."

"Steady as she goes, Dave," I said.

Moods. The moods on that watch. Connie was in one too, when she came up. And she was ten or fifteen minutes late, not that she wasn't welcome to the extra sleep.

"Sorry, watch mate," she said. "Dreams. I couldn't be sure which was sleep and which was waking. I thought Helen was my brother, Buddy."

"Like your dreams?"

"I like it now."

"Me too. Tell about the dreams."

"No. Sad dreams. Sort of, slow and sad. I kept wanting to speed up the projector, but then the . . . pitch of sound would have risen, too. Wouldn't it? From a murmur to a kind of keening . . . ."

"Wake up, Connie," I said.

"Yes. Talk, will you Barney?"

I said there was something I'd been thinking of telling her.

"Politics. The nation?" Connie asked. "Whither are we drifting? . . . I'm sorry."

"Never mind."

"I said I'm sorry. And I did ask you to talk."

With Helen I'd have told her to talk to herself. With Connie, even when she thought she'd been sharp, there just wasn't any edge to her.

"All right. I was telling you when I first felt old?"

"Yes. You were trying to catch a jet in a sewing machine. On the slag heap at 23. Poor Captain Barney."

"There was another time, connected to it, when I first felt wise. Is that a good dogwatch topic?"

"Dogwatch doesn't start till four," she said. "But don't wait."

"Truman was in it," I said. "MacArthur later. Korea. That's bitter stuff, that wise."

"Yes," Connie said. "It's different from old. Old's just . . . what you said, Barney. The taste of mortality. But when you start tasting the wise, you're beginning to feel ready for it, too. Aren't you? A hint that there could be a time when you won't care too much if you do die. That's how the wise tastes. What happened, Barney?"

"I liked Korea when it started. I was on a business trip, to Boston. There was pretty heroic stuff going on. Inchon. The world learning to prevent crimes against peace—sounds pretty dumb, now, I know, but that was before MacArthur turned it into a regular little stupid war. Anyway, I was in Boston, the world was in Inchon. And I went to see about reenlisting, getting retrained. Flier with combat experience reporting for duty, world."

"Why not?"

"Man wasn't interested. He said if I'd wanted to keep my hand in, why hadn't I joined the Air Reserve?"

"Oh, Barney." I could see her fine warm smile in the starlight. "They wouldn't let you be a minuteman."

"That's it, of course. I must have thought it was still some quaint, old democratic time. When being a citizen meant you were supposed to be able to step out of your front door and fall in with the militia. March off to defend the right."

"They could have used you. They found a use for Buddy."

"They didn't want any damn citizens fooling around with their expensive airplanes," I said. "When the government gets away from the people, the armies get professional."

"And sometime, somewhere, they start getting licked."

"MacArthur made Korea into the Punic War," I said. "I about

choked on my newspaper, the morning that he crossed the parallel. It was that . . . bitter taste of wise, I guess, I choked on. Helen had seen the paper first, and wasn't a bit surprised. Maybe she was born wise."

Connie said: "Even little girls know that when boys start fighting, they aren't going to stop until someone stops them— or one of them is badly hurt."

"What did Buddy say about it?"

"He was sorry he'd gone back in. But all he did was work for the judge advocate. My minuteman brother."

That was one of the things we talked about on our long watch, sailing a little east of north now, up between the islands.

Once, later on, Connie said: "Barney, what's it like in Scott's Fort?"

"Like any town. Like your town—no, it's not. Your town's grown, so there's more new in it. Scott's Fort is pleased to be about the way it always was."

"That sounds nice."

"There aren't any signs at the city limits, asking travellers to join the community," I said. "No one's out scouting up new industries, the way Dave did for Wonamasset."

"He might take that job," Connie said. "If there really is one."

"With us? The fiberglass division?"

"A day or two ago, he spoke about it. I don't know how seriously."

"I wish he would."

"I like those signs," Connie said.

"What?"

"The town signs, on the city limits. I remember one, 'Learn our History. Join Our Future' And another, so simple and nice: 'We're Growing. Stay and Grow With Us.'"

"The West," I said.

"Oh, and I remember one. I forget the name of the town. Let's say it was, oh, Fairfield. Can we call it Fairfield?"

"Sure. What does the sign say at Fairfield?"

"Joe and I were driving into it, and it was dusk. Somewhere in the Middle West. And we were tired—I guess it's an ordinary enough sign, but it touched me like poetry. It said: 'If You Lived in Fairfield, You'd be Home Now.' Do you like that?"

"I like the way you tell it," I said.

Probably an hour after that, when she had the wheel, Connie was singing to herself. I was in the galley, but the door stood open as it always did in clear weather, and her song was on the wind. Often she sang that way, a lullaby kind of way without much tune to it, and any nonsense words that came to her. I don't think she was very conscious of what syllables she sounded, when she sang that way. I always felt that trying to make them out, on my part, would be a kind of eavesdropping, but I couldn't miss the ones she was singing. They were my children's names:

Lum, lumla Goober, Brad and lumma deeda Mary Bliss. And la, lalam . . . .

I went up on deck quickly, and she stopped singing as she always did when I reappeared. All I could do was hope she hadn't heard herself as well as I had.

"Shall I take it now?" I said.

"Yes, please." As she stood up, she pressed against me all of a sudden, still holding the wheel with one hand. Our cheeks went together. My arm went around her, and she said:

"Oh, Barney."

"Connie, Connie, Connie."

"My cheek's wet."

I pressed my own cheek harder against it. "There's salt in the air tonight, shipmate," I said. God I ached for that lady, every way there is to ache. "Turn loose," I said. "You'll sail us . . . into a great big coral rock, or something."

She pulled away, and said, "I just wish I could. I'd do it." I sat down. "Then you'd have to save me. You'd have to swim with my life preserver strap in your teeth for miles and miles."

"Not unless you hurt your leg," I said.

"I'd hurt it, darn you . . . ." And she kicked me, damned if she didn't, with the toe of her topsider, hard in the shin.

"Ouch," I said. "I'll send troops." But neither of us could quite get the other laughing that time.

Just before I went below to call Helen for the sunrise, we spoke for what was, I guess, the last time that trip, about Kennedy. I'd have said we were pretty well talked out there, but Connie had one other angle:

"I thought of something odd. I think he meant most to you of any of us, but . . . well. He pinned a medal on Art, once. Kelso used to see him sail. Dave knew him, of course, and I once shook his hands at one of those coffees that his sisters ran in Massachusetts. Even Helen, when she was dancing school age, probably saw him. You're the only one of us who didn't."

"I'd call that truer than it is significant, chief," I said.

"Probably, old and wise Sir Barney. Probably. Sir Barney of the Slag Heap."

"Anyway, you could be wrong. About which of us takes it hardest. Remember how upset Art was, the first time—second time—I saw him?"

"Art gets cross at our being proprietary about Kennedy," Connie admitted. "He didn't seem old to Art. Did he seem young to Kelso?"

It was light enough now so that I could see coloring. Her tone of voice was getting light now, too. Enough intensity.

"Kelso told me that he would have voted for Kennedy," I said. "And ruined a perfect lifetime of Republican ballots. I don't think Kennedy seemed so much young as he did a . . . oh, a kind of new incarnation of Theodore Roosevelt. 'The strenuous life.' The books. The enjoyment and concealed anxiety. Teddy was president when Kelso was my boy Goober's age. . . ." I hurried by that, before I could start feeling awkward for having said it. "And he admired Wilson, but his first vote was for Warren G."

"Warren G. and Calvin C.," Connie said. "We've had some honeys, haven't we?"

There were islands in sight on both sides as we sailed—small ones, and quite distant. I was glad for once that the watch was ending. I'd loved the long quiet hours with Connie, but it had reached a point where it was hard on both of us. A kick in the shin, or a try at laughing, was like water on a hot day; you got thirsty again so soon.

"I'm supposed to get Helen up," I said. "For the sunrise."

I went below and into the main cabin. Kelso was lying awake.

"Land in sight?"

"On both sides."

"I'll get us located." Kelso swung his legs out of the bunk, sat up, and scratched himself. He looked okay.

I went into the forward cabin. Helen was sleeping very deeply, and I looked at her for a moment, feeling hardly anything except that it was rather a shame to wake her. I was surprised, when I did, to have her reach her arms around me, pull me half into the bunk and kiss me.

"Gracious, Miss Sweets," I said. I hadn't closed the door coming in, and felt I'd better push away. Kelso might have been embarrassed. At the same time, what with the intensity over Connie, and the fact that the trip had gone on so long without permitting intimacies, I also thought about closing the door and staying there. I was still on watch, but Kelso, getting up, would have taken my place. We could, Helen and I, have worked out some time alone there in the forward cabin whenever we liked, during the trip. Concealment, if not privacy.

But this was a sexless trip, really, for all hands. With so much continence being practiced, the married thing would really have been out of tone. It seemed to me that Helen felt that, too, and that when I kissed her back, lightly, neither of us was really much inclined towards more than an exchange of promises. And I did wonder if she might not have preferred, on some ideal yacht, some perfect Helen cruise, that it were one of the other three men on board, coming in to where the cabin was warm with her sleeping. It wasn't a disturbing thought, especially.

I went humming back up, bantered a little with Kelso, and was about to trade off with Connie at the wheel when Helen arrived.

She was wearing slacks, a light sweater and no lipstick. She had her arms crossed in front, hands close to her neck, so that her shoulders were pulled forward, making her look small and guarded.

She registered Connie and Kelso, big-eyed, nodded a silent good morning to them, and avoided looking at me. She went quietly away, up towards the foredeck.

I waited till she reached the bow, and asked Connie to excuse me. Kelso was busy with his sextant.

I went forward to where Helen stood, and said to her back: "Did you want to see me?"

Helen shook her head without turning it. Her hair had a nice luster to it, I thought, under where the sun had faded the strands on top.

"Okay."

So I turned and started back.

"Barney?"

I stopped. Now she was looking over her shoulder at me. "I just want to be alone to think."

"Hard to manage these days," I said. "But we'll do our best to let you."

"It is hard," she said. "That's why I asked you to get me up. Barney?"

"If madame will command me?"

"Please don't be flippant."

"I wasn't planning to be any way at all," I said. "Except absent." Fifty-two feet absent, if that's what the pretty girl wished.

"I wanted you to get me up so that ... when Dave was sleeping."

"Okay."

"He asked me to marry him last night."

I stared at her. Finally I said, and not very flippantly, either: "The man's a marrying fool, isn't he?"

"You think he's a fool?"

"I think he's partway out of his head, Helen. Not for wanting to marry you—that might make some wild kind of sense."

"He loves me."

"You real sure about that? What'd you tell the man? I thought you found him kind of erratic."

"No. Not recently. He's much different now. I said I'd think about it." She said that as if it were an absolutely natural and reasonable thing, as if she and I were friends and she was telling me something interesting, a little impatient that I was slow to savor the situation.

"You're a little out of your head, too," I said.

"Go away."

"No. I don't think I will. You want me to believe Dave was serious?"

"I'll tell you about proposals, my friend," Helen said, standing taller. The wistful girl voice and pose hadn't worked so well. "I've heard my share. They don't start serious. They start with a certain kind of joke, to see how you take it. So the man can pull back chuckling, if you're cool and sorry."

"What was Dave's little joke?" I asked. "Let's you and me jump ship, and fly to Guanahani. Where nobody will ever find us."

"New York," Helen said.

"Pretty drab." It did start to sound as if Dave expected this to be taken seriously, but I wasn't going to show I thought so.

"Because I'm leaving for New York when we get to Nassau."

"Tomorrow? I'd call that a fast move."

"For God's sake, Barney. Can't you see that I'm upset by it?"

"Attracted?" I couldn't really believe she was. Helen, like many of the women who pass for wild, isn't really—if wild means impulsive. What Helen does can be totally careless as far as consequences go, but it's rational enough as far as her deciding coolly what it is she wants. It would have made her nicer, I suppose, if I could have thought her hesitation was caused by some concern for Dave, who had apparently become to some degree her lover in their series of midnights. And who was not a stable man, any longer. I started to tighten up, in spite of myself. "I said, are you attracted?"

"If I knew, I'd tell you," Helen said. "Go away, please. I came here to be by myself, and find out."

"Then you shouldn't have spilled it," I said. "I don't feel a thing in the world, oddly enough, like strolling back to the cockpit and chatting with the folks while we wait for your decision."

"Oh don't you? Dave says Connie is in love with you."

"Connie is so damned unhappy she'd be in love with anyone who was decent to her," I said.

"That's you. Gallahad just isn't in it."

"Oh no," I said. "No fight this morning. Thanks just the same."

"Shipboard romance. How conventional of you."

"Oh boy. Get those tables turning."

"I'm supposed to fly off to the children, and leave you two

265

crossing the Gulf Stream with your sweet sorrows and your dear crew of friends?"

I took a deep breath and said: "Helen, sometime this morning Kelso's going to sail us into a cove somewhere, and there'll be a beach. What do you say we wait, and take the dory, and go off where you can raise your voice without people who don't need to be involved hearing you?"

"I'm going to the beach with Dave." She said.

"I suggest you plan to spend a few dull moments talking to your husband first. After that I don't give a damn what you do."

I could have wished that last part was less of a lie.

3

Kelso found the cove at noon. I'd been asleep five hours by then. I'd gone down and taken a belt of 120-proof, Hudson's Bay Rum, straight, told myself that whatever I was going to do, I'd do it when I woke. And surprised myself into believing it and going right to sleep. I didn't even wake at ten when Dave must have got up, across from me, to go on watch.

When I did wake, it was because I heard chains clanking in the dark, and opened my eyes to find it light. The anchor was going out, and the motion of *The Bosun Bird* had almost stopped. Then it did stop, with a little tug, and I was fully awake and very clearly aware of how I meant to go about things.

I put on swimming trunks and sneakers, and scrubbed hell out of my teeth. Then I pulled a light grin over them and followed the flash they made up onto deck.

Art and Kelso had broken out face masks, and the first thing they were going to do was dive under the boat to fix a gadget that sticks into the water and tells you what your speed is. The thing had got fouled going through some fishing weeds, a hundred miles back up the creek. There were only two of the masks, and no help needed.

I hollered, hearty as a scoutmaster: "Come on, Dave, let's sling the old dory into the water."

There was pretty swimming-beach around us on three sides, a couple of hundred yards away, and the small cay seemed to be uninhabited.

We climbed the hatch covers and started undoing lines, and I kept the Rover Boy chatter going all the time. "We'll check that beach, and make sure it's safe for a landing party. Get rid of the lines, yeah, and get back here. Go into the ferry business. Right? We'll commandeer those face masks, and do a little skinny skin diving. . . ." Stuff like that.

By the time we had the dory over the side, I'd managed to establish by sheer loudness, because Helen didn't gather herself to object as loudly and Connie didn't care, that Dave and I would make the first trip to the beach alone.

Actually Helen did call, as Dave and I were floating away, rigging the tiller and raising the little, red, leg-of-mutton sail: "Barney. Wait. We want to go, too."

By that time I had my head of silly steam built up to where I could yell back: "At ease, sailor. We'll test the defenses. Cover us."

I handed Dave the mainsheet, he tucked the tiller under his arm, and we went bouncing off in the Caribbean breeze. It was natural to him to do the sailing; I'd counted on that. I didn't let myself off being assinine until I was standing on sand, water around my ankles, pulling the little boat up towards land.

Dave said, suddenly: "What are we doing this for, Barney? We could have brought some others."

I hung on to the floating dory, and had him caught.

"Come on, Dave," I said, soberly now. "Get out a minute, will you?"

He looked at me, mild and inquiring.

"All right. Stay there if you want," I said. "I hear you tried to make another bet last night."

"Helen told you?" he sounded pleased. "Good."

"It is?"

He smiled, with some kind of crazy confidence. "That means that she's considering it."

"Oh. Passionately," I said. "Thrilled to have it to consider."

"Don't be unfair . . . oh, well. It doesn't matter, does it? I don't suppose she's always been fair herself. That's part of that strange, rather lovely essence. You know what I suspect, Barney? I suspect you understood Helen quite well once, but that you've ceased to care to."

"Whereas you do?" I said. "After ten days acquaintance."

"In ten days we've spent eighty hours together. Forty of them by ourselves. In a normal situation, that much acquaintance could take years."

"I'm familiar with the abnormality," I said. "I've been putting in some hours like that myself."

"Of course. Helen and I realize."

"What?"

"That you're in love with Connie."

"For Christ's sake," I said. "Sure I am. And in love with the Caribbean Sea, and *The Bosun Bird*. And her captain and all members of the crew." I wanted to take it easy on him. I really did. "But it hadn't occurred to me to sign on for a life cruise," I said.

"But why not?" Dave seemed excited, as if I'd really given him some sort of opening. "Why shouldn't you? What's wrong with you, Barney? Change your life, if you don't like it. That's what Helen and I are talking about, dope. We're thinking about four people, not just two. I'm sorry it's so abrupt, but let's recognize it, when something good happens to us, huh? Why waste another day, another hour?"

"Oh, come ashore Dave," I said, and I gave the dory a big heave, stepped out of the water and beached the man. "We're on land, now. It's morning."

He sat in the boat, still holding the useless tiller. I felt the solidness of earth through the bottoms of my feet, the absence of movement, and for an instant it made me dizzy. Then steadiness came up my legs, and a tentative feeling, like being light-headed all over, left my body for the first time since St. Thomas. "I won't have any more of this, Dave. I'm surprised I even have to say so."

Something left his face when I said that, some kind of radiance. I felt like a bully, and yet I doubt that what robbed my friend of energy was what I said so much as his own, stodgy sanity returning.

"You don't really need a reason," I said. "But I'll give you one. It's an old and settled habit of mine, protecting Helen. Left over from something, if you like. If you were in love with her. Or looking for anything but another bet, it could be different. I won't let her be your desperation move."

"I guess you won't."

"It seems to me the wheel's been spinning a long time, boy, for you and me. I think we've both made all the bets the house allows." Then I added, being brutal: "Lousy one anyway, for you. Helen's mother's money is safe as Fort Knox. She can get a thousand for this or that, like a kid getting extra allowance. Even so, it's more like hundreds."

Dave looked away. When he looked back he said: "Think what you want of me, Barney. I hardly know what to think of myself this morning. When you cool off, I'd like it if you'd ask yourself if my motives could have been that simple."

"Yeah?"

"I guess it sounds . . . nutty and sudden, in the light of day. But Helen seemed to . . . I really didn't think it was going to offend you. And maybe, maybe I've got someone whose protection I was thinking of, too? Less of a habit, but the same responsibility. If you'd felt the way Helen and I believed you felt, she might have been okay."

It took me a moment to realize he was talking about Connie.

"Oh God, Barney. I used to be able to trust my judgment of anybody." Some kind of spasm twitched across his face; he closed his eyes. When he opened them he said: "Today I'm wrong about my oldest friend. I don't know what's happened."

I said: "We're just not twenty any more."

"You want me to get out so you can clobber me, I will. I go down easy these days."

"Leave it to the twenty-year-olds," I said. "We got a day with Helen to get through."

"Want me to tell her?"

"Might be best."

"Okay." There was a pause. Then he said, "There's something else I've been wanting to tell you for a while."

"What, Dave?"

"Did you ever wonder why I made such an ass of myself that day, the day Kennedy was shot? Trying to get you and Helen to come along, as if it hadn't happened."

"I think I understand. It was for Connie."

"And myself. If we could have had a trip like this . . . ?"

"Things might have been different," I said. "I wish they were, Dave. I surely do."

Then, being me, I stewed all the way back to *The Bosun Bird* over the dumbest question people ever ask themselves: if I could have known, would I have acted any differently? Felt Goober in my arms and had to make the flat admission that I couldn't have.

After that our day on the beach was as quiet and pleasant as I hoped it would be, except for one muddled-up half hour. We'd been collecting shells to take back home to the kids, sand dollars and periwinkles and conches. We'd dived and got some coral fans. Now Art and I were playing catch, with a piece of driftwood we'd found, worn splinterless and into the general shape of a football. You could even get it to spiral a little.

Helen, who'd been in a slight pique all day, predictably enough, was sunbathing again. She's a strong swimmer, and had swum to the beach instead of waiting for us to get her with the boat, and that took some of the energy out of her irritation.

Near her, but not really close, Dave lay on his stomach with his eyes closed. He was back to wearing a tee shirt with his swim trunks, to cover the scars.

Kelso was letting Connie sail him around the cay in the dory.

"The long bomb," Art announced, and I went sprinting down the beach and caught the driftwood in high style, over my shoulder. But I couldn't reach him, throwing it back; the kid had a tremendous arm. He started running out into the water for the short passes I threw him, and after a time, when we had run ourselves half-silly and out of breath, I overthrew, and he yelled,

"End of the half," and I came panting in without our ball.

"Let's hit the locker room," I said, and we fell onto the sand, heaving and happy, between Dave and Helen.

After we'd got our breath, Art grinned in Helen's direction; she was up on her elbows, with her head thrown back, letting the rays get at her throat.

"Look," Art said, pointing up into the world's clearest sky. "It's a U-2."

"What?" Helen opened her eyes.

"Spy plane," I cried, getting into the game. "Just finished flying over Cuba."

"I don't hear a plane," Helen said.

"Now, Mrs. Barney. It wouldn't be much of a spy plane if you could hear it," said Art.

"Do you actually see anything up there?"

"How could he?" I said. "Too high."

"Too fast," Art zoomed his hand. "Wasn't it, Barney?"

"Hot dog." Dave Doremus said it, bitter as a curse, there behind us, and I realized then that he must have sat up abruptly and looked when Art cried *U-2*. "Got some more childish games we can all play?"

"It isn't all that childish," Art said, none too placating. "As a matter of fact, I don't consider anything childish that you big boys are getting up for me to play war with."

"How come you're not, Art?" Dave said. "They don't draft athletes, huh?"

"I'd like to fly a U-2 plane just once," I said. I'd wondered about Dave's question, but it didn't seem to me a proper one. "I'd like to try that camera, just because it's such amazing equipment."

"That's what scares me," Art said.

"What, Art?" Helen asked.

"That amazing equipment Barney likes. You know what? My world's got no privacy in it. Privacy's gone, like the horse and buggy. They got big ears to hear you with, Mrs. Barney, and little bugs, too. And cameras that take your picture in the dark. Felt like we were isolated out at sea, didn't it? Well, we weren't. They really do have U-2 planes, or something even higher and faster, out over the Caribbean. All day long, taking a thousand pictures an hour. There's a man in Washington right now who could show you our course and position every hour we were out there, if he wanted to. Thanks Dave. Thanks Barney."

"Don't mention it," I said. "Ever again."

"Go picket the White House," Dave said.

"Boy's got a case, though."

"Half time's over," Dave said, lying down again. "Go play football, big team, will you?"

I saw that Kelso and Connie had come sailing back into sight again in the dory, and a minute or two later Art and I were hauling the little boat onto the beach. Then it was Helen's turn. In fact, that's exactly what she said:

"My turn to go sailing."

"Who'd like to take her?" Kelso asked.

"I'll do the sailing," Helen said. "If Connie can, I can. But I'll pick my crew." She smiled at me, she smiled at Dave, and she said: "Come on, Art. You need the lesson."

"Let's stop at *The Bird* and get the Skipper's sextant," Art said, jumping up. "I'll navigate us all the way to Nassau, Mrs. Barney."

They did go out to *The Bosun Bird,* as a matter of fact. They both went aboard, and below, but almost immediately we saw Art come back, capering around and holding up the bottle of Hudson Bay Rum for us to see, and a box which turned out to have glasses and a bottle of water in it. He put those things in the dory, cast it off, and sailed it around by himself for a few minutes. Then Helen came back up, and, though they sailed out of sight for a while, it was plain from Art's manner when they got back that nothing more than sailing had gone on. He was still clowning and unruffled, and I figured that if Helen had had any sort of fast play in mind, she was too skillful to have exposed the intention. The lead would have been his; he couldn't have been allowed to know he was declining anything.

She got a little drunk on the overproof rum they brought back, kissed Art once—I wondered if he wasn't being given a sense of lost opportunity, to pay him back. Then she amused herself by going over to Kelso and being cuddly, which embarrassed the Skipper nicely. That made Art pant around a little, too. He was a beautiful kid, but the time and place and situation were wrong for Helen. Still, I sensed that his failing to respond more seriously made her feel unattractive. Maybe it was the same kind of time for her that Dave and I had shared on the beach in the morning, when we had to agree that we weren't twenty any longer.

All that being so, I made the married move, after all. Sailed her off to the boat, leaving the others for a time. Going below, giving her a hug.

"What's this for?" Helen asked. "Pity on the old hag?"

"Lust, Miss Sweets," I hissed. "Do you realize I won't be seeing you again for ten long days?"

And actually, I was quite excited by her as we went into it, but candor makes me confess that as we moved along, my mind wandered a little, to other people, other places. And just before the simultaneous-engineering part of it got my attention back, I was remembering, for some reason, a trip by plane, and the green "No smoking" light on a stewardess's short blonde hair.

4

We went through Nassau harbor at high noon, under power with the sails down.

It was a dreary noise, and a lurching feeling, but it was interesting to see how surely Kelso took her in, hardly even looking at his harbor chart.

Helen was packed to leave. We were a day late for her evening plane reservation, but it seemed likely we could change it. She was dressed, and so was I to take her to the airport if it could be arranged. Otherwise, and it was really an attractive alternative, we planned to find a hotel where we could spend a night ashore. Dave was going with us so as to get a room for them, too, for a night off the boat, if it worked out that way. We talked about going dancing, and trying to find some steel-band music, and felt self-conscious in our summer suits with wallets bulging in the pockets, after ten days of shorts and no trading.

"I've always docked with Perkins," Kelso said, turning towards a private marina as we came in.

"Old home day," Art said. "Wait till you see the other charter boat boys come around, and start asking questions and telling lies about how much money they made this winter."

"There are some very nice people," Kelso said.

"Pirates were awfully nice, too," said Art. "Have we got harbor clearance, Skipper?"

"I've chartered out of here so often," Kelso said. "They all know me and the boat."

"There's Perk waiting," Art said. There was a man standing on the end of the short dock, watching us move slowly in.

"Not unless he's gained a lot of weight," Kelso said.

"You sure, Skipper?"

We got closer and closer, but it wasn't until the man waiting was close enough to throw a line to, so unexpected was he, that we recognized him and Connie called his name:

"Stiggsy! Stiggsy Miller!" She and I were at the bow. We'd thrown the line.

Dave came running towards us, twenty feet, and jumped the gap between boat and dock.

"Stiggsy, what is it?" I heard him say, and then there was too much creaking of timbers and backing of the motor to hear the rest. Stiggsy was hanging onto our line, and talking low and fast. Dave went red, under his tan. He started to move past Stiggsy, towards the street at the end of the dock. Stiggsy let go of the line with one hand, and reached the other out for Dave but couldn't hold him. Dave came running, past me and Connie, reached the steps, climbed fast to street level. There was a cab standing there. I could see the driver put his newspaper down, start up, and make a U-turn, driving Dave away.

"Wait," Stiggsy had called. "Will you wait Dave. I got to tell you." Then, as I jumped out and took the line from him, he turned to Connie. "I'm sorry, Mrs. Doremus."

"What is it, Stiggsy?"

"I shoulda dropped your line and cold cocked him."

"But why? What's happened?"

"To keep him from the cable office," Stiggsy said. "There's a cable for him there."

Sunny Brown.

"Let's go after him," I said, looking around for Art to hand over the mooring lines to. I didn't see him, and it took a couple of minutes to get *The Bosun Bird* firmly docked. Then we ran up, and got our own cab, and going to the cable office, Stiggsy told me.

Sunny had come back to Wonamasset two days after Dave and Connie left. She was looking for Dave, and hiding from Buster.

She'd come to Stiggsy when Dave's phone didn't answer.

We moved past palm trees into downtown Nassau traffic.

"That was what Dave told her," Stiggsy said. "She could always reach him through me, if she ever needed him. God, Barney, how I hated to see that sick little face come into the shop. But what could I do? Dave wanted me to let him know. I gave her some money and what address to cable—I guess he was pretty sure she was going to send word, wasn't he?"

"Acted like it sometimes," I said. "Dave's pretty sick himself Stiggsy. Oh, he talked a little bit about ... staying in New York. Getting a job in New York."

"I bet he could get a good one," said Stiggsy.

"Where'd Sunny stay?"

"I put her in my place. In the office. I didn't want her out around town, picking up with everybody."

"She have dope?"

"That was supposed to be the thing. She was all cured, see? I wouldn't have told her where to send the cable if she wasn't."

"Doesn't she know Dave's got a wife?"

"She said it wasn't like that. She just wanted money for clothes and stuff. To go out West where Buster wouldn't follow her, and maybe Hollywood. I don't know. I tried to give her a couple of hundred. But it had to be Dave."

"Sure," I said.

"The cable office called me to check the charges. I wouldn't say all right till they read me the message," Stiggsy said. "She says, 'I'm cured.' You know? 'Got a big chance out West. Must see you.' Stuff like that. And 'Buster doesn't know where I am, so hurry'."

"Maybe Dave'll get home and get her out of there," I said.

"No," said Stiggsy. "That's what I was doing on the dock. Buster's come back."

I was too appalled to answer.

"You know what?" Stiggsy said, gloomily. "He's just as bad as Dave about her. Do anything she wants. He's let her get hooked again. Hell, he gets her the junk. Imagine, hook your own sister."

"Dave wouldn't let you tell him that?"

"Oh, I said it," Stiggsy said. "I said, you got a cable, Dave, but a couple of things have happened since it got sent. Hell, I said Buster and I said hooked, and I might as well have been talking about catching mackerel."

We couldn't see anybody in the cable office. I tried asking if there was a message we could pick up for Mr. Doremus, but the girl said he'd got it himself. I guess that's what we wanted to know, but then of course we already did.

"We'll find him at the airport," I said, and Stiggsy and I ran back to our cab.

"Where you been?" Stiggsy asked. "I been around here three days, hanging around with the charter men and helping them. Waiting on you. You were supposed to be here yesterday, huh?"

"We made a side trip, Stiggsy. You think we can stop him?"

He shook his heavy head, sharp as if something had stung him. "I thought so when I left the Cape, but I guess I just wasted my money. I can call Buster, though."

We did see Dave, at the airport, on the other side of a barrier they wouldn't let us through. I think what he said was, "Don't worry, Stiggsy. Barney, you stay out of it this time." Then he was gone.

"I call Buster and tell him to take her to Boston," Stiggsy said. "Buster don't want anything like before. Dave gets there and she'll be gone."

"Try it, Stiggsy," I said. "Can you reach him?"

"Damn right I can. She's still at my office, and he's with her all the time."

So he went into a phone booth, while I waited ten minutes. He was smiling when he came out.

"Right on the button," he said. "Buster was right there, person-to-person. If you call Buster a person."

We went back to the boat. Connie was changed and packed by then. There was plenty of space on the evening plane; she and Helen and Stiggsy could all get on it.

"Would it help any if I came, too?" I asked them all.

"You can't, Barney," Connie said. "It's just you and Art and Kelso. Suppose the Skipper got sick again. Who'd navigate?"

"Maybe Art and I would make a deckhand between us." I said. "I don't suppose old Kelso'd change his schedule. Or hire a crew. Nothing reasonable, like that."

"He thanked us very kindly," Helen said. "I offered to stay. Kelso informed us that he and Art could manage, if all of us were needed."

I went below to speak to Kelso about it; he and Art were sitting at the table. Art had a glass of that powerful rum. They wanted to know whether some emergency had claimed Dave, and I thought it easiest just to agree to that. They were both unusually solemn.

"I'm staying with the boat, Skipper," I said.

"Are you quite sure you're not needed?"

"I haven't thought of anything I could do back there."

"Art has something to tell you, then. It may influence you."

"What's that, Art?"

"You tell him, Skipper."

"No. But I'm sure Mr. James noticed that you went below. When we were coming in."

"That fat man on the dock," Art said. "I thought he was there for me."

"Yeah? What for, Art?"

"The draft," Art said. "I guess they've been looking for me for about a year now."

"Once we reach the United States," Kelso said. "I can't carry Art on board any longer. He's a fugitive. I feel he should . . . seek out the authorities."

"Couldn't we take him up to Boston?" I said. "That where your draft board is?"

Art nodded.

Kelso said: "I have never knowingly broken a law in my entire life. Art may leave the boat here. If he chooses to take passage with us across the Gulf Stream I must consider that he is submitting to a form of citizen's arrest."

"You going to walk him right to the police station, when we get to Florida?" I asked.

Kelso said: "No. I shan't interfere with the operation of another man's conscience. I'm only concerned with my own. I was never in the service myself, but you were. How do you feel about . . . walking him to the police station."

"I'm not even very big on the citizen's arrest idea, Skipper," I said. "I like Art."

"I have willed this boat to Art," Kelso said very stiffly. "And enough in trust to maintain it if he chooses to do so, should I die unexpectedly."

"Skipper!" Art said.

"I have no intention of changing that." Kelso said, stiffer than ever. "Whatever you decide to do."

"All right," Art said slowly. "All right, Skipper. Wherever we land, I'm hopping over to the draft board. Like a nice little rabbit."

"Very well," Kelso said. "Now Barney believe me, I am grateful for your offer of help. But Art and I can quite well sail the rest of the journey, if you feel you ought to go with your wife and Mrs. Doremus."

I shook my head. "I signed on for the trip, Skipper." I thought of them, trying to go watch and watch across the Gulf. Four hours on, and four off. Even if Art were an expert sailor, that could be punishing for him; even if Kelso had been my age, he couldn't be allowed to try that. "What about the rest of it, when Art leaves?"

"I would simply go up the inland waterway under power, and sleep at night," Kelso said.

"Gentlemen," I said. "I wouldn't miss this leg for anything."

So we saw the others off, Art and I. I was glad for Connie that she had Stiggsy to arrive at home with. Tempting as it was to imagine that it might indispensably be me, and Stiggsy who could stay and help sail, I thought: no. Stiggsy will be loyal to her, and tough with Dave, in a way Dave can accept. And make no intellectual or emotional demands on his own behalf. I didn't like admitting it, but he was a better man for the job.

Helen asked if I had doubts, and I admitted them. "You'd be more use, really Miss Sweets. Except for the navigating."

"Kelso wouldn't carry me alone," Helen said.

"No," I said. "I guess it's like choosing a pitch to swing at. I'm committed. Nothing to do but follow through."

Nassau and Essex, Connecticut (outside).

I was glad I stayed with the boat, but not because it turned out I was indispensable. Like a fire extinguisher, I was there if something drastic happened; as long as it didn't, I was merely useful. My work only made Art and Kelso's lighter, so the pleasure I took in the crossing was chiefly selfish. It felt like what I needed.

The problems flew themselves away on airplanes, and the feeling I had, standing with Art at the airport as Helen and Connie and Stiggsy's flight left the ground, was like the moment on the boat, starting out, when Kelso would cut the motor and that silence of small sounds would start. And all the power we needed would come naturally, moving to us out of the sky. So we could blow no faster than the world blew, and didn't want to. If this seems ungracious, it may be more so when I add that it would have been no different feeling if Dave and even Stiggsy had been standing with us, ready to resume the voyage.

It was the departure of the ladies that I couldn't help enjoying.

Helen and Connie, I loved them both, but there is something in a man that rocks more gladly with the wind womanless, I think.

It was six in the afternoon. I turned to Art. This had to be one sailor who'd want his night in port before he went along to submit himself to a society that never gave him anything he didn't fight for, until Kelso Clark came along.

"Leave tomorrow morning?" I said.

"Let's see if Kelso's ready," Art said. "If he's got ice and meat, let's go tonight."

"You really want to?"

"Let's sail even if he hasn't got ice and meat."

"If he wants to."

"He will. Skipper hates being in port."

"Okay," I said. "Fine with me."

"You might be able to talk him into a steak dinner before we go, if you want one."

"Corned beef at sea'd taste better as far as I'm concerned," I said.

"Me too," said Art, and as he'd predicted, Kelso hardly had to be consulted. A really silly smile broke onto his face when we got to the boat, and Art cried: "Come on, Skipper. Let's put the cork in this tub, and get out of here." Of course the smile was partly because a speech like that from Art restored the good tone between the two of them, too.

So we were out again before dark, all three in close accord, and the harmony was never marred, all through the next four days.

I tell myself that it was no more than a lull, and of course that's true. And then I tell mysrlf the first lesson of our times: take all the false security you can get in this world. It's the only kind there is.

Kelso Clark, we had to concede, wasn't going to do any very lengthy sleeping with either of us duffers sailing single-handed. So Art and I went watch and watch, leaving Kelso to wake and sleep, supervise and relieve as he chose. It suited the Skipper, apparently. He'd be up an hour and sleep for two, up for two and sleep for one. He was a man tuned to time and weather; he took his short sleeps during the night, and in the daytime could stretch out, resting and snoring a little, for as long as there was no particular change in the boat's motion.

The instant it started to pitch differently, or the wind changed sound, he'd be up, yawning, letting on that he'd just happened to finish sleeping, and generally find me or Art or both of us at work. We worked, those four days, in the crazy way Americans do, for pleasure. We got up when we didn't need to, put a lot of energy into cooking for each other, cleaned and polished and went over lines. We scrubbed the decks, turned out all the bedding, aired spare sails and refolded them. We found metal polish and did the bright work. Even Art insisted on backing Kelso's navigation with me, taking a turn with Dave's sextant when I got done, and coming out right, now.

"Slow down a little, boys," Kelso'd say.

And I might groan and say, "Yessir, Captain Bligh, sir. We're trying, sir." And we'd scrub even harder.

Or Art would deliver a little lecture on irresponsibility in young fellows, and whether he could really trust an impetuous man like Kelso with the boat, after he left.

Art and I even cleaned the engine one afternoon, with kerosene, getting gloriously dirty and then wearing the grease off our skins afterwards with buckets of sea water and a coarse brush.

Sleep? I have the impression that I never slept at all, and yet was never tired. And of course I did sleep, sometimes four hours straight, corking right off, hardly turning over in the bunk. There wasn't much lolling around the deck, that leg. When we weren't working, I drank some rum, Kelso told tales, and Art cut up.

"Did this sailor," Kelso was at the wheel and pointed to Art. "Did this sailor tell you about the time the little girl pushed him overboard? When we were cruising in the islands."

Art was hoisting a bucket of sea water to heat for dish washing.

"Now Captain Kelso," Art said. "You didn't understand that. Not at all."

"I don't know what he was trying to do to her," Kelso said, severely. "He probably deserved it. There they were, standing in the moonlight on deck, looking over the stern. And suddenly she pushed her little hand into the middle of his back, and splash. In he went. We were making about six knots . . . ."

"The time has come," Art said. "For you to know exactly what I said to her. I said, 'Please, my dear. Push me in. My good old skipper needs some man-overboard drill, to keep him awake. He's rusty, dear,' I said. 'He may not remember what to do . . . .'"

"You've given me constant practice in areas like that," Kelso said, smiling.

"Skipper, sir. You seem to doubt me."

"No!" Kelso cried, too late, for as he cried it, Art had set the bucket down and yelled,

"Man overboard, sir." And fully dressed, for it was a chilly day, he jumped backwards over the side.

"For God's sake," Kelso said. "Throw the life preserver."

I grabbed the white doughnut and heaved it back towards Art. The water was different from what we'd sailed before, green and glistening with murky undertones, and a perpetually heavy swell. Art went away in it quickly, as if it were he that was moving.

"Ready about, Barney," the Skipper said, and we had to sail

an enormous circle, a mile probably all told, to get behind where Art bobbed with his life preserver. We completed it, so that we were heading again in our original direction, then had to turn into the wind, at just the right time, to drift down on Art. Kelso did it beautifully, cross at first, but he couldn't stay sore at Art's damn foolishness. For it was an act of perfect trust in Kelso. I don't suppose there was any land within two hundred miles.

Kelso played his flute. He hadn't on the first part of the cruise, but now, just as he talked more easily, he seemed to feel free to play every day for half an hour or so.

Sometime in his boyhood he'd been rigorously trained, and while it took the first two days for him to get his lip in shape and sound well, he was very fluent and perfectly correct. I heard it first waking late one afternoon, and couldn't believe the music for a moment, it was so sweet and unexpected.

When I peered out from the galley, I saw that Art was at the helm, listening, and Kelso sitting on the cockpit edge. He was playing some ornate, nineteenth-century meditation. Another man might, I suppose, have stopped playing out of diffidence when I appeared unexpectedly. But Kelso Clark was never diffident when he was doing something that he felt to be correct.

I stepped out and sat down across from him, while he finished the selection.

"What's that called, Skipper," I asked.

He shook his head.

Art said: "He'll run you crazy, Barney. He doesn't know the name of anything he plays."

Kelso smiled. "I learned thirty or forty studies and recital pieces when I was young. Sometimes one comes back, sometimes another."

"You say, hey Skipper. Would you play that soft pretty thing you played yesterday—he doesn't even know which one it was."

"Do you improvise, Kelso?" I asked.

"No. When I remember something, I seem to remember all of it. I can still hear my flute teacher, and the way he played them. He was an old Frenchman, who'd been a dancing teacher down South, and fought for the Confederacy." He started playing again, something much livelier.

"Skipper," Art said, when he finished that one. "I think you've whistled us up a breeze."

We were already going along quite smartly, but over to the east, across the water, charcoal lines appeared, drawn vertically on the flat evening sky. Then we could see a squall move, taking ten minutes or more to do it, and cross behind us, turning the surface dark, breaking up the gleam.

The next squall started across in front of us. We sailed to meet it, and that is how our storm came.

"Will you take the wheel please, Barney?" Kelso said, and quite deliberately put his flute back in the case, joint by joint. He carried it below. When he seemed to come back up instantly, carrying a small sail, I realized he must be moving quickly though he never had the look of hurry. Art was already at the foredeck. Kelso had me turn into the wind, and they had our jib changed to a smaller one so fast I didn't realize they'd done it until Art scooted past carrying the wet one. Then they reefed the foresail. The main already had a reef in it, I noticed now as I hadn't before. Kelso must have done it back in Nassau, while we were at the airport.

By the time rain started blowing at us, Kelso was ready to take the wheel from me, and start us sailing again. Art brought raingear to him, and then Art and I checked hatches and closed doors, checked the stowage and the ropes on things that were tied down.

Then we came to sit with Kelso in the cockpit, waterproofed and watching. It was a wild couple of hours.

The rain came very hard, and the wind and sea grew so noisy that we couldn't hear each other. Sea water gushed along the deck and there was a steady sound of wood creaking. While the rain lasted, I couldn't see much. Then it stopped. A full moon started ducking in and out of the tearing clouds, and I gasped to see what we'd been riding: waves taller than our mast.

I'd seen them that way only once before, twenty odd years earlier on a troopship when everyone got sick. But the iron ship had lunged and wallowed through the waves; the wooden one sailed them. Buoyant as cork, keen as a blade, *The Bosun Bird* went over the hills of water like a perfect skier, sliding down into the moonlit valleys, coursing back up to the next crest with no loss of speed or smoothness.

It wasn't until after midnight that anyone went to bed. Kelso had gone below a couple of times, to get warm, but he couldn't stay below until the moment when he could say: "Sea's going down."

Then they both went down, and left me with it. The waves didn't seem all that much smaller to me, but the sky was clear and I felt unalarmed. I'm not sure I held the course too well. There was a lot of westward drift, and our heading was about due north to compensate. It wasn't until the sea was almost calm again, about three o'clock, that something happened that scared me. I wasn't dozing, but I probably wasn't absolutely alert, either, nor can I say what made be look behind. A change in the way the wind felt on my ear, probably.

I looked behind, and I saw running lights, high above the sea, both red and green.

If you can see both colors, Kelso'd told me then the ship is pointed toward you. I panicked for a second. I couldn't see the thing clearly in the night, had only a sense of ponderous size and speed. After the panic, though, I gripped the wheel and gritted my teeth and told myself to sail calmly. We had running lights, too, and their helmsman couldn't help but see us.

But I kept staring back at the damn thing, getting bigger fast, and there came a moment that wasn't panic at all but a true recognition of danger. That was when I yelled.

"Skipper."

Kelso Clark was at my side so fast he might have been standing there all along.

"Ready about," he cried, not taking the wheel but going for the main sheet. "Hard alee, Barney. Swing it." And I swung, knowing as I did that Art was there, too, now and that whatever they were doing was all that could be done. We started to sail off the collision course, and the thing kept coming up. It passed close enough behind to kill our wind, and as it went by Kelso yelled:

"Ahoy, up there. Wake up, you stupid fools."

It was the strongest language I ever heard him use.

We rearranged ourselves then. Kelso took the wheel, and I asked about our lights.

"Why didn't they see them?"

"I don't know," Kelso said. "Because we're small. Or more likely because they're all asleep, and running on automatic pilot. That's contrary to maritime law, but they do it."

"A tot of grog, mates?" Art said.

"I think I will have one at that," said Kelso. And we got back on course, and, at Kelso's suggestion, toasted Admiral Vernon, Old Grog, the man who first put water in the sailor's rum.

For a while, because of the fright I guess, and because we felt so comfortable together in the dark, Art and I continued to sit up with Kelso. We talked about the storm:

"I never stopped wishing Dave was here," Kelso said. "Wouldn't he have liked it, though?"

"I don't understand about Dave," Art said. "We got along so well at first."

"I wish you could have known him, really," I said. "Dave's a man over the edge and falling, Art. I wish you'd try not to hold him responsible."

And Kelso said: "He'll stop falling, Barney. With that nice wife he has. He'll be the man he was."

I didn't have anything more I felt like saying on the subject. Shortly afterwards I went below, and was lying on the bunk, finishing my grog when Art came down carrying his, and did a very young thing:

"Hey, Barney," he said. "You're a lonely man."

"Am I?"

"Do you mind my saying that?"

" 'Sokay," I said. That Hudson's Bay Overproof was reaching into me now; I guess it was into Art, too.

"Skipper'd never let me say a thing like that."

"I doubt if it's so," I said.

"Oh yeah. Oh yeah. I'd like to see you with your kids.

"Hope you will, some time."

"But kids ... are they company? I mean, can you let them get close to you? You're ... you're very attentive to your wife, but you don't let her get close, do you? Or your friend, or ...."

"Or who, Art? You talking about Connie."

"Yes."

"Been keeping your eyes open, haven't you?"

"Am I making you sore?"

"No, Art. But let's go to sleep." I was touched, I guess. Not sore. In some clumsy way the kid was concerned about me.

"Ever get homesick, Barney? For Missouri?"

"Do you for Boston?"

"No."

He let me go, and I lay there drifting off, in the middle of the Gulf Stream, wondering if I ever got homesick for the Middle West. I thought of the long golden autumns, and the muddy springs, the tropic heat of midwest summers, and the winters when cold winds come all the way from the Arctic Circle. And I thought, yes, those are the only Octobers, and I went to sleep.

2

We stayed out one more night. Kelso said we could make Florida the next day, and Art said that was all right with him.

Then it was Kelso who weakened, and said, no, let's go on up to Morehead City, in North Carolina. So we did, the morning of our sixth day out, about three A.M. We slept at anchor, and received the coast guard, when day came and it was time to prove that we weren't hauling Cuban refugees.

When the chief petty officer was done looking over the boat and examining our papers, ready to get back on his launch and wave us in, Art said:

"Skipper, here goes."

Then he shook hands with me, and winked, picked up a small suitcase and called to the boarding officer,

"Just a moment, sir."

He was grinning as he walked along the deck, forward. Kelso, with his face rigid, started to follow along after him but Art waved.

"Thanks, Skipper," he said. "Good passage. I'll write you a card, to the boatyard."

"Essex, Connecticut," Kelso called back. "Remember. General delivery, Art."

The last thing I heard Art say, to the coast guard officer, was very polite: "Sir, could I talk to you for a moment? I think you might have to take me in custody."

They rode away together in the launch.

Kelso and I did feel very much alone then, Kelso more than I, I'm sure. We didn't want to stay around Morehead City long. Kelso went to a marina, and got fuel and ice. I went uptown for groceries and whiskey, and called home.

Mary Bliss answered. It was teacher's meeting today, she said, and a day off from school. I damn near cried at the surprise of hearing her voice, and suddenly began wanting the trip over so that I could see her again, and Goober.

"Brad will be home next week, Daddy," she said, and I remembered that his prep school let out earlier than the public schools.

"Maybe I'd better talk to your mother," I said.

"She's not here."

"When's she coming back, honey?"

"She's collecting today.'"

"Doing what?"

"Collecting. With Mrs. Stetson." I laughed. That would be a long, hard day of sherry drinking, Helen and Betsy Stetson going from house to house, picking up Community Fund contributions from their friends. I felt fond of that image.

"Okay," I said. "Have you got something to write with?"

Mary Bliss went and got a pencil, and I told her to write that we'd be arriving at Essex, in the Connecticut River, at the Steamboat Dock, in the early afternoon next Wednesday.

Didn't say it was me and Kelso Clark alone. From what he said, the inland waterway trip was nothing to fret about, anyway.

I took a cab back to the boat with the provisions I'd bought, and while I was paying the driver I overheard two men talking. They may have been crewmen on the deep-sea fishing boats which ranged the dock. One was pointing to *The Bosun Bird*, and saying:

"That came in from outside last night."

"I wouldn't go outside in nothing like that," the other man said, and I felt proud and sad.

3

"Quiet, isn't it?" Kelso said, as we left under power. The old man missed his boy. "I never thought, when we all six left St. Thomas, it would end like this."

I sympathized with him, but I didn't want to see the trip turn melancholy. The inland waterway was a long, green tunnel, of canals and small rivers and not many towns. We fell into teaching one another things. I did birds with him, and he gave me lessons on the flute.

There were towns now and then, and locks. We tied up at night, and Kelso slept a lot during the day, too, while I steered us along. He didn't really cheer up until the afternoon I ran us aground.

We didn't often meet other boats, but that day there was quite a big motor sailer coming the other way, a house boat almost, and I moved over towards the edge of the canal to make room. We needed nine feet of water, and suddenly there wasn't that much under us. Without any special noise or anything, the boat, rather firmly, stopped moving. The motor sailer went on happily south, away from us.

It was a feeling of utter, bewildering suspension, and my first impulse was to pat *The Bosun Bird,* to reassure it, as you do a dog when you step on its foot accidentally.

"What the hell?" I said, knowing Kelso'd be up in a moment. I reversed the motor, and gave it some throttle, but I was too slow. Our keel had moved on into the mud and we were stuck, tilting slightly, settling.

Then I had the damndest sense of loss and shame; I kept listening for something to break or bust loose, and at that Kelso came up. He was calm, almost jaunty, and he carried his instrument case.

"I suspect we'll have time for a flute lesson," he said, reassuringly, and I smiled. What he'd been needing, to come out of his blues, was some sort of nautical challenge to rise to.

He opened the case and started putting the flute together. "Be a power boat along sometime," he said, chattily. "We'll wave him down, and get him to go by full speed. When the wake floats us, we'll just back off."

It was as simple as that, if you knew what you were doing.

I'd already learned how to produce some pretty wretched scales on the flute. While we were waiting, Kelso put me through them all.

We went along cheerfully after that, sometimes through bodies of open water into which the canals and creeks of the inland waterway flow. We could have sailed across the bigger ones, I suppose, but Kelso seemed content to chug along until we reached the lower end of Chesapeake Bay, at Newport News.

"Barney, shall we? Go outside again?"

"I've been waiting for you to say that, Skipper," I said, and I had. I'd had enough of noise and diesel smell and long green tunnelling. I played my first arpeggio in celebration.

It wasn't an ordeal, but I won't deny that it was arduous. It took us sixty hours, with a contrary wind, and we changed every two. Thirty short watches and thirty rests. It took a total output of each man's physical energy to keep going that way, but when I suggested, off New Jersey, that we go in and anchor overnight, Kelso wouldn't admit that he was tired.

There wasn't much to navigating with the Atlantic coast in sight, so we sailed, slept, ate and took turns on the flute. Kelso, now that he had his lip back, was really something of a marvel—those meditation and gavottes, transcriptions of operatic arias and lullabies, those jigs and unaccompanied laments. That's what I remember best, that and being tired and starting to improvise a little myself, especially at night as we went by the lights of the eastern seaboard.

It was first light when we reached the outer markers of New York harbor.

"Mind making some coffee, Barney?" Kelso said, as he came to relieve me.

"I'm not planning to turn in," I said. "I want to see it." Buoy after buoy stretched along towards the harbor mouth, which was still hidden in dim light and mist. "It's a pretty well-worn road, isn't it?" I said.

"Barney, would you make some coffee?"

It was pretty uncharacteristic for him to show impatience for the wheel.

"Sure, Skipper," I said.

I made some coffee and took him a cup for which he thanked me, making some effort to control his sharpness now.

"What's wrong, Kelso?" I asked.

"It's this harbor. I'm afraid you'll see what I mean."

"I expect it to be quite a sight in the morning sun," I said. I was making the obvious connection between dawn here and dawn at Guanahani.

"It's beautiful up above," he said. "It can get pretty ugly here at water level."

At first I thought he meant the water. It was true that it was turning dirty already, with grapefruit halves and oil and floating boards, and the farther in we got the more garbage and flotsam there was. Once we went through an island of garbage.

"That's probably from a liner," Kelso said. "They discharge it just before they enter."

But he was talking about another kind of ugliness. I'd cooked us some breakfast and carried the plates up, and we were eating when I noticed the tugboat. I noticed it because Kelso had stopped eating to watch it.

"What's a collision course?" he asked, in the tone of an examiner.

I knew my lesson: "If the angle doesn't change as you go down the legs of it, that's a collision course," I said.

"We're on one, with the tugboat."

"He has to yield, doesn't he?" I said. "Since we're under sail?"

"He'd love to have us try to stand on that rule," Kelso said. "Ready about, Barney. I don't want to be anywhere in front of him."

"You mean he'd try to hit us?"

"Or pass close, anyway, to see what his wake might do to us. He's changed course twice already to maintain the angle."

"What in hell for?"

"This is a rich man's toy to him," Kelso said. "Cluttering up the space he works in." He said it quite impersonally, neither bitter nor sympathetic; he was simply describing a normal hazard of navigation. I suddenly thought of the people out in the Caribbean on the cruise ship, waving to us, and our lordly feeling towards them. "He's in one of the harbor unions, I suppose. They don't care for our kind of traffic. Ready about."

We sailed behind him, and the tug didn't turn again. But it slowed down enough so that we didn't cross very far behind. There was plenty of wake, as he gave it some throttle, to toss us and make our sails flap. I looked at the tug, angrier and less tolerant than Kelso, and could see the man at its wheel motioning crewmen to the back rail. Three of them lined up there as we went bobbing past, losing way. We were quite close enough to see them unlimber and urinate in our direction, but a little too far to see their smirks or hear whatever it was they were yelling.

"That's in the hope that we've got ladies aboard," Kelso explained. "No they don't usually chase you down. But I know of sailing yachts that have been turned over and damaged."

After that we took the sails down. We were getting into quite a bit of traffic, steamers and barges, coast guard, fishing boats. A fire boat, all shined up. But every time I raised my eyes, I'd see something that I liked seeing: the Statue of Liberty, first grey, then rosy-green in the dawn. The skyline, emerging clearer and clearer.

But the amount of junk bobbing around in the water was incredible.

The wharves were busy as we came closer, and the traffic actually thick. A ferry boat went by us, close and slow. Staten Island ferry, I think—the passengers were commuters, anyway. Men in business suits, girls in cloth coats with fur collars, reading papers, or talking, or just hunched against the wind, still partly asleep.

They took no more notice of us than the Statue of Liberty had.

"But it's like watching a parade, Kelso," I said, recognizing downtown office buildings, feeling pleased to do so. "You can be stirred by the music and the marching, and the flags and colors. Or you can think about the wars and killing, and the sore feet and stomach aches that the guys have marching."

"It's all there, isn't it?" Kelso said.

We fought tide across the mouth of the Hudson, went around into the East River and up that side of Manhattan where the shipping grew lighter, the boats themselves much smaller. The tide turned. Kelso, who'd been fretting over tide tables, began to smile again.

"The rip tide through Hellgate is more than our engine could go against," he said. "Now we want to catch it before it gets going too strong the other way."

He'd been at the tiller for five hours by then, but I knew he wouldn't change over.

So we came to Hellgate, past some sort of police boat and the slums of East Harlem, under bridges jammed with morning traffic. I'd decided against New York for myself long ago, when I chose birds and children, but it still had power to excite me, even if it was a soiled and troublesome place.

We turned through a kind of wide channel then, whose banks were concrete. It was two or three blocks long, and we could see dead-end signs, garbage cans, a playground. Kelso was looking at his chart of Long Island Sound and steering when the shouting started: colored and Puerto Rican kids of various ages were gathering, trotting along the edge of the canal in pace with us, staring and hooting: "Rich bitch. Rich bitch."

One of them pegged something at us. It looked like a rotten orange, but it fell short.

But I couldn't mind them. Hell, they were kids. I waved, and yelled, "Hey, where's your arm?"

That made Kelso smile. "Why don't we play them a selection?" he said.

"Yes, sir," I said, went and got the flute, put it together and handed it to him. He let me have the wheel, he stood up and bowed to the children.

"Rich bitch, rich bitch," they yelled at him.

"Here's one I know the name of," said Kelso, and he stood, facing our adversaries, and began to play, high and spirited, *Yankee Doodle*, with trills and variations.

I began to laugh. Someone of them reached the side of the boat, with a piece of garbage, plunk, and I could have drawn away a little. But I wanted them to hear Kelso, so I held it steady.

"Your turn now, Mr. James." We exchanged positions, and while Kelso steered us past through the gauntlet of hoots and cauliflowers, I tried *Begin the Beguine.* Didn't do badly, either. As we cleared the end of Hellgate, most of the kids were still cursing and throwing, but a couple had started, however satirically, to wiggle and dance.

"We'll get satin jackets made, Skipper," I said. "With KELSO'S CRUISERS written on them."

Up in the sound, we found that we could run rather grandly before the wind. It could have been a spinnaker run, I guess, but once we were back on home turf, Kelso gave out. He'd had an anxious six-hour stretch, and he confessed quite plainly:

"I'm exhausted," and went below.

So I went on for an hour or so, up the middle of the Sound. When we got to what I thought might be New Haven, I called out. When Kelso didn't appear right away, I called again but instead of coming up he called back:

"What is it, Barney?" The voice wasn't too distinct, but then there was the galley between me and the cabin where he'd gone to lie down.

"I think I see New Haven, Skipper," I called, and then I saw him. There wasn't a galley between us at all, because he was in the galley, supporting himself on the counter.

"Be there in a minute," he said.

"Are you all right, Skipper?"

I could see him push himself up, down there in the dimmer light, and push towards me till he reached the companionway.

"Having a hard time waking up," he said. "Really went to sleep down there." And he slumped against the door frame. He looked very pale.

"Where can we put in?" I said, remembering how sick he'd been two weeks before.

"Let's go . . . on to Essex."

"No."

"Promised we'd be there. Today."

"You need to be looked at Skipper," I said. "As soon as possible."

"No, Barney."

"And put to bed."

"We'll make Essex," he said, took a step into the cockpit and nearly fell. He caught himself on the edge of the cockpit, looked off to port and said, conceding: "The lighthouse is Old Saybrook. Essex, just a little way."

"We'll go to Saybrook," I said.

"All right. All right, I'll take it."

"No. Go back below, Skipper. Please."

"Can you . . . do it by now, Barney?"

"I can do what Art did once. I can get the sails down and motor in."

"Let me hold it," Kelso said. "While you do."

That sounded like it would save time. I reached out a hand to help him to where he could sit by the wheel. He looked absolutely miserable by then, and I lowered the canvas as quickly and neatly as I could, and tied it loosely around the booms, left the jib on the deck. We were drifting now, and I let us while I helped Kelso down to his bunk. Then I took *The Bosun Bird* to Saybrook.

We got a doctor to come to the dock. He wanted Kelso off the boat, taken to a hospital. Kelso was pretty well collapsed, but conscious enough to protest.

"I'll take her up to Essex, Skipper," I promised. "And get your boatyard friend up there to take her over. Don't you worry."

He wasn't really strong enough to disagree but he was smiling when they carried him away. He might not have made a sailor out of me, but at least I could be trusted with his boat.

So I crept out again, just *The Bosun Bird* and me, around the point with the lighthouse on it, and up into the Connecticut River mouth. I went slowly, three or four miles an hour I guess, up the five miles to Essex, wishing I was under sail, hoping the kids would be there to see me come in anyway.

The big wharf on the left, Kelso'd said, would be the Steamboat Dock. It had a building on it, with a restaurant on the second story. Seeing a restaurant up there made me wildly hungry, and I hoped it would be open.

Then I saw Helen, a familiar figure standing at the edge where I would come in, her skirt blowing in the wind, and waved.

I couldn't see any children, but there were men there to catch my line, and the gap between me and the dock was getting narrow.

I concentrated on getting the motor into reverse at the right moment, so as not to bump hard when I docked, managed it.

Felt a sense of small triumph for that maneuver, as one of the dock men jumped on board and threw my line to the other. I felt *The Bosun Bird* tug, and stop, and looked back to see Helen running to catch up with me like a commuter's wife at a train station.

Okay. Good work, Ozark Seaman.

"Hi, Miss Sweets," I cried, salty and self-satisfied.

"Oh, Barney," Helen said. And I noticed belatedly that she was crying. "Barney. Dave's dead."

If you lived in Arlington, you'd be home now.

"*CORINNA*," said the title.

When to her lute Corinna sings
Her voice revives the leaden string,
And doth in highest notes appear
As any challenged echo clear.
But when she does of mourning speak,
Even with her sighs the strings do break.

And as her lute doth live or die;
Led by her passion, so must I.
For when of pleasure she doth sing,
My thoughts enjoy a sudden spring;
But if she does of sorrow speak,
Even from my heart the strings do break.

"Thomas Campion," said the book. "1601." And the book went on, as if nothing had happened, to the next poem. But I kept reading that one and in place of *Corinna,* I read *Connie.*

I don't read modern poetry. I can't say I much give a damn for romantic poetry, either. In fact, I can be sweeping: I don't like anything since Milton well enough to spend an evening reading it, and I wouldn't take Milton to a desert island, either.

It's the Elizabethans who can get to me. Those were men who wrote poetry for other men to read, and one rather mannish woman but she was a queen and didn't count. I like their lyrics, I like their sonnets. I like their plays. I like the way they can make a sentence turn out.

And of course, all of that was the throw-in when I made my big buy, which was Shakespeare. I'm conventional enough to think he's the greatest of the writers. He was my father's choice, too.

To my father's kind of people (but he was an older man than most of my friends' fathers, and country-raised) you either settled on knowing the Bible or, if you were a worldly bastard, Shakespeare. It was a surprise to me to grow up and learn that most people didn't choose either one.

Now I read Shakespeare, or some other piece of Elizabethan stuff, like any man with too many interests, inconstantly. But once or twice a year, with short-time intensity, I skip the highball after dinner and about the time the cocktail hour booze wears off and the house quiets down, I start a play and sit up with it till I'm done. If its a late play, and I want to go slow and think about the lines, I may take two or three evenings in a row for it. I like knowing how many plays there are, and that I get through all of them, even *Timon of Athens,* in about ten years, in an unsystematic way. And ought to make it through two more times, or even three, before I die.

You know what the most Elizabethan thing is that we do, this century? Space launches. Yeah, I'd go.

"But if she does of sorrow speak . . . ."

I thought of Connie, and the cemetery for heroes down where we took Dave's body. Down there where the South begins. And I found myself remembering the moment on the boat, when she quoted a line she liked and called it folk poetry. From a little road sign on the outskirts of a midwestern village, seen at dusk. . . .

And I thought about Dave, and Kennedy, and about the rest of us, and I thought: if we lived at Arlington, we'd all be home now.

2

I went right up to the Cape, as soon as I'd driven Helen home, hugged the kids and made two phone calls.

The first was to the doctor in Saybrook, who said he was amazed at Kelso.

"His body would be phenomenal in a man fifteen years younger," the doctor said.

"Is it the ulcers and malaria?" I asked.

"No sign of it. I think he just needed sleep. I imagine he'll be out of here tomorrow morning."

"And cross at the bill," I said. "Thank you, doctor."

The other call was to Uncle Troy. Things were fine at the plant. Tully'd done a fine job. It was fine that I was back. Well, yes, Barney, we were still a little behind on production. Like two weeks.

That meant they'd lost almost another week, in the time I'd been away. Sure, Tully'd done great.

"We're ready for a vote of the board on the glass canoe division, Barney."

"A little something for the west end of the plant, huh?"

"I think the board will like it, don't you? The cost figures are very encouraging."

"I think the board will like it, but I won't," I said.

"Really, Barney? Why not?"

"A canoe is something made of wood and canvas," I said. "Not out of glass or aluminum or quick-drying jello."

"But you understand, from the buyer's standpoint, there's no maintenance problem with a glass canoe."

"A man should love his canoe," I said. "And think it's too damn beautiful not to take care of." And I remembered Dave saying once: *Manufacturing can be a heartbreaking thing, if a man's not proud of what he makes. He needs a product for sale, not a bill of goods.* And I'd replied: *Like a farmer needs to tell himself, that's the best corn around. That's a real pig.* "Anyway," I said to Uncle Troy. "The man I thought I could get for the fiberglass division. Isn't available now."

"I've asked Tully to run it," Uncle Troy said. "He's agreed."

So they were handing me the plant back, the main office, the big desk. What Tully'd won of my authority was going to be wiped out, after all. It was coming out my way, for now at least, without a fight. I was almost disappointed about that. I could have used a fight along in there.

Dave had been dead two days, then. I didn't call Connie to say I was coming. I didn't want to give her a chance to say it wasn't necessary.

I felt so numb on the drive up that when I went by the park where the Mustang had been, and saw it replaced by some already obsolete jet fighter, I couldn't seem to care. Maybe some Korea joker would stop by and love that one up, sometime.

I went straight to the house when I got to Wonamasset, no problem finding it this time. Even if I hadn't remembered, all I had to do was follow traffic. People were driving by, slowly, looking at the Doremus house out their car windows, and Stiggsy was there in the yard, in a cop's hat with billy club, waving them all on.

I pulled in to the curb, and he came running at me, grimly, yelling:

"All right there, in the Pontiac. Move on." Then he saw who it was, and said: "Boy. I'm glad you're here, Barney. I thought you were another damn reporter."

"How is she, Stiggsy?"

"I don't know. Trying to be calm and dignified."

"Of course she is."

"She's like a queen," Stiggsy said. "Whose country lost the war."

I got out of the car. "There isn't any question how it happened is there?"

"You just off the boat?"

"I didn't even take time to read the papers all the way through," I said.

"He killed himself all right," Stiggsy said. "She wouldn't have been able to."

"Sunny?"

"They did it together. Some say she was passed out, and didn't know about it."

"I guess it was a hose on the exhaust pipe, and in the window?"

"Yeah. The car was still running when they found it."

"Who did?"

"Buster."

"What did Buster have to do with it, Stiggsy?"

"Everything, except put the hose on. I got back, see, from Nassau. The son of a bitch was still here. 'She don' wanna leave,' says Buster. 'I can't make her leave.' Girl didn't weigh a hundred pounds, I asked him why didn't he just clout her and carry her off? 'Oh no, Sunny wouldn't like it.'"

Dave had had eight days in Wonamasset, only three of them at home. On the fourth, he'd figured out where Sunny and Buster must be staying.

He'd been watching, and asking around quietly. Stiggsy, who couldn't lie to Dave, admitted he knew but wouldn't tell him. It was Stiggsy's bargain with Buster; he'd prevent Dave from finding

Sunny, just as long as possible. Buster'd get the girl out of town as soon as possible.

"You gotta understand how it works with her," Stiggsy told me. "See, whichever one she's with, that's the one she hates. Now she's with Buster, she loves Dave. The one she's not with, he's supposed to come rescue her. That's how me and Buster got in partnership. She's shooting heroin. Buster's going to get something to put in her needle that will knock her out. Simple. We'll put her in my panel truck, and haul her away to Vermont."

But the plan scared Buster, Stiggsy said. He wanted a doctor to prescribe what to put in the needle, and the only man he knew he could ask a favor like that was in Boston. Nervous when Stiggsy decided to tell him, on Dave's fourth day back, that their time was up, Buster'd agreed to go to Boston that evening. But in the afternoon, Dave's scouting paid off. He saw Buster on the street.

Dave was driving. He'd pulled over to the curb, and watched Buster go into the moving picture theater. Dave knew damn well there was no matinee on Tuesday.

Stiggsy's store, of course, was directly across from the entrance to the movie house. Dave didn't know then about Stiggsy's office, but he went into the store anyway.

"I just saw him, Stigg."

"Yeah? You suppose he's down here collecting or something?"

"They're over there, aren't they? In one of those rooms, over the theater."

"Those are offices. They ain't for living in."

"Buster could make the manager let him stay in one."

"How would he do that, Dave?"

"Come on Stiggsy. You know who owns the theater. The same men Buster works for."

"Yeah. The same men."

"No wonder we get such lousy movies." Dave stared over at the building. "That's a great way for her to get well. Lying up there in an empty office, full of dreams. When the show's on, the soundtrack would get into her dreams."

"It ain't empty," Stiggsy said. "It's my office."

"Thanks a lot," Dave said. "You're a real help, aren't you?"

"What do you want from me?"

"I'm going to wait here, Stiggsy. Till I see him come out again."

"I'm not going to let you take her out of there, Dave. Not unless you leave me unconscious first."

"Stiggsy, this is my affair," Dave said. "I've got to be sure that she's all right."

"That one's never been all right."

"She's sick. You know that. I'll get a doctor."

"It'd take some doctor, to fix her up," Stiggsy said.

"All right, Stiggsy. I'll do it the right way. I'll call the judge. We'll arraign her, for use of heroin, and get her sent back to the hospital. All right?"

"Call him," Stiggsy said.

"Let me see her, first. I'd look pretty silly calling the judge if the evidence isn't there."

Stiggsy said he was unconvinced. Sunny would never agree to that. Dave would do as she wanted. Stiggsy decided to play for time. Buster and he would be able to carry out their own plan in just a few hours.

When Buster came out of the theater, Stiggsy gave Dave his key to the office. He thought about going up with Dave, but decided he'd better wait and watch, so that he could intercept Buster if the big man should come right back again before Dave was through looking. So he watched, anxiously, for Dave to get back out.

It didn't occur to Stiggsy that Dave might find Sunny fairly rational, able to walk, and that there are many exits from a theater.

"I felt great when I saw Dave come out again," Stiggsy said. "I'd told him he could have ten minutes, and he wasn't up there more than five. He came in, and gave me the key, and said, 'Thanks,' and I asked about the judge. Dave said he'd make that call at home. I saw him get in his car and drive away."

Then, he supposed, Dave must have gone around a couple of blocks, circled, and driven in behind the theater building, where an alley was. "He's got her waiting there. She gets in and he backs out of the alley, and they're gone. And I don't know it till Buster walks into the store, about an hour later, and belts me one. Wham. Just like that. I never got hit so hard in my life. Before I could get organized, Buster's run out and jumped in the car with his boys and they're driving away."

It seems odd that Dave didn't take Sunny farther away, but he was hardly rational. They'd gone to a motel at Wonamasset Beach, and hid there for the next three days. On the night of the fourth, about ten o'clock, Dave must have seen Buster and another man get out of a car, and walk into the motel office. The driver, who'd stayed in the car, spotted Dave, hurrying Sunny out of their cabin. The driver started his engine and blew the horn, but it took a minute for Buster to realize what the signal meant, and come running out, and by then Dave was away.

No one knew or could know where he'd driven between ten o'clock and two next morning, but he probably followed beach roads and country lanes; Dave knew them well. He seemed to have kept circling around Wonamasset, possibly stopping for a time now and then. Stiggsy thought he might have wanted to get back to the motel for the needle and the heroin they'd left behind. Or was Dave wondering who he could go to for help? Stiggsy was mournfully, incurably worried that Dave might have felt their last meeting so harsh, the deception that followed it so flagrant, that Dave didn't think he could call on Stiggsy any more.

No one knew or could know, but it seemed to me I did. I didn't think Dave would have hesitated to come to Stiggsy. Or to drive six hours to my house (though I wasn't back yet). Or even to go to the authorities, for protection. If Dave had felt that anything was left to save, either of Sunny or himself. I think he was just driving around by then, knowing it was the end of the line, looking for a place to stop.

He chose a kind of headland, above the beach, where he could see out into the night mist towards the water, and see above the mist to the stars he'd read so often. I feel that in that place he might have got out of the car for a little, leaving Sunny in her dream—Sunny had had her heroin, the medical people reported, before they left the motel and the equipment behind.

So I see him getting out, and standing by the car, listening to the sea; listening, perhaps, for the sound of a pursuing motor. There was no turning around now. Buster and his friends had not always been out of sight, during the drive, and Dave must have felt that he was cut off. I see him getting the hose out of the trunk of his car—it was green rubber garden hose—and a roll of black tape. I see him doing his invariable neat job, wrapping the tape to the pipe, fitting it to the end of the hose in such a way that the diameter would be reduced from tailpipe-size to hose-size. He had left a rear window open just an inch. He put the free end of his hose through the crack, so that it hung down inside the car. He taped newspaper along the car frame and the window glass, on either side of where the hose entered.

I even feel that I know what he said to the girl, when he got back into the car, after taking his last look towards the misted sea. I hear his voice saying, my voice saying—for I can feel myself close to the car door once, on the driver's side as I get in; and it doesn't quite latch, and I open it and pull it closed more sharply—I hear, feel, the voice say:

"Let's play the radio, Sunny. Let's hear music. I'll turn the motor on, so the battery won't run down."

I do not feel that Sunny was unconscious already from her drug, but I do not suppose, either, that she consented or was consulted. I see her slumped there beside Dave, half conscious who he was, as Dave, with his arm lightly across her shoulders, breathed the more deeply and died first. And I don't think Sunny knew it. I hear her move her fingers in a light dry snap, as something in the music catches her, and she murmurs, singsong:

> "Three. Three.
> Three bees.
> Honey Bee.
> Bumble Bee.
> Useta be."

And then, after a minute, like a little girl about to cry:
"Sailor?"

I do not hear, or feel, or know, what the music was that played on the car radio.

3

I went in to see Connie, and knew she was glad that I had come. I stayed with her all afternoon. I answered the telephone, which she wouldn't let me leave off the hook, and told reporters that she was unavailable, and that I was a family friend from out of town, who didn't know anything and had no name. Stiggsy caught one of them trying to get in the back door, and chased him away. A little later I found one in the house, who'd got by Stiggsy, and was making off with a framed photograph of Dave's two kids. He wasn't a very big reporter, and I took it back.

That persuaded Connie to do what I'd been urging on her. She packed some overnight things, crying a little because some of what she wanted had to be got out of the suitcases she'd had with her on the boat. I heard her, and she stopped crying when I came to the door of the room.

"Don't fuss over me, Barney," she said.

"I like to."

"All right. Then do."

I was going to drive her to her parents' home, in Rhode Island, where she'd agreed to stay until Dave's body was ready for the train trip to Washington.

"A military funeral's the only way I know to keep from doing something local and awful," she said.

"It seems all right."

"That way there'll be no one there, except me."

"And me," I said. "When the time comes, I'll see you down, Connie. If I may."

"I didn't want to ask, but I accept," Connie said. "My brother called. Buddy. He'll come if he can, but he doesn't think he can."

"I know," I said. "Marches and murders. Judge Buddy's still at war down there."

It was after that she packed her clothes.

I left the house first, to check that there weren't any newspaper men around at the moment, and tell Stiggsy we were ready to break out. He seemed soberly relieved that Connie had agreed to go, and went around back to check there.

It was as he left that another car started past, then stopped in the middle of the street, and I learned the last, secret detail about Dave's end.

Buster Brown got out. I recognized him, of course, but he didn't seem to know me.

I went to meet him at the sidewalk, and said:

"Yes?"

"I want to see Mrs. Doremus," he said.

"Who are you?" I hoped it would stop him for a minute, and it did.

"Listen, it's my sister got killed."

"I'm very sorry. I know Mrs. Doremus is sorry, too."

"I gotta see her."

"No," I said. "She can't see anyone today."

"What are you, a doctor?"

"She's in my charge. You'll have to arrange a meeting later on."

"Look, Doc," he said. "I need some money to bury my sister right. It costs."

"This wouldn't be the time to take that up with Mrs. Doremus."

He hesitated. Then he said: "All right. Now I know what you think," and started to walk around me. I looked at his size, thought about his age, and decided to take the fifteen-yard penalty. I'd let him get by far enough, and I'd clip him. I glanced at the impassive men in the car, started to make a slow turn to do it, when Stiggsy came charging around the house, with the billy club above his head, red-faced and yelling:

"Let me have him."

I don't know if Buster was frightened. I would have been. Stiggsy was as heavy a man as Buster, and as strong. Even if he was nearly fifty, fury took the years off, and he had a stick.

But he used the club first to feint with. Buster's arms went up to take a blow that wasn't struck. As the arms raised, Stiggsy's head went down under them and he dove. Running hard, he left his feet and went headfirst into Buster's stomach. It was a terrible blow. Buster crumpled, went down and twisted sidewise, moaning from it.

Stiggsy was on him then, with both knees, beating him with that weighted stick, beating ribs, kidneys, arms, legs, the stick moving so fast I could hardly see it.

"Dead man, huh," he kept yelling. "Fight a dead man, you bastard."

I yelled myself. "Stop it, Stiggsy. He's out." I went to grab him. "Come on. He's out of it."

Behind me, the two men came out of the car. I was pulling

Stiggsy away, and onto his feet when they reached the lawn, and we turned towards the two together.

"Get him out of here," Stiggsy rumbled, his huge chest heaving. "Get him out of here before I kill him."

I don't know whether they'd come to fight, or to help me stop it, but no one in his right mind would have tried Stiggsy Miller frontally just then, unarmed. They collected Buster, whose groans were pretty loud now as he humped his body along the ground, trying to get away. They pushed him upright, and half carried him to the car.

"I shoulda killed him," Stiggsy said. "For what he done."

I guess I still thought this was for Buster's having cold cocked Stiggsy in the cigar store, but I was wrong. That had been taken as a just blow.

"Hitting the body," Stiggsy said. "Pulled Dave out of the car, and was hitting the body. . . ."

I put my hand on Stiggsy's shoulder. The shirt was wet. "The man's a lover, Stiggsy," I said. "He loved his sister. He wasn't a sane man."

"He better . . . not . . . bother. Mrs. Doremus," Stiggsy said, panting now that his fury was leaving.

Then we heard Connie's voice. She was standing in the open door of the house with her overnight case. "Barney? Stiggsy?" We went to her. "Were those . . . reporters?"

"Yes, ma'am," Stiggsy said.

"You didn't hurt him, did you?"

"No, Mrs. Doremus. No. It's all clear now."

We put Connie in the car. I walked Stiggsy to his truck.

"You've got some money of mine," I reminded him. "That I won on a bet?"

"Yeah. Sure, Barney. A hundred bucks or so."

"I want you to send it to Buster, for his sister's funeral."

"You don't want to do that," Stiggsy said.

"Send it in Connie's name. It'll keep him away from her."

Stiggsy nodded, and we shook hands.

4

I made two trips to Washington that summer. For the first I got a uniform together.

I was glad enough, for Connie's sake, that the veterans' organizations around Wonamasset wanted to take charge of the arrangements for Arlington. Dave hadn't had particular friends among them, except for Stiggsy, but he was their medal-winner and it mattered to them.

It was Stiggsy who advised me about the uniform, which I don't suppose I would have thought of otherwise, calling long distance: "I don't know if I can come, Barney, I'll try. I don't know but listen: you can just buy a uniform at army surplus, you know? Don't try letting your old one out. That old fabric, it don't hold stitches. It don't pay, and you might want to wear it again sometime, for a parade, you know?"

I couldn't really tell him that I hadn't kept my air corps things, any more than Dave had his marine dress. It was going to be a closed casket, that's all. But I thought Stiggsy might be likely to show up. For him, and because I couldn't be sure it wouldn't somehow mean something to Connie, I got the uniform together. Some bought. Some borrowed. I even had more or less the right row of ribbons. Maybe it meant something to me, too.

I put it on, feeling like an impersonator.

"Have a safe trip, Captain," Helen said, with such a studied lack of irony that its absence was ironic.

I drove to New York, took a shuttle plane to Washington, and was there half an hour before the ceremony.

Stiggsy hadn't come down after all. The Legion Post in Wonamasset was having a simultaneous memorial service, and he'd put himself in charge of the detail which would fire three volleys in the local cemetery. Old Sergeant Stiggsy.

At Arlington there were just Connie and me, following the marine honor guard who carried the box.

There were three volleys there for Dave, too. Then taps. An echo. A white cross, like all the others.

Afterwards, I took Connie to the Shoreham and we drank bourbon and told each other it was okay. From there she'd go stay with her folks again, in Rhode Island, for a while. Then she thought she might go south to see her brother. Perhaps there'd be something useful she could do down there.

But she was spooky about making the plane trip north alone, so I turned in my New York ticket and rode the Boston shuttle with her.

Part of the way we held hands like kids.

Connie's father met her at the Boston airport, and I got another shuttle plane, back to New York.

The second trip to Washington was in late summer with the children. Brad was finishing his first job, as a counsellor at camp in Virginia. He would come up to join Mary Bliss and Goober and me, on the visit I needed to make to my brother Alex.

There were first cousins there for my kids to renew acquaintance with, and I always liked seeing Alex and Tanny. Through the years it had become one of the things that could cheer me up.

Helen thought she'd let us go without her. She wanted to play in the club golf tournament. She was partners with the new pro, so she had a good chance of winning something. The pro had been to our house for drinks. I supposed he'd be there for more while I was gone.

We did our family business. Alex and I sat up late, talking and drinking wine. Alex loves wine, and is one of the men who can often tell what he's drinking from the taste of it. It was Burgundy, and we ate walnuts with it; he could crack them cleaner than I could.

A good deal of the evening I spent telling him about Dave. I hadn't called, when I'd been down for the funeral, but Alex was the kind of brother who understood why not.

Around midnight he smiled his beautiful, blind smile and said:

"Come on, Barney."

"I can't," I said. "I haven't been practicing."

"Come on anyway."

I couldn't refuse him. We went to their music room where there were two grand pianos. Tanny played four-handed classical stuff with him, but Alex hadn't anyone with whom to play jazz. And he'd gotten better and better through the years, though always as an amateur.

Once in a while, Tanny told me, he'd play for friends. Not very often. Even less often, he'd play at a party and the people who heard him might boast of having been there. He could play in the manner of any pianist he'd ever heard, people like Monk and Mingus included, but his personal style stayed close to Art Tatum. It made him pretty hard to keep up with, and I was rusty.

But he knew my playing so well that he could come close to anticipating my mistakes, and fill in over them.

We played *Ain't Misbehaving*, and *Grand Piano Blues*. We played the half-forgotten swing songs of our boyhood, testing one another's recall. We went on *Deep Purple*, swapping fours for ten minutes till I hollered uncle. We played *Sweet Lorraine*, which is a good piano piece, and after a while I let him persuade me and we played *Skylark*, at the tempo that meant so much to me. And *Don't Be That Way*.

In the morning the first cousins had a summer class to go to, and I told Goober and Mary Bliss I'd take them to the Smithsonian.

Goober thought that was great. Mary Bliss had another idea.

"Daddy," she said. "Couldn't we see Kennedy's grave?"

"No," I said, with the automatic negative built in to answer children's suggestions. "We couldn't. Anyway, Goober and I want to see Lindbergh's plane."

"I'd like to go to the grave, Dad," Goober said.

"Marlene did," Mary Bliss said. "When they were in Washington. She said it was neat."

"Okay, honey," I agreed, somewhat to my own surprise. "I guess I can't ignore a recommendation like that."

"Daddy. I don't like teasing."

"Sorry. Goober will have to put a tie on."

"I'll change my dress," said Mary Bliss.

While the younger kids were changing, Brad phoned from the bus station. His voice sounded unexpectedly deep:

"Shall I come to Uncle Alex's, Dad?"

I told him where we were going, and he said he'd meet us there.

"You don't need to, Brad. It's going to be children's hour out there this morning."

"That's all right," Brad said. "I'll see you all at the cemetery. Hey, don't tell the kids, okay?"

"Okay."

Goober came down with a tie on, a jacket and a white shirt, too. His hair was wet and combed. Mary Bliss had changed to a grey and green plaid jumper with a white blouse under it. She has dark, fine glowing hair, like her mother's.

I was very proud of the way they looked.

We took a cab to Arlington, the kids sitting very straight and silent, but as we stopped, Mary Bliss broke it with a squeal:

"Daddy, look. It's Brad."

I'd seen him there, and though I was expecting to, she recognized him first. For Brad was dressed in khaki pants, a sweat shirt and a cap, and standing by a dufflebag, all neatly pressed, like a slim, young soldier waiting for a ride.

Mary Bliss jumped out of the cab and threw herself at him. Goob was more restrained.

"Sorry, Dad," Brad said, hugging his sister, tousling his brother's slicked-down hair. "I didn't stop to think you'd all be dressed up." That deep voice, and pleasant manner; Brad is a deceptively relaxed, courteous boy but you could see authority in the firm line of his chin, if you weren't misled by fair hair and glasses. Gave him a hug myself, while Goober backed away, trying to get his hair back in place with his fingers.

"Here, Goob." Brad took a comb from his pocket. "Shouldn't have done that, should I?"

Goober took the comb, and said: "You can wait till we come back down."

"Brad can come," said Mary Bliss.

"That's all right. I'll wait," Brad said.

"Come on, Brad," I said. "If you want to." And I said to Goober, "Brad's in his working clothes, Goob. He's just come from work. That's all right, isn't it?"

So the four of us climbed steps, and stood by the white picket fence and watched the lamp burn, as so many thousands of other people have. We were by ourselves, though, that morning.

I really don't know what it meant to the kids, but they were as quiet as I was.

I thought about Kennedy. Then, after a while, I thought about Dave, out there in some one of those thousands of graves. I couldn't have found it again, without help.

What I thought about Dave was: it could happen to anybody. Hasn't there ever been a time when you were getting yourself home from a party, and might quite justly have been busted for drunk driving? Lost your license? Might have started having to depend on others to get to work? Lost your temper about that, started making bad decisions, drinking a little more, till suddenly you wouldn't belong in an office, you'd belong in a bed? . . . Hasn't there been a time when you overdrew quite a bit at the bank, and when you might, instead of being able to borrow, extend notes, piece it out, have run into some bad financial luck that would have kicked the bottom out of the hole? . . . Or a time when you were a little bit infatuated, and if she hadn't turned out to be more decent about the thing than you deserved, you could have had your own house staved in by a predatory girl?

No, little Ozark buddy. It doesn't matter how strong you've built your position, you better have pretty tough skin on your teeth, too. Otherwise the lesson seems to be that you can be the richest, the best looking, the most powerful. You can be witty, charming, married to the prettiest girl, the one whom fashion copies. You can be the son of a strong man, surrounded by fierce brothers, father of lovely children, friend and patron of the wisest poet, survivor of a dozen deaths. The youngest leader ever chosen by your people; by the world. . . .

And a screwy, jittering little clown can dream his hand to a gun, fantasize his way to a window, be a make-believe marksman through a nine-dollar scope—but if the finger of diseased imagination presses a real trigger, you will, in the next moment, be truly and terribly dead.

Every man, even the most blessed, needs a little more than average luck to survive this world. But damn it, Dave, I thought . . . and then I tried to tell myself: "Leave the organ keys alone, Missouri Boy. Go back to your honky-tonk piano."

That could not have been said to work.

I made my arm firm around Mary Bliss, standing still for once with her eyes wet. Looked at solemn old Goober and slim Brad, side-by-side, Goober heavier already than his older brother and nearly as tall. And didn't know whether I wished Helen were there or not, but I suppose I did.

I know I wished there were some way I could say the lines that came into my mind to a twelve-year-old girl and two boys, fourteen and seventeen, without sounding sententious. From the speech, of course, accepting the nomination, *we are not here to curse the darkness, but to light a candle.*

Out loud that was translated: "Don't cry, honey." I wanted them all back with me now. My honor guard. "Come on, Mary Bliss. Brad and Goober, shall we go along?"

We started away, and in a minute Mary Bliss was skipping ahead, in the dark plaid jumper. Goober had actually started to run, and then stopped to look at some enormous black ants. Brad and I, walking shoulder-to-shoulder, almost like friends, caught up with them.

"Hey, can we still go to the Smithsonian, Dad?" Goob asked.

"Keep your voice down here, Goober," Brad said.

"Sure we can," I said, smiling and keeping my own voice down. "There's plenty of time."

"Will they have the kind of plane you flew in the war?"

"I don't know. I hope so."

That was all Goober wanted to know, but I felt very much like keeping the little conversation going. The boys fell in walking side-by-side in front. Mary Bliss tucked herself against my side and under my arm, and we followed.

"Shall I teach you guys to fly?" I asked. "Brad and Goober?"

Brad looked back, and nodded, yes, and then looked away, as if I'd tricked him.

"We can start this year still," I said. "When we get back to Scott's Fort. I'll rent the plane from the company. Okay, Goober?"

Goob's attention was on something else. The war, I imagine. I know he heard me but he didn't answer. Mary Bliss answered. She did it by tugging at me, and when I looked down I could see that she didn't want her brothers to hear her ask, but her face was beautifully hopeful.

"You too, Mary Bliss," I whispered, grateful to her. "I'll start teaching you, too, honey."

Brad heard, and looked back at me, and nodded again. My tall son. Approved of me. And was about ready to start smiling again now, to run pick up his dufflebag and whoop, and wrestle Goober for it, and they'd all three get on to the next thing, as kids do.